CW01475765

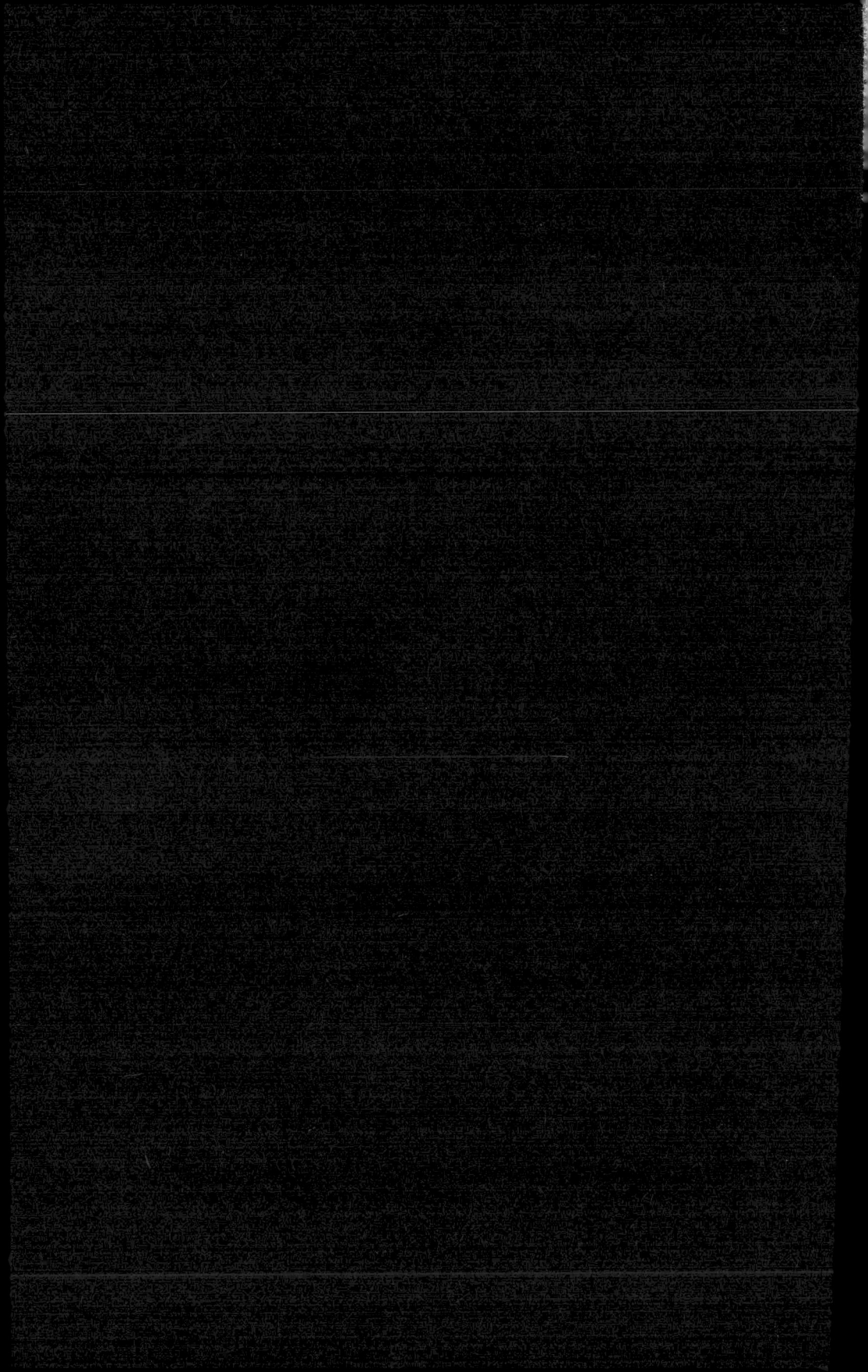

GOD STORM

SOLITAIRE TOWNSEND

Also by Solitaire Townsend

Non-fiction
The Happy Hero
The Solutionists: How Businesses Can Fix the Future

GOD STORM

SOLITAIRE TOWNSEND

Bedford
Square
Publishers

First published in the UK in 2026 by Bedford Square Publishers Ltd,
London, UK

bedfordsquarepublishers.co.uk
@bedfordsq.publishers

ISBN
978-1-83501-259-8 (Hardback)
978-1-83501-260-4 (Trade Paperback)
978-1-83501-261-1 (eBook)

2 4 6 8 10 9 7 5 3 1

Printed in Great Britain by CPI Group (UK) Ltd, Croydon, CR0 4YY

The manufacturer's authorised representative in the EU for
product safety is Easy Access System Europe, Mustamäe tee 50, 10621 Tallinn, Estonia
gpsr.requests@easproject.com

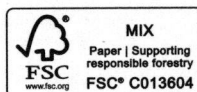

To my parents, for taking us to museums.

The Kalends of Februarius, Londinium Arena

MDCXXXVII Aurelian Calendar

PROLOGUE

Blood and oil. Arena sand always tasted the same.

The girl spat the filthy grit back at the man's shoe, but he didn't even glance down at her. Puce mouth gaping wide, a fleck of spittle flew as he roared at the sky, punching his fists in the air. Kicking up more sand into the face of anyone her height.

Fans. No wonder her mother hated them.

She pushed past him. Bumping her head against spectators' hips, worming forward between sweaty adult bodies.

Thick dark fumes from wide copper bowls of burning crude oil mingled with the tangy body odour of the frenzied throng. As she wrinkled her nose, the corner of the girl's mouth twitched into a half-smile. The smell of home.

These votive basins of flaming oil were merely theatrical, of course. A show of piety from the Arena bosses to the goddess Gaea, whose blood the fuel was said to be. Today's stink was nothing compared to race days, when war charos chased each other around the Arena, spouting plumes of gritty smoke from their exhausts, and then from their engines as they crashed and mangled each other for the audience's entertainment. Her hair, clothing and even meals carried the tang of burnt oil for days after.

A flash of Imperial red in the sky distracted her determined progress through the crowd. The Emperor's small red dirigible hovered just ten feet above the sand. Whatever was happening had caught even the jaded attention of the Imperial family.

She needed to hurry.

Moving down through the stands, the girl passed the invisible line dividing working Plebeians in the cheap seats from the noble Citizens. Flat-caps and mop hats were swiftly replaced by silken top hats, lace bonnets and neatly starched toga sashes closer to the front. The Arena was strictly ordered by Citizen and Plebeian with the Imperial family literally floating above. The only three classes anyone in the Imperium Romanum cared about. A few of her kind might be lurking in the crowd; the forgotten fourth class cleaning up puke or emptying latrines.

The girl didn't care. Her lowly rank made it easier to reach right to the front of the crowd. The Citizens simply didn't see people like her, just as they ignored the crumpled food wrappers at their feet.

Damnatus! Thick fingers jerked her head back, tangled in her hair. Half-lifted, someone shook her as the crowd screamed their appreciation for action happening on the Arena floor, drowning out her own yelp of pain. Scalp stinging, she twisted to bite her assailant's hand. Before her sharp little teeth could find his skin, the stupid fan released her to pound the back of the Citizen beside him. Their top hats and toga sashes knocked askew in jubilation, taking no heed of the scowling urchin at their knees.

She considered biting him anyway, risking a lashing. But then a tiny gap opened between the wall of bodies against the front balustrade. The girl pounced at it. Just tall enough to peek over the wooden railing, she was too small to interfere with important people's views.

The screaming horde of fans gorged on the show before them.

The girl stood where she shouldn't be and stared at her hands — bloodless white and trembling as they gripped the front railing. This was what she'd wanted, plotted for, and risked punishment, finally, to see. Her fingers stilled their shaking as she glowered at them.

Grinding her teeth against each other, she forced her eyes up to look at what everyone in the Arena was shouting about.

It was a sunny day by Londinium standards, clear and almost warmish. The light glinted on the tiny granules of Arena sand, except where slicks of red-black stained it. Enough had been shed to build sandbanks where feet pushed and slipped in the struggle. The girl noted all the blood. But, no bodies, yet.

Mother still stood, out on the Arena floor.

The tall gladiatrix tightened a leather strap in her breastplate. The girl's nose crinkled. That was a calculated show of vulnerability, designed to entice the enemy to attack when he thought you distracted. Why would Mother use such an amateur ploy?

Slitting her eyes against the light, which had promised clarity but instead flattened sight, the girl scanned for injuries. Leather laces of sandals reached just below her mother's knees. Her muscled legs, skinned bloody in places but not pierced through the scar tissue from past fights, unprotected by the ridiculous short red skirt studded with bronze. The bare midriff that her mother feared, but that spectators expected for a gladiatrix. Her breastplate, clean enough in places to catch the sun, despite smears of blood flecked with sand.

There, Mother had been struck in the side, blood slowly pulsing out and staining her short tunic. Perhaps this wasn't a feint; every gladiator knew that tightening the breastplate could slow bleeding beneath it.

Her mother's face was obscured by an ugly Spartan helmet, uncommon on female fighters. It had two spikes pointing down below the chin, and her mother's long dark hair waved out from behind it.

Her plait must have unravelled in the battle.

That morning, the girl had carefully tied it, while her mother sat, sharpening her gladius sword with a slice of marble. The rhythmic swoosh of stone against metal as familiar as a lullaby.

'Please, I promise I won't bother anyone.' The girl had begged to watch the fight.

5

'Dearest, the mind moves matter. I must have no distractions on the sand.'

It was an old argument. The girl was allowed to watch training bouts and charo races but never true combat. War is hated by mothers, the girl was taught, but not even the gods fight necessity. Her mother battled only because if she refused, the Arena bosses would whip the gladiatrix. If flogging didn't force her back to combat, they'd sell the woman and child onto the oil rigs, or whore pits.

The girl knew that women don't yearn for battle, as men do. Mother risked her life on the sand only to protect her daughter.

Whenever the gladiatrix left their tiny room for another bout, the girl would sit, huddled in a corner. Listening to the roars of the crowd through the stone, not knowing if they cheered her mother's victory, or her death.

Days ago the girl had decided that the next time her mother left to face the Arena, she'd watch rather than wait.

Flinching now as thunderous cheers rocked the stadium, the girl stood back up, ramrod straight and eyes forward. The Imperial dirigible had banked upwards, hovering high as if the gods themselves played audience.

Out on the sand, Mother's giant opponent was minotaur-headed with matted black fur and blooded horns.

It's just a mask, the girl told herself, hoping that reassurance would release her breath.

He charged forward, bellowing a war cry, spiked cudgels whirling in each muscled fist.

Mother turned towards him, her guard up and feet grounded, unflinching. Then she leapt forward, raising her own sword to meet the towering nightmare. The girl's chest tightened, barely able to contain her pride and fear, all caught in one small ribcage.

Sunlight glinted off the gladiatrix's sword.

But blood-soaked sand is treacherous. A pace away from her enemy, her mother's foot skidded, then she stumbled, one knee pounding the ground. Her blade flew from her hand to land yards away in a puff of sand.

The entire Arena silenced; the girl, every Citizen and every Plebeian breathless as the eyes of the famous gladiatrix opened wide. Mother flung her body forward as the beast-man raised both cudgels to pummel breath, blood and brain-matter from her.

Landing prostrate beneath him, still too far from her own weapon, Mother's long tanned legs fell akimbo. Her hair tumbled around as she tore off her helmet. The masked gladiator loomed over the fallen woman.

This was what the crowd had paid for.

Every throat, all ten thousand of them, erupted into a baying thunder for the death blow to fall. The Imperium Romanum might rule most of the known world, using oil-fuelled engines to impose civilisation onto barbarians, whether they liked it or not. But from the most powerful Citizen to poorest Plebeian, everyone agreed civilisation included glorying in the death of a slave woman, born to kill, and die, for their pleasure.

The watching girl slammed hands over her ears as they yelled, not knowing if she screamed too.

But no killing-blow fell.

The wild cheers jerked to silence.

The minotaur-masked man just swayed where he stood. Then, the heavy cudgels dropped from his grasp onto the sand with two thumps. Knees crumbling, the weight of him collapsed with a slap of skin and bone onto the woman prone on the ground beneath him.

As he fell, he revealed the gladiatrix's helmet, its razor-sharp chin points sticking out of his colossal rump like a tail.

Mother had skewered him from below.

After a stadium-wide inhale that the girl knew she'd never forget, the crowd went berserk. Men either side of her punched and pummelled each other, almost crushing her in their frenzy at the bold move. The stink of them caught in the girl's throat.

But the gladiatrix didn't move, trapped under the fallen carcass as dark blood gushed from the opened sluice of his severed groin artery. The girl's hands pulsed in and out of fists as the crowd rumbled back to quiet. The watching men pointed and sniggered.

They would call for your death in the same breath as your victory.

The girl stared at the giant corpse. It wasn't cold that day, but all her insides shuddered as if she was freezing. Mother had warned her that panic floods the blood with poisons, chilling and confusing. Right now, the girl couldn't remember what she was supposed to do about that.

She stared ahead, refusing to look away. Mother wouldn't leave her alone. Most gladiatrixes drank bitter-fennel tea to prevent birthing more slaves into the Arena's clutches, their bosses looking the other way. But *her* mother had wanted a child. The girl knew she'd fight to come home to their small room, as she promised to do whenever she left.

The monster's leg jerked, and his trunk started to rise.

Her mother still fought her enemy, now for freedom from being crushed under his dead weight. Slowly, the gladiatrix dragged herself out, her blood staining the sandy stage alongside the widening pool spilling from the corpse.

The victor gulped air, then pushed herself up off her knees, panting too fast, clutching at her side wound. The girl gasped along with her, no longer trying to force her body from shaking. Thank the gods, it was over.

Straightening, the gladiatrix swept back her long hair and frowned at the heavens.

The girl now understood why she shouldn't be here. Who wouldn't hate killing for an audience? The gods might decide your fate, but they didn't demand you thank them for it.

She turned to hurry back to their rooms, where, she promised herself, she would be quiet and obedient from now on. For the mother who risked her life, forced to fight, for her daughter.

The faces of the crowd stopped the girl's retreat, thousands of eyes glinting with anticipation. Turning back to the sand, the girl's shoulders tightened. Mother should be hurrying away from this pit of blood and death, seeking treatment for her wound, coming home to her daughter.

Instead, with a grunt of effort, the gladiatrix thrust her sword to the sky. As if it was a signal everyone but the girl understood, the Arena stilled to silence.

A muffled clap of hands wafted down from the Emperor's airship.

Mother's eyes closed at the sound, her chest filling with a deep breath and smile fainter than the applause.

Then she roared, 'LET US LIVE, SINCE WE MUST ALL DIE!', which unleashed a wave of deafening cheers from the stands. Turning to each corner of the Arena, Mother soaked in the glory pouring down upon her. Ignoring the blood running down her side.

'Brit-ann-i-a! Brit-ann-i-a! Brit-ann-i-a!' the gathered hordes in Londinium's famous Arena chanted. That wasn't Mother's real name, but the gladiatrix saluted the crowd, fist over heart, as they screamed themselves hoarse calling her battle-name.

Kicking her fallen foe onto his back, the gladiatrix tore off his mino-taur mask, revealing a pale, dead face younger than the girl had expected. Thrusting the trophy above her head, her gore-spattered mother stood with blood running down her arms and from her side wound.

Mother's smile grew to be wider and sharper than any her daughter had seen before. She laughed louder and deeper than the girl had ever heard.

The girl didn't stay to listen to the wild screams of jubilation from her mother's adoring fans. Ducking behind the balustrade, she still panted as hard as the gladiatrix. The mother who, despite what she had assured her daughter, loved the fight.

The girl wanted to be sick. She wanted to laugh.

But more than anything, she wanted to hit something.

The Ides of Maius, Londinium

MDCLVII, Aurelian Calendar

CHAPTER I

The scroll pierced the governess more efficiently than any blade.

Just a few lines of neat black script, secured with the crimson seal of the Academy. In civilised life, a mere slip of paper can crush the dream of who you thought you were.

Arrow's heart stopped even as her nail sliced through the thick wax.

She and her young charge, Livy, received so few letters that it had nestled, unnoticed, in their postbox for far too long. Now, Arrow held a summons for Livy to the Academy. The girl was expected by Lunday this Ides: in two days' time.

Arrow's lungs fought to take even a single deep breath against the stays of her cheap corset. For Hades' sake, the letter must be a trick or administrative error. Although, the glorious Imperium Romanum wasn't renowned for having any sense of humour and its tolerance for mistakes was homicidally low. She scanned the letter again, searching for any hint of why Livy was being thrust out into a world Arrow had been warned to protect the girl from. But it read more like a delivery order for a sack of potatoes than a life-changing pronouncement on a child's future.

Of course, there was no mention of Arrow herself. Bondsmen would likely secure her once Livy was gone, as removers cleared out their garret.

Livy sat at her small desk with unusual meekness as Arrow stuffed the document into the sash at her waist, alongside the sharpened dagger she always kept there. As the soon-to-be-no-longer a governess's hands fumbled, Livy's eyes widened.

Arrow's fingers itched to pluck the paper back out of her sash, ball it in her fist, and burn it to cinders in their hissing oil grate. Instead, she smoothed a tiny crease in her fading green skirts and picked up a battered book, hands barely shaking.

Disturbance comes only from within.

Livy was too polite to ask about the letter directly, as Arrow had raised her to be. But no eight year old could battle curiosity indefinitely. The girl lasted less than five seconds.

'Miss, do we venture into town today?'

'No, dearest.'

'Or I could run a reply for you?'

Arrow tried to force a smile into her voice. 'What sort of governess would allow an unaccompanied girl-child onto the Londinium streets, alone?' She coughed to cover her throat tightening – clearly, one whose unusual talents were no longer required in this post.

Arrow began reading out the day's lesson.

Sighing, Livy kicked her toes against the table, knocking over their nux game board with old salt and pepper pots in place of missing pieces. The girl's head snapped up as if expecting a rebuke, but Arrow ignored the mess and continued to recite Horace, lips remembering the oft-repeated verses while her knuckles turned white gripping the page.

She had just two days. To pack up their life together and prepare the girl for the Academy, of all places. Two days to say goodbye. Arrow stumbled, losing her place in a stanza extolling the perfection of a mediocre life. It took her longer to regain proper composure than anyone with her training had the right to.

Gods, she hated Horace, and it dawned on her that this lesson was pointless anyway. Before the week was out, these humble classes would be replaced by proper lectures from the educated Dialectics of the Academy, an institution beloved of the Emperor himself.

Since the seat of the Imperium had moved from old Rome to Londinium, the new capital city had sought to outshine its predecessor. While the ancient republic continued to be revered for its poetry and piety, Londinium was widely considered, mainly by its own denizens, to shine more brightly in science and oil-engine industry. For over a thousand years the Academy of dialectic scientists had funded itself by educating the children of Citizens, and a smattering of rich merchant Plebeians.

Arrow pictured Livy perched in a school amphitheatre, scratching notes onto a scroll before running back to her dormitory with the other Academy girls, laughing and playing nux with all the pieces intact. Meanwhile, her former governess would sit shackled in the slave pits, waiting to be sold on, alone.

An old pain stabbed low in her belly, below her corset binding. Arrow thrust the feeling back, refusing the memories that threatened to escape the cage she'd shackled them in.

Freedom begins with the clear understanding that some things are within our control, some things are not.

With a rough push of her chair, Arrow stood, unsure why she had done so. She stared down at the girl she had cared for, taught, nursed when sick and been surprised by every day for almost eight years.

The dismal odes of Horace couldn't be their last memory together.

'Dearest, shall we venture out to the Imperium Museum?'

Livy leapt up, eyes ablaze. The girl adored the museum but rarely did Arrow risk visiting such a public place.

'Really, Miss?'

'Well, educating the mind without educating the heart is no education at all.'

Livy ran off to grab oiled boots and Arrow tightened the ties under her own plain bonnet.

Later, in a different world and with another name, Arrow would wish she'd taken a last look around their tiny home before she latched the door. Their few precious books and scrolls, Livy's drawings in wooden frames Arrow had made for them, the threadbare but comfy armchair by the oil grate. But we rarely notice the moments when reality becomes memory.

As the cold of the Londinium street hit them, Livy looked up at Arrow and grinned. The girl's unruly brunette curls framed a broad fawny face, with eyes so dark as to be almost black, and her smile promised glee and mischief, if she could get away with it. Arrow's own smile ached in reply, feeling every day of the twenty-seven years she knew she looked older than.

As they turned from their quiet neighbourhood onto the wide avenues of the city, three charos sped past them, engines roaring, taxa lamps unlit. Arrow waved at them anyway, but the taxa drivers, hunched over their steering apparatus, didn't even glance sideways. Both she and Livy coughed on the exhaust fumes from the vehicles that a rising wind couldn't snatch away fast enough.

On their rare trips this far from home, the streets usually bustled with top-hatted Citizens and wealthy Plebeians promenading with fashionably bonneted and parasol-twirling ladies on their arms. Livy and Arrow would weave between them, giving a wide berth when they spotted a toga sash.

Today, being alone on the street made for greater speed and anxiety.

As they pressed on, a vast swirl of bruised clouds darkened to black above them. '*Damnatus*,' Arrow mouthed. She'd thought this morning's dreary sky was merely Londinium's habitual brooding against Sol's light. But a Godstorm could hit like an unexpected punch to the jaw: hard, fast, and liable to break bones.

A judgement from Jupiter himself, the Priests called the new spate of wild weather. On the few occasions that Arrow allowed herself the expense of a newspaper, she read of ever more crops blighted by searing heat, or floods that could sweep away entire Plebeian villages. The major Temples had suspended their usual squabbling to agree; the gods punished the Imperium Romanum for lack of piety. The sky now regularly blackened with smoke from burnt sacrifices . . . but the Godstorms worsened. Ever more destructive, no matter how many bulls were dragged to the altars.

Arrow knew she and Livy should retreat back upstairs – but then there'd be no excuse to ignore the Academy scroll for a second longer.

If they moved fast, they'd reach the museum before the tempest grew too perilous.

Arrow waved her charge forward, the woman and child clutching their hats with chins tucked into the high plain lace of their collars, overcoats tightly buttoned. Darkness fell like an oil lamp being doused, and the wind probed their defences, whipping the rain sideways against their skirts, then lashing from another direction. Arrow thrust forward, her muscles welcoming battle against the storm, as they were useless fighting destiny.

The scroll in her waistband refused to be ignored, like an untreated wound. Questions pounded inside her skull. The foremost of which was: *What the Hades?*

Livy was hardly of age for the Academy. Arrow hadn't expected such a summons even in her worst nights of sleepless worry. As governess, she been ordered to keep the girl safe and secret. But as the years went by, the only evidence that Arrow had that she and Livy weren't entirely forgotten was the small monthly stipend for food and necessities Livy's legal guardian provided. So, Arrow had protected the girl from a threat never explained to her, and educated her without much direction. Considering her own circum-stances, Arrow couldn't have found a better position. She remembered the squirming infant first being placed into her inex-perienced arms. In that moment, she hadn't understood all the other duties her arrangement would include: bedtime stories, tending scraped knees, anxiously nursing illnesses and sudden flashes of joy at Livy's burgeoning if roguish humour. Secrecy came easily to Arrow, but protecting the child eventually fell far second to raising the child.

However much she wished otherwise, the summons couldn't be ignored and there wasn't a soul whom she could ask why it had come. Livy was to leave their little garret and enter the company of the sons and daughters belonging to the most influential, and publicly visible, families in the Empire. Which brought Arrow back full circle to not knowing what the Hades was going on.

The blinding white light of Jupiter's wrath spiked down from the heavens.

Thrusting Livy against a brick wall, Arrow held her own body between the girl and the sky. She could hear Livy counting until Juno's lament boomed in reply a few seconds later, echoing across Londinium, even over the hammering rain on the grey pavement. Livy had remembered the science that thunder followed lightning, but the lesson had become perilously practical.

Arrow clenched her teeth against curses bubbling on her tongue. *Fear is the foundation of safety.* She should have fixed the wooden slats across their windows and refused to budge until the storm had passed. Two days wasn't enough time to tidy away their life together anyway. Hadn't her own mother always warned her rashness was a liability?

Or perhaps it was cowardice.

They struggled onwards through a Citizen suburb – Doric-columned mansions set back from the public street, with warm yellow oil lamps visible in a few windows. Tempting, but a far more severe violation of her orders than she was already risking. In a Plebeian neighbourhood, she might have begged refuge until the storm passed.

Their cheap bonnets lost shape under the wall of punching rain-drops, and their skirts swirled around their ankles, threatening to trip them even as they ran. At least the sideways gusts could only hit them with leaves and street litter. Nowadays, people bolted down anything a strong boreal could lift. The few trees left standing in Londinium bent and swayed beyond what seemed natural.

Head so low, it took a while for Arrow to recognise the tall black railings surrounding the museum grounds. Hanging onto the firm bars, Livy smiled up at her again, despite reddened cheeks streaked with tears from the wind. Arrow would say a prayer of thanks, but she didn't deserve the gods' graces for taking such a stupid risk.

'Spare a few denarii, lass?'

A shape blocked their path, and even with the high winds its acrid smell hit Arrow before she saw the filthy rags.

'Avant!' Arrow jerked Livy back behind her, fingers tangled in the girl's coat.

Under the vagrant's hood hung a mottled beard with small plaits in it. He wasn't even trying to hide them. Plaits meant a follower of the old Anglish religion. One of that kind mustn't be allowed near a child.

'Just a couple of denarii, to help me out on this 'orrible day.'

The beggar crouched, blackened nails on unstable knees, staring at Livy. Arrow squared herself before him, hand hovering over the thick green sash at her waist.

She had spotted, and avoided, a few bedraggled Anglish skulking in corners of their neighbourhood recently, all begging (or pick-pocketing). But she hadn't expected one to accost visitors to the Imperium Museum.

'Back, I warn you. Or I'll—'

A small arm shot out from behind her, and the man's hand darted to meet it. A chip of silver flashed in the murk as it passed between them.

'Gods bless,' Livy said, her smile unsteady but holding for the old man, and with a final stare he sped out into the tearing winds and rain. Arrow quickly lost sight of him in the murk and uncoiled her fingers from fists.

'Livy, that was your allowance for a honey cake in the museum.'

The child replied with the tiniest of shrugs, dislodging a cascade of rain from her bonnet, 'Being poor means you don't have lots of things, but being greedy means you haven't got anything.'

Despite winds biting her cheeks with their frozen teeth, Arrow stopped to stare down at the sodden child. She must have taught Livy that maxim, but so long ago she didn't remember when.

Then she turned on her heel and pushed her way through the rain, dragging Livy behind her like a bobbing balloon at a Floralia fayre. They battled up the shallow steps and between the museum's high entrance pillars, granite as dark as the sky. A few steps in and the thick walls muffled the Godstorm's thunderous song down to a dull drumming.

In the wide vestibule they had their choice of hundreds of hooks to hang their drenched overcoats, so few others were taken. Livy shook off the remaining rain in the frenzied manner of a puppy – her bonnet, dress and curls all spun back and forth.

'Livy, must you?'

'But it works, Miss.'

Such unladylike behaviour deserved a chiding. Instead, Arrow smoothed out the misshapen edge of Livy's blue bonnet. Then let her hand rest for an instant longer than necessary on the small shoulder. Imperium propriety required all children be raised with a minimum of tenderness, lest the Roman character be weakened. And as a servant, any feelings she might harbour were irrelevant anyway. But, life without the girl was hard to imagine, just like her life before Livy was hard to remember – at least, if she worked to forget it. Arrow closed her eyes for a second, willing the right words to occur to her, a way to explain to a child that everything she'd ever known was about to change.

Nothing came.

After another second, and sacrificing any last vestige of decorum, Livy pulled free from Arrow's hand and dashed up to her favourite exhibit, her feet echoing on the marble.

The giant skeleton of a long-dead lizard dominated the grand domed space. Three fathoms high, his pale skull proudly faced the tall doors, while the ever-decreasing bones of his tail extended across the entire length of the gallery. Far above the carefully reconstructed beast, an elaborate stained-glass window usually lit the bones. Today, the Godstorm's gloom left only the fizzing oil lamps, hidden in notches along the walls, to warm the scene.

The little girl grinned up at the fang-filled skull.

'Hello, Sire,' she said, making a solemn curtsey.

Arrow arranged a smile for the child. 'Livy, were he alive, with all his skin and muscle back on, he would gobble you up if you tried that.'

'You wouldn't, would you?' Livy addressed the bones. 'I'd tame you, and we'd be great friends and have adventures. I'd ride up on your back like a giant charo, and you'd live in the park near home.'

'He certainly would not,' Arrow said, lungs struggling against her corset as Livy talked of home. She shook her head. 'He would get far too chilly in Londinium. I taught you about reptiles being cold-blooded, and I wouldn't like to sew him a giant coat or a dress; my fingers would get sore.'

'A dress?' Livy squealed. 'But – he's a boy!'

'How in Juno's name do you know that? This might be a lady lizard, so it would only be right and proper for her to wear a dress, with full petticoats – ' Arrow paused, tapping her finger against her chin – 'and perhaps a nice bonnet?'

At the image of her darling beast as neatly dressed as the pair of them, Livy burst into laughter, which echoed out across the hall. Arrow hushed her and cast around for any affronted Citizens. Crowds usually shuffled around the enormous skeleton, but today the hall remained theirs – almost.

A tall Legionary lurked within the inner museum doors, watching them. Arrow cursed herself for complacency. She'd been following Livy's antics rather than checking for threats. Managing not to flinch or stare, Arrow glanced over, using the peripheral vision she'd clearly neglected lately. This was no mere honour guard, kicking his heels, waiting for some Citizen to emerge. He was the picture of a fully-armed munifex in dark leather, glinting breastplate and red uniform, with an arc-gun on his right hip and short sword on the other. Heart pounding but head clear, Arrow's eyes narrowed. While he radiated alertness, she couldn't detect any taut edge of a warrior expecting imminent action.

The museum had been one of the few public spaces still free of City Legion patrols. Arrow's stomach clenched at the thought of soldiers prowling the halls of the Academy itself. She should have taught Livy less poetry and more politics.

Disconcertingly, a quarter-smile had claimed some territory on the soldier's face as he watched Livy. He glanced at Arrow, but so swiftly she knew he saw merely a tired servant woman in a cheap but respectable green dress. She briefly resented how easily he dismissed her and was tempted to change her stance into one any warrior would recognise.

Shaking her head at her foolishness, Arrow reminded herself of the arc gun slung at his side. She ushered Livy up the grand marble staircase behind the skeleton into the welcoming upper halls of the museum itself.

As they wandered through rooms filled with the treasures and oddities collected from every nation the Imperium Romanum had conquered, Arrow's fists finally unclenched. With damp skirts drying, she and Livy pointed out favourite exhibits to each other: the giant stuffed ice-bear standing with raised claws and teeth bared for Livy and the delicate soul vases from the East for Arrow, hundreds of them ranged on shelves, the flickering lamplight revealing their mysteriously moving colours.

The scroll screamed for attention, but Arrow ignored it, bearing the wound of their imminent separation for a few moments longer.

Despite a few half-heard murmurs and footsteps in galleries they passed, it was easy to imagine they had the labyrinthian museum to themselves. Livy weaved between glass cases like a bright blue bird, fluttering with inquisitiveness. Arrow was nothing but dust and shadows.

They reached a chamber displaying the unruly past of old Britannia itself, before the civilising age of the Imperium Romanum. Although they usually rushed past this room to more sensational exhibits, today Arrow slowed her step and looked around. Livy stopped beside her, facing a monolithic black stone, near the height of the space itself. It didn't suit the confines of the exhibition, speaking instead of rain on green hilltops, brooding under moonlit skies.

'What do you think it is?' Arrow asked, grasping a final chance to expand her charge's interest in the world, however primitive the example.

Livy bounced on her heels. 'It's an egg with a dragon inside . . . Or a giant who fell asleep, and maybe he'll wake up!'

'If he does, he might be rather affronted to find himself propped up, with a note on his toe – 'Arrow peered at the white square – 'saying he's carved from obsidian quarried near the Slavia seas.'

'That's why he's asleep.' Livy grinned. 'He must be knackered after walking all the way here.'

A snort of laughter escaped Arrow before she could rein it back. 'Knackered is a vulgar term,' she admonished.

Livy grinned and Arrow yearned to ruffle the girl's curls like she had when Livy was much younger. Instead, she settled a sterner countenance. She must act like a respectable governess while she had the chance – it hurt less.

'Consider the effort it took, without oil engines, for the ancient Anglish to drag those tonnes of rock across half the world.'

They peered into nearby cases filled with metal gauges and dials, with ornate animalistic swirls like tails or fins. Gods only knew what they were actually designed to measure. No wonder the old Anglish tribes had been obsessed with geometry: before the brute force of oil, they would have needed ingenuity instead.

Outraged newspapers reported that Druidic rituals still held sway with the Plebeian classes, with floridly written reports of supposed animal sacrifices, and hints of worse. As seat of the Imperium Romanum, Britannia was supposed to shake off the last vestiges of those uncivilised creeds. Returning to stare up at the brooding obelisk, Arrow didn't think the Emperor would have much luck. She'd never cared much for either the familiar Imperium gods or the old Druidic spirits, as none of them seemed to give a damn about her. But in the maze-like alleys and overflowing tenements of Londinium, she suspected the ancient creeds might be almost impossible to root out.

Arrow sniffed as if she could still smell the Druid beggar, who had braved Anglish plaits right beneath the proud SPQR carved over the entrance. Here inside the museum, of course, the Anglish religion was represented as being as outdated as any other weird creed the Legions had rolled over.

Livy walked towards the next room. But Arrow hesitated. A little lump at the black rock's base caught her eye. She looked around, but they'd only seen a single old custodian, nodding asleep, rooms away.

Scooping up the dark stone, she turned it over. It was a tiny version of the obelisk, but with a silvery lattice symbol engraved upon it, perhaps depicting two arrowheads crossing each other. Her hand hovered; it wasn't a part of the exhibit but too like the large stone to have accidentally fallen just here. It felt heavier in her hand than its size suggested.

To overcome an inclination and not be overcome by it is reason to rejoice.

It wasn't made of anything valuable, and it felt solidly pleasing, snug in her palm. The wind beat upon the small windows above her, and she felt as if, below her senses, the Godstorm vibrated the very walls. She'd lose everything that mattered in two days anyway. Arrow frowned and slipped the stone into the sash at her waist, then caught up with the bouncing dark curls of the child.

Livy was on tiptoe, peering into her favourite exhibit case. Within it, a multitude of tiny birds perched, dived and were caught mid-flutter. Glass eyes, silent wings and iridescent feathers were artfully poised with invisible wires. None of the birds were recognisably from Britannia itself, and some were no larger than Livy's thumb, which they had once used for comparison. A close study would even reveal miniature green and blue mothers, perched forever at the side of their thimble-sized nests.

Arrow watched her young charge's rapt expression, wishing the two of them could be caught in this moment.

Livy strained forward. 'I see eggs in that one,' she whispered, as if afraid to frighten the dead birds away.

It was time.

Every old scar on Arrow's body, and there were a lot of them, started to twinge as she drew out the Academy summons and smoothed the crinkled paper against her palm.

Futuo, futuis, fututum, and the gods too.

'Livy dearest, I have some exciting news for you . . .'

The girl turned from the mother-birds, her face a picture of simple trust in the woman who had raised her.

Crashing boomed down the hall. Livy jerked back, jostling the huge glass case.

The din bounced off the walls, drowning out the unending rage of the storm outside. Grabbing the girl as she turned, Arrow pulled the small body against her own.

'Ware!' she said, one hand holding the child's arm, the other hovering over her own waist.

Another roar layered in tortured screeches as if the ancient fossil skulls had all gaped open at once and emptied their death screams into the museum.

CHAPTER II

Arrow scanned the room full of large, quivering glass cases. 'We're moving, Livy,' she said. 'In step with me. Now.'

The child's eyes widened, but she didn't cry or query. Arrow prowled to the archway out of the gallery, thankful the girl's well-trained tread was firm behind hers.

The crashing booms bounced off walls and cases built for murmurs and soft footfalls in a crazy cacophony, making it hard for Arrow to get a clear read on direction or cause. She stopped at the arch itself, torn between seeking the source of the uproar or retreating to a farther gallery.

'Livy, stay close.'

The girl's reply was clear, if shaky. 'Yes, Miss.'

They weaved through upper galleries until they neared the top of the grand staircase down to the main hall. As Arrow peered around the corner, a sharp wind slapped her and she grabbed her bonnet.

The Godstorm had punched out the stained-glass window above the hall and now raged in through broken shards.

Blown askew from its wires and delicate wooden scaffolding, the lower body of the giant skeleton had collapsed. The lizard's skull spun, its neck bones hanging almost to the floor, while the massive vertebrae twisted at the end of their wires, crashing into each other with an echoing thud.

Arrow inched to the top of the stairs. Livy gasped, peeking from behind her. The beautifully mosaicked floor of the grand hall was littered with large spikes of coloured glass and chunks of creamy bone, sharp wires and splinters of wood.

Arrow sighed and turned to Livy. 'They'll need a charo to drag out that mess.'

The girl stared at her decapitated monster, eyes wet as she shivered in the cold. Arrow suppressed an unseemly urge to comfort the girl with a great hug or stroke her hair. Instead, she bent a little to meet Livy's stare.

'Look at me, dearest. They'll repair your lizard, I'm sure.'

'But how? He's all in little bits everywhere.'

Arrow caught the catch in Livy's voice even over the winds. Gods, the girl was still so young. *We gather strength as we go.*

'He was in pieces, buried in mud, when they first found him. I promise you, it will be so much easier now. Like a test when you already know the answers.'

Livy took a deep breath and nodded.

Clamour interrupted them and, as Arrow glanced down the stairs, her lips narrowed into a hard line. Despite the danger of broken glass and the dancing bones twisting around over their heads, a ragtag of vagabonds and rough beggars were pushing into the museum. The Godstorm must have become ferocious to have driven them inside the doors. A few of the most raggedy wore small plaits in their hair, and some had even dared to weave in tiny silver amulets.

Deus-damnatus. Those amulets were only worn by the Anglish.

Typically, you rarely saw anyone wearing them outside the poorest dens of the Old Town. They were an invitation to a Legionary to arrest or beat you on the street. Arrow had thought the plaited beggar outside the museum was madly bold, but now a troupe of them were blithely pushing into the museum itself.

Thankfully, the solider at the door ignored their blatant blasphemy as he struggled to handle the growing crowd, while more outsiders pushed in from behind, shouting, 'Oi, c'mon! Move it!'

What if more soldiers arrived? If they saw the ruin in the museum and the provocative plaits on the mob, things would become ugly. Arrow had to suppress the urge to roll her shoulders and bring up fists. *During a riot, the law is silent.*

Well, it was a bad plan that couldn't be changed, and she was trained to be decisive in crisis.

'Let's leave, shall we, dearest? There's no place nicer than our own hearth.' At least for a little while.

'Yes please, Miss. I'd like to go home now.'

Arrow hurried Livy down the grand stairway towards a tea room tucked behind it. She couldn't imagine delivery boxes of fig pudding were traipsed through the majestic main hall, so there must be a service entrance back there. But as they turned into the niche of richly carved wooden tables, Arrow's tread faltered. Others had already taken shelter there, or had been enjoying tea when the window blew out. Citizens, all loudly bemoaning their situation to each other. She spotted a small door in the corner. Perhaps the nobles would ignore a plainly dressed woman and child slipping behind the counter?

A mature matron was seated at one of the tables, her ample corset and overabundance of lacy puce frills straining against deep cuffs. A man sporting a gaudy patterned waistcoat paced beside her, and a blonde woman fluttered around them both. They all wore Citizen toga sashes as golden as the young woman's hair.

'Mama, please don't fret so,' the blonde woman's voice fluttered.

'Something must be done!' the seated dame demanded while her attending acolytes failed to comply. 'Where are the servants? I demand assistance. Oh, I may faint!' she rasped.

Watching from the corner of her eye, Arrow thought the ashen-faced younger woman looked more in danger of collapse than the ruddy doyenne.

As she and Livy inched closer to the inconspicuous door with its 'Staff Only' sign, the loud woman turned and shouted at them, 'You, girl! What is going on here? Where are the guards to help us? I will be taken to my charo!'

Arrow stiffened, as if someone held a blade at her throat.

'Hush, Mama,' the blonde woman said. 'I don't believe that lady works here.'

'What?' the madam replied. 'She's behind the tea counter! Girl, assist us immediately!'

As Arrow faced the Citizen, curse words curdled in her throat. She managed a careful medium curtsey and kept her eyes lowered. 'I'm sorry, Citizen, but we also are just visiting the museum. I hoped to find an exit here, to hire a taxa.'

The old woman snorted, ignored Arrow's explanation, and heaved herself up. 'There.' She pointed at the door Arrow was headed towards. 'Let us leave this awful museum at once.'

While the man gathered bonnets and fans, the younger blonde woman came towards Arrow and Livy. She was dressed in expensive yellow flimsy rather than practical cloth, but her smile seemed genuine.

'We have a large charo and driver waiting. Perhaps you would allow us to help you and your little daughter?'

Livy's head jerked up at the word. As a tiny child, she used to tell shopkeepers and street sweepers that Arrow was her mother. It had taken years of scolding to stop her.

'I am Livia's governess.' Arrow's polite smile felt like it was cutting her mouth.

'Ah, of course. Nevertheless, this isn't the best place for a child today,' the young woman insisted as she smiled at Livy, who dropped into the neatest curtsey Arrow remembered her ever managing. Then the girl's cheeks pinked up, a sure sign of impending brazenness.

'We're going to ride home on the back of the big skeleton, once he's put back together,' Livy said, radiant under the gaze of the beautiful Citizen.

The woman patted Livy's cheek with a tinkly laugh that knotted Arrow's stomach, 'What a charming idea!'

'You can come too, if you'd like?' Livy replied, almost breathless at the rarity of speaking to a stranger.

Arrow was at a loss as to how to intervene without causing offence, frozen in her polite smile that was harder to maintain by the second.

'Livia, was it? How sweet of you to offer.'

Livy nodded with that ancient expression of wisdom that sometimes can pass over children's faces and said, 'Kindness forever begets kindness.'

It was Livy's favourite proverb. She'd even sewn a messy needlepoint of it as a gift to Arrow. The Citizen woman's hand fluttered at her chest as Livy recited it, as if she were struggling to catch breath. 'Oh, to understand and be understood,' the woman sighed.

The skin on Arrow's neck prickled, watching the eyes of the young Citizen on Livy. *The first punishment of the sinner is the conscience of sin.* Her smile now a rictus, Arrow tugged Livy forward.

The girl was supposed to be kept secret, especially from Citizens. Museum trips were meant to be out of the question. If only Livy didn't love the damn place so much.

Arrow took control of her lungs, and her tread didn't falter – much. Citizens had so much on their minds: power, politics and parties. The woman in yellow, who probably wasn't that much younger than Arrow herself, in chronological age at least, would soon forget this exchange. The strong-willed matriarch was unlikely to accept two extra evacuees in her vehicle. Arrow's disobedience in bringing Livy here would never be revealed to her master.

In two days, none of it would matter anyway.

Arrow almost tripped – had it ever? Late into many nights, she had curled up in their battered old armchair by the oil grate, mending Livy's clothes or reading a rare newspaper, pondering her orders. The most obvious explanation was that Livy was some rich man's bastard, maybe even sired by her guardian himself, hidden away as an ignorable shame. What remained entirely inexplicable was why Livy had to be taught, and protected, by someone with Arrow's unusual skills.

And why those unspoken dangers now seemed so irrelevant to Livy's guardian that she could be snatched from near total seclusion and dropped into the extremely public Academy.

Arrow held a little more tightly onto Livy's arm.

The Staff Only door was small, but, once through it, the kitchen revealed itself to be a messy warren crammed with towering boxes and dirty pans.

'Damned ridiculous!' the brightly clad man in the group huffed as he toppled a box and a gentle drift of paper cake cases fell around his head.

Arrow started a quick perimeter search, pulling Livy with her, as the winds pounded against the small windows. It felt rude rooting through this private corner of their beloved museum but, between gangs of Druids and chatty Citizens, she'd happily drag Livy back out into the storm.

Behind a shelf stack, Arrow spotted the outline of a plain wooden door set into the outer wall. With a sigh of relief, she glanced back to see if the Citizen family had followed them. Instead, she spotted a handful of raggedy street people who had wandered through the open kitchen door and were now blithely opening boxes to help themselves to whatever they found. One scruffy old man with an outrageous plaited beard hung with silver amulets stood and stared at Arrow. Then winked when he saw her looking back at him and started stuffing pastries into his pockets.

She remembered that face. If she'd seen those amulets under his hood in the rain, she wouldn't have let him within ten paces of Livy, let alone take her coin.

Druids and Citizens. She needed to get Livy out of here, right now. She hunted for the door handle, which was hidden by fallen boxes.

'Step back a little, Livy.'

Arrow's fingers found the cold metal of a large bolt at the bottom of the doorframe. But as she was about to pull it open, she hesitated, listening to the tempest still raging outside.

The flowery man from the Citizen family spotted her; he strode over and demanded, 'Move away, girl, I'll get it open.'

She jumped up, curtseyed and humbly lowered her eyes. Nothing else was thinkable after a direct order by a Citizen, but she couldn't let him open it.

Inching in front of the door, she said, 'Sorry, sir, but I'm afraid that—'

He snorted with outrage as if she'd tweaked his nose. Then his arm shot down and tugged the bolt open. Even as she bent to stop him, the raging winds outside punched the door inwards and hurled him against the wall. Arrow's hip smashed against the metal table as she stumbled backwards.

The Godstorm rampaged in like an army taking the gate of an enemy stronghold.

'Ware! Livy!' Arrow shouted, scrunching her face against the gritty gale. More boxes tumbled, and a great clatter of pans fell. Ignoring the pain in her side, Arrow braced her boot against the table, and heaved her back against the door with all her strength, battling to close it. The wind cut her like a lashing, but she slid down and felt behind her skirts for the bolt.

Bracing against the struggling door, Arrow rammed the bolt closed. She turned to where Livy waited. Everything in the large room was a tumble of boxes.

The girl wasn't standing where she had been.

Arrow jumped up. 'Livy! The door's closed!' She reached up on tiptoes, searching for a flash of blue. 'Come out now, dearest!'

No answer.

Arrow shoved past people, ducking to look under tables and throwing aside boxes to check the corners of the kitchen. Bile caught in her throat and her heart ran riot, not being able to set eyes on the child.

'Livy – LIVY!'

Holding still, she hoped for an answer or even the sound of tears. The girl couldn't have gone far in the minutes since the door blew in. But Arrow could only hear the rough voices of adults shouting. As she ran back out into the tea room, a raggedy man grabbed her arm, dragging at her. Arrow bashed the side of her hand into his elbow joint and raised her forearm to connect with his falling head, then pushed onwards, not even looking back to see if he dropped.

The pale Citizen woman in yellow was windswept and swaying in the chaos. Arrow seized her. 'Have you seen Livy? The little girl with me?'

'What? No. Don't hurt me!' the woman wailed through rising tears.

A scream rang out from the main hall – older and deeper than Livy's light voice, but Arrow ran towards it anyway, guts wrenching. She drew the blade hidden in her waistband and turned into the hall, scanning its far corners, her blood pounding in her ears, but found no hurt child, no lost girl, no Livy.

Arrow stood in the middle of the great room, glass crunching beneath her feet, dagger drawn, loosed hair swirling with the howling winds, as the bones danced crazily above her. Growing panic and her old training warred with each other, heart racing but senses coldly alert.

Once before, the girl had gone missing while they played amongst trees in the small public park near their garret. Arrow's heart had raced then too, but she waited, trusting the girl to either find her or shout out. Livy had popped up from behind a tree within minutes, but it took hours for the panic-poisons to leave Arrow's muscles. The girl's drills had started in earnest that very day, in how to stay calm, find her governess, and never, ever, to hide again.

Arrow fervently wished that Livy had forgotten all of that and was about to slip out from a corner with a sheepish look. But wishing wouldn't make it so, and Arrow knew how to listen to her instincts and make swift judgements.

Even if she had failed both her duties today – Livy was neither secret, nor safe.

The riffraff had slipped away as she searched, leaving only a handful of the museum's usual patrons wandering forlornly around the devastation. Her worries about a riot were unfounded. The only person panicking was her.

Livy wasn't in the hall.

Arrow took two sharp breaths, focused her mind and sheathed her knife. Why did her instincts scream at her when the girl could just be lost?

Those blasphemous Druids with their plaits and bravado.

The wrongdoer often is the one who has left something undone, not always the one who has done something.

She raced back to the kitchen and, on hands and knees, she searched the floor. A smear of blood by the door? No, that was from the ass who'd opened it.

The Druids had no reason to push into a dangerously damaged museum, guarded by a Legionary. What did they want? There were dark rumours, ones that until now Arrow had dismissed, that the followers of the old religions still gave sacrifice to their spirits. Horrible images crept into her mind of plaited hair, and drums, and Livy screaming.

She scrambled around on her knees, scanning and fingers searching every inch of the gritty floor.

Livy would have struggled.

Arrow's fingertips touched a small lump of cold metal under the largest table in the kitchen. She drew out a silver amulet, a flutter of bright blue fabric caught in its geometric tracery.

It was from the cloth of Livy's bonnet, torn off where it had snagged on a Druid's talisman.

'LIVY!' she screamed into the devastated museum.

But she knew the girl wasn't lost. She'd been taken.

CHAPTER III

Every second counted. But Arrow couldn't move.

A lifetime ago, a much younger woman, so unlike Arrow that she sometimes struggled to admit they were the same person, had felt this before. The sinking dread of loss and terror, clutching for answers when there were none.

For years, that old memory had hidden deep below the daily routine of lessons and meals, stories and sewing. Now it leapt back up, wielding grief in one fist and shame in the other, pummelling Arrow as she held her head in her hands, breath slicing through gritted teeth.

She'd lost a child, again.

Never do what you'd blame others for doing.

That was one of her mother's favourite sayings, especially when her daughter's wayward nature caught up with her. Arrow herself had started repeating it whenever Livy was being particularly impish.

Arrow straightened her shoulders. Panic was poisoning her, and no governess, especially not one with her skills, should be kneeling on a kitchen floor when there was a child to save. She forced a full inhale, and another out, like regimented soldiers marching – I, II, I, II.

If Livy had been deliberately taken, then there was only one person she could turn to. She pressed the amulet so hard into the palm of her hand that her heartbeat throbbed against it.

Her orders to avoid contact with Citizens or soldiers were now irrelevant. Arrow strode over to the tall Legionary as he tried to appease a group of nobles. The broken glass was already being swept from the doorway, but the fine Citizens didn't appreciate having to wait even a moment longer in the wreckage.

Arrow forced herself to modify her voice to that of a worried but reasonable servant woman.

'Sir, a young girl is missing.'

The Legionary turned to her, leaving the Citizens with raised eyebrows and huffs at the slight.

'A child, lost in all this? Is she hiding?'

'She was taken. I must tell her guardian that his ward is missing . . . abducted. He will order a proper search.'

'Abducted? Come now, surely the child simply ran away from the fuss. We will search every cranny of this place. She'll be found soon, no doubt.' He reached out as if tempted to pat her shoulder.

She only needed to flash the amulet to convince him. But then he might call for reinforcements, hold her to be interviewed by his superior, or even lock down the museum itself. Arrow tucked the small ornament with its blue fabric into one of the concealed pockets in her sash.

Better to be thought hysterical then be held here. She knew one name that would open any door: a name she'd been ordered never to use on pain of a lashing or return to the slave market.

Hades to that. Livy was gone.

'I must tell Consul Derain. He is Livy's legal guardian. If you do find her, send a runner to his office in the Spire, and I will return.'

The Legionary's eyes widened at the Consul's name, but, before he could answer, a booming voice interjected.

'The *Consul*, you say?'

The large puce-clad matron from the tea room strutted to Arrow's side.

'The Consul must, of course, be informed about the loss of the little child!' the old lady went on, the full force of her imperious gaze bearing down on the Legionary. 'I have our charo outside. I was only waiting for Tarquil to gather his wits. I will transport this young woman to the Consul immediately and offer all our aid to recover the dear, sweet − ' she paused and narrowed her eyes at Arrow − 'girl, was it?'

'Yes!' Arrow seized on the unexpected offer. 'May we leave at once? I don't want to delay the news to Consul Derain.'

At the magical name of the second most powerful man in the entire Imperium Romanum, the old dame gave a twisty smile. 'Yes, yes,' she said, then huffed. 'Tarquil, Octavia. We're leaving − now. Octavia, straighten your hair.'

The fop who'd opened the kitchen door sat on the edge of a plinth, the young woman nursing a tiny cut on his forehead. His yellow toga sash was dishevelled, and he moaned, while the young woman called Octavia had turned grey. She looked up and shuddered − any warmth from earlier evaporated, replaced with a little shiver when she saw Arrow.

Damnatus. In her fervour to find Livy, Arrow had handled the pale woman roughly.

'Oh, Mama.' Octavia's eyes fluttered away from Arrow. 'What about Tarquil? He's terribly hurt.'

'Ridiculous,' the matron huffed. 'On your feet, boy. We mustn't keep Consul Derain waiting.'

With that, she strode out, the last of the unswept glass crunching underfoot. Octavia took a skipping step to keep ahead of Arrow, and Tarquil slouched behind. The Legionary merely saluted fist to chest, although his face flashed disquiet.

Arrow ached to sprint to the Spire through the downpour, but a charo would be faster. She must think logically − how to brief the Consul and what grid search to order for the Druidic haunts in the Old Town. Her back teeth ground against one another. Her mother had scolded her about that. 'Clenching the jaw weakens the shoulder. Your enemy will spot the muscle pulse and know to strike high. Victory requires tranquillity.'

Grinding her teeth even harder, Arrow lifted her skirts and climbed into the charo. The smartly uniformed driver finished cranking the starter handle and jumped into the open forward compartment to fire up the engine. With a spluttering shudder, the vehicle pulled into the wet street. The enclosed cabin was upholstered in a sickly yellow with gold tasselling, although Arrow couldn't see much detail in the weak light from a small lamp hanging above, throwing wild shadows.

'Well then, my dear,' even the old woman's gums were puce, 'that girl is Consul Derain's ward? How *very* interesting. Have you been with her long?'

The madam's heft was set diagonally across from Arrow, and, when the pile of flounce leaned forward, Octavia was obliterated from view even though she sat opposite Arrow. It made little difference. Despite being almost knee to knee, Octavia didn't meet her eye.

'I've been Livia's governess for eight years.' Arrow wanted to shove the florid face away, roll down the window and scream Livy's name into the wet streets. Clasping her fists together in her lap, she prepared to pay for her ride. 'I am so grateful for your assistance, Citizen. May I enquire to whom I am indebted? I will inform the Consul of your generosity,' she managed.

'I am the Citizen Regina Troak.' The lady paused with her eyebrows raised. When she didn't receive any note of acknowledgement, she flapped her hand at Octavia. 'My daughter you've met, and that brave warrior who fainted from a drop of blood is my nephew.'

'More than a drop!' The young man sprawled over most of the seat next to Arrow, who shuffled against the window away from him. 'It's stained my toga. How am I expected to be seen in this state? I look like a street brawler.'

'You look like you hit your head leaving a brothel,' Madam Troak sneered back at him.

Arrow managed not to gasp outright. The one time she'd met Consul Derain, he'd spoken as if the muse of history hung on his every word. All nobles did, yet this wealthy Citizen was bickering like a fishwife. Madam Troak and her nephew continued to argue in low, hissing mutters about Tarquil's other vices, which ranged from gambling to not even having reached the political office of quaestor. The charo grew stuffy with all their moist clothing warming up, the window closed against the rain.

Arrow could barely see through the glass anyway; it felt like they weren't even moving. The panic was threatening to overpower her again – she wanted to rip at her cheeks and scream at them all. These Citizens should be frenzied too; the whole city should be. Livy was gone. But the faster her heart raced, the stronger her training forced her breathing back to even. The more her fingers wanted to punch out, the firmer she held them still. Damping all that fire back down her own throat, Arrow bottled up her roiling dread and guilt. She must become a carefully controlled metal mechanism, like the oil engine that drove this charo. Hard and precise with their fire shackled within.

Perched opposite, Octavia fiddled with one of the garish seat tassels. Then her ashen face lifted, voice whispering below the noise of her arguing family. 'I saw what you did to that poor vagrant – you broke his arm! I didn't tell Mama, but I don't believe you're a governess at all!'

The noblewoman's slender shoulders twitched under the damp silk of her impractical gown. Even though she tried not to, Arrow couldn't help noting that the pale neck would snap with a single hard punch.

Oh, gods.

'I am a governess, but . . .'

Sod the smug omnipotent bastards. She deserved to be despised for losing Livy.

'I am indentured.'

Long ago, Arrow had learnt it was safer to watch people's reactions rather than hang her head when revealing her status. Octavia's eyes widened like a city fox caught in charo headlights, but she didn't call out for her mother to demand the slave be thrown from the vehicle.

Arrow didn't even blink. She knew what Octavia – what anyone – would be thinking. The indentured must be irredeemably brutal, witless or debased, otherwise why would the gods make them slaves? It was the perfect rationale for her ferocity in the museum. One such as she would lash out when afraid, like an animal.

Octavia tilted her head a little. The exulted noblewoman might never have conversed with one of her kind before. Citizens ruled above the common Plebeians, and then far below them all huddled the indentured. Officially, even the heretical Plebeian rabble in the museum enjoyed higher status and protections in the Imperium Romanum than Arrow. In this city, the indentured cleaned latrines, carried bricks or whored for soldiers, far from genteel eyes. Many more toiled and died in the oil rigs, the never-ending convoys of oil ships and the vast fire plains, counted only on an Imperium Romanum tally. Few wore bonnets, even the cheap ones Arrow allowed herself. None were trusted to teach children.

But the Consul had bought her as guardian as much as governess.

Octavia looked a little flushed and leaned back. 'Oh, I see,' she went on, quite politely. 'The poor child is motherless?'

'Livia is without family. I was bidden to teach and protect her.'

'Protect? The Consul knew she faced peril?'

In her interview with Consul Derain, he'd commanded Arrow to guard the child and never do what she now did: speak of her. He hadn't explained why, and she wasn't allowed to ask.

Arrow tried to swallow but her mouth was too dry.

'I don't know.'

She should have assumed the worst and hidden Livy in some corner, ready to cut down anyone who came near. Maybe she indeed was just a witless slave, to have been so negligent. The Anglish had grown bold, and she'd watched them slope into her neighbourhood. But she'd merely tutted with distaste as if she were a normal governess, rather than raising her guard. Arrow gulped back the rising darkness, looking down at her hands twisted together as if locked in combat.

Octavia leaned forward a little and her hand fluttered out, skin almost translucent, without scar, blemish or callus. Then, with the hesitancy of a butterfly coming into land, the hand rested on Arrow's knee. So light, yet the touch of it burned though Arrow's thick skirts to the skin beneath.

'I'm sure you'll find her.' Octavia's words carried a soft smile.

No Citizen had ever touched her before – well, not without wearing armour to do so. It took Arrow's breath away.

Both their heads jerked up as the charo came to an abrupt stop.

'The Spire,' Octavia said.

Arrow jumped out before the driver could open the door for them. The rain had slackened into a nasty drizzle as she ran across the processional square to the towering spiral of black marble that pierced the sky. The tallest building in Londinium looked brutal beside the slim columns and sweeping porticos of the surrounding civic buildings.

Arrow conjured a lecture about old Emperor Aurelius. How he'd commissioned the huge, coiled building to honour the deep drills in the fire plains, which pierced through Gaea's hard skin to find her thick, black, sacred blood.

Since the time of Augustus, the newborn Roman Empire had used the steam engines devised by wily Cato (or his Anglish slave if historical gossips were to be believed). They pumped water, powered mining drills and even ran small chariots. Then one fateful day in the ninth year of God-Emperor Aurelius's reign, he was blessed with divine inspiration by the Goddess Gaea. Lifting a crude black oil lamp used by farmhands unable to afford olive oil, he'd seen a destined future for the Imperium.

43

Over a millennium later, that near-magical oil now fuelled ever more powerful mechanical engines and made the Imperium Romanum invincible and everlasting.

It would be a good lesson, but Livy was not there to teach.

Arrow collided with the first checkpoint: a small cabin punctuated the fencing, twenty feet from the Spire itself. A tall Legionary in wet-weather armour stood behind the cabin, two large guard dogs at his feet. Their tiny eyes bored into Arrow, hefty jaws open, mountains of sleek muscle coiled for any command to claw and shred.

'I must see Consul Derain,' she rasped.

A prematurely balding young clerk's face was half-obscured by the scratched cabin window, more dilapidated than an official building should be. The ravaging Godstorms didn't respect protocol.

'Do you have an appointment?' he drawled, without looking up from his scroll.

'No. This is an emergency.' Arrow's voice rose.

The soldier stirred and one guard dog rumbled a warning, not yet a growl but it rippled the large animal's muscles. If they discovered she was indentured, there would be trouble.

'Are you a Citizen?' the clerk droned on. 'You may visit the Spire with an escort at any time if you are a full Citizen of the Empire. Otherwise, move along.'

The Consul had never given her any papers or password to reach him in an emergency. If she tried to send a message now, it might take hours for a response to get to this gate. If it ever came at all.

Could she fight her way in? At least she could cause such disturbance that someone would carry the story to the Consul. Her hand gripped the handle of the concealed dagger at her waist. The dogs both sat up, intuiting a threat from the bedraggled woman that the Legionary remained oblivious to.

'Excuse me. I am Octavia Troak, daughter of the widow Regina Troak, and Citizen of our Imperium.'

Octavia had come up behind her, and, despite now being as soaked as Arrow, she managed to remain ladylike. A yellow toga sash fell from her shoulder, the passport of a Citizen to anywhere in the Empire – immediate death to anyone who wore it without the right to do so.

'I am in great urgency here, dear man.' Octavia smiled, but an edge had slipped into her voice. 'The legal ward of the Consul has gone missing. This is the child's governess, an employee of the Consul himself. I require entrance and escort for us both.'

The clerk stared at the two women with a slack jaw, then down at his papers and back up again. Arrow felt nearly the same state of shock; she had expected the charo to speed off once Octavia informed her mother they had conveyed a slave.

The soldier standing guard beside the checkpoint said, 'Follow me,' and he opened the gate, barking a command at the dogs, which both immediately sat at attention as the Citizen passed. Their eyes never left Arrow.

'Quickly,' Octavia whispered, 'before Mama catches up and makes a scene.'

Arrow managed a nod. They walked off over the slate paving with the only available escort. He led them to a side door, then up marble staircases and along corridors lined with plinths carrying the carved likenesses of Emperors, Consuls and famous political heroes from across the Empire.

'All my father ever wanted was a Troak bust on one of these plinths,' Octavia muttered. Arrow didn't know if she was supposed to answer.

How long had Livy been gone? Not even a full hour, although it already felt like years.

At the end of a long corridor, the guard rapped twice on a large door of Britannian oak and pushed it open for them. 'Visitors,' he grunted into the room and then left with more haste than he'd led them there.

The room was well lit and packed with heavy desks from which emerged the sound of busy scribbling. A few washed-out faces of clerks looked up, without showing much interest, then returned to their scrolls. At one end of the room was a closed silver door, with the broadest desk before it, from which a heavy-lidded pale man stared at them.

As he slipped from his chair and walked towards them, Arrow noted that his eyes were the only heavy thing about him.

Her right hand jerked as if grasping for a weapon. Although dressed in the simple dark cloth of a clerk, this man was a killer. He moved like she used to.

'I am Caligo. You are . . .?' he said without any welcoming formalities.

Octavia should speak first, but appeared aghast at the man's rudeness, so Arrow attempted politeness. 'Forgive the intrusion; I am governess to the Consul's ward, Livia. She is lost, I suspect abducted.'

'Well,' the clerk raised one eyebrow, 'the brat lost herself, did she? I warned Derain. Oh well. I will tell the Consul when he has time to deal with housekeeping matters.'

Octavia gasped, but Arrow felt her pulse speed. Consul Derain was responsible for the girl's safety.

'Livy is the Consul's ward,' she managed. 'He is legally responsible, and answerable, for her welfare.' She pulled out the small amulet, with its scrap of Livy's blue fabric, and held it out. He must take this evidence seriously. 'Livy was taken by Druids.'

Before her hand could curl back around it, Caligo snatched the amulet from her palm, then he flicked it, and caught it again as if he played with a coin. Arrow shook where she stood, jaw so tight against the urge to strike out she wasn't sure she could speak.

'I'm afraid that is *not* going to happen,' he said, and, with a small smile, Caligo slid into a stance she recognised. It was an invitation to attack and a warning that her opponent was ready. He knew her training. Just as he knew her skills would be pointless in this room, except to have her dragged out and hanged before the sunset.

Arrow fought the urge to lash out. *Men act as wolves to other men.*

Octavia dropped beside her.

Rather than the faint Arrow expected, the young woman knelt before the clerk. One hand clutched her heart, and the other reached up to him in supplication.

A Citizen begging a man without a toga? Arrow's muscles seized with the shock of it.

Octavia's yellow bonnet had been lost somewhere in the storm, and her golden hair waved out behind her. The dishevelled lace and slick of her dress clung damply to her body in ways Arrow suspected Madam Troak would not approve of. As if by order, a single sliver of sunlight broke through the clouds and lit the scene through a high window.

'As supplicant, I, Octavia, a Citizen of this Empire, do entreat you. Find pity for a small girl lost in our city. I'm sure the Consul cannot be so hard-hearted as to overlook her plight.'

Tears fell from the big blue eyes staring up at the dark man. Octavia's pose recalled a mythical figure from old Rome, one of the Vestal Virgins begging for the life of a wrongly accused man.

Octavia's plea astonished Arrow, but nothing about Caligo indicated that he would succumb to a woman's tears, even those of a Citizen. Until he struck his chest with his right hand and bowed his head. The other clerks similarly bowed with their hands over their hearts. The Consul remained in his office, so had Octavia's plea somehow moved them all?

Arrow turned to see that a group of soldiers had entered the room. The closest and youngest was staring at Octavia's kneeling form caught in the sunlight. Three bearded Centurions stood at attention behind him, each fully armoured in white and gold. The younger man, clearly entranced by Octavia, wore the simple armour of the Wolf Legion, but his uniform carried gold braid upon the shoulder, and he wore a fresh green laurel across his brow.

He ignored Arrow, who fell into her deepest curtsey, head almost to the floor, as he held his hand down towards Octavia.

'Lady, I know not what brings a Citizen to her knees, but I swear, if it is within my power, or the power of this Empire, then your entreaty will be answered.'

He raised Octavia to her feet. The two stood, Octavia in her yellow dress, elegantly dishevelled, as the broad-shouldered young soldier, a head taller than she, delicately held her hand as if she might float away. The room watched from under lowered lashes as mere audience to their play.

'Sire,' a deep voice broke in.

The Consul had come through his silver door behind Caligo's desk while they were all transfixed by Octavia. Arrow recognised the tall man with an arched nose and greying hair, wearing the white toga sash as only Consuls and the Imperial family were permitted. His grey eyes stared at the laurelled soldier, except for one flick towards Arrow.

'When the Heir to the Empire enters, a mere Consul such as myself should be ready to greet him at the door,' Consul Derain said.

Octavia started to tremble as she gazed up at the Emperor's son.

'If you did that,' the Heir answered, 'then I wouldn't have been able to aid this noble lady. Indeed, I still don't know the cause of her distress or how we shall answer it.'

Octavia sent a pleading glance down to Arrow. The young Citizen appeared entirely overcome.

With her head bowed, Arrow tried to radiate meekness. 'Sire, Consul.' She took a quick breath to steady her voice. 'The Consul's ward has been abducted from the Imperium Museum. Citizen Octavia kindly offered to bring me here to inform him, so we might search for her.'

Caligo whispered into the Consul's ear as she spoke, and a flicker passed across his careful face.

'Ah yes, my ward. How unfortunate.' The Consul spoke to her but looked at the Emperor's son. 'The girl went missing in the museum?

48

Well, that place is a warren. I'm sure she'll be found asleep in a corner. Children do that sort of thing, I believe. I will direct my staff to search the place.'

'You have a little ward, Derain?' The Heir's smile widened, showing teeth. 'My, you are full of surprises. You've never seemed the paternal type.'

'An unexpected responsibility, Sire. An old acquaintance from my Academy days died without fortune. I have provided for the child's education as best I could.'

Livy would be enthralled by even this snippet of information. The girl read every story about families with an intensity that sometimes worried Arrow: from the evil stepmothers of fairy tales to the tortuous familial lineages of the gods, Livy studied them like an alchemist searching for the elixir of life. When she asked about her own family, Arrow had nothing to tell her.

'But, I expected her to be taught strict obedience and Imperium propriety.' The Consul turned towards Arrow and his brow furrowed, 'Why did you leave the museum rather than finding and disciplining her? I bought you to stay with the child.'

Arrow flinched. Although correct, that word was considered impolite even when applied to the indentured. No matter, Livy was still lost, and the search hadn't started.

'Sir, there were street people in the museum, some clearly followers of the old religion. They took her.'

As she spoke, the Emperor's son dropped Octavia's hand to clutch at the handle of the arc gun on his hip. His face paled to ash, and he stared at Arrow.

'Nonsense,' the Consul snapped. 'Sire.' He stepped towards the Heir and his voice softened, like one trying to appease a scared child. 'Augusto. Panic easily infects the brains of women. This is nothing but hysterical fantasy.'

The Heir's knuckles showed white on his arc gun. 'What . . . what if it's true? What if the filthy Druids are here? Stealing children?

They bewitch the very sky, sending these storms against us. Now this! Derain, we must send the Legions in – all of them, against their foul Anglish magic. We will raze the Old Town to the ground. I'll burn them out, like rats!'

The three guards behind him stood immobile while the Emperor's son ranted, although Arrow did notice the telltale twitch of muscle in the jaw of the closest Centurion. He, too, ground his teeth, it seemed.

'Sire, there is no need.' The Consul's voice was sing-song. 'I've already placed new military guards across the city, and my people watch the Old Town at all times. We have dirigibles tracking them from the sky. Nothing moves in Londinium without my knowledge, you know this.' He touched the arm holding the arc gun and nudged it away from the hilt. 'The Plebeians were merely sheltering from the Godstorm, poor wretched things they must have been. This is just a soft-headed indentured girl, with no sense or education. This whole bizarre story is nothing more than foolish female imagination, I'm sure of it.'

Arrow knitted her brows. The Consul knew her education in military tactics and combat decision making was equal to any Centurion. Why would he dismiss her report as fantasy? With ten men, she could search the Old Town, or at least find someone with plaits in their hair to wring information from.

She thought of Livy smiling up at the giant fossil in the museum. Heir or no, the time for delay was over.

'But, I found—' she started, watching the clerk Caligo's fingers close around the amulet he'd taken from her.

'Enough!' The Consul's voice resounded as it must on the senate floor itself. 'That child will be running amok in the museum right now, disturbing worthy people, because you are derelict in your duty.'

It was perilous to contradict a Citizen, and a Consul no less, but . . . Livy.

'We must—'

'Be silent . . . slave.'

Arrow's stomach churned, but she stood silently. The armed Centurions had all turned towards her, hands on the hilts of their arc guns.

Was it her imagination or did Octavia gasp at the word 'slave'? It couldn't be shock, because she already knew Arrow's status. Perhaps the delicate woman was affronted by coarse language.

The Consul moved towards Octavia, dragging the Heir's attention with him. His voice softened again, 'Now you, my dear Lady. May we be of help returning you to the museum, or your family? Your delicate feelings in this matter do you great honour.'

'But, Livia,' Octavia said, looking over at Arrow, 'will she truly be found?'

'Of course, she will. I give you my word of honour upon it,' the Consul said.

Arrow blinked – his word could not be questioned. A Citizen's honour was the rock upon which the Empire rested.

The Heir took Octavia's hand again. 'I'll order my own guards to the museum to search for her, no effort will be spared. Now, do you have a charo nearby, or may I offer my own?'

'Oh, my mama is downstairs in ours, she must be worried by now.' Octavia's gaze drifted up to the handsome face of the Heir.

'Then let's go down together and assure her you are well,' the Heir replied, smiling back at her.

Octavia blushed a little, and, despite her fury and terror for Livy, Arrow couldn't help but imagine the raptures of widow Troak when her daughter reappeared from the Spire on the arm of the Emperor's only son.

The couple went to leave, followed by the white-clad Centurions. Arrow stared at the woman's retreating back, but then blond hair swished as Octavia spun, face glowing.

'For dear Livia.' She stepped back and pressed a handkerchief into

51

Arrow's fist. 'Nature loves nothing solitary. Please assure her that she has friends!'

With a shining smile for the whole room, Octavia rejoined the Heir, and they processed out. Arrow gripped the slip of silk, then almost dropped it when she spotted three yellow nasturtiums and a small O and T embroidered on the corner. The initials made this handkerchief Octavia's official signet. Giving it to Livy constituted an offer of legal patronage. If Livy were standing here, by accepting the signet she would have immediately, and legally, become part of Octavia's family. With all the rights and protections that status bestowed.

Arrow fumbled the silk into her sash while all the men politely faced the Heir's retreating back. To offer patronage to another Citizen's ward without asking his blessing first was either boldness or flighty folly. Hopefully, Consul Derain hadn't noticed the initials.

Once the door clicked closed, the Consul turned to the dark clerk, all softness gone from his voice. 'No clerk will speak of this. Make them understand that my displeasure will fall upon their necks if they do.'

Caligo nodded, and the sound of diligent scribbling from the other desks raised a notch.

'That was a near disaster, but a pretty face has more than once diverted him.' The Consul's lips were a mere line of displeasure. 'Do not attempt to manage a situation like that again, Caligo. The moment a Citizen enters my rooms, you will inform me. Your skills are useful, but your sense is limited. As you would do well to remember.'

'I apologise, Sire,' Caligo replied meekly, like a shamed schoolboy, 'I feared the slave girl might say too much.'

Derain closed his eyes for a moment, as if looking at Arrow were a chore he'd rather avoid. If his voice was displeased with his clerk, it was disgusted when he finally turned to her.

'You, little *fool*. As of this instant, your contract as governess is revoked. You will seek no further contact with me, this office, or the child. Return to the bonds market until my men can sell you on.'

'But . . . Livy,' Arrow said. Her heart had soared when Octavia pressed the handkerchief into her hands, but now her nails pressed into her palms so hard her skin began to break.

'Forget that name.' Derain scowled, then gathered himself. 'That child is no longer your concern, as you are no longer her governess. You have no references and no right to be here.'

This was her last chance, for Livy.

'That clerk has the proof. An amulet—'

The slap hit her worse than a punch. It was leisurely, Caligo's fingers almost caressing her cheek after the impact. She held herself immobile for it, even though it would have been easy to block.

The pain burst in like an old enemy so familiar they were now indistinguishable from a friend. Hair spilling out of her hastily tied bonnet with damp, cheap skirts and boots muddy from the rain, she wasn't a governess anymore.

Arrow's heart calmed, and her head cleared.

The clerk ran the tip of his tongue across his lip, staring at the rising red welt on her cheek.

The Consul strode back to his office, throwing his orders to Caligo over his shoulder.

'You caused this mess, so clean it up. Take her down the back stairs, not via the atrium. Then speed her to the bonds market to be sold immediately.' The Consul paused, without looking back. 'To a buyer outside the city, even at cut price.'

Caligo grabbed Arrow's arm and towed her towards a low door in the back corner of the room.

Fear was the first thing on earth to make gods.

As they went down a steep old stairway at the back of the Spire, Arrow dragged her skirts above her ankles to keep herself at least a step ahead of Caligo.

If she was sold outside the city today, would she even hear if Livy was found? She would have no one to ask, and no right to do so. With a word, the Consul had taken the name 'governess' from her.

Stumbling on the precariously high steps, Arrow threw out a hand to steady herself.

'Halt.' The clerk's voice made the skin on her back crawl. But she stopped, hand out and skirt held.

'Poor little slave.' Caligo stood just one step above her. Gods, having an enemy behind you, back unprotected, went against everything she'd been trained since birth.

Which the bastard clearly knew.

His voice mocked sympathy: 'Come on now, girl, why in such a hurry? You know you're nothing now. No one.' He ran his fingers into the small of her back, pushing just enough that if she didn't steady herself, she'd fall forward. His fingertips were hard, like weapons.

'Are you so very eager to reach the slave pits?' His voice sounded like there was too much saliva in his mouth. 'Or do you crave knowing how many denarii you're worth? Which master will use you next?'

The pressing fingers reached her waist.

'You know the pit bosses strip and fumigate the merchandise before parading it for sale? You'll lose this nice dress, I'm afraid.' His hands searched for the ties of her skirt, body looming behind her own. 'They auction slaves naked.'

'The Consul said we should go quickly.' Arrow hoped threats of more displeasure from the Consul might distract him.

Caligo laughed and grabbed the back of her bonnet, dragging her head against his chest, breath speeding against her still smarting cheek. 'Right here, I own you, not Derain. And I will use you however, and for as long, as I wish.'

For earning him Derain's displeasure, the clerk would debase her.

As he pulled her bonnet back, Arrow's neck strained, tiptoe high on the narrow step. His other hand fumbled with her skirt ties.

'Remember. I know exactly what you were, little slave. That stupid brat has finally gone. So, you can stop pretending you're some sweet nursemaid.'

He was right, she wasn't good or gentle. She'd never deserved a soft life raising a little child. She was nothing, no one.

The clerk had almost opened the back of her skirt, his body pressed against hers, warm breath against the skin of her straining neck. Two of them on an empty stair, insulated against screams.

They were all right about her. She wasn't a governess anymore.

Necessity has no law.

Arrow dropped.

Knees sharply buckling, she tore her head forward, despite the bonnet ties cutting her neck. Hips and elbows thrust back with all her strength.

Years ago at the Academy, she'd been taught a falling body would stay in motion unless acted upon by an outside force.

The clerk went right over the top of her, with a grunt. His spine smacked down the sharp steps below, head cracking against each one on the way down.

Arrow had forgotten how satisfying the sound of bone hitting stone could be.

She carefully followed, until he came to rest, sprawled across the bottom step. His pose was reminiscent of a resting satyr, apart from the blood gushing from a crack in his forehead, quickly obscuring his face.

Standing over him, Arrow massaged her neck.

Her hand floated, almost of its own accord, to the sash where her knife was hidden. One slash would stop his shallow breathing. But when her hand slipped into her waist belt it closed on Livy's summons to the Academy rather than her dagger hilt.

Arrow wasn't a governess anymore. But Livy didn't know that.

Did they all expect her to forget the last eight years? Forget the dark curls, the bold smile, the rolled-eyes during lessons? Forget the feeling of Livy's hand in her own?

The gods demand absolute obedience of an indentured slave to their master. There were terrible consequences for those who rebelled against the gods' laws.

But, what had her mother said to her, so many years ago?

If you can't sway the heavens to your liking, then you must raise hell to your bidding.

The Nones of Junius, Londinium Arena

MDCXXXVII, Aurelian Calendar

CHAPTER IV

'They say, those who the gods love, die young.' The training Lanista gave no other welcome to the novicii gladiators. 'And the gods are jealous in this Arena. Most of you will die before the year is out.'

The girl wasn't sure if he was trying to motivate them, terrify them or merely offer fair warning.

She stood in a raggedy line with five other children. By their heights, she thought she must be one of the youngest, at nine years old. Some she knew well; they'd grown up together as Arena brats. Others must have been recently bought.

She was the only girl.

'Some of those standing beside you, you'll kill soon. If you're lucky, others you'll kill later. Each of you will wound, scar, and leave the others racked with pain. Often, every day.'

If their Lanista wanted to ensure the novicii gladiators didn't become friends, he was going about it the right way. The girl shuffled a little further away from the unfamiliar blond boy next to her.

The Lanista bent and scooped a handful of gritty Arena sand, letting it slowly trickle out between his fingers. 'This sand is now your mother and father, it is your lover, your master and it will embrace you on your death.'

The girl froze, blinking in the weak sunlight as if it were a blaze.

She knew how thirsty the sand could be: it had drunk her mother's blood and left no trace.

Yet here she stood, desperate to test herself against it.

'You'll grow muscles you didn't know you had, and you'll train in strategy to thrill an audience. Perhaps, you'll fight so well you'll win your freedom – ' The Lanista surveyed them, the girl watching his old, scarred face wrinkle with distaste. When he looked at her, he even snorted – 'doubtful as that seems. Each day you'll train here, you'll be tested, and you'll prove if you deserve a glorious death on the sand. If you fail to impress me, then we'll send you to the bonds market.'

The girl didn't expect glory or freedom here on the Arena sand. If she had any choice at all she'd never have stepped foot on it again.

But she would fight men, rather than the only other fate for an orphaned slave girl – whore for them.

'Your tests begin, now.' The Lanista brushed the last grains of sand from his hands, then looked back up at them with more interest than he'd yet shown. 'Fight. The worst combatant will be sold on – today.'

The children stood, shuffling their feet, staring at the Lanista. He gave no further instructions, no direction on who was supposed to fight who, or how. The mountainous former gladiator stood with thick arms crossed, eyes boring into them with more heat than the weak Britannian sun above them.

The girl heard the unmistakable thud of fist into soft tissue.

A short lad on the far end of the line had punched the boy next to him in the stomach. The other child keeled forward, crying out, but the attacking boy kept pounding his target's skull and ribs.

That unleashed chaos.

All six children sparked to panicked battle. Thin arms crashed into smooth and spindly legs. Small fists connected with jaws years away from the first wisps of a beard.

As the youngest, and a girl, she would have to fight twice as hard to be considered half as good. Her chances were slim.

SOLITAIRE TOWNSEND

While there's life there's hope, only the dead have none.

She had no inheritance except this moment. As orphaned child of a popular gladiatrix the Arena bosses had gifted her this trial for gladiator school. But that right extended no further than today. If the girl failed to impress the bosses, they wouldn't hesitate to profit off her sale to the whoremongers.

Her mother's death had won her the chance of learning to kill.

The blond boy was a head taller than her, but slower. She kicked out his bony knee, but as he went down he managed a hard elbow in her ribs, winding her.

Her chest hurt and her breath burned. She imagined her mother's lowered brows and shaking head watching her daughter stumble.

Up on his knees, the boy smashed forward, trying to tackle her to the ground, where his weight would be the advantage. But his grip wasn't strong enough. She grabbed the back of his tunic and tugged herself through his arms, kicking out at his head without success.

Rolling forward, she gained her feet just as he did. Both swung punches at each other's face. She blocked his blow with her left arm, but hers missed the nose she'd tried to crush.

He missed a grab at her arm, and she slipped, failing to land a kick at his ribs. They were fighting air . . . and losing.

She'd watched enough Arena battles to know how pathetic this was.

The other children grunted and shrieked in pain beside them. Panic threatened tears, but her fear kept them at bay.

Gods, she must look like a little weakling girl to the Lanista right now. Perhaps that's what she looked like to the boy, too.

She heard her mother's voice as clearly as if the tall woman stood beside her. *If courage cannot defeat an enemy, then cunning must do so.*

Flopping her shoulders, the girl let a tear escape, not entirely faking. She clutched her side, as if this was the first time her delicate skin had felt a blow.

The boy grabbed his chance, face bright with victory, and safety from the slave pits.

He charged her again, shoulder headed for her midriff to tackle her down. Exactly as he had before. He'd obviously not yet learnt that gladiators studied each other, watching for any repeated moves.

A pace before his body would have slammed into hers, the girl whipped sideways out of her slouch. Leaving her bunched fist at eye height. It wasn't a perfect alignment, but her knuckles connected with the side of his eye socket with greater force than any blow her own little arms could have generated, gifted by the boy's weight and speed.

His head jolted back, and his feet skidded on the sand below him. He landed on his rump with a satisfying thud. The girl's arm thrummed with the jolt and the skin on her fist was broken, droplets of blood already welling up to feed the hungry sand. The pain of it sent a thrill up her arm and to her heart. Victory was always the best remedy for any injury.

She'd brought down a boy both older and bigger than her.

'Enough!' the Lanista barked out, shaking his head. 'That was like watching kittens squabbling over a saucer of milk. On your feet.'

The children scrambled back up. The boy she bested didn't meet her eye. There was blood trickling down his cheek, but he didn't wipe it away. The girl heard soft weeping further along the line.

'I've never seen such a pathetic group of novicii gladiators in all my years in the Arena.' Their trainer paced along their line, 'You have no strategy, no style and no strength.' He stopped at the far end from the girl and shook his head at them. 'It would be easier to sell you *all* off and use the income to buy more weapons. But I doubt the bosses would get enough from you to afford a single decent sword.'

With that, he seized the upper arm of the boy who'd taken the first punch. Tears ran down the youngster's dirty cheeks and he was covered with bloody scratches and sand. The girl judged he'd taken a beating after the boy beside him had launched the surprise attack.

'One down, five to go.' The trainer near lifted the lad off his feet.

The boy cried out, but the girl heard sighs of relief from the others. Hers was the loudest.

'The rest of you will sprint the perimeter of the Arena while I hand this lad over to the bondsmen. Go.'

With that, their Lanista turned on his heel and strode off across the quad, dragging the sobbing loser behind him.

'Bundle of laughs, isn't he?' the boy she'd been fighting quipped. His white-blond hair was the same shade as the Arena sand caught in it. The boy's nonchalant smile clashed with the swelling bruise around his eye and blood trickling from a bust brow.

The girl had expected to make her first enemy by beating him. A small price to pay for winning another day free from the slave pits. But while his lopsided grin and bruising wound both occupied the same face, neither owned it.

'Guess so,' she answered, unable to match his smile but loath to reject a truce. She doubted she'd be offered many.

The boy winked at her. 'Race you? Bet I can make it round the Arena before old latrine-breath gets back,' he shouted over his shoulder, sprinting forward.

Was this a game to him? He was so pretty; he should fear the whoremasters too. Maybe if she kept bashing up his face he'd have less to worry about.

The girl ran after him, at the back of the pack, but catching up. Most of the boys were half-limping or cradling damaged elbows and shoulders. She imagined they were a ridiculous sight. A bunch of raggedy, skinny and bust-up children, dwarfed by the huge Arena they stumbled around, red pennants fluttering high above.

But as they ran, the girl laughed for the first time since her mother had been butchered on this sand.

She was in pain, and still in danger. But she had won her first fight.

The Ides of Maius, Londinium

MDCLVII, Aurelian Calendar

CHAPTER V

Carefully stepping around Caligo's blood, Arrow left the Spire.

In the sharp light outside, she spotted red pennants flying high over tall limestone walls. Her only hope was a name that, until now, she'd firmly convinced herself that she had forgotten.

To save Livy, she had to find Barro.

Thinking of him made old injuries ache, and, even worse, her heart flutter a little. Although that was probably just the exertion from attacking the clerk.

Arrow started to walk, then run, away from the Spire, in the opposite direction to the bonds market.

A little watery sunshine lit the alleyways. Grateful for her sturdy boots, Arrow skidded on the drying cobbles. It must be early afternoon, and if she could find her way through these back streets there might be a chance of reaching the Arena during training hours.

Was she panting so hard because of her desperation to find Livy, or were the gods already reaching down to punish her? Arrow stopped, hands on knees, lungs burning. *Breathe.* She'd be no use to Livy if she passed out in a back alley. After a moment she was able to go on, although she couldn't shake a feeling of being exposed, hair on her skin raised.

Now she'd escaped from the Spire, it was like a clock had started ticking in her chest, counting down the time she had to rescue Livy before she herself was caught.

Within the hour, sooner if Caligo regained consciousness, Arrow would be marked down as a bonds breaker. Special teams of bondsmen scoured the city for those few slaves who dared insult the gods by betraying, assaulting or running from their masters.

Confine yourself to the present. She repeated her mother's maxim to herself. The hunt would start, but so had she.

The blood-red flags fluttering on the Arena's turrets kept peeping over the top of pitched roofs as she ducked under lines of washing and around piles of city detritus. A few faces peered at her from low doorways, but she knew better than to ask for directions. She was too smartly dressed to be welcome, but obviously not a Citizen who could demand assistance.

Keep moving. Forcing her ribs to expand as far as possible under her corset, Arrow took a deep breath in – which turned into a coughing fit as she stepped out of the passages behind the Spire and into the wide criss-cross of roads that ran around the Arena itself.

A haze hovered over the road that even the Godstorm hadn't cleared.

Thankfully, mid-afternoon wasn't rush hour, but the charo fumes still slipped up her nose, drying out her mouth and leaving an oily taste in the back her throat.

Arrow wasn't the only one choking on them. A shack perched perilously close to the wide roadside and an ashen child, not more than three years old, slumped inside its doorway. The cough rattling from their small chest could be heard even over the traffic. The wide eyes spoke of a life comprising nothing more than gulping for breath between each hack.

Charos of every shape and colour raced by in both directions, engines thumping as drivers enjoyed one of the few wide roads in the city. The nearest safe crossing was a mile's stride further along, but the entrance Arrow needed was closer, directly across this road.

Looking both ways, she waited for the perfect moment, then darted out into the stream of traffic, holding her skirts up tight against her legs. A few taxa drivers screamed at her from their open seats as Arrow dodged between them, horns blaring. One big red charo with high gold headlights topping off its prow almost clipped her, the shocked faces of its occupants behind the glass pane whipping away. One slip and she'd be under the wheels. But Arrow had played this game as a child, and she'd lost none of her reaction speed. She dodged and spun, and even held back her coughs until she could safely press up against the large sandstone slabs of the high Arena wall. Then she hacked until she bent over, and a little rage fell out of her with each barking cough and splutter.

Before her coughs became sobs, Arrow started walking along the thin strip of land between the high Arena walls and tarmac road, stepping over trash and even a discarded charo wheel rim. She traced the old familiar roughness of the pale stone with her hand as she headed towards the door she needed. The creamy walls were enormous, running up so high that the red flags were just tiny fluttering dots. The scuffs on her palm from the stones reminded her how soft her hands felt compared to when she left these walls to become Livy's governess.

Arrow picked up her pace despite sudden weariness. There wasn't time to be tired, nor for nostalgia.

Forgetting the road, she took a deep breath and almost choked again. For generations, gladiators had grumbled that the roads should be moved further from the Arena because the thick fumes affected their fights. She stomped through the miasma, but her feet nearly failed her at an unmarked but oh-so-familiar shadowed entrance. For Livy, Arrow squared her shoulders and stepped into the tunnel cut deep into the proud Arena walls.

Dusty old shields and spears were the only ornamentation hung along it, unchanged since she'd last been there. But a thick-armed man she didn't recognise now sat behind a high desk by the small wooden door to the training rooms themselves.

Arrow tried to swagger, but her skirts made it feel like a sashay.

'I'm here to see Barro; I'm an old pard of his. He inside?' she asked, trying to mimic a confidence she'd all but forgotten.

'Ain't no entry here, girl. Best go back to your charo and take it round front, that's the public entrance,' the man drawled.

Even a few years ago she would have known the man – if he was a Retiarius or Secutor – and which quads he trained in. That she didn't recognise him at all showed how long she'd been away, and how carefully she'd avoided all news of the place.

'Look, friend, I have the right to enter,' Arrow tried.

He huffed without looking up and continued rubbing down his long dagger. For Hades' sake, she needed to say it.

'I was a gladiator.'

Why did that sound like a question even to her own ears?

Arrow couldn't manage more. Couldn't tell him that she had fought as the first ever female Murmillo, carrying a heavy sword and shield. Her victories. The men she killed to the roar of the adoring crowd. The thrill of standing in blood-drenched victory under the sun followed by the heart-pounding doubts in the dark. Nor that she left eight years ago through that very door, at the height of her power, her eventual freedom likely. With Barro's blood on her knuckles as she walked out.

The guard didn't even look up. He just sniffed and kept running the filthy cloth along the sparkling steel. Other than attacking him right here and now, what else could she do?

Actually, she might be able to take him. But then wouldn't get far into the quads uninvited. You can't fight an arc gun with a hatpin. While there were far fewer female gladiators, her kind were welcome in the training quads and offered most of the same privileges as the men. The last time Arrow had stood here, her hair had been slicked back into a tight bun. Her suntanned skin strapped under leather training greaves, with fighting sandals laced up her legs and a sword on her hip. At the sight of the red and gold champion laurels pinned to her shoulder, this man would have struck his chest and opened the door with bowed head.

Today, with skirts muddied around her ankles and hair wisping out from her crushed bonnet, the contrast with a warrior woman couldn't have been starker. The heavy feeling in her gut dragged at her as panic for Livy made her heart flinch.

'Can you just tell me if he's in there, or send a message? I must speak to him, please.' Arrow begged where once she would have commanded.

'I'm not a message service for angry girlfriends, now bugger off around to the front.'

She gaped. Of course, this must be what it looked like to him, a dishevelled woman pleading to see her lover, who'd probably thrown her over. With horror, Arrow felt a deep blush rise up her chest. She wanted to leap the desk, rip that dagger out of his hands and silence him with a single slash across the neck.

Instead, she stood there, fighting back her pinking skin. Before giving him any further confirmation of jilted womanhood, Arrow turned and strode out of the tunnel back into the daylight, without another word.

Not a governess, not a gladiator, just a *bloody* girlfriend. He would never let her in. Perhaps she should tell him she was a runaway slave searching for a girl no one wanted. A child she had raised, taught and woefully failed to protect.

No, stop that. *Either don't try at all or make sure you succeed.*

When she found Livy, could she take the girl to Octavia rather than back to the Consul? The pale woman had risked personal shame to plead with a mere clerk. Octavia could be like a mother to Livy, showering her with all the luxury a Citizen could command. Perhaps she would even buy the girl's governess's contract, finding a place for her in the household. The handkerchief from Octavia was folded up and tucked into a pocket like a talisman.

We suffer more often in imagination than in reality.

Arrow ground her jaw to force out the silly fantasy from her mind. The Consul was Livy's legal guardian, and he was more powerful than any mortal man, second only to the Emperor. Octavia was just a soft-hearted young woman who perhaps even now was missing her handkerchief, not realising that was what she'd handed over.

The only person looking for Livy was her former governess, and Arrow must find the girl before the bondsmen found her. A few deep gulps of the oily air controlled her heart and also nudged her memory. Not only gladiators needed access to the fighting pits of the Arena. An entirely different type of fighter also needed space to live, train and prepare to die. A few minutes' walk further around the edge, and Arrow could hear, and smell, the other entrance.

She plunged into a corridor plastered with warning signs.

It took a minute to adjust to the gloom, lit by a few old oil lamps. The dark filled by growls, barks and squeaks harmonised with the familiar sound of snores coming from one corner.

'Mustard! Hey Mustard, wake up!' she called, walking towards the sound.

'Wha'?' A coughing began and then a frailer voice than Arrow remembered said, 'Oi, no one can be down 'ere. Din'ya see the signs?'

'Don't worry, Mustard, it's just me. I need your help,' she answered.

As he stood up from his chair and stepped into the faint oil light, she saw how much time had passed. In eight years, her old friend had gone from ageing but spry to an old man. Mustard was made of sinew wrapped in leathery hide and a thousand scars. But today that skin looked significantly looser, his remaining hair relegated from the peppery grey she remembered to a shock of white.

But his eyes cleared when he saw her, and he stood a little taller in his leather apron, with thick protective pelts wrapped around his arms.

'That can't be young Arrow, now, can it? All dressed up like a proper lady in a green frock. It looks like Arrow, but it can't be, she don't have a weapon in her hand!'

It was both alien and familiar for someone to say her name. She was Arrow in her own mind, but Livy called her 'Miss' and no one else had called her anything much at all for years.

Arrow wasn't even her real name.

It had been chosen by the other gladiators as her battle-name. Arrow had Arena sand ground into her skin; small but tightly muscled and faster than any man, she fought for respect as fiercely as victory. Some called her cold. While other gladiators earned real gold by granting bed-sports to fans, Arrow couldn't be bought. For a long time, she hadn't even been kissed. But out on the Arena floor she wasn't cold, she thirsted for blood almost as much as the sand itself. At least she had, at the beginning.

'Hello, Mustard,' she answered his welcome and even stepped forward to slap her arm against his in a gladiator greeting. 'Yes, it's Arrow,' she hurried to explain, 'but I'm afraid this isn't a social call. I need your help: I've got to find Barro.'

Mustard hesitated, but then said, 'Well now, that Barro-boy ain't been a gladiator hisself for years, he left a while after you did.'

Barro had been sold on? Her stomach crunched in panic, but Mustard went on, 'I sees 'im here somewhat still though. Comes in afternoons to train with the Arena lads, and even with the Citizens. Why you keep coming back here, now you've got away? I asked him. You should know that Mustard man, he answers me, once a beast has a taste for blood it never leaves him be. He might be here now, I reckon. If you really want him?'

'I do, please. Can you get me into the training pits? I can't pass the gladiator's door.'

'Not much surprised by that, Arrow-girl, in the get-up you've got on. Big Jacko would have pegged you as a dam spitting for her darlin'!'

Mustard laughed to himself, but he tugged up the leather straps on his arms and waved her forward.

A stab of guilt pierced her; if not for her desperation, she probably would never have come back here to visit the old beast-master ever again.

'How are you, Mustard?'

'Shouldn't grumble, but I do,' he said with a wink. 'Need more help down here than them slack-jaws they send me to muck out and feed the beasts. Got so many new 'uns coming through. Now me, I've been handling Arena animals' man an' boy. But e'en I don't rightly know how to cage some of what they send me now. All teeth, claws and even feathers. Comes from the edge of the world, a few of 'em, I reckon.'

Nodding in sympathy, Arrow rolled her shoulders as she walked, although the tight buttons of her blouse didn't allow much movement. Then she stopped, arrested in place with a chill on her neck.

Turning, she saw a pair of yellow eyes with black slits staring back at her from a dark corner. The observation felt unnerving, deadly still and unblinking. This was unlike anything from the other cages in which animals either slept or threw themselves at the bars as they passed. This cage contained coiled feline blackness, perfectly at rest, but watching. Arrow knew she was being sized up with as much intelligence and skill as any gladiator in the Arena, judged for her strength and calculated for what it would take to kill her.

Mustard turned to look at them, the energy passing between the woman and the slitted cat's eyes in the cage.

'Yep, take that one there. Barro himself told me when she'd be coming in. Panthera they say she is, from away there in the River Kingdoms. Not a large cat by a lion's scale, I give you, and they weren't sure if she'd fight. Some Citizen fool-boy wanted her first. Said he was gonna beat a river queen in front of his rich mates. Show her how the Empire treated "dusky she-cats from the old forest" or some such dribble. Warned him I did. Seen ev'ry animal passed through here in forty years and I knows a killer, whatever shape she's in. Laughed, he did, when he saw her, disappointed she was so small. But Arena bosses paid a packet for her capture and shipping so the lad could only afford a fight to blood and ground. Hold 'er down for two minutes and cut her fur and he'd have won. All his mates come to watch it, pouring posh wine down 'emselves and talking dirty bout them river women.'

Here the old man paused and looked into the cage. The yellow eyes moved to meet his.

'She tore his face half off in the first seconds,' Mustard said. 'He screamed an' thrashed on the ground and then she laid right across him, like she was sat on a pillow, ripping off great clumps from his legs with her claws like a pussycat. It all happened so fast it took us a while to get the nets and fire to pull her off. Couldn't kill 'er, see? He'd just paid for blood and ground, and he'd signed away blame for 'owt else. Arena law. Only when I got 'er back 'ere and it all calmed down, I worked out she'd held him down for the full two minutes. I swear she knew the rules. No one's asked for her since. Though I reckon the Arena will find a way to use a killer spirit like that. They always do.'

The look on Mustard's face as he finished his story made Arrow pull her gaze away from the Panthera and stride onwards. Although she could still feel the cool eyes on her neck as she did.

Mustard led her through a small door, and Arrow blinked in the light. They walked out on the vast sandy base of the Arena floor, the huge ranks of empty spectator rows rising all around them. Her dress and dirty petticoats suddenly felt too heavy and the bones of her corset, even though she wore the cheapest one, seemed to compress her ribs unbearably.

She wrestled to breathe against the constraining clothing she had so desperately wanted just a few years ago.

'Where might Barro be?'

The vast sand was sectioned off into training grids. A handful even sported large rattan screens around them so wealthy Citizens could train without prying eyes.

'Barro usually fights over in Venus quad, right up by the sharp corner, you 'member it?' Mustard answered, shielding his vision against the light.

'I remember,' Arrow replied, 'thank you, Mustard. I'm glad to see you, and I'm sorry I didn't come before.'

'Well now. I never said it, y'know, back then. But I was right pleased you got away.' Mustard couldn't quite meet her eye. 'Might sound strange, coming from the likes of me, considering what I do an' all. But I don't like to see a wild thing caged. You owned the sand, Arrow; I never seen nothing like it when you fought. But you got away a'fore it owned you. I wish you well wit' the troubles I can see you got.' The old man ran his thumb along an old scar on this jaw. 'I'll say this: 'ware of Barro. He ain't the boy you knew back then. Man now he is, and got more sides to him than any creature I ever met.'

'Well, Mustard, I'm not the girl from back then either, and he's my one hope, and a faint one at that. Goodbye. I will come again, and I would love to bring someone for you to meet . . .' Arrow said, but on the last words her voice cracked, thinking of how thrilled Livy would be to visit Mustard, and how inappropriate she would have considered that meeting even a few hours ago. She squeezed the beast-master's arm and strode off across the sand.

Venus quad was the closest to the main entrance, and Arrow dodged around gladiators, city-folk and even a few Citizens training. The public training hours on the Arena floor were supposed to be one of the few times where rank didn't matter; just skill and sweat. Of course, in reality the official Arena law of equal-sized quads, freely bookable for training by anyone, didn't quite work like that. She passed a group of about twelve scruffy young lads practising wrestling with focused concentration all crammed into one quad. While in another, a weak-limbed older man, with the bearing and training clothes of a rich Citizen, gently stretched alongside a well-oiled and somewhat scantily clad gladiator, with suspiciously empty quads all around them.

Across the sand, she spotted a female fighter's silhouette against the afternoon sun. The woman practised her sword swing, raising and sweeping the blade in tight, deadly arcs – working on her sharp-stop to a falling weapon, harder on a woman's trapezius muscles.

After staring at the training woman, Arrow hurried ahead, lifting her heavy skirts to move faster.

She saw Barro and his opponent while many steps away, their outlines as they wrestled coming into focus. Arrow recognised Barro by his white-blond hair, so rare here in Londinium. But the rest of him had grown and hardened from the boy she had known. It took an effort of will not to straighten up her own hair. The last time he'd seen her she was leaving the Arena to be sold on, after refusing to fight any more. She'd had to knock Barro out cold to reach the door.

After a few more years, if she'd survived, there would have been a chance of winning her own contract back. Those gladiators who endured could become full Plebeians, and over the past decades a handful had even reached Citizenhood. Folks liked it when gladi-atrixes earned their freedom. Until then, Arrow had been one of the most respected, and even feared, of the indentured.

She'd also been very good at it.

By refusing to fight, Arrow had forced the Arena bosses to open her contract for trade. She condemned herself to a lifetime of servi-tude and contempt, just to escape the sand, and him. Of course, that's what all the Arena gossips believed, but no one, not even Mustard, knew the truth of it.

Barro had been furious, hurt and confounded as to why she was throwing everything, including him, away. The heavy pit filling in her stomach tried to convince her to walk away again now: she'd find no help here. Arrow shook her head and ground her jaw against it. What happened years ago didn't matter.

Livy had been taken today.

Barro sparred with a darker man. Both wearing only trousers, their bare feet gripped into the sand. Barro was the taller of the two, with broad, well-muscled shoulders. Arrow noticed, although she must have known before, that his bare chest was covered with thousands of tiny freckles merging into skin tanned by years in the Arena. His opponent was shorter but wider, his thicker muscles giving him an advantage in strength but at the cost of speed. A long purple scar disfigured the brawny man's face from eyelid to lip, moving like a snake as he scowled at Barro.

Both men had golden sand stuck to the sweat sheen on their ribs and backs. Circling, they blocked swift kicks and jabs. By the heaviness of their breathing, Arrow judged they had worked up towards a final clash. If she'd taken much longer getting here, Barro would have been gone.

The scarred man sprang into a drop-kick, knocking out Barro's knee. Barro grunted as he thumped clumsily on his side, fingers grasping at empty air.

Arrow's muscles strained in the traces of her joints as she watched them. She still drilled with the exercises her mother had taught her, late every night after Livy went to bed. But she hadn't sparred since leaving the sand. Her knee ached on cold mornings, from past blows like that one.

Barro's opponent pushed his advantage. Not bothering to correct his footing, he grasped towards Barro's neck. But Barro wasn't where he should be. A feint: Barro had twisted, flipping the other man with a clap of skin hitting hard muscle. Now above, Barro's toes curled in the sand as his forearm thrust against the man's windpipe.

The men panted in and out in time. Arrow's own chest fell into rhythm with them.

No time for that, for memories of skin against skin.

'That was a dirty trick when you tried it on me, Barro, and it still is.'

Barro's head tugged up wide-eyed at her, and he was the boy she knew. But his forearm also wavered. Undistracted, the other man used his bulk to flip his opponent; now Barro spluttered face down in the sand, the darker man's body on top, yanking a wrist up in a painful lock.

Barro spat out sand and said through gritted teeth, 'Mal, meet Arrow.'

The dark man backed off, and both scrambled to their feet – Barro with a lopsided grin and Mal with a nod.

Barro brushed himself off, eyebrows raised. 'Well, Mal, it's hard to believe, I know, but that prim miss standing there was the most heartless gladiator ever to spill men's guts on this sand. We called her Arrow in honour of the single weapon she couldn't master. I think it bored her killing from a distance rather than being close enough to taste the blood. Arrow, this is Mal, who owes his victory entirely to you.'

His teasing always landed on her with the same weight as his punches.

'I need to talk to you, Barro,' she said. She'd hoped to catch him alone – the last thing Arrow needed was someone who might remember her when the bondsmen came asking.

Mal handed Barro a water jug, and he winked at her, then upended it over his head. The water washed away the sand and sweat from his torso but left his smile in place.

'I need your help.' She wanted to run. 'Please.'

'What's up? I thought you'd buggered off to be a schoolteacher. Don't think I'd be much help in a classroom.' He laughed, and Mal snorted.

Arrow wanted to curl her arms around and rock herself, the dark pit in her stomach growing. Or smash her fist into something.

'Barro, can we talk? Privately?'

'I've got places to go, dear old Arrow, people to please. Spit it out or scurry back to your chalkboard.'

He'd always been a killer, but she didn't remember him being this callous. She'd leave right now if she had anywhere else to go or anyone else to ask. But Livy was somewhere in Londinium, scared and alone, or worse.

The words tumbled out of her. 'Yes, I am a governess now, but the little girl I've cared for since I left here – Livy – she's been taken, and no one else will properly look for her. It's been hours now, and she's just eight years old. I need your help.'

Barro glanced back at Mal. 'Sorry, Arrow, but I'm not hired muscle anymore. Now I help old Mustard find animals for the ring and seek out the little niceties of life even the richest Citizens can't find in the Grand Arcade.'

A merchant must have bought his contract. Barro had always been bartering and dealing on the side, even stealing bits of armour after he'd dented them in bouts. Arrow had nursed him when the Arena bosses lashed him for that. After she left, they must have finally tired of his pilfering and sold him on to a trader who valued a slave with commercial instincts and a killer's training. Her heart lifted a little: he might be even more helpful than she'd thought, if he agreed.

'If you find things, then help me find Livy. Barro, I'm begging you.'

'I usually take cash.'

Arrow could feel her heart beating in her temples. The man Mal watched her from the corner of his scar-mutilated eye. He wasn't like any gladiator that she remembered; he moved like a soldier. Swallowing her anxiety, she stepped forward and touched Barro's wrist, a fingertip against his skin. He froze.

'I'll find you money if that's what it takes, Barro.' If he wouldn't help her, then nothing mattered anyway. She dropped her voice to a whisper. 'You can even hand me over to bondsmen, for the reward, after we find her.'

Barro's eyebrows were high, but his voice stayed low. 'You defy your master for this?' His hand gingerly reached up towards the welt from Caligo's slap. She turned her face slightly away; this wasn't about her.

'I must find Livy, even if I've been ordered not to. She's just a child and I was supposed to protect her.'

Saying the words unleashed tears that had been testing her eyes since the museum. She tried to shake them away; she wasn't a girl who *wept*. Barro had fought her right here in this Arena, they both carried scars to prove it and she'd never cried even when sewing her torn skin and muscle back together. But today, she stood there in her prudish dress and stupid petticoats and couldn't defend against a single tear. The darkness inside her lapped up the shame.

Barro's blond eyebrows creased like she'd asked him a question that he didn't understand.

'All right, Arrow, all right. What do you need?'

The clerk Caligo had stolen the evidence she had that Livy was taken by Druids. The Consul himself spoke about the girl's abduction like a minor inconvenience. Days might pass without any real effort made to find Livy, if they tried at all. Days when the Anglish could do whatever they wanted with her.

'I need to get my hands on some Druids.'

'You don't need drunks with dirty plaits to throw runes to find her,' he said.

'I don't need them to help me, Barro,' Arrow's rage steadied her voice, 'it's them that took her.'

Barro looked down at her face for a moment, but she refused to wipe the tears from her cheeks. Then he walked back to Mal. They exchanged a few words and Barro slapped the dark man on the shoulder. Mal nodded and strode off, without a glance at her.

Barro turned back. 'Let me chuck on some clothes, and then we'd better go see Scratch.'

CHAPTER VI

'Scratch? How in Hades can that little rat help us find Livy?' Arrow demanded.

The two of them marched along the path beside the traffic-choked Pretorian Way.

'That rat is now a minor Pontifex, priest of Gaea's blood and keeper of the flame in the Academy Temple.' Barro swept into a mockery of a Citizen bow, eyes lowered and arm across chest, but almost tripped trying to walk as he did so.

'I don't believe you. Scratch is a Pontifex?'

Arrow remembered a gristly slave boy with a pinched nose and nasty temperament. The Arena had bought Scratch after his previous owner sold him at a loss. Despite the rigorous training and discipline they were all subject to, Scratch never quite made the grade as a gladiator. He would switch between sneaky fighting moves to then exploding in a roiling rage that was all bellow and not much bite. The other trainees learnt to check their weapons and armour before a bout, because he'd loosen breastplate ties and blunt off your blades.

He'd been whipped more than once. The Arena bosses needed entertaining brutality on the sand, not sabotaged farce.

In his last days, Scratch was subject to incessant gossip amongst the other novicii gladiators about his likely onward sale. Things got nasty. If you beat him in a bout, then he'd try to get back at you.

He'd poisoned Barro's drink with a sickness draught and smashed up another pious boy's makeshift altar to the Goddess Vesta.

Arrow had tried to stay out of his way.

But one night, after she'd thrashed him in a bout while the Arena bosses watched, he'd cornered her alone in a corridor. Arrow was unarmed, but Scratch hefted a long knife in each hand. He'd spat at her, grinned, and then ordered her to strip naked.

When the bosses came to find out what all the screaming was about, they'd ordered Arrow to clean his blood off the walls, as Scratch was carried to the infirmary. The boy was sold on the next day.

Arrow had heard that some Temples now had to buy indentured children to raise as subordinate or assistant priests, because Citizens preferred to send their precious offspring to the Academy, and Plebeian families would only raise traders. That they required slave-born priests was another irreverence the Temples blamed for the Godstorms.

Barro winked and said, 'Scratch doesn't just nurse the Temple flame, he's obsessed with the old cults and digging up their secrets. Tips off the Inquisitors to Anglish festivals so they can be rounded up. If it's true them old Druids did take your girl, he might know why.'

Arrow nodded and picked up pace, forcing flashes of what might be happening to Livy down into her chest to curdle around her gut.

The Academy was a swift trudge along the Pretorian Way from the Arena. Arrow had been barely eleven years old when she had first made this walk, with a nasty bruise across her cheek bone from her morning's training on the sand and clutching an old writing slate in her bandaged arms.

A few weeks earlier, Mustard had told her a story about ancient rights of wards of the Arena. If a child had been born to a gladiator within the walls of the stadium itself, then apparently, as a 'child of the sand', she should be permitted to study at the Academy if she also trained as a gladiator.

At first, she'd scoffed at the idea as a tall tale, like stories of unicorns and dragons Mustard told her that he'd wrangled. But a few wizened Arena clerks nodded when she asked them. Finally, she screwed up enough courage to ask a Plebeian, an old gladiator friend of her mother's with a missing eye, and he told her the short ritual phrase she needed to recite while standing on the Academy steps on intake day. Then he'd firmly warned her to never use it.

Arrow shivered a little remembering the long-robed Dialectics' dark brows and curled lips when a bloodied and scruffy Arena brat turned up on their Academy stairway reciting the sacred words – demanding entrance.

'Docendo discimus.' By teaching, we learn.

The Citizen and rich merchant Plebeian parents, proudly presenting their perfect little darlings, had been perplexed and then outraged.

To all their chagrin, ritual was ritual, and she had to be admitted, though the Academy Dias loudly predicted that she'd quit within a week anyway. Arrow was granted no personal tutor, not permitted to ask any questions, exiled to the side of lecture halls below the ranks of proper students. Often, those Citizens' sons and merchants' daughters mistook her for a servant, and she never corrected them. Not once had she raised a fist when they spat at her or cracked her tablet. Mostly, they all ignored her.

Arrow trained in the Arena every morning, then patched up her wounds and walked, or limped, to the Academy every afternoon. Without that education her only buyers would have been rig owners and whoremongers when she finally forced the Arena to sell her contract on.

The Academy had hated her, but it had saved her.

Every evening when she came back to the Arena after classes, thrumming with shame from being laughed at, spat at or ignored, Barro joked with her, or sparred with her. Without him, the Dias' predictions would have been proven right, she wouldn't have lasted a week.

'Barro, are you sure you want to do this?'

'A half-hour ago you were begging me to help.'

'I mean, I could go to Scratch myself, now that I know.' Arrow looked behind to check no one was walking close to them. 'There are consequences for aiding an escaped slave.'

She didn't mention what she'd done to the vile clerk.

He shrugged and Arrow thought that, even if Barro had the responsibility of Atlas himself, he'd shrug off the world. 'Everyone's a slave, Arrow, even the Citizens. They just don't know it.' Barro threw his arm out to encompass the streets of hurrying Plebeians, heaving charo traffic, and the few Citizens strolling along browsing the shop windows. Arrow was going to say they looked bloody well free to her, but Barro went on with his half-smile playing around his lips. 'Take us, for example. I reckon you owned me more than the Arena bosses ever did.'

She almost lost her footing.

'What? I never owned you, Barro.'

'No, you made that perfectly clear when you punched my lights out, then when I came round, I learnt you'd had yourself sold on rather than stay with me. Bit of an excessive way to end a love affair, I always thought.'

Arrow was glad for the corset holding her straight up.

She hadn't told Barro why she forced her sale, because if he knew, she'd never have been able to do it. Hurting him, and ruining her own chance of freedom, was the only way to avoid sharing a truth that would destroy them both. She'd welcome any fate rather than the horror of honesty.

Being bought as Livy's governess had felt like receiving a pardon from an inescapable prison.

Livy. Once Barro helped her find Livy, he could criticise her past choices as much as he liked. Crunching her fists, she walked ahead of him, without answering.

They weaved between the growing crowds. Many of the younger

86

Citizen ladies had taken to wearing light silk masks over their noses and mouths. Arrow didn't blame them; the filth from the exhausts dulled the bright awnings of the smart shops selling silk parasols and the latest cravats.

Arrow didn't notice the growing smell of evaporating oil because it was laced into the charo fumes, but it became overpowering as they reached the jet black Temple. The building suited the patina of charo soot deposited from the road. Both she and Barro coughed as they stepped between the dark pillars.

The Gaen Temple sat on the Pretorian Way, mingling the smoke from its bowls of burning crude oil with the fumes from the city's charos. Its neighbouring Academy shone in white marble cleaned daily by a small army of slaves, set far back from the street behind a long immaculately manicured garden with shading trees. To the relief of most new Academy students, they didn't have to pass through the Gaen Temple itself to reach their classrooms, instead using an entrance to the garden. Many managed to never set foot inside the black building during their entire Academy tenure.

Their last few steps had been made in uncomfortable silence, but now she and Barro tripped over each other.

'Do we need to—?'

'It's by the entrance. No, the other side.'

'Sorry.'

They inelegantly jostled to reach the libation tray, nodding but not looking at each other enough to avoid missteps.

On the rare occasions she had ever entered a Temple, Arrow usually half-dipped her fingertips in the Gaen libation and then would surreptitiously wipe off the oil on a handkerchief. But, if Scratch truly was a Pontifex now, even a minor one, then she had no doubt he'd be a stickler for ritual. Arrow plunged her hands into the crude oil up to the wrists, every tiny cut singing on contact with the thick, dark liquid with its muted rainbow sheen. Most of it slopped off again, the oil acting as its own lubricant. But enough was left to make her nose wrinkle if she brought her hands close to her face. The smell wasn't unpleasant – they used the purest form of Gaea's blood in her own Temple – but it prompted tears anyway.

'Arrow?'

It was like a picture of the troubled young Scratch had been painted over with that of a holy Pontifex. Still bony, but taller and wearing a long black robe adorned with small silver drill heads. If you'd never seen the original Scratch, you wouldn't know he was there. But, around the eyes, she recognised the boy she'd known, and it took a force of will to curtsey rather than raise her fists.

'Pontifex.' Barro gave a slight nod and Scratch walked forward with that non-committal semi-smile of all Temple men.

'Well, by Gaea's grace! I bid you enter the Sanctuary of Oil. Arrow-girl, the gods themselves rejoice to see you in such womanly attire. I prayed throughout my novitiate for you to repent from the Arena. I see that heaven, in its wisdom and mercy, heeded my prayer rather than gutting you for foul arrogance in attempting to fight as only a man should.'

It was hard for Arrow to smile with her jaw locked tight and fingernails pressed into her palms. Scratch better have some information.

'That's right, Pontifex. It was unfair for the gods to gift our Arrow here with such speed, strength and skill, compared to yours.' Barro's voice always carried a wry smile that covered its bite.

'The gods had greater plans for me,' Scratch snipped, then held his hands before his face, sniffing the thick oil ground into his skin, and his shoulders settled back down. 'No matter,' his Temple smile resettled, 'the gods have chosen our paths and Gaea's blood fuels our journeys along them. Does our patron have a message for me?'

Barro stepped forward before Arrow managed to ask what patron he was talking about.

'No, Pontifex. This is another matter. Arrow's charge, the little kid she's a governess for, was taken from the big museum today.'

'Scratch – sorry, I mean, Pontifex,' Arrow forced another another mollifying curtsey, 'Druids took her. Can you help us?'

Scratch looked between them, eyes widening.

'The heretics took Consul Derain's ward from the Imperium Museum?'

Arrow's jolted up from her curtsey. 'You know I was governess for Derain's ward?'

Barro's hand almost grabbed her arm as he stepped between them. Sensibly, he let it hover.

'Just because you hid yourself away with the girl, Arrow, doesn't mean no one else knew. The Pontifex here trades with a lot of powerful men, don't you, Scratch?'

'Barro, take care. I will only accept so much of Mercury's wit from you.'

'My humble apologies, holy Pontifex.' Barro swooped into a proper bow with arm and fist crossing his heart.

Scratch fiddled with his drill bits but seemed appeased. 'It's true that I know a great deal of what happens under the gods' eyes. But this? Anglish heretics in the city's most eminent museum? That alone should chill us! I hesitate to tell you, but I have darker fears.' He took another deep inhale of his oil-soaked fingers. 'Gaea's blood must guide us.'

Scratch spun and strode into the Temple proper. The tall domed space of the blackest marble was lit with thousands of tiny smoking oil lamps. The choking fumes explained the lack of casual weekday worshippers who tended to snatch some rest in other Temples.

They passed a statue of Gaea herself: a generous and motherly naked body with sad countenance, her hands reaching down from the pedestal as if to lift a supplicant. The statue had oil rivulets running from her eyes, her breasts, and from between her legs. It was supposed to represent her great gift and sacrifice for the Roman people. Arrow thought it looked painful.

They stopped under the large silver model of an oil rig that dominated the centre of the room, glinting in the lamplight. Arrow's nose stung with the evaporated chemicals rising from the huge bowl of crude oil the rig stood within.

Grand as the Temple rig was, it was merely a symbol for the colossal metal pyramids that dominated across leagues of the fire plains in the East. It was said you could walk for a month across the plains and see nothing but rigs, slaves and the giant charnot convoys transporting millions of barrels of oil to ports for trade. During the Festival of Gaea, the rig bosses would burn up entire lakes of oil, releasing thick black clouds a hundred leagues high, proving their piety and guaranteeing the gods would keep the liquid gold pumping for another season.

Scratch gathered himself before the ceremonial rig, as if preparing for a sermon.

'If the Consul's ward was taken by these animals, I fear it may already be too late.'

Blinking back tears from the rising fumes, Arrow said, 'Scratch, I'm begging you, please tell me. Where have they taken her?'

The Pontifex shook his head as if answering her would be too much for him and crossed his hands before him.

Arrow just needed a lead, a hint as to where to search. Livy would be alive, and she would save her. Nothing else was thinkable.

Begging hadn't helped. Lying would have to.

'Pontifex, I wouldn't want to tell the Consul you'd been unhelpful in my search.'

Barro widened his eyes a little but didn't contradict her.

Scratch pulled up straight, coughed and said, 'Well now, of course, I shall assist with all the abilities the gods have granted me.' He was playing with his drill-bit jewellery again. 'The Anglish refuse the bounteous gift of Gaea's blood, which frees men from toil and holds up our deified Empire. Instead, the heretics scrabble about in their hovels to survive, ignorant and without honour. They live to rob and debase us, ignoring the god-given stations of Citizen, Plebeian and slave.'

Barro sniffed at that, but Scratch went on, 'I believe they manage to evade us through conjuring foul spirits and dark magic against our Legions. They are in league with our enemies and raise tempests to hide their sedition!'

Arrow had heard rumours like that all her life. That the Anglish were somehow both stupid lazy peasants and also dangerous powerful magicians. She'd always ignored it, until now.

'Why would they take Livy? They must know she will be searched for.' Well, by her anyway.

Scratch closed his eyes as if in prayer. 'The foul Anglish are monsters. They use human sacrifice to summon their magic against us.' Scratch brought his hands up to sniff his fingers again, as if in benediction. 'Please tell the Consul I will pray for the girl's soul.'

If her heart had really stopped, she would have fallen to the floor. That's what her vascular lessons in the Academy had taught her. Somehow, Arrow was still upright.

Barro's voice lacked its usual lilt. 'Perhaps so, Pontifex. But I doubt they'd try a bloody ceremony in the heart of the Empire's capital. They'll take her to their own territory, maybe out into the country-side somewhere. The girl was only snatched a few hours ago, and they'll need to get past the gate guards to leave the city.' Barro snapped his fingers. 'Smugglers' routes! Druids smuggle more than they steal.'

Scratch lowered his hands. 'I know these beasts, Barro. They have already gutted her in some alley.'

'C'mon Scratch. Where's their Londinium base for all that contra-band they bring in?'

'The Empire's shores are secure. The blasphemers are nothing more than common thieves. I won't hear of smuggling.'

Scratch was sweating. He started to walk back towards the door, fussily straightening his robe.

Barro nodded and grinned at him.

'Ah, I see. Playing both sides, are we, Scratch? Squealing to the

Inquisitors about a few Anglish rituals while taking backhanders from them to keep their smuggling secret?' Barro flicked her a wry smile. 'Scratch wouldn't be the first. Even I've wandered through the Old Town to find a contraband trinket or two for my customers. I never knew who the biggest Anglish boss was. Bet you do, though, don't you, Scratch?'

The priest's shoulders tensed like they had in the Arena when he knew you'd got the better of him. But he ignored Barro's insinuation. 'I will send word to the Consul of my conviction that his ward has been sacrificed and offer my services to entreat her soul's release from Tartarus.'

'Gods, man. The girl might still be alive, at least for now. Tell us what you know.'

Scratch sniffed. 'It's time for you both to leave. I must pray.'

He had always been a gods-damned coward.

Arrow reached out and caught Scratch's elbow, almost as if seeking solace. Then she applied hard slanted downward pressure to a spot on his distal humerus – the same part she'd repeatedly smashed against the wall when he'd tried to molest her when they were kids in the Arena. Injuries like those she'd inflicted that day never truly heal, as teenaged Arrow had known well when she dealt them out.

His face went white as she ground his bones against each other. 'Answer the question, Scratch.'

'Arrow, no!' Barro whispered beside her, but she ignored him.

Scratch was staring into her eyes, his own widening, she didn't know if in shock or pain – she hoped both. Arrow squeezed harder and wrenched the joint, watching his agony. The hard dark lump in her belly warmed.

'Unhand me!' he managed.

'Where, Scratch? Tell me where to look for her.'

Arrow felt his joint shift unnaturally in her fist. Scratch knew better than to scream when an enemy's hand is on you, but he whimpered, tears running down his face. She'd either opened the old fracture or fully dislocated the joint. *Good.*

'The Green Man, it's the Green Man!' he choked out.

'Who?'

Barro answered, 'That's a where not a who. The Green Man is a pub in the Old Town. Who do we ask for?'

'The Green Man isn't just a pub, it's a person!' Scratch rasped as Arrow maintained pressure. 'He's their leader, their high priest. Tell the barman that Scratch has information for the old man.' He sagged against Arrow's skirts.

She let go and the Pontifex fell to the floor, cradling his arm like it was a newborn.

'You bitch,' Scratch spat out through tears. 'I'll have the Consul whip you. You'll beg on your knees for my forgiveness.'

'You know this pub?' she asked Barro, ignoring the blubbering Pontifex.

'Yep. Even had a pint there a few times.'

'You must both return to your master,' Scratch shouted at their backs. 'I order you in Gaea's name!'

Damnatus. Even though he was technically as indentured as they, any Pontifex had the power to command a slave.

Arrow turned to him. 'You always were a piece of crap, Scratch.'

'What kind of language is that for a governess?' Barro said, his wry smile now a little shaky.

'I lost that job, Barro. Are you still with me?'

He stared at her. Arrow had no doubt the implications were clear. After what she had just done, Barro should seize her and try to prevent her escape, to save himself from her fate.

Instead, he shrugged, looking up at the sad-faced statue of oil-bled Gaea.

'I'm going to regret this, aren't I?'

Arrow wouldn't have been surprised if the marble Goddess had nodded.

They could hear Scratch shrieking for guards as they ran out of the Temple together and dodged down the nearest side street. She had no doubt the Pontifex wouldn't hesitate to condemn her as an apostate.

Not just a bonds breaker, she was now a heretic.

CHAPTER VII

After weaving through back streets to confuse their trail, Barro steered Arrow towards a large red-brick building on a street corner, with 'Funiculus' carved onto its pediment.

Arrow stumbled, and Barro raised an eyebrow at her. 'What's up? We need to jump on a chain-train and we'll be in the Old Town in ten minutes. It would take hours to walk, and we need to get out of the city.'

'Let's hire a taxa instead.'

Barro snorted. 'The city taxas won't take a fare south of the river, you know that. And we'd be remembered.'

'It's just that – ' Arrow shivered – 'I've never been on a chain-train.'

'Well then, it's about time you did. The funiculus is a wonder of the modern age – fast, smart and safe.' Barro placed his hand on her back and nudged her forward.

'Safe,' Arrow muttered, but she walked across the road, once or twice letting herself glance up to the suspended rails hanging overhead.

The station wasn't as crowded as she'd feared, and Barro didn't have to queue to buy their tickets. He dropped his shoulders and slowed his speech to mimic a hard-working, and hopefully unmemorable, Plebeian worker. Arrow hovered in a shadowed corner, staring up at the large board of destinations with time-slates hung beside them. Barro slouched back to her, giving way to anyone who cut across him. Neither of them glanced at the four Legionaries patrolling the station.

'Which is our train?' Arrow tried to sound unconcerned.

'Well, they've all been delayed because of the Godstorm,' Barro looked her up and down, 'and I'm not sure this will work with you like that.'

'What do you mean?' Arrow looked down at herself and then tried to straighten up her bonnet. 'Am I such a mess that I'm going to draw attention?'

'That's not what I meant. Never mind, let's get the next one, we can just catch it,' he said and strode towards one of the staircases leading up from the station floor.

Arrow followed him up, and they stepped out onto a high platform that jutted out above the main station building at the level of the nearby roofs. Winds whipped across the open space, and the few ladies there huddled towards the back of the raised platform, holding their hats. Arrow contemplated the precarious chain-rails dangling out in the air alongside the station, swaying a little in the wind. They snaked off beyond the platform and out over the city, suspended between giant pylons and threading through entire buildings, plunging into gaping dark holes around which people had just kept building. The upright hair on her arms wasn't from the cold.

A guard blew a loud whistle, and the chain-rails strung above them started to rattle. Other passengers walked forward, but Arrow's legs were unwilling to move.

Barro chivvied her forward with a pointed look. She shouldn't stand out, even for being nervous. As an oil-heated wind blew across the platform, she managed to step towards the edge. The long set of carriages slowed to a stop, hauled by the engine at the front, venting fumes, all hanging from the chain-rails. She could smell the metal in Gaea's blood as it burned. The guard dropped the handrail, and the carriage doors opened, tipping the carriages towards the platform as short walkways pushed out.

A few people got off, and all the other passengers hurried on. Barro took one look at her and then took her arm in his, like an old couple, and led her over a walkway and into a carriage. Arrow gripped a burnished bronze handle over a chair and dropped down on one of the solid wooden seats.

'I would never have believed it.' Barro grinned as he slipped into the seat beside her. 'The great Arrow, unafraid of any weapon in the Arena, who once beat a man twice her size by biting a chunk off his nose; the girl who regularly thrashed me, no matter how hard I trained, is afraid of a train ride.'

'We are sitting in a big lump of metal and wood, hanging off a string, and hurtling across the city powered by burning fuel that could easily explode, sending us to the ground in a deathly fireball,' Arrow answered between her teeth.

'Well, yes,' Barro conceded, 'but look at the view!'

Arrow forced herself to look through the window and back to the distant Spire, towering over the buildings around it from this vantage point. As they pulled away from the station the clickety-clack of the chain-rails above them sped up, and all of Londinium spread out below: from grand houses to squalid tenements, Temples to the many gods and long boulevards of shops and arcades. The roads teemed with tiny charos, almost invisible below the fumes they sent upwards, broken by green patches of parks and formal gardens that she and Livy loved to visit on rare warm days.

Londinium, seat of the greatest Empire the world had ever known. Gifted by the gods with oil, to ensure it never fell.

'This little girl we're risking our lives to find, she's who you left me for?' Barro was nonchalant as he spoke, but he didn't look at her.

He deserved an answer, for everything he was risking. Not the truth, but an answer that perhaps he could live with. Something so plausible it was almost real.

'I didn't leave you, Barro, I left the Arena. I just couldn't fight anymore, on the sand, or with you.'

'Maybe I could have helped, did that occur to you? I didn't intend on bleeding out for the damn fans' entertainment either. I had *plans*.'

'Perhaps, Barro. It all seems so long ago now.' She looked out of the window, but noted his shoulders were tighter than when he had been sparring with Mal.

'It makes you happy, just looking after some kid?' he asked.

'You and I didn't have anyone, Barro, we were a couple of orphan brats, fodder for the Arena bosses. So yes, I guess it has made me happy, seeing Livy grow up like a . . . real child.'

That was all she could say, and it was more than she'd intended.

'The gods gave children magic to charm us,' Barro recited, flatly.

Arrow stared back down the track, but she couldn't see the Imperium Museum from here.

What if Livy had just wandered off, and they were moving further away from her? Maybe the diligent young Legionary had already found the girl and sent a message to the Consul. If she'd only waited, they could now be heading home together, as she listened to Livy's excited stories of her adventures lost amongst the treasures. She'd make them both hot tea and continue teaching Livy nux on their board with salt and pepper pots standing in for the missing pieces.

Arrow shook her head so violently her bonnet shifted sideways.

Her mother warned her of this. Before heading into battle, the doubt would come. 'Little one, always 'ware your own mind. Standing in the dark, waiting to step out onto the sand, every warrior doubts their training, doubts their instincts and even doubts the gods themselves. Each must fight against their own fear before they ever fight each other. You must conquer yourself first, before victory over another.'

Arrow must find Livy. Nothing else mattered.

The train stopped at a few stations, and Arrow's hands lost the bloodless white grip of when she first embarked. Barro wandered off to speak to the guard. He slipped back now with a sheepish look on his face, as if their earlier conversation hadn't happened.

'Looks like you're getting used to train travel, Arrow, that's great. Because, well, we're going to need to get off soon.'

'Don't worry Barro-boy, you won't need to lead me like a kitten over the walkway again. I can step off at the platform myself.'

Barro spoke as fast as the rattle of the train. 'Well now, that's the thing. When I told you that taxas won't go to the Old Town, well, neither do these chain-trains, really. They do go over it and on down to the big villages on the edge of the city. But there isn't a proper platform stop anywhere near the Green Man.'

'So,' said Arrow, a horrible thought dawning, 'how exactly do we get off?'

'The train doesn't stop, but it does slow down, a bit. Today it's going to slow down a lot, because I just fixed it with the guard. He'll let us onto the footplate at the back of the train. It will be so slow by then it will feel like stepping off onto a platform,' he said.

'You want me, in full skirts, to jump from a moving train and onto a rail pylon, at roof height, above the cobbles of the Old Town?'

'Well,' Barro shrugged his shoulders, 'the next stop is Herne village in another twenty minutes, or so. You could wait and get off there. You might be able to find a cart to bring you back into the city. Eventually.'

Arrow closed her eyes. *Livy, shaking her hair and hat in the rain, laughing.* She nodded at Barro.

The guard looked unwilling once he saw Barro was with a woman, but a few more denarii changed hands, and they waited for the whistle the guard said would be their signal.

'Have you done this before?' Arrow asked.

'Once or twice. It's the fastest way.'

Arrow closed her eyes, then flicked them open when she felt Barro's warm breath against her neck. His hand slipped across her shoulders, pulling her close against his body, an arm wrapping around her waist. Which she was tempted to snap.

'Ware,' he breathed into her hair.

A Legionary had entered their carriage and was asking for occupations and destinations. *Damnutus.*

Arrow turned her face towards Barro's with a coy smile, while slipping her hand into her sash to rest on her dagger.

She and Barro were at the end of the carriage, by the rear of the train itself. There were a few other passengers between them and the soldier.

The whistle tooted out – their signal.

The Legionary was having trouble with a pinched-faced old woman in severe grey. She had an affected accent and was questioning the soldier's right to know her destination, as her mistress hadn't given her permission to speak of it.

They had to get out of the carriage.

Giggling in a low tone, Arrow brushed her lips against Barro's cheek, cocked her head in the most coquettish manner she could muster, then slunk up and slipped out of the end door, throwing a kiss back at him. Through the glass pane she saw Barro give a big sleazy wink to the workman behind them, who gave an approving nod back. Perhaps the man would try to slow the soldier a bit for the sake of two lovers. Barro clicked the carriage door closed behind him.

'Ready?' he shouted over the wind on the back plate of the train, once again all business.

Arrow slowly untied her old bonnet, and let it fall from the rear of the train, green stays twirling. She pulled her hair back into the tight bun of a gladiator. She'd treasured her respectable hat but jumping off a train with ribbons tied around your neck would be unnecessarily tempting to the gods she was already defying.

She nodded at Barro, and he swung himself up and around the railing to face forward. Arrow came up behind him, leaving space for him to manoeuvre. The train slowed, and, as it did, the carriage wobbled a little.

'Almost there; I can see the pylon!' Barro shouted without looking back.

Arrow wasn't sure if it was better or worse that she couldn't see the pylon coming, but then, as the train slowed almost to a stop, Barro stepped up from the footplate as if into the air.

Arrow moved to where he'd stood and leaned out, almost enjoying the sharp cold on her skin after the performance in the carriage.

Barro's arm grabbed down to hers and pulled her to the edge of the footplate. She girded herself to jump up to him. He was balanced to the side, standing on a pylon spur, holding her with one arm and the pylon with the other.

'Now!' he shouted.

Arrow stepped upwards.

Then jerked to a stop – one foot on the train handrail and her arm being pulled by Barro on the pylon.

Checking behind, she saw the Legionary, who was clasping a handful of her petticoat.

He looked as surprised as her and hadn't yet pulled his arc gun.

'LET GO!' they both yelled at each other.

The train juddered and inched forward.

'Arrow!' Barro shouted as her hand slipped in his, and her body stretched out between the train and pylon. The train gave out a loud whistle, the sign it would start speeding up again. As it moved forward, she was strung in the air between Barro's hand and the captured petticoat, her legs dangling.

Arrow kicked against her skirts and the soldier was pulled up against the back railings of the train as he tried to hang on.

A partly torn hem was clutched in his hand, trapping her. The rest of her was strung between that and Barro's slipping fist. Arrow gripped onto Barro with whitening fingers and kicked at her skirt again and again. Stupid, unnecessary, hard-to-wash, always-snagging, bloody petticoats!

The Legionary blinked as if remembering himself and drew his arc gun with the hand not tangled in fabric.

Arrow booted out as hard as she could without dislodging Barro's hand from hers. Two fathoms down on the hard cobbles, a mangy dog looked up at her.

As the barrel of Legionary's arc gun came up, the hem of her petticoat finally tore free, and the train jumped forward. Arrow dropped, then jerked and spun at the end of Barro's arm, clutching at his hand above the sheer drop.

The strip of white lace fluttered from the Legionary's fingers, waving to her as he shouted incoherently at them. The shot of adrenaline almost made her laugh out loud. But she'd been trained better than that. The smell of arc-gun powder laced the air.

Thankfully, a dangling woman doesn't make an easy target.

The train rattled off around a bend.

'Swing me!' she called up at Barro and got a grunt in reply. His arm started to move her back and forwards. She arched her back to gain momentum. As she moved closer to the pylon, she kicked her legs out to catch at a pole – but couldn't quite reach.

'Again!' she called, aware that only Barro's lifetime of sword training, building his grip and shoulder sinews, prevented him from dropping her from sheer pain.

Once more, Arrow swung back and then in towards the pylon. Her foot touched metal, and she wrapped her ankle around it, using her legs to pull herself closer. She let one of her hands go from Barro and grabbed at the metal. Fingertips catching, she released her other hand and hugged the pole, slipping down a few feet until she landed on a crossbar. She sat there, skirts billowing out around her, arms wrapped around the pylon pole like a lover.

'You hurt?' she finally shouted up to Barro.

His reply held some strain. 'Hurt? Why would I be hurt? My arm was just used as a rope for a circus stunt by a woman in full bloody formal regalia. Of course I'm hurt!'

Arrow smiled with relief. She had worried that her weight in full skirts might have dislocated his shoulder. If he was complaining, then it couldn't be that bad.

'Give me a minute to tie my arm back onto my body, and I'll climb down to you.'

He would be rotating his shoulder, fingers seeking for any dislocation or serious tear. That's what she would do, it was what she'd helped him do after their Arena bouts.

The only times they didn't help each other patch up, massage or medicate was when they'd been forced to fight each other. Neither wanted to see the damage they'd inflicted until it was bandaged or salved. Sometimes it had taken Barro days to look her in the eye, if he'd blackened one or both on the sand.

As Arrow clung to the pole, she remembered the night following their last ever fight, after they'd been battling to settle a bet between rich Citizens. She'd thanked the gods through her tears and gags that Barro wasn't there that night. Grateful that he didn't witness her useless attempts to stop the bleeding.

Barro's boots stepped onto the nearest pole, dislodging the memory.

'I need a week in the hot springs and a bevy of massage women,' he quipped.

'Well,' she took a deep breath, pushing the encroaching dark back down to her belly, 'I needed an actual platform to end my first ever train ride. So, let's call it even. Now, how do we get off this thing?'

'There's a maintenance ladder not far below us. Can you get down to it yourself? Not sure I'll be much help with this shoulder,' he said.

They gingerly climbed down the few crossbars to the ladder. Arrow went first, with Barro coming behind, favouring his left arm.

They reached the bottom of the pylon and touched their boots to dirty cobbles. A dilapidated high fence had been set up to protect the pylons' feet, but its gate had been pulled aside by travellers years ago.

103

Before they ducked through it, Arrow hesitated. Without looking up she said, 'I needed that rope. Thank you.'

'Don't mention it, you can hang from me anytime. Look,' his brows lowered from their customary arch, 'you've been out of things for a while. What do you know about the vox populi right now?'

'I don't see many people. Well, anyone,' she answered. 'Why does it matter?'

'It matters. You remember back in the old days, if things got tricky in the city, or when big shenanigans went on at the top of the Empire, then the seats at the Arena would be heaving full? As if people wanted to get away from it all, or vent their anger watching us?'

Arrow nodded, remembering the packed stadium whenever political scandal rocked the Imperium Romanum.

'Well, for the last few months it's been standing room only for even the minor gladiator bouts.' Barro kept looking around as he spoke. 'The old Emperor is dying, folks say, and the young Heir . . . people don't know him. Everyone's jumpy and ready for a fight. Like in the gladiator mess hall before a big battle up in the Arena. Someone's likely to die soon, and everyone's determined it won't be them.'

'So, things are tense,' Arrow said. 'What's that got to do with me, or finding Livy?'

Barro frowned. 'You're a bit less done-up now, without the hat and stuff, but you clearly aren't a normal Pleb. People notice a well-dressed woman, and bondsmen don't always wear uniforms.'

Arrow's stomach filled with lead. Why hadn't she followed politics, alert for any threat? She and Livy had lived in their little bubble together, and she'd relished their separation from the hurly-burly of the main city. Another way she'd failed the girl.

'I get it, Barro – keep my head down and mouth shut. I promise. Right up until I find someone who knows about Livy. Get me to this

Green Man; he sounds like someone who knows every filthy plot. He'll tell me where Livy is.'

'It might not be quite that simple,' Barro said.

'Leave me alone with him, Barro, and it will become very simple, very quickly.'

CHAPTER VIII

They strode into a bustling market street.

Unlike the calm boulevards of neat store awnings in the city centre, here a mass of people hawked, bargained and thieved from each other. The smell of baking bread, spices and sweaty bodies fought through Arrow's senses. Within a few steps, people were pushing them back and forth, and her wide skirts slowed them down in the press. When Barro leaned back and clutched her hand to help pull her through, she didn't resist. It was that or lose him in the heaving crowds.

His hand was larger and more calloused than she remembered, but he clasped hers with a perfectly balanced pressure. As if they held hands every day.

They passed stalls sticking out from people's homes. Some of the market produce was familiar, fruits and cakes. Other stalls were crowded with things about whose use she had no clue. One was laid out with what looked like dried roots; when she peered closer, she saw strips of old animal skin and unpleasant green tinctures in small bottles.

The stallholder looked like a fairy-tale witch from one of Livy's storybooks. The hag spotted Arrow staring and shouted out, 'A little taste of old man's mettle for your young gent there, my lovely? Or perhaps he doesn't need it, strapping fella that he is. Maybe some mayday myrtle then for you? That'll get your juices flowing,' the crone cackled.

Arrow hardly understood a word, but she grasped the tone and felt a blush rising. If Barro's warm grip hadn't tightened on hers, she would have dropped his hand.

Other stalls sold the geometric amulets worn by the rag-tag crowd in the museum. A few silver, but mainly wooden, Druid icons were displayed by nervous-looking traders, with their barrows ready to be folded and wheeled away upon any sight of a Legionary's helmet plume.

The market was overwhelming and the most Anglish place she'd ever been. Plaits and charms. Arrow tried to clear her mind, but the spices, sweat, hawks and yells cracked any attempt at composure. People were everywhere, pressed up against her. Her rage swept back up her spine and she almost choked on it.

The child-stealers had taken Livy into this filthy pit of stench and shrieks.

A man pushed himself up against her in the throng, his hands low on her body, lifting handfuls of skirt. She dropped Barro's hand and elbowed into the man's ribs, sharply upwards and hard, hoping to crack one. Then she thumped her shoulder into another man who hadn't even tried to make any room for her. It hurt and it felt good.

Damn kidnappers.

A mottled woman dropped her tattered basket of turnips when Arrow pushed forward past Barro. A few rolled under the feet of others, and a man cursed as he fell. The florid turnip woman turned on Arrow, fists raised. 'Stupid cow, look what you done!'

Arrow spun back to face the woman, staring at the plaits and amulets in her filthy hair. The fallen man behind cursed as others tripped over him and a stallholder bellowed when someone jostled produce off his barrow. People shoved and shouted. Arrow lunged towards the angry woman, noting how easy it would be to break the arm that was pointed towards her. There were bodies between her and her opponent and with a grunt she started to smash them away.

Then gasped when Barro pulled her sideways into an alley.

Arrow slammed him back against the dilapidated wall and thrust the hard edge of her forearm against his throat. Barro didn't resist. He just stood there, palms outward, breath held.

'What in Hades, Arrow?' he croaked.

She was almost vibrating with every muscle screaming and teeth gripped together. Her ridiculous green dress felt like a costume. If she ripped it off, she imagined her gladiator armour and leather greaves would somehow be underneath.

Barro didn't raise his defences. They pressed against each other in the musty passage. Two people overhung by wattled garrets, with the smell of rotten food permeating the air.

She conquers who conquers herself. How many times had her mother made her repeat that whenever she wept in the dark.

It took effort, but Arrow forced her shoulders to drop. Stepping back, she managed to turn her palms up, the signal to end a bout.

'Fear hides behind daring, remember?' Barro said.

Arrow nodded, not trusting herself to speak. Fighting the urge to lean back in and rest her forehead against his chest, hiding her face and admitting how scared she was.

How guilty.

Barro cocked his head, watching her, with that look as if she was a puzzle he hadn't solved yet. Satisfied she wasn't going to start a riot, he led them down the back street and out into a different part of the busy market.

He took her hand again, and Arrow carefully twisted herself to avoid touching anyone.

She hadn't come here to beat up any Anglish, but to find the ones who had taken Livy.

They turned a corner and left the din as quickly as they'd entered it. A square opened before them, almost entirely filled by a giant ramshackle building, patched up and generally thrown together. Every one of its chimneys was a different design, various creeping plants vied for space and the large pile of bricks tossed to one side had either fallen down, was about to be built up, or both. Roads ran around the bizarre structure and alleys led off in all directions. A cryptic pub sign, empty but for a fresh sprig of holly, rattled above a large gaping door.

A road bridge was just visible above the pub, with a chain-rail criss-crossing it, so proper people wouldn't have to travel through such an insalubrious neighbourhood. For a spot at the crossing of so many paths, the quiet in the square surprised Arrow. Barro stopped and stared at the pub.

'This is like the edge of the Styx on a market day whenever I've come before, with folk queuing up to get in or passing out beers. Maybe it's in quarantine,' he said.

Now Arrow tugged him forward. 'There aren't any plague signs,' she said, 'and anyway, everyone's in that market rather than here.'

They crossed the empty road, pushed open a heavy wooden door and walked into a wall of darkness and heat. A miasma of pipe smoke and moist air from wet clothes struck them, all laced over with the stink of stale beer and unwashed people. Arrow hadn't smelt worse since her Arena days.

As her eyes adjusted, she noted a few patrons in rough chairs and stools around what looked like upturned beer barrels. Men in working clothes and a few women in the tattered aprons of washerwomen or seamstresses. Every single one wore multiple plaits and silver amulets. They looked up and stared at Barro and Arrow with expressionless faces, not a flicker of recognition. But Arrow knew what it felt like to step into a room of enemies and her hand convulsively gripped Barro's harder.

He walked them up to the rough bar, no more than two planks of beer-stained wood between barrels.

Barro's smile was wide. 'Hello, friend, we'd like a quiet word with the Green Man, if you please,' he said to the back of a well-built man standing behind the planks, who was lining up wooden steins on a shelf.

'Well, he's there if you want him.' Without turning the barman stubbed his thumb towards a carving above the bar.

Unlike the rough workmanship everywhere else in the pub, the wooden image hanging over the bar was as expertly carved as anything Arrow had seen in a Temple. Four broad intricate leaves emerged from the face of an old man. Two of the leaves came from his eyebrows and the other two his beard, with their stems growing out of his mouth. At first glance, it looked perfectly symmetrical, but her brain couldn't quite agree with her sight. She narrowed her stare and realised each leaf's veins and edges had been deliberately carved askew, and even the eye-curve and lips didn't match. The first impression of perfect symmetry was in fact perfect chaos.

Even their religious icons were lies.

'Scratch sent us,' Barro went on, 'it's urgent.'

The barman didn't even turn back from organising the mismatched glasses on a rough shelf. Gods, she didn't have time for this.

Arrow leaned forward over the counter, 'So you don't care that Consul Derain is planning to burn this pub to the ground, probably today?' She raised her voice a little. 'I'm just an indentured charwoman who cleans the mud from their boots in the Spire, but I heard it all.'

The barman turned and raised his eyebrows at Arrow in the same way Barro did. The whole room went silent. Then a younger boy who had been sitting in a corner jumped up and scampered off behind a dirty rag of a door. The low bubble of talk from the other patrons started up again.

'Well. Something to eat while you wait?' The barman leaned in a little, now all warmth. 'Let me get you a little bread and a hunk of cheese. It'll be a few minutes till the boy comes back.'

At the mention of food Arrow's appetite woke up and demanded her attention. She almost said no, thinking that it would be a betrayal to eat when Livy might be cold and hungry. But she remembered her training; hunger inhibited reactions and strength alike.

She nodded.

The barman led them to a side table with four proper legs, and one of the women bustled over with a surprisingly good-quality platter of simple, fresh bread, sharp Britannian cheddar and even a rare spoonful of sweet winterberry pickle.

The room lost interest in them, although Barro still watched the others while she ate. Arrow had dropped his hand when the food arrived and was surprised that she missed its warmth. Barro didn't eat, even though she saved half for him, and she became aware that he was even more on edge now than when they entered.

Leaning forward as if to scoop up a little more pickle with the bread, she hissed, 'What's up?'

Barro started to massage his shoulder. 'Just struggling to recover from saving a hapless maiden from certain death.'

He grinned, and his voice held its familiar teasing edge, but Arrow felt strain behind it. Barro's careful bravado put her on guard, even more so as he clearly didn't want to tell her why he was nervous.

'Your master, the new one, he knows you come here?' Arrow asked.

Barro raised an eyebrow. 'No one cares where I go, as long as I track down what they want, at the right price.'

'Your new master, he treats you all right? You seem to have the run of the city. Does he tell you what to get, or do you report everything? It's almost evening, won't you be missed soon?' Sitting in the decrepit pub, Arrow was seized with an unexpected and burning curiosity about the last eight years of Barro's life. What adventures, what loves, what lives had he lived since she left? After refusing to let herself think about him at all, now she wanted to know everything. Although she didn't think for a second that he'd tell her.

'Oh, you know me, Arrow,' Barro answered, eyes circling the room, 'I'm like a cat, I always land on my feet. Don't you worry.'

That was less than even she'd expected.

The boy tapped the table, having returned unheeded while they talked. He said nothing but waved them to follow him. The barman didn't even turn to watch them leave.

The barefoot lad, in trousers too short for his growing legs, took them behind the filthy curtain and through the back rooms of the pub. He led them down corridors filled with empty boxes and barrels between mismatched doors. Barro tried to engage the boy in a little banter but was so steadfastly ignored Arrow began to wonder if the boy was deaf, or just terrified.

They traipsed down short staircases and ducked under low doors, and she couldn't work out the plan of the vast, rickety, place. Finally, they came to the lowest doorway of all. The boy took an oil lamp hanging beside it and crouched over to enter, his head moving down what must be stairs. Barro followed with Arrow behind. The ceiling wasn't much higher above the long staircase behind the door, and she heard Barro quietly curse as he hit his head on the long walk down.

They followed the boy into a series of cellars. Much bigger than Arrow expected, almost another building down here below the pub upstairs – equally confused, with small rooms and side corridors branching off who knew how far. She was impressed. Londinium sat on quite marshy ground: cellars like these couldn't be dug out just once; they'd need constant repairing, otherwise the ooze of the city would seep in. Down here it felt dry, surprisingly cold and with a tang in the air.

Arrow ached to kick open every door they passed, screaming out Livy's name. Instead, she rolled her shoulders. Her heart was beating steadily, and her fascia moved smoothly over her joints. All the rage, terror and guilt were now locked up tight in the heavy pit behind her wall of gladiator-trained calm. The lamp-lit corridor reminded her of the walk towards the Arena floor before a battle. All that was missing was the muffled sound of thousands screaming her name from the stands.

The boy carried the oil lamp through the subterranean rooms, although here and there other lights hung from the walls. Eventually, they reached an unremarkable door, but this time, rather than pushing it open, the boy waited, and then, through no signal that Arrow could discern, he opened the door, then ran back the way he'd led them. So, the Anglish even scared their own children?

She let Barro enter first, following as a woman should, silent and modest.

'Scratch is a piss-ant squealing damsel. We've heard nothing of a plot against us!' a voice boomed out.

The words belonged to a huge, seated man, bigger than any she'd faced in the Arena. Two thick plaits hung down either side of his craggy face, above arms covered with deep blue tattoos in strange spirals that moved with his muscles. Woad. Only criminals wore woad in the city, along with gangs of thieves, highwaymen, and worse scum out in the wilds.

'Things have changed, fast,' Barro answered. 'A child has been stolen and Citizens are screaming for Anglish blood. Scratch sent us to warn you.'

'Well, that's as might be. If any of 'em comes looking for a fight,' here the man stood, his head reaching near the ceiling, 'then they'll get more than they bargained for. Tell Scratch to stop telling tales about missing kids, it won't profit him none.'

Arrow's teeth flashed as she smiled. 'I'm the child's governess, and I know who took her.'

'What? I thought you were some scullery girl. Screw this, I'm busy. Bugger off back to Scratch, the both of you.'

Arrow's smile inched up and she said with a sing-song softness, 'If you've touched my Livy, I will gut everyone here. Starting with you, Green Man.'

For the first time in years, she squared her shoulders into a full fighting stance and flexed her hands to attack. The big man didn't react, he just looked over his shoulder at the other men around the table, who stood as one. Now Arrow could see another, smaller figure, sitting behind them all. Old and tanned, wearing ratty rags and with a long, plaited beard hanging with amulets. The man who had winked at her in the museum before Livy was taken.

She had been a negligent fool to let him palm Livy's coin outside the museum.

'I'm the Green Man here, woman,' the old Druid proclaimed, 'and you should rejoice. Livia is held in the god's embrace now. I have freed the girl's spirit!'

Even the dust motes held motionless in the air as Arrow blinked.

The Druids had sacrificed Livy.

The darkness that had been locked in her guts burst upwards, burning through her heart and plunging down every vein.

What was the point of living even a breath longer? Soon, she would let the darkness take her, and pull her down into blissful oblivion.

But first, she had men to kill.

Spinning low, she cracked her elbow down into the back of the huge, tattooed man's knee. His leg started to collapse before he could grab at her.

'Arrow, no!' Barro shouted.

She slammed the heel of her hand up to meet the soft underside of the big man's nose. Cartilage broke, but she kept pushing with all her strength until a giant swell of warmth hit her fingers.

A shattered nose wouldn't drop a brute that size, but the blood and pain might blind his senses, long enough for her to reach the old man. Once her hands grasped the Druid's neck, then no one would pull her off.

Arrow swung herself, dress and all, over the crumbling mountain of the now roaring big man and landed on one of the others behind him, and they went down together in a tangle of her skirts.

But she had years of taming those folds to her will and managed to raise her knee while the other man struggled to unravel himself. He soon regretted having opened his legs to get clear as Arrow rammed the sharp edge of her knee between them. Using this unstable foundation to push herself up, her entire weight pressed down into his groin.

His breathless screech fuelled her.

As he folded forward in agony, she brought both her elbows up together to meet his eyes, knocking his head back with a crunch and leaving him unconscious, or dead, it didn't matter. She sprang up and heard Barro still yelling, 'Arrow, Arrow, stop.'

Her brain registered injury to her wrist and hip.

Gods-damn, let every bone break if she could just reach the Green Man.

One more enemy stood between her and the old Druid, and this thickset opponent had learnt caution. He circled to her left, trying to lead her away from her target, but she inched closer, keeping her peripheral vision on the Druid. The man between them crouched into a wrestling stance, and then he drew a short sword over his shoulder.

Arrow felt warm blood on her hands and arms; she could even feel a trickle run down her cheek where she'd been cut. Her hair had loosened from its bun and her skirts bunched askew. An unhelpful state to face an armed enemy, so she feinted to the side to give herself a moment's space. Then used that delay to draw her own dagger from her green sash. He might be larger than her and with the bigger weapon, but she'd reached the throat of opponents worse than him.

Raising her blade to attack, she registered a tiny thud as something hit the floor. Arrow allowed herself a quick glance down. It was the black onyx stone she'd picked up in the museum. It had fallen from her sash as she drew her dagger.

'Hold! All ye' hold!' the old Green Man screamed. "Tis the Inguz stone!'

The enemy opposite her was transfixed by the little dark stone with its silvery carving at her feet, and his sword arm started to waver. Which was the opening she needed. The only one not captivated by the old man's gabbling, Arrow leapt forward, raising her dagger across her body and towards the man's neck. She could almost taste the kill.

The day before the Arena fight in which she'd died, Arrow's mother had lifted her daughter's chin, searching her face for something the girl wasn't sure if she found. 'Life is just one long struggle in the dark, dearest, remember that.'

Under the Green Man pub, Arrow froze, arm raised.

Then her whole body convulsed. She'd been hit in the back, and it was like nothing she'd experienced in the Arena. Pain poured into her. She could do nothing except clench her jaw with her hands clawed into a crippling tension.

No blade ever touched her like this. It felt like being scourged with fire, but with no flames.

She burned inside. While a white light crackled in her vision.

On and on the flood of pain came, breaking into every sinew of her body and careful barriers in her mind. Millions of lines of anguish burning from her back and down each vein from her scalp to her toes.

She was stiff as a statue, caught in the everlasting now of agony. *Please, gods, please.*

The huge pulse of pain stopped as quickly as it started.

The screaming tension gave way, but now her every fibre collapsed – first knees, then shoulders, and finally her head crashed onto the dusty floor. Compared to the screaming agony of before, the thuds barely registered as pain.

Every bone turned to water as she fell, and her mind crumbled with her limbs. Her senses, fried by the searing torture, fled.

As the darkness swallowed the last wisps of her, she heard Barro calling her name from far away. Although he sounded like Livy.

With that last stab to her heart for the child she failed, she was gone.

The Kalends of Sextilis, Londinium Academy

MDCXLII, Aurelian Calendar

CHAPTER IX

Arrow hadn't expected the Academy to be more brutal than the Arena. But here they cut you with disdain rather than daggers.

She tilted her damaged face away from the other students, willing herself to remain stoic.

These last few months Arrow had striven to become part of the school's furniture. No more notable than a desk or chalkboard. If she sat on the floor at the far end of the raised student seating, no one, not even the Academy Dialectics, acknowledged her.

Although, she had to admit that ignoring her might be their choice, rather than her skills. After all, absolutely no one in the entire Academy wanted a violent Arena brat amongst their number. Pretending she wasn't there most days suited them.

Today was not one of those days, unfortunately. Arrow had entered the schoolroom later than usual, after all the other students had taken their seats. And as she crossed the room her giant, purple-black eye was impossible to conceal.

The girls looked disgusted, and the boys stared in fascination. She wondered if in their twelve years they'd seen someone beaten up before. She wanted to shout out, 'I gave as good as I got,' and tell them how Barro would be limping for a week after their training bout this morning.

But this lesson was taught by Dia Agrippina Severina, one of the few female scientists. She was young and prickly, known for demanding strict silence. Arrow was more afraid of her critical stare than any thrashing in the Arena. Legend had it, Dia Severina had once failed the Heir himself on a test.

All attention moved from the girl's battered face to the tall, fashionably dressed lady scientist. Not least because the table before her was covered with vials, a glass balloon-like contraption and a cage with three cooing doves.

While Dia Agrippina Severina might be feared for her strict temper, she was beloved for her impressive experiments. Compared to the never-ending droning of their Rhetoric, Poetics or Calculi teachers, this looked to be a more exciting lesson.

'My young Ladies and Gentlemen,' Dia Agrippina Severina did not need to yell at them to quiet down, 'today we delve into the invisible, but fascinating, world of vapour. Those insubstantial gasses which surround us every second of our lives, but that most people walk through ignorant of the wonders they contain. A century ago, a discovery thrilled through this very Academy – the finding of *spiritus* vapour. The noble Dias of the time revealed that everything that lives and breathes depends upon spiritus. Every inhale you take gathers spiritus into your lungs. In many ways, it is the most precious element in existence. And today, we shall experiment with it!' She paused in the impressed silence. 'However, experimentation requires effort. I require a student to pump the gas.'

The affront from the room was palpable. Citizens did not *assist* in experiments, doing *labour* in front of others. Despite being little more than twelve, each child was perfectly aware of their family's relative prominence in the Empire. The few boys of rich Plebeian families looked distinctly uncomfortable, as if they might be singled out.

Well, there was one twelve year old in the room with no standing at all. Maybe they'd all appreciate another look at her shiner anyway.

'I'll do it,' Arrow said, coming to her feet. It was the first time she'd spoken in any Academy class.

Dia Severina's perfectly manicured dark eyebrows shot up, contemplating Arrow, as if trying to remember why this damaged entity was in her classroom.

'You . . . are the Arena ward?'

'Yes, Dia.'

'How fascinating, I was not aware you were in my class.' The Dia's cheekbones inched even higher. 'However, unlike the *gentleman* scientists of this Academy, I welcome anyone truly seeking knowledge.' Arrow wasn't sure, but she thought the woman might be smiling at her, but in such a genteel way it was hard to tell. 'After all, if a debutante such as myself can reach the dizzying heights of becoming a Dialectic, why shouldn't a gladiator girl aspire to a little learning?'

Arrow nodded as the other students chittered behind her. That was the most anyone had said to her since she'd joined the school.

'Place the doves in the jar, girl. Seal it tight, with no way for spiritus gas to enter.'

Arrow had been taught by Mustard to handle worse than a few doves. Once all three birds were sealed inside, the Dia proclaimed, 'The doves will soon consume the spiritus gas trapped within the confined space. Observe.'

The three grey-white doves had calmed from their fluttering when Arrow had first placed the bell jar over them, and now they just perched, cooing, in the sealed space. After more time than Arrow felt comfortable standing in front of the silent class, the cooing and preening fell quiet, and the birds stopped looking around them.

One began to sway, and another gave a squawk. The doves had inhaled all the natural spiritus that had been in the tightly sealed jar. Denied it, they would soon faint, then eventually perish.

Arrow thought it was a stupid experiment. If she wanted to watch things die, she'd have stayed at the Arena.

But Dia Severina snatched up a tube, and attached it to a dock on the side of the jar. She indicated for Arrow to grasp the thick-handled pump on a great metal tank beside the desk.

When the first dove finally fell sideways into a faint, she nodded to Arrow to begin pumping gas into the chamber through the rubber-stoppered seal.

'Students, over many arduous years, we of the Academy have discovered the concentration of spiritus each animal requires to live. The correct amount is now being provided to the doves, via this hose.'

As Arrow pumped in the calibrated amount of spiritus needed by three doves, the birds stopped swaying, the fainted one roused and they all began to preen and coo again, revived.

'Continue. There is more to prove here.'

The room had become restless and Arrow's arms tired with the rhythm. She wondered if this lesson would last much longer. They'd already learnt most of this anyway. Everything needed spiritus to live, inside a bell jar or out. Why couldn't they let the doves go?

But Dia Severina was watching every wriggle, head turn or feather ruffle of those birds as if her life itself depended upon it. Only glancing away occasionally to check Arrow pumped at a continuous speed. The intensity of the Dia's gaze drew all other eyes to the fat, contented little doves preening in their bell jar.

Arrow's trained muscles started to throb as she continuously moved the handle and she desperately needed to scratch her nose. Nevertheless, she held her place, slowly pumping spiritus into the jar at a constant rate. What did Dia Severina expect to happen?

Time and silence stretched on and the muscles in Arrow's arms went from aching to starting to scream at her as she kept the constant pressure of the spiritus moving into the jar.

Without warning, one dove dropped on its side.

Dia Severina jumped, wide skirts jiggling, and then stood as tense as if beside an unexploded bomb.

'Do not stop, girl, you are making history!'

The students bobbed up from slouched positions.

'Observe . . .' Dia Severina murmured.

The second dove beside the prone bird also collapsed, dead or fainted. The final bird swayed and even ruffled its feathers a little. Arrow kept pumping.

Finally, looking up at her with what could only be construed as accusation, the final bird fell. Despite the constant flow of life-giving spiritus gas into their jar.

'At last! Today is no mere lesson of well-worn principles, children. You have witnessed a true experiment.' Dia Severina's brown cheekbones shined in the afternoon light. 'This is the first proof that our air is a Janus, of two sides. If *spiritus* is the air of life, we've just proven that rising concentrations of *effula* is the vapour of death. A deadly pollutant that every living thing exhales, in exchange for the spiritus we all inhale.'

Arrow wondered if she was the only one who held her breath.

Dia Severina's voice calmed and retook a teacher's aspect. 'The existence of this effula in our air has been long known, of course. If spiritus is inhaled, then something must be exhaled when our lungs compress. Before today it was believed to be a mere waste, like other parts of the body produce. My fellow Dias believed exploration of this gas was beneath them. Worthy of study only by a woman. I have no shame in telling you I procured the spiritus for this experiment only because I agreed to teach you. However, we have now shown effula to be worthy of study, as all deadly things are. If we had placed four doves in the jar, then the effect would have been swifter. A multitude of doves in a closed space might survive mere minutes. A city of them would build concentrations of effula perhaps even higher than that of the spiritus that blesses our air. Effula is a poison. Therefore, I propose—'

'Can I release them?' Arrow interrupted.

'What? They have served their purpose, girl. We have proven high concentrations of effula are lethal.'

'I don't think they're all dead, yet.' Arrow gulped at the air that she now knew was a battle between spiritus and effula. 'I know what dead things look like.'

The woman stared at the girl and then down at the doves.

'Very well, release them. The point is proven. Now, where was I? Yes, my great discovery will upturn . . .'

Dia Severina went on, but Arrow was no longer listening. With her exhausted arms she managed to lift the glass jar off the doves without breaking it. Two of the birds had the glass-eyed stillness she'd learnt to associate with death. But the fragile little chest of one moved, at least to Arrow's eye.

She carried it towards the window.

The rest of the class left the room, voices high as they gossiped about what they'd seen, and complaining at the length of the lesson.

'Well, does it endure?' Dia Severina had followed her.

Arrow nodded; the bird was struggling in her hands.

'I hadn't expected such a soft heart from one trained by the Arena,' the Dia said.

'Well, the way things die can be sadder than death itself,' Arrow answered, even though she wasn't sure if she'd been asked a question.

The Dia's head cocked to the side, much like the birds had done, and she spoke as if to herself. 'To understand the things at our doorstep is the best preparation for understanding those that lie beyond.' Then she took a step back, observing Arrow as if she were another experiment.

Arrow had been appraised by opponents on the sand, judging her strength and stance. This felt like a different evaluation, of what was behind muscle and bone. It was more uncomfortable. So, Arrow allowed herself the impudence of glancing at the Dia in return.

Citizen Dia Agrippina Severina's dress was likely the finest that money could buy, an ivory cream shot through with darts of dark jet, matching the ivory and jet bangles circling the flawless brown skin of her wrist.

Study of the great families was as compulsory at the Academy as study of law and science. Arrow had learnt that the Severina family ranked high, their line a long one. They could be traced back to the time of God-Emperor Marcus Aurelius, who had released the power trapped in Gaea's blood. Such a momentous event that the calendar of years was restarted on that date.

The wealth and power of the Severinas was near to that of the Consul himself.

Barefoot, with a bruised face and not-too-clean smock, Arrow stood before this grand scion of Citizenry. She ground her jaw but didn't flinch.

'Well, child, as you aided me today, perhaps I shall succour you in return. Come to my lab tomorrow and you may transcribe my notes on effula.'

'Thank you, Miss.' To Arrow it sounded like she'd be doing the helping. But without tutor or time to study back at the Arena, she knew she was falling behind.

Assisting Dia Severina would teach her more than silent lurking in corners.

The Citizen went to place a hand on her shoulder, then hesitated and brushed her skirt instead. 'Perhaps together we will affect more than just the lives of doves. That must be our purpose here at the Academy, to improve the world around us, not just understand it.'

Arrow didn't think she'd have much chance to change the world. It was too busy constantly pummelling her. But she nodded anyway, grateful to be included in Dia Severina's grand vision, even as a scribe or gas pumper.

Pulling open the stiff window, Arrow sat the dove on the sill outside. The silly thing wasn't in any hurry to fly away, but nevertheless Arrow quickly closed and relatched the glass pane.

The window looked out over the Gaen Temple and no one wanted the smell of burning oil in the room.

Almost as bad as effula, the girl thought.

The Kalends of Junius, Atlas Sea

MDCLVII, Aurelian Calendar

CHAPTER X

Damnutus in deum.

Arrow's head swam as if rocked by tides in deep water. It wasn't pleasant.

A sharp pain throbbed at her temples and a rhythmic pulse of sickness washed along her body.

Where the *Hades* was she?

Rough fabric was tucked under her curled-up limbs. Trying to piece together her situation, all Arrow could imagine was that she was severely ill . . . or poisoned.

A bark of laugher jerked her fully awake, although her body was still numb.

'Consul Derain? That old crow can peck at me if he wants.'

It was a woman's voice, with a strange lilting accent. 'I know the risk I take, more than you do, sunshine boy. Old man Llund and his charge, those I gave my word to carry. Now I have a god too,' the woman sniffed, 'unlikely as that seems. And a blond boy who smiles too quickly.'

'You can't keep us here. What did they call her? She's the Inguz!'

That was Barro's voice.

Arrow struggled to force sticky eyes open. Her queasiness wasn't helped by the scene that came into focus. She lay on a small bed, although it was far too high off the floor, suspended against the wall,

131

with a barrier running along it, like one set for a baby to save them falling. The space beyond was both huge and yet confined.

A wooden hall, but a few feet away she could see metal bars. A cage in a cavern?

Rolling to her side, fighting nausea, Arrow blinked when she saw the woman who faced Barro. Tall, dressed in long crimson skirts and wearing a leather jerkin pulled tight at the waist with fur stitched onto her sleeves. She was missing the respectable high-necked blouse any Empire woman would have considered obligatory. Instead, she had several thin strips of leather strung around her bare neck, loaded with what looked like pieces of bone, or even animal teeth, a few nestling scandalously low. More striking than beautiful, the woman didn't look happy, dark brows frowning under even darker curly hair.

'She is the Inguz, you say,' the leather-clad apparition said. 'This weak little woman? Strange vessel for a god. Would sail in a stronger bark, if I was he.'

Barro was turned away from her and swaying. It wasn't just him, her guts told her that everything around her – bed, window, Barro and the woman – were all moving. Gods, she must be very sick.

'Please,' she managed to croak. 'Water, please.'

The leather-clad woman and Barro's heads snapped around. Barro was sporting a nasty blackened and swollen left eye. She couldn't see any other injuries, and he wore nothing but trousers, his chest and feet bare, with hands bound with twine before him.

Front-tying the hands of anyone with their training was asking for trouble. However, Barro's shoulders were deliberately relaxed into a non-threatening posture and his hands held almost in suppli-cation.

'God or no, can you help her?' he asked the strange woman, whose curls framed her furrowed brow, and she looked him up and down with a hard stare. Then she walked towards the raised bed with a strange gait, her skirts swinging with each step. Despite the sway, she reached the end of the raised cot and picked up an oiled leather pouch stoppered with a cork. Holding it within reach, she stood, staring, and giving the pouch a tiny shake.

There wasn't to be any gentle holding of head or dripping of water into a parched mouth.

Damn it, Arrow was thirsty.

With an effort, she awoke her arm, reached out with a tremor, and took the bottle from the woman, who raised an eyebrow. Managing to lift her own head a little, Arrow tipped the bottle up to drink. As the liquid hit her mouth, she coughed and spat. This wasn't water but some thick liquor with a strange bitter taste. More poison? She went to throw the bottle away, but the woman stopped her, wrapping a warm hand around her own, holding the bottle in her grip.

'Fool,' the woman said with her thick low accent. 'Drink. Valuable that is – only way to heal from lightning. Drink or die, Inguz woman.'

Another wave of queasiness hit, and it was all Arrow could do not to vomit. If she was already poisoned this badly, it was unlikely anyone would bother wasting more on her, so she raised the oilskin pouch to her lips. After the initial shock, the tang did taste almost familiar, reminiscent of medicine as a child. She managed a few large gulps from the bottle, and her head started to clear, although the rhythmic sense of everything swaying didn't leave her.

'If the Inguz you truly be, then may you forgive me for keeping you here. But I will not risk my ship and crew till we are in safer waters.'

The woman then strode out, bending to get through the small door to their cage, and locking it behind her with a jangle of keys.

Ship. That was why everything was swaying. She and Barro were prisoners in the brig of a ship.

After watching until the woman had climbed a ladder out of the hold, Barro came over and placed the back of his bound hand against her cheek, then he brushed a wisp of hair back from her forehead.

'Arrow. Sorry. Perhaps I should salute, you now being a god and all. How do you feel?' he said.

'What in Hades is happening?'

'You've been out for three days since the fight in the pub. Llund, that's the old Green Man, he hit you with what for all the world looked like Jupiter's wrath. He said it was to stop you killing his bloke, but without killing you. Although you looked white as a corpse after it anyway.'

'I was hit with . . . lightning?'

'Gods, it was a terrible thing to watch. Llund just touched your back with a rod, then white light sparks streaked all over you. It was over by the time I could get to you.'

'I thought I'd died.'

Barro wasn't wearing his customary half-smile, and his eyes were younger than she remembered, even the blackened one. 'So did I.'

They had both expected to die almost every day back when they fought for their living on the sand. She'd forgotten how much that feeling hurt until seeing it reflected from his face.

Managing to hitch up at least the corner of his smile, Barro said, 'Well, then there was a bit of commotion I had to deal with.'

Arrow had a good idea what kind of commotion resulted in a black eye.

'Men ran in from all over the place. I was told not to touch you, and four twitchy blokes sat around me with their knives out to make sure of it. Llund left after you fell and, eventually, he came back with this sea captain lady. Seems they have some arrangement, although the lady didn't appear overly pleased about it. Walked right over and put her hand against your neck, then she says, "the Inguz lives", and everything happened at once. Llund looked like Venus herself had winked at him and ordered me to pick you up. We headed off down those tunnels under the Green Man, I'd always suspected they went a'ways, but turns out they span across half the city. We scurried through them to the docks. Smart for smuggling, I thought.'

'You carried me?'

'I hoisted you over the other arm than the one you'd already used as rope.'

Her breath started to feel raggedy in her chest. 'For Hades's sake, Barro, what have I done?'

She'd convinced him to help her, risking his cushy indentured position with a merchant. Now he was technically an escaped slave, and a prisoner. Barro shrugged and tugged at the ties around his wrist with his teeth, so Arrow pulled his hands towards her, not quite well enough to sit up yet, but able to unpick restraints tied by someone more used to tying sails.

Barro snorted. 'We're on a damned Frisian ship.'

'The Frisians? Gods, they're the Druids of the sea. I'm sorry, Barro. All you did was try to help but now you're on a pirate ship to who knows where.' She concentrated on the ties. 'It was all for nothing. Scratch, damn him to burn in Hades, was right all along.' It had to be said out loud, but the words almost didn't come. 'They sacrificed Livy anyway.'

She was wrong, she hadn't been ready to say it.

All the death she'd seen, all the death she'd doled out. Losing Livy should just be another loss on top of all the many others.

But once the words were out of her mouth the truth of it hit her and her breath fought with a scream. God, why had she taken that drink? Better to die here in the deep belly of a boat then live any longer. It would have been more of a mercy if they'd let the lightning take her.

She felt like she was falling; her stomach curled and extremities were losing feeling.

It wasn't the scream she expected; instead a choked sob escaped her.

Barro's hands on hers were all that kept her in the world. His voice was softer than she'd heard it in years. 'Scratch? Damn it, he's never right about anything. Commotion, I said? Well, the biggest upset was none other than – your Livy. She ran in after you fell from the lightning rod and threw herself at you. I went to pull her off and your little she-cat punched me in the eye.'

Heartbeat, movement, even the dust motes in the air stopped as she looked at Barro. His lopsided smile softened as he watched her face.

'Livy's alive?' she managed.

'Yes. Your girl's alive and was scratching and shrieking in the Captain's arms as I carried you behind them.'

'Llund didn't sacrifice her?'

'Nope, seems to think snatching her from the Consul was freeing her soul, or so he ranted on about in the tunnels.' Barro's hands were free, and he wove them into hers. 'Do you think anything other than your kid turning up could have stopped me killing every last one of them after I watched you fall?'

Shaking her head, Arrow pushed herself up on the cot. 'Is she . . . hurt?'

'I don't think they've harmed a hair on her head. Although a few blokes are sporting bites and bruises from trying to pull her off you.'

Arrow's heart had restarted and, if anyone had listened, she thought it was now beating in a different tone.

'And one shiner,' she said, nodding at Barro's purpling eye.

'Your girl's got quite a right hook; been taught well. The she-cat stopped pummelling me when I said I was your friend. Then I got a hug.'

Livy was well, and even angry and belligerent. Livy had hugged Barro for being her governess's friend. Livy was alive.

'Thank you, Barro. Oh, gods, thank you.'

She threw her arms around Barro like she used to when they were gladiator brats. But holding each other from the strange bed was too convoluted so she managed to slip her legs over the slide and both she and Barro fell to the floor, clasping each other. Bruised ribs, healing cuts and injuries she hadn't checked yet all squealed at her. Arrow didn't care. She wasn't sure if she was sobbing, laughing, or both, with her face buried in Barro's warm bare shoulder.

'Hmmm, I didn't think you'd be this grateful,' he chuckled into her hair.

'*Damnutus*, Barro.' She pulled back a little. 'If Livy's on this Frisian ship I need to find her, now.'

'I thought you might.' He lay, sprawled with one arm propping his head below her. 'I've already picked the lock and had a nose around the nearest boxes. Couldn't go further with you getting your beauty sleep though.' He raised an eyebrow at her, hand on her back.

Too much. Arrow pushed herself off his chest, ignoring the feel of muscles wider and harder than those of the boy she'd known. She went to brush off her skirts and realised for the first time she wasn't wearing them, but instead was clad in brown trousers with a pale hessian shirt.

'Barro. Where is my dress?'

'Dress, corset and petticoats were covered in blood, the Captain ordered them taken away.'

'So who, in Juno's name, took me out of them?'

Barro stared at her outrage, then laughed. 'Your honour's intact, m'lady. The Captain herself changed you, and she did it fast, like she was handling a toddler into festival clothes.'

Her shoulders dropped a little, but then Barro added, 'Just me, Llund and four or five sailors were around to watch.'

She'd punch his other eye black, but what did it matter? Livy was found! But Arrow ground her jaw. Finding wasn't the same as saving.

The Frisians were notorious brigands from the frozen northern seas above Britannia, untamed by the Empire even after centuries of skirmish and rigid sanctions against trade. Londinium's newspapers luridly reported their vicious assaults on innocent merchant fleets and even plebeian villages in the Hebudes islands. She was surprised a woman could become Captain of a Frisian ship – she must be a bloodthirsty harpy to have achieved such eminence amongst the rapacious pirates.

Livy was being held somewhere on their ship. It was time to get her back.

'Any weapons in the crates you checked?' she asked as Barro sat up from his languid sprawl.

'Nope, but I think I've found the source of most contraband that passes through Londinium. Silver amulets, Eastern silks, spices and even tea, all nicely packaged up. Gods know who they'll sell them on to.'

'Well, I don't fancy fighting through the Frisians to reach Livy with a fistful of cinnamon. We'll have to make do with anything we can pick up on the way.' Arrow pulsed her fists. Livy might be just a few feet away up those stairs, surrounded by bloodthirsty outlaws and in the clutches of that Green Man, Llund.

Barro's face was impassive, like back when she had tried to teach him some of the history or alchemy she'd learnt at the Academy.

'You'd cut your way through a pack of pirates to reach her, wouldn't you?'

'Of course, she's mine,' Arrow answered automatically, then pulled herself straighter. 'She's my responsibility and I need to get her back to Derain.'

The Consul had mentioned an 'old Academy acquaintance' who had fathered Livy. Derain wouldn't name a lowly Plebeian as a friend, and if Livy's father had been a Citizen then the girl held those same rights.

The whole Imperium Romanum existed to serve its Citizens. Arrow almost snorted at herself for the heartbreak and worry she'd first felt receiving Livy's summons to the Academy. After the last few days, she'd give every drop of blood in that heart for Livy to be ensconced in the Academy right now. Whatever fate her former governess found at the bonds market should have been nothing compared to knowing that Livy was where she should be.

'Livy has a life waiting for her and I will fight to secure that for her with my last breath.'

None of their enemies, Captain or Llund, were likely to suspect that both she and Barro were trained killers. She could use that to force them to hand over Livy, perhaps.

'We need leverage. Maybe if I held a blade to the Captain's neck?' she mused out loud.

'That's an option. But I think the Captain herself might have gifted us another way. I saw her slip some things back into your pockets after dressing you. Not your dagger, Llund took that after you flattened his men in the pub, but maybe something more helpful.'

Her trouser pockets were deep, and she touched first the silk of Octavia's handkerchief. Her heart skipped a little knowing she still had it, but it couldn't be what Barro had meant. Then Arrow's hand felt something hard and cool, and she drew it out.

In her palm was the Inguz stone. Black and smooth with its strange silvery pattern.

'Apparently, finding that thing means you've been possessed by the divine spirit of Inguz, whoever that is.' Barro made a florid bow. 'And what's the point of being a god if you don't boss people around, eh?'

Arrow recalled one afternoon when, as rain hammered against the window of her small Academy office, Dia Agrippina Severina had leaned back from her lamp-lit scroll. It had taken a moment for Arrow to realise the Dia was staring down at her, where she organised notated papers on the floor. 'The existence of the gods is a helpful thing,' Dia Severina proclaimed. Arrow had nodded, wondering if she should call on divine help for deciphering the Dia's handwriting. 'So let people believe in them.' Before her assistant could conjure a suitably erudite reply, the Dia was already back scrawling more notes.

Arrow smiled now. The Captain had mentioned a god, and back in the Green Man everyone had stopped fighting when they saw the Inguz stone. The idea she was harbouring a god just because she'd picked up a pebble in a museum was clearly absurd. Luckily, she didn't need to believe it, as long as their captors did.

Barro popped the brig's lock and at the top of the stairs they found a low corridor with more steps and ladders running off in dizzying directions. Everything was rich chestnut wood, smoothed and glossy as if often scrubbed by many hands. Neatly coiled ropes, stacks of dark barrels and wooden poles with various hooks took up every corner. Lamps hung at points, giving off a strange blue light rather than the familiar yellow glow of oil lamps.

Both she and Barro selected sharp hooks and pulled out their poles. They then had to stuff the hooks into their trouser waistbands because walking took both hands. Arrow worried it was the after-effects of the lightning she'd been hit with, but Barro also kept swearing as he bumped into corners, stumbling over his own feet with every roil of the waves. The whole place creaked and moved underfoot like being trapped inside a giant child's toy.

Sunlight cut through the blue-lit gloom from one open hatch, and she tottered up small steps onto the deck.

As Arrow felt the sun warm her face, the tang of the sea hit her. Back in Londinium she had walked down to the docks a few times to pick up fish for a special dinner for her and Livy. It was always grimy, stinking of fish guts and thick brine. She'd thought of the sea like that, a larger version of the pools of filth in the wharves. The fresh smell on deck took her by surprise. If anything, the ship was cleaner than most of Londinium: large creamy sails whipped overhead and men strode across the place, pulling on some things and pushing on others.

The ship was large, at least two times the length of the great hall back in the museum, with a high prow towards the front and dotted with hatches and more equipment Arrow didn't recognise. The sun glinted off the water all around and watching the small, white-tipped waves helped her body adapt to the sway of the ship. Barro beamed at her, and her own smile met his.

Considering how angry she was, the sunshine felt wonderful.

'Cargo belongs in the hold!'

The Captain strode down the length of her ship towards them, like an irate nereid, chest moving in ways that would have caused a charo pile-up on a Londinium street. Out here, her scandalous clothes and accent fitted with the ship and wide expanse of sea. The Captain didn't stumble at all, while the supposed-to-be-god was struggling to stay upright.

Trying for a supernatural resonance, Arrow declaimed, 'I demand you return the child you've stolen.'

The Captain stopped opposite them, hands on hips, with fingers close to a short sword hung at her waist.

'They say you are Yngvi, who they call Inguz, and I must deliver you and the child to a fated shore.'

'I say you must take us back. The girl you carry is the legal ward of Consul Derain of the Empire. You have been tricked into kidnapping us.'

A few crewmen wandered up behind their Captain. Arrow had expected peg legs and eye patches over leering grins, but these were just large, hard-looking men, carrying hammers and ropes. The weight of the vicious hook at her waist called to be drawn against them. But that wasn't the plan.

Barro stood beside her. 'You hazard war with the Empire over this. Does your Frisian crew know you've put them in such danger?'

'You risk much, sunshine boy, here on the deck of my own ship. Extra cargo you are, with all men aboard on part-rations to keep you fed and watered. You'd best trip back down below, before we start questioning if you're worth carrying at all.'

The sailors started to fan out around them, ready to return the packages to the hold. The Captain stood, now with arms crossed, and brows lowered at them.

Arrow was horribly aware that all around was nothing but water. She'd hoped to see sight of the Britannian coast, or even pursuing ships. Her knuckles curled into fists. She would get Livy back even if it meant skewering her hook into the woman's ribs. This god could fight dirty.

'The Inguz rises!'

The old Druid Llund was paler than she remembered, but just as scruffy with his plaits and silver trinkets clinking as he scuttled across the deck. His arms were raised, and he looked like a Pontifex about to bless an oil libation.

'Where – is – Livy,' Arrow demanded through gritted teeth, and felt Barro's shoulder touch hers, nudging her towards the railed edge of the ship.

'Livia is well, Inguz. Eiocha herself protects her, and she will save Eiocha in return!'

Eiocha was their pagan word for the goddess Gaea, wasn't it? Arrow tried to remember. The man's crazy mystic talk had got to a few of the gathering crew. Arrow spotted men making signs, as if to ward off evil or welcome her as a god. She couldn't tell which.

'Livia will stop the Empire strangling us. Save us from the storms. The god is risen and the child is ready!' Llund was in full rant, arms thrown open to the sky.

Right, time to see how far this god thing could get her.

'Yes, I am the Inguz! Bring me Livy and take this ship back to Londinium.'

The Captain rolled her eyes, but Llund held his hands out as if placating a hysterical child, or animal.

'Livia must reach the fated shore.' Llund grinned at her with mossy teeth.

Sailors were gathering, more than Barro and she could take down with nothing but boat hooks. The mad Llund's face shone with feverish belief as he nodded at her.

Well, if they wouldn't listen to their gods' orders, they might listen to the stone's loss.

Turning the stone over in her pocket, Arrow reached the rail edge, with Barro at her side. She reached her hand out over the water, turning her palm upwards so the criss-crossed jet-black stone was visible, its silvery tracery glinting in the light.

'I don't know why this thing matters to you, old man. But by whatever name you call me, I *will* drop it to the depths unless you return Livy to me.' She watched Llund as she spoke, her arm swaying in the wind.

If possible, the old man went even paler, pinned to the spot. Even the Captain took a sharp intake of breath. Good, the stupid stone did have a value to them.

Llund stepped forward, as if terrified to rock the ship, his eyes bulging.

'Please, take care!'

Arrow leaned out a little further. 'Bring – me – Livy.' On each word she tossed the stone in the air above the waves, catching it without watching.

Llund quivered, hands entreating.

'All in time, Inguz. You, and that man, must return below. I beg of you, stay there until we reach our port. Then the fates will decide our destiny.'

'If you think I'd leave Livy in the hands of a crazy Druid, you're about to learn what kind of god I can be,' Arrow spat out, her free hand clutching the handle of the hook at her waist.

The gathered pirates were muttering, and the Captain had to bark an order to silence them. Arrow locked eyes with the strange woman. She knew almost every man aboard would underestimate her, including Llund. But perhaps this woman would understand what she'd be prepared to do to save Livy.

The Captain's dark eyes were like a stormy sea, below a brow crinkled with the worry of responsibility. But a light danced in them too, and the few lines fanning out from her lashes could be from laughter rather than anger. The pirate faced her with a boldness no Empire woman ever matched.

Arrow wasn't sure what she saw in her own face. But with a deep sigh, the Captain turned away first.

'I will not stand between this woman and her child, Llund.'

Without waiting for an answer, the Captain strode across the deck to a small door opposite the one Arrow and Barro had come through, pulling it open. For a moment, there was only darkness, then a small form dove out.

'Miss! Oh, Miss, it's really you!'

Livy was wearing brown trousers and a seaman's shirt, her unruly dark curls tied back with twine. Her cheeks were flushed and eyes shining as she ran across the planks with steady feet.

'Livy, dearest.' Arrow felt like a tie had been cut and she threw herself across the deck, skidding on her knees to Livy and pulling the girl into her arms.

They hadn't hugged in years, but right now Arrow couldn't care less about Imperium propriety. The Inguz stone rattled to the deck. Any plan Arrow had didn't continue past this moment.

'Livy.' Arrow rocked the girl. 'Dearest. I'm so sorry.'

'Oh, Miss. I thought you might be dead.'

'Don't worry about me, Livy, I just felt a bit ill. All the better for seeing you now.' Arrow didn't have to force her smile.

'I wanted to look after you, but Barro said he was your friend and would make sure you woke up.'

Arrow just squeezed the girl, trying not to think about Livy alone and scared, wondering if her governess would survive.

A young boy peeked at them from behind the stocky sailors. His wild hair was the colour of flame, like nothing Arrow had seen before, although the governess in her noticed it needed a cut. She and the boy were in almost precisely matching outfits, and Arrow realised she must be dressed in his spares. He stood with that indeterminate stance of every lad between the ages of ten and seventeen, as if he wasn't sure he was doing the right thing and was both worried and defiant about that.

'Well now.' The Captain sounded tired. 'The girl has her governess back. And some of us have work to get on with.' The crewmen muttered behind her. 'Tor, my boy, see to the Inguz and young Livy. They will bunk together.'

The red-haired boy stepped forward and nodded at the order. The old Druid shuffled over to the Captain muttering, but the woman cut him off.

'Llund, we are at sea, the child is going nowhere. My word on it.'

The Captain then smiled as sweetly as a Londinium debutante at Barro. 'You now, my sunshine boy, are no deity. You'll be eating our food on this voyage, so perhaps you are of more use in the galley than the brig; Cook always needs help scrubbing pans.'

'Bloody pleasure cruise this is turning out to be.' Barro huffed, but Arrow worried about the smile that followed it.

CHAPTER XI

A loud caw rang out.

Two white seabirds, with a wingspan three times the size of any crow or pigeon at home, circled far above them, as if they were tethered to the mast.

'Freyer's goslings. Good luck to have one, and two have followed this sailing!' The boy Tor nodded at Arrow and Livy like an over-enthusiastic market-stall owner who hadn't made a sale all day.

The Captain had ordered the deck cleared. Barro winked at Arrow, then slouched off towards the galley as she and Livy stumbled to their feet. A deflated Llund disappeared below before Arrow could grab his scrawny neck.

She should chase Llund to question him or try to plot an escape with Barro. But in this moment, all Arrow really wanted to do was hold Livy's hand.

Tor was nattering on in what became clear was a tour of the ship. Arrow kept a professional smile plastered on her face for the boy, but Livy was silent.

Tor was grinning. 'We're almost the largest in the fleet! See, we have two sails and four light-lenses.' The boy slapped his hand over his mouth at the last words. Arrow had heard that sailors were superstitious; if the large birds were good luck perhaps naming light-lenses was bad.

Livy stared out to sea as if nothing on the ship mattered but was gripping her former governess's arm as if she might float away.

Arrow's guts twisted with worry, but she hitched her smile up higher for the boy, encouraging him. Livy might need the undivided attention of the woman who had raised her after such a shock, but she needed information to assess the new situational parameters. The Inguz stone was back in Arrow's pocket and Livy was hers again. But the ship was still headed away from civilisation. One objective secure, others slipping away with each wave.

Arrow wasn't sure if her growing headache was an after-effect of the lightning strike or punishment for being so coolly strategic when Livy needed her heart rather than her head.

Fore, aft, midships, long lines and brackets, curl knots and cuzziners. Amongst the barrage of new terms Tor reeled off Arrow learnt that the ship's name translated from the Frisian as 'Flyer'. They had set off from Svalbaer in the far north a few weeks ago and arrived at the Londinium docks quite soon after, under a Gaulish flag to avoid impounding. Arrow suspected the Captain must have paid a hefty bribe too, but didn't correct the boy, not least because Tor kept saying 'mother' rather than 'Captain' and that information was worth knowing.

'Is your father also on board?'

'No.' The boy looked down as if his bare feet were suddenly fascinating, and his voice dropped so that Arrow had to strain to hear over the rhythmic beat of waves and creek of wood. 'Thorl took him three winters ago, during an ice storm in the Vestsea. He saved the *Flyer*, for me.'

'Ah, so you are the real Captain around here then, good sir?' Arrow smiled, hoping a little teasing would nudge the boy out of his sudden dark mood.

Tor looked like she'd spat at him. 'Captain Baja is my sworn commander, and every sailor aboard will kill or die at her command!' It sounded like words learnt by rote, but Tor also stood a little taller and the righteous indignation flowed off him. Even Livy turned from her thousand-mile stare.

The boy was a loyal sailor, not just a son.

'Of course, she is, Tor.' Now Arrow was nodding to placate him. 'Well then, your *Flyer* is well named, she moves faster even than a race-charo!'

But the now grumpy Tor strode off towards a small door, glancing back to check they had followed. They climbed down steps and dodged under beams to reach what could only be called a cupboard, where Livy had been staying. The girl climbed up into the small raised pallet bed and curled up, while Tor scampered off.

If we truly learn from failure rather than success, Arrow felt she deserved an Academy diploma. She kneaded her temples to try to release the pounding that was building. Well, she wasn't in the brig anymore, had learnt more than was comfortable, and had regained what she'd lost.

Looking over at her former charge, Arrow hovered, not sure where to start. An ideal Imperium Romanum governess would probably use this moment for stoic instruction or to pray thanks to the gods. It was harder to perform proper decorum without her bodice and skirts.

On this ship, Arrow wasn't sure any gods would heed them, especially as she was now apparently a competing deity. She fervently wished she and Livy were back in their little garret tidying away schoolbooks, all this lunacy just a dream.

'Livy, dearest. We'll find our way home.'

The girl lay silent, with Arrow holding the edge of the bed to steady herself, then Livy turned, her face a picture of childish disquiet.

'Do you have a god inside you, Miss? Mr Llund told me you did.'

'Not unless it's a seasick god, Livy. I'm just me and I've been looking for you.'

'That's what Mr Llund said he was doing too, after I woke up.'

Arrow kept her voice steady but knew her knuckles gripping the bed turned white with the effort. 'Did Llund hit you in the museum, hard enough to fall over asleep?'

'I don't think so, my head didn't hurt or have any bumps. I remember something on my face that smelt sweet, and I went to sleep. I woke up in a room that smelt of beer. I was on my own, but there was a plate of honey cakes on the floor, like the ones in the museum. I was very hungry, so I ate all of them.' Livy looked like she expected a chiding for eating too much cake while being abducted and held captive alone beneath an Anglish pub.

'Oh, Livy, you've been very brave, as I knew you would be. I'm so proud of you, dearest.'

That was all that was needed for the girl's sobs to start. Arrow lifted Livy down, her heaviness a reminder they hadn't sat like this, with Livy in her lap, for many years. She hummed snippets of nursery songs, not trying yet to explain or understand.

Gods, how many ways had she failed this child?

Right now, she could, perhaps should, tell Livy that the woman she'd only ever known as governess was in fact a murderous gladiator, and now an escaped slave. But the girl had gone through so much. Arrow thought that maybe she could pretend to be a governess again, at least for a little while.

Anyway, it would be too strange to hear Livy call her by her battle-name rather than their familiar 'Miss'.

Tor peeked his head around their door again, and furrowed his brow, so like his mother, seeing Livy curled and sniffling. Arrow smiled a little and nodded at the boy, resting her cheek against Livy's curls. He crept in and placed two bowls on the floor nearby, from which a rich spicy fish smell rose. Then he laid a stoppered pouch alongside: the medicine the Captain had given her earlier.

Tor stood, twisting the corner of his hessian shirt and looking anywhere rather than directly at her.

'My mother, Captain Baja. She's a very good captain, as good as my father. She doesn't look like it, but she's worried about this sailing. She sent the medicine when I told her you were pale again.'

'Thank you, Tor. I'm worried too. I just want to take Livy home.'

Tor nodded, then he left them alone again when Livy didn't speak. The stew smelt delicious.

'You should eat, dearest.'

'You want to take me home?' Livy sniffed.

'Londinium is our home, dearest. Llund took you, and he's taken Barro and me too. We don't matter much, but you are the legal ward of Consul Derain.'

'Do you think he's my father?' It was a question Livy hadn't asked before, but here their careful politeness seemed pointless.

'No, Livy. Although, I do think you come from a Citizen family. Oh, Livy, that could mean so much for you.'

Arrow's stomach growled but one more thing had to be said.

'Livy, I only want the best for you. All the best things in the world.' Arrow took another deep breath and forced some excitement into her voice. 'A letter arrived, just before we went to the museum. It was an invitation for you to study at the Academy! Consul Derain arranged for it. That's what's waiting for you back in Londinium. Isn't that exciting?'

One day this abduction by pirates would fade into nothing but a thrilling anecdote for the girl's new Citizen friends. Livy would graduate as an eminent Dia, wrapped in fashionable silks and a precious toga sash. Arrow imagined Citizen Livia walking on the arm of her besotted husband, teaching her own daughter to play nux, and laughing when she won.

'Would you come too?' Livy asked between sips of the soup.

'Perhaps,' Arrow lied.

If Derain refused Livy's return, there was still Octavia's embroidered handkerchief as a thin thread of hope for the orphan girl. No need for Livy to know that no option included amnesty for a runaway slave.

Arrow hoped her own execution would be swift, and private.

After every drop of the stew was eaten, she and Livy washed as best they could, with a few clean rags and a little water from a pouch hung by the door of their tiny cabin. Then they climbed into the pallet. Since swigging from the medicine, Arrow's skull had stopped thumping and now was filled with fluffy sleepy clouds.

'Miss, Tor told me that Inguz is a boy-god. He has the power to change the winds, tides and times.'

'Well, Livy,' Arrow said snuggling down beside her, 'perhaps tomorrow I will be able to change the wind to take us back.'

Livy yawned, 'Maybe, but you need Captain Baja to turn the sails. She's the only one allowed to order that.'

The waves rocked while Arrow thought about the proud woman who had inherited her dead husband's ship, ordering men to work or fight at her word. The Captain seemed entirely sure of who she was. Arrow fell asleep wondering what that might feel like.

When she woke, her arm was wrapped around Livy.

The unfamiliar swaying room was disorientating, but that wasn't what had awakened her. She could hear the muffled sound of voices raised in anger – many of them. They must be loud to have reached her asleep down here.

Arrow slipped out of the pallet without waking Livy and walked over to the small door. She inched it open and the sound of angry men became clearer. She thought she could make out the Captain's voice . . . and Barro's.

Arrow didn't want to leave Livy, nor take her into danger. But if Barro caused trouble it would fall on all three of their heads.

Stepping back, Arrow pulled the cover up over Livy and stared at her sleeping face, which looked so much younger without its grins and frowns of the day. Then she turned and left the cabin, closing the door tight behind her.

Up the stairs it was night, the deck lit by blue lanterns flickering as the waves swung them a little. Barro was standing towards the prow with the Captain between him and a pack of sailors. Two other men leaned over the side, their shoulders heaving in what smelt like sickness. Arrow moved closer, hugging to the shadows between the swinging blue lights.

'Farlen nova! It is not liquor, it is poison!' one of the crew shouted, gesturing to the two men retching over the side.

'I drank it myself, we all did – even you, Tarven, my friend.' Barro was open-palmed and held his voice soft.

The scene was painfully familiar; if not for the roll of the ship and tang of the sea air, this might be a brawl in the Arena mess hall. Which Barro had often been the centre of, even back when they were nothing more than children.

'Did you, Tarven? Did you all?' The Captain scowled. Arrow recognised a woman struggling to hold her temper. 'When this man offered you a drink and a game of cards, did none of you follow my orders?'

The man Tarven looked dishevelled, and his face was flushed red. 'You said to leave the woman and child alone, Captain, that other one was just scrubbing dishes, we thought. But he brewed up poison in the kitchens, gave it to Akurk and Josha so he could cheat them at cards!'

'Is this true, sunshine boy?' The Captain turned to Barro.

'My friend Tarven here has it all wrong, my Lady. I made a little scrumpy with what I found in the kitchen, to ease my homesickness. When Akurk, Josha and the rest wanted to win back what I'd taken from them earlier tonight, I offered it around. We all drank from the same spout. Perhaps our Empire spirit is too strong for your delicate Frisian stomachs?'

The men roared at his slur.

Why would Barro deliberately provoke the furious crewmen? The Captain was unmoved by the taunt, but Arrow's jaw tightened.

'They can puke all they want; they do that enough when we make port, and they head to the taverns. But you, my extra cargo. What did you hope to gain from this? You are not what you seem. Tarven

153

already wants to give you a beating, yet you insult him. You stand there with your hands open, but I feel like you are playing cards, now, with me.'

Barro rose up from his apologetic stoop and the lopsided smile fell from his face, replaced by stony indifference.

'Like any prisoner, I wanted to win my way to freedom, or at least information about where my jail is heading. But if Tarven is to beat me, then you should tie me down first. Else I will break his neck as easily as I snapped the carrots for your stew.'

Arrow recognised this side of Barro from their Arena days. Back then, when his smiles ended, the blood started. Here, the crew jeered at the idea of the young man beating the rugged Tarven, who was a head taller and hands wider than him.

The Captain shook her head as if done with the whole situation and took a step back to let Tarven thrash the interloper. Barro cracked his neck and flexed his fists. Arrow knew he was maintaining his training at the Arena. It wouldn't be a fight, it would be an execution. And after Barro killed the sailor, Arrow wondered how long it would take the Captain to draw her sword.

For Hades' sake. Hadn't Barro himself warned her not to try fighting her way out of this mess earlier?

Arrow jerked out into the light of a blue lantern. 'Stop . . . or there will be death here.' The crew fell silent, staring at her. 'Captain Baja, please listen. Barro is gladiator-trained, as am I. He has killed more men in the Arena, with nothing but his hands, than anyone you have met before.' She swallowed. 'Except me.'

The Captain's chest heaved as if rage blocked her breath and then she turned to another dark corner of the deck.

'Is this true, old man? Did you bring gods-forsaken *Arena killers* aboard my ship?'

From the darkness, a man in scruffy rags and plaits shuffled out. Now it was Arrow's turn to clench her fists. But if she moved against Llund now, the whole crew would come down on them. Despite her threat, she wasn't sure she and Barro could take them all at once.

Livy lay asleep below.

Llund ignored her and spoke to the Captain. 'Lady Baja, I should have warned you about Barro. What the Inguz says is right, that man is a gladiator.' Then Llund's nose wrinkled. 'He's also a cheat and fraudster – not to be trusted.'

'So says the stealer of children,' Barro spat out.

The crew roared and pushed towards Barro.

'Silence!' the Captain barked. 'Llund, if this is true, you will explain why you let me take this snake aboard. Killer or no, he must be punished.'

'Over the side!' one of the crew shouted out and others joined, as they surged forward towards Barro, who stood bouncing on the balls of his feet, with fists raised. Arrow started to calculate how many of them she could incapacitate.

'ENOUGH!' roared the Captain.

The leather-clad woman drew her short sword from the scabbard. It was the single weapon Arrow had seen aboard. All the men fell silent. But rather than pointing it towards Barro, or even Llund, instead the Captain spun, took a few strides, and rested the tip of the sharp blade against the hessian of Arrow's shirt. She heard Barro inhale sharply, but she flashed an Arena hand sign at him. *Back off.*

The weight of the weapon pressed against Arrow's heart.

'You, the woman chosen of Yngvi. Now I understand why Llund wielded Thorl's lighting against you.' The woman's nose wrinkled. 'Of all the horrors of your cursed Empire, your Arena of blood is the worst. Killing for show.'

Arrow didn't move, meeting the dark eyes of the Frisian woman even as the sword tip pressed on the edge of breaking skin.

'So speaks a pirate,' Arrow answered.

Interestingly, at those words the Captain regained control of herself. Her dark brows smoothed, shoulders dropped, and breathing slowed from a ragged pant.

In that moment, Arrow saw a woman who had to protect a son, placate a crew, fulfil some promise to the mad Druid and now had two murderers aboard, one carrying the name of a god. If their roles were reversed, with Livy at risk, she would let the crew heave Barro over the side and slam the other gladiator in the brig until they made port. It was the only sensible option, as Barro had proved dangerous.

The Captain sighed, perhaps even with regret at what she was about to order.

The entire ship would be a bloodbath within minutes.

Bloody stupid *men*.

Arrow reached up and gently clasped the tip of the razor-sharp blade between her fingertips. Then slowly moved it up from over her heart and leaned forward for it to rest against the skin of her own throat. The tip was so sharp she felt it scratch and a little blood trickle, although the Captain's sword arm was steady.

This had better work.

'Captain Baja of the *Flyer*, I offer my sworn fealty to you. I will kill or die at your word while on your ship, like every man here. In return, Barro must live.'

Barro snarled, 'No!' but Arrow didn't break eye contact with the Captain. Their breathing now matched as if they wrestled on the deck planks rather than stood unmoving, facing each other.

The Captain was the first to look away.

'Take that killer back to the brig, unharmed. All here bear witness: the Inguz now serves the *Flyer*.'

Several of the crew gasped, whether with astonishment or outrage Arrow couldn't tell.

'This is a mistake, Captain. That man is not to be trusted.' Llund's face was shiny in the strange blue lights strung around the ship.

'I am not trusting him, Green Man. I am trusting her,' the Captain said. Then she walked over to Barro, sheathing her weapon and nodding Barro towards the door down to the hold.

He flourished a bow towards Arrow, throwing in two hand signs.

The first meant 'you lead, I follow'. The second wasn't informative about anything other than Barro's forceful dislike of her choices.

Despite her boiling blood, Arrow took a long look at Llund, then headed below to Livy. As she left, the crew grumbled and dispersed behind her.

Barro was alive, although she wasn't entirely sure why she'd saved him.

Saturnalia,
Londinium Arena

MDCXLIX, Aurelian Calendar

CHAPTER XII

Long ago, the Londinium Arena had looked beautiful at least once.

Thousands of tiny candles nestled into the sand, the flickering light of them masking the gladiator blood spilled there over the preceding days.

Gladiatrix Arrow bit into a honey cake an Arena boss served her, bowing as he did so. She chewed obligingly, but it was hard to summon the expected jollity. Each candle reminded her of a life she'd taken.

No one could fight, and kill, as well as Arrow did without admitting they enjoyed it. The rip of flesh, pound of fist into bone, the weight of a bloodied weapon victorious in her hand. Crowds roaring her name.

But once the fans' jubilant calls fell silent, she started to remember the screams.

Arrow ground the honey cake in her jaw.

Tonight, the fighters' sacrifice was supposed to be forgotten, and the survivors required to at least feign merriment as they were feasted and waited upon by their Arena bosses.

Because the rules of Saturnalia dictated that, on this most beloved of festival nights, the masters should serve their slaves.

As every Empire child was taught, long ago in the arcadian age of Saturn, all men were equal, and the world was at peace. Every

Emperor promised his reign would return the Imperium Romanum to that glorious golden era. Arrow wondered why then they pursued war, enforced slavery and hoarded the wealth that Saturn supposedly despised. Perhaps the oil age was gilded for some.

Her pondering was interrupted by another loud 'Hear me!', by Barro, who had been proclaimed the Saturn King, empowered to order around everyone in the Arena.

For one night.

An Arena boss had already failed to juggle hot potatoes when commanded, much to everyone's hilarity. Another was dressed as a gladiatrix, his large belly hanging over the studded skirt. He was thoroughly enjoying it, prancing around in a way that would invite instant death if Arrow tried the same in battle.

'As Saturnalia Rex, I do hereby decree that only gladiators have freedom of the Arena for tonight. On this most auspicious of festivals, the sand is ours. None but a gladiator may have entry until sunrise tomorrow!'

A huge cheer rose to meet Barro's pronouncement, not least from the Arena bosses now free to head home to their proper Saturnalia revelries.

It was obviously planned, Arrow thought, as she picked at the remnants of the feast. It was no surprise Barro had been chosen as 'king for the night'. Arrow suspected a boss had slipped him a golden coin to release them early. None of the other gladiators minded though, drunkenly stumbling off to poke around in places they weren't usually allowed. If they were found the next morning asleep on the couches in the boss's offices, they might even avoid a beating. It was Saturnalia after all. The priests had unbound the feet of Saturn's temple statue, and for a few hours at least all were equal – Citizen, Plebeian and slave.

Which was all damn stupid, especially as the days leading up to the feast were the bloodiest and most dangerous for gladiators. The stands had been packed until this morning to watch Arrow's bouts.

She'd even missed her Academy graduation, a Saturnalia tradition the Arena bosses didn't deem worthy of her skipping a battle re-enactment for. Arrow secretly hoped Dia Severina might send her certificate and hated herself for such sentimentality.

Well, if she had freedom of the Arena, Arrow decided she'd use it to go back to her bed.

'Gods, you look like you're chewing sand rather than honey cakes, Arrow.' The King of Saturnalia was one of the few gladiators left at the table, finishing off his drink.

'Well, your highness, maybe I'd have ordered the bosses to clean up before they left. Now, we'll have to do it ourselves, tomorrow.'

Barro's eyebrows came together with drunken exaggerated confusion. 'Bugger, you're right, Arrow. Tell you what, I do hereby decree you are Lua Saturni, Saturn's wife, for tonight only of course. All my power is yours.' He leaned down, fist over heart, in a mock salute.

Just that morning a man had given her that salute for real. An hour later she'd slipped her sword between his ribs after crushing his windpipe with the edge of her shield.

The Saturnalia crowds had gone wild.

'That's flattering, Barro, but if you'd ever listened at Temple, then you'd know she's a goddess of utter destruction, endless war and human sacrifice.'

'Suits you then, Arrow, I guess, considering how many men you've sent to Tartarus this past week.' Barro winked.

She hadn't meant to hit him quite so hard, but Barro fell back onto the sand scattering candles and leaving a pool of darkness amongst the light. And if she hadn't heard him laughing then Arrow might have left him there, alone as all the other gladiators had left.

Instead, she threw herself forward, her fist slammed into his midriff and forearm raised to punch into his throat as the belly blow keeled him over. Instead of curling up he grabbed her fist and pulled her body into his. Bloody stupid move; she had the advantage now.

'I'll will fight you if you want, Arrow,' Barro gasped out, the stomach punch having winded him at least. 'But *is* that what you want?'

The hand that should be knocking her sideways instead reached up to brush hair from her brow.

Arrow stiffened as if she'd been impaled.

Barro had always been there, teasing, fighting, teaching and learning as they both grew up in the Arena. In the past few years, as they'd become full gladiators, they'd been drawn against each other, but never in a death match. She'd always assumed her relief at that was because he was such a good fighter he might beat her.

Or perhaps it was because she couldn't bear the idea of killing him as she'd done to friends before.

As she'd done to a friend on this very sand today.

She thrust down and kissed him with the same ferocity as when she fought him. The smell of honey cakes and wine mixed with the scent of him, that she knew almost as well as her own.

Her kiss was almost a bite. But Barro didn't bite back; his hands moved up instead to stroke her hair. She leaned back and ripped at his bright-coloured wrap tunic, pulling it off his body like armour wrested from a fallen enemy. But he just kissed the inside of her wrist, then each finger more used to gripping killing steel than caressing a lover.

'I will fight you, Arrow, or I will make love to you, not both at the same time,' he whispered into her hair, his large, calloused hands slipping inside her tunic.

The light touch of his fingertips on her bare skin sent prickles up her spine. It was almost the same sensation as the first moments of facing a new enemy, when your body thrilled for combat.

Did she want to fight? Until now, it had been the one thing she'd known she could desire from Barro. His hands moved up her ribs, feather-light as they reached breasts usually protected by steel.

Breath by breath, the blood pumping through her body for a fight started to slow. Their tunics became blankets on the sand.

Arrow had lain on this sand before, when injured or defeated. Always under the bright sky and watched by the bloodthirsty crowds. Tonight, the wide Arena was more like a waving sea, with floating candles around their patch of darkness.

Her fingers traced over a body she already knew. Arrow could tell the story of his scars; some wounds she'd sewn up herself, others she'd given him. His hands did the same down her back and up the inside of her thigh. It felt like they both owned part of each other, bodies made by their bouts. As he kissed down her chest, he chose the spots without the bruises he'd seen her receive in today's bouts. Finding pleasure for her in the places without pain. As he got lower, she tangled her fingers in his hair. But even as she lost herself in the feeling, she didn't pull on his scalp, knowing a deep cut she'd given his forehead was still healing.

They moved together in a rhythm learnt in fights on this same sand. Yet each avoiding the places where it hurt, gentling the wounds, taking care with injuries they would mercilessly exploit if facing each other in battle. Kissing between where the punches had fallen.

It was the most tenderness that Arrow had received, or given, in a long time.

As Barro's lips again found hers, their bodies wrapped together, she wondered why she could taste wet salt in their kiss.

Perhaps, she thought, those few tears would wash away all the blood she'd shed on the sand.

Then she forgot about everything, for the night of Saturnalia at least.

The Ides of Junius, Atlas Sea

MDCLVII, Aurelian Calendar

CHAPTER XIII

The deck brush scratching against the *Flyer*'s planks set Arrow's teeth on edge. But she scrubbed harder to dislodge memories of the Arena, of a sea of lights under stars.

The past weeks of cleaning decks, polishing rails, coiling ropes and hosing out the latrine had started to re-harden her callouses and awaken muscles that years as a governess had softened. From morning to night there was another dirty or boring job to be found somewhere on the damn boat. The crew had swiftly got over their brief hesitation in allotting their least favourite tasks to a god.

As the newest crew mate sworn to the *Flyer*, apparently it was tradition that Arrow got the worst jobs aboard. If they tired of her asking questions, a senior sailor would order her to be quiet, and it was her newly sworn duty to obey.

Arrow still ate with Livy and fell into their shared pallet exhausted every night. The girl tried to help, carrying sloshing buckets or tidying up what Arrow had to clean. Often making so much more mess that Arrow sent the girl away to play with Tor.

The Captain's son was teaching Livy impressive (if terrifying) tricks, where they hung from the ropes, or ran across them, then swung across the deck. Arrow declared the dizzying heights of *Flyer*'s nest, the lookout high up top of the mast, off-limits for Livy. Although she suspected the prohibition was broken as soon as she turned to another chore.

Leaning backwards, Arrow released muscles in her aching spine. No matter. Barro still lived and the Captain had left them alone.

Kneeling down again in her uncomfortable little puddle of water, Arrow rhythmically scoured the planks, with the sound of gulls above and the sun warm on her neck.

Livy flopped down on a nearby crate, chewing her lip.

The two had snatched a little talk about escape and return to Londinium. The girl wanted to know why Llund had taken her, but the old Druid had kept himself locked away in his cabin. Arrow would have kicked the door in, but that would break her promise to Captain Baja. *Gods-damned Barro.* Arrow hoped he was enjoying lazing around in the brig.

She missed her and Livy's little garret in London, with their soft beds, old books and the rhythm of days passing in lessons and walks around city parks.

That thought sparked another memory. So many years before, her own mother, with a cut lip and splinted arm, had dragged herself up from her cot the day after a brutal bout in the Arena. Mother had waved her towards their wooden training swords. 'Today, we practise your compound attack. Your feint must draw the parry, but your sword arm keeps dropping too low.' Mother limped over and hefted her own sword in her left arm, wincing as she did.

'But, you're hurt!' her younger self had protested. Arrow remembered begging because no daughter should spar with a mother so broken and in pain. Her mother was having none of it.

'Dearest, for the prosperous, education is an ornament. For unfortunates like us, it's our only refuge from death.'

Practice is everything.

An older and wiser Arrow sat back up on her tired arches. 'Right then, Livy. We don't know where we're going, but we don't have to waste all the time getting there.' She dropped the brush in the bucket.

'Even here, I can still teach you a few things. Please recite the twelve principles of rhetoric to me, each with an appropriate example.'

Livy didn't know she wasn't a governess anymore. And although Derain had stripped Arrow of the title, he couldn't wipe away the Academy knowledge in her head.

The girl wrinkled her nose at the idea, but, after Arrow gave her the option of taking over the scrubbing or restarting lessons, Livy remembered her love of learning.

Teaching without books, pens or even a desk forced Arrow to improvise. Sitting on the deck, she pulled snippets of poetry from her memory. Taught Livy funny rhymes to recall the names of the emperors going back before Marcus Aurelius moved from old Rome to Londinium. She even recited scientific principles from her days in Dia Severina's lab, telling Livy about the doves and effula experiment.

'So everything breathes out effula, all the animals and the people. But . . . it can kill you?' Livy asked.

'Only in high enough concentrations. Dia Severina was trying to measure the levels in the countryside compared to the city.'

'What does it smell like? Would I know if there was too much in the air?' Livy was not so subtly sniffing.

'Thankfully, you and I will never breathe enough to know that,' Arrow assured her. 'But I suspect undiluted effula would smell quite nasty, perhaps like charo fumes.'

At the last words, Arrow heard a gasp and looked up to see Tor seated, quite comfortably, in a curl of rope above them.

'Hello, Tor, how long have you been up there?' Arrow asked.

'Oh, he's been there for ages,' Livy answered for him, smiling up. 'He likes the idea of school, don't you, Tor?'

The boy looked sheepish and darted a gaze over to where his mother was standing at the other end of the deck. The tall woman was looking out over the waves through a twisted metal instrument and was engrossed in noting down some sort of measurement.

171

'I like learning things, Lady Inguz, I hope that isn't wrong?' Tor said.

'Not at all, Tor, every teacher enjoys an audience. But did you have a question about effula?' Arrow used her best teacher's smile to invite the boy into the lesson.

'It's just the bit you said about charo fumes. My mother and Llund keep talking about them. They're really bad, aren't they? They might kill Eiocha,' Tor said.

Livy was sat primly as if in imitation of a governess. 'That's not the lesson, Tor, you're getting mixed up.'

Arrow thought she'd better take over to avoid a squabble. 'Livy's right, it's effula that's dangerous. Charo fumes aren't very pleasant, but they're not dangerous. We put up with the smell because oil fuels everything.'

'That's why we've got light-lenses instead,' Tor said.

'I didn't know that, Tor. Livy and I are also eager to learn, aren't we? What is a light-lens, and how can you use it instead of oil?' Arrow probed, idly pushing her brush around. Every night blue lights burned bright across the deck. It occurred to Arrow that she'd never been tasked with the dirty job of refilling their oil.

Tor looked horrified by her questioning. 'No! Umm. It was the bit about charos. I'm sorry, goodbye,' the boy stammered out and then scurried off back up the rigging higher than she or Livy could climb.

Arrow wondered what the boy had meant and if finding out might prove useful, but Livy looked forlorn as she watched Tor leave.

Well, if effula science was going to cause problems, there were more distracting subjects to learn.

'Livy dearest, shall we start your other lessons too? I was teaching you wrist-locks and drop-kicks, before the museum, wasn't I?' Arrow asked.

Livy jumped up, forlornness forgotten, ready for fighting practice. The deck was almost clean, no one had given Arrow another job yet, and she needed to stretch out her rebuilt muscles. Comfortable in their trousers and shirts, Livy and Arrow started to spar, the small girl and the not-much-larger woman both focused as they practised twists and kicks.

Tor and a few crewmen stopped what they were doing to watch, from a distance. Arrow didn't much care. Livy's lips were pressed together. Arrow snatched at her wrist, gripping enough that tugging wouldn't free the girl's arm, but not so tight as to bruise. Twisting, Livy yanked the hard side of her wrist bone against the weakest part of any grip, the fingertips. She stamped her own foot towards Arrow's instep as she did. Dodging the stomp on the rolling deck lost Arrow's footing, and she stepped on the scrubbing brush that had been kicked out of place. She let her arms and legs flail as she fell, in hope of a laugh from Livy; there had been too few of those lately.

'If that's how you fight, perhaps I'll let your sunshine boy back up from the brig.'

The sky was darkening behind the Captain as her hair caught in the wind. The watching crew laughed.

'Perhaps.' Arrow's smile was tight.

'She could beat you, I bet my supper on it!' Livy defended the woman she still only knew as a governess, as the sailors chuckled louder.

'Ah, but, young Livy,' the Captain turned to the girl, 'I couldn't fight against a god. She might smite me.'

Arrow couldn't help a loud sniff at that, then dropped to her knees and started scrubbing again. 'And I couldn't allow myself to beat my Captain, that would be mutiny.'

There were a few grunts from the sailors, but also sniggers.

When Arrow looked up again, Captain Baja was handing off her sword to another sailor and then tying back her wild black hair with twine. Tor and Livy were both watching with glee and the grins on the sailors' faces ran from calculating to lecherous. What had her mother said? Never provoke an enemy you're not obliged to fight. Arrow knew she should provide Livy a lesson in self-control by begging the Captain's forgiveness and refusing to engage. Take the punches, if they came.

But it felt good to be limbering up in shirt and trousers rather than skirts and corset. What could it harm? The sun had dimmed but the air was fresh, and the roiling waves no longer befuddled her step. Bouncing on her heels, Arrow grinned at the frowning Captain.

'A friendly bout . . . to the first pin down?'

The Captain gave one curt nod – then charged, slamming her shoulder into Arrow's own.

Damnatus.

Just about keeping her footing, Arrow managed an elbow punch into the woman's ribs as she pivoted. She heard a cry, but that was Tor. The crew were shouting out, mainly for the Captain but with a few 'Inguz!' and 'Yngvi!' thrown in.

Captain Baja bent with the blow but then grappled Arrow from behind, body pressed close, trying for a lift and slam down onto the deck. Barro would love this, watching the only two women aboard fight. Served him right to be missing out.

Arrow tried to kick out Baja's knee, but the woman's skirts dulled the blow. Gods, the Captain was stronger than she'd expected. Arrow struggled to think of a move that would free her without seriously injuring the other woman. That ruled out the classic back headbutt into the face, breaking her nose. *Pity.*

Instead, Arrow lifted both feet, feeling Baja sag a little with the weight, and pushed herself up and through the woman's arms, leveraging off her opponent's bent knees, and rolling out of the high fall.

Baja's body slammed into hers and they both went down. Gods, the reflex to break the woman's neck as they fell was so hard to resist. Arrow's hand ended up twisted in her opponent's hair instead. The Captain's cheeks pinked, and she huffed, trying to pin down across Arrow's neck. *Break her forearm?* The angle was right but she shouldn't do it. *Smash her head to bloody pulp on the planks?* No. Gods, she couldn't kill someone in front of Livy.

The Captain was struggling to get purchase on the deck, rolling harder. Fighting without killing or maiming was harder than Arrow remembered. She couldn't think of any way to win without damaging Baja, badly.

Well then, maybe she should just lose.

In some ways, falling limp under the other woman's strength would almost be a relief. Livy merely thought of her as a governess anyway. No shame in it . . .

Arrow yanked at the handful of soft curls her fist was tangled in, hard. If it was too dangerous to fight like a gladiator, then she'd try like a governess. She pulled the hair harder, aided by a hard roil of the waves beneath them.

Both of Captain Baja's hands flew to her scalp as she yelled in the pain, sitting up astride Arrow, necklaces jangling. Arrow laughed in a way she'd never have risked in a real fight.

Then, Baja's shout of pain stopped, and the woman tensed like she'd been turned to stone. Beneath her, Arrow felt the muscles of Baja's legs almost spasm, then harden around her waist. But this wasn't another attack; the woman was staring out at the horizon as the boat suddenly heaved beneath them.

'*Soroinn*,' Captain Baja breathed, unheard by anyone but Arrow, then she roared, 'Veor! Flotnar, maor sailsrinn. VEOR!'

Arrow released her hair, but the Captain was so intent on the horizon she could have hung on, as the woman stood without noticing. Arrow sat and followed the Captain's gaze.

Deo-damnatus.

Scrambling up off the hard planking, Arrow threw herself over to where Livy was trying to stay standing with Tor clutching her on the now treacherous deck.

'Livy! GODSTORM!' she shouted over the growing roar of winds.

The expanse of pale blue and green waves was now so dark as to be almost black, and the surges that rocked them were hitting the side with force, throwing swathes of water up across the deck.

175

Tor ran off after his mother. The crew were all dashing about, hauling or stowing with a frantic energy Arrow hadn't seen before. She recognised the panic, controlled by relentless training and discipline. Their fear was more worrying than the darkening horizon.

By the time they reached the hatch to their cabin, she and Livy were crawling on the deck that would drop away from your feet, then slam back up from another direction.

Everything they passed on the ship proved not just to be neatly placed, but also strapped down with ingenuity. The same could not be said for their meagre belongings. As they opened the door to their cabin, she saw that even their bedroll was tipped to the ground and their plates, cups, and the Empire dresses and petticoats they'd found and been repairing in the evenings, hurled everywhere.

'Climb onto the cot, Livy, and hold onto the slats,' Arrow said while hanging onto the side of a small shelf nailed to the wall.

Arrow managed to pile a few things alongside Livy on the bed, crashing into walls and bed corners with every wild swing of the ship. She wanted to get the bedroll at least partly under Livy, but the girl's fingers wrapped around the slats of their pallet were all that was keeping her small body from slamming around the room as Arrow was.

'Miss! Be careful.'

Tor entered as Arrow fell back for the third time away from the pallet and hit the wall.

'Put it on her, not under,' Tor shouted over the loud creaking of strained wood. Together they lifted the thin bedroll onto Livy, and Tor showed Arrow the fabric ties in each corner to hold it down. Livy looked a little squashed, but she was no longer hanging onto the bed for dear life.

'Can you breathe?' Arrow shouted to Livy over the sound of tortured wood, and the girl nodded with a grimace. She'd be able to wriggle out, but for now the thin bedroll gave her some protection.

'Mother said I must stay below, to look after you!' Tor shouted.

Arrow nodded, although she suspected the boy's instructions were as much for his own safety as theirs.

Tor showed Arrow how to wedge herself in a similar position to him, between the pallet and the wall, and Livy was able to reach out her hand from the bedroll to squeeze hers. Arrow wasn't sure which of them was most reassured by that. The rolling and screeching of the wood got worse, and there was nothing else to do but feel the wild riding of the waves as each tip and then drop pulled at her stomach.

Barro, hidden away in the hold, would have no idea a Godstorm was attacking them.

'Tor. The brig, is it safe?' she yelled. The boy nodded while bracing his body against another slamming roil.

Then a noise louder than Arrow thought possible overrode even the storm. A deep boom that dazzled her senses, reminiscent of the feeling when the lightning hit her back at the Green Man pub.

Tor screamed, 'Thorl has struck us!' The boy lurched up and flung himself across the room. 'Mother!'

'Tor, stay. Come back!' Arrow called after him, but the boy managed to wrench open the door, and he careened out.

She looked towards Livy. The girl was wide-eyed but secure under the lashed-down bedroll. 'Get Tor. Please, Miss!'

'Stay put, Livy, I'll come right back,' she shouted. Livy nodded, and Arrow made her uneven way across the room slower but steadier than the panicked Tor. She hated to leave Livy, but the boy was wild with fear for his mother, and she knew he had been sent to them for his own protection. Arrow hoped she'd find him at the top of the stairs and could drag him back down to the relative safety of their cabin.

The ship rolled in three different directions at once, and she fell backwards twice before grabbing the edge of the steps. Crawling up them on hands and knees, she braced herself as her shoulders and hips slammed into the sides with each giant swell of the waves.

'Tor!' Arrow shouted out into the raging wet darkness at the top step.

A flash of light near-blinded her, and a deep shiver of recognition ran through every sinew. Any doubts about Barro's tale of the fight in the Green Man disappeared. Her body knew that the lightning flashing out of the sky was the same that had hit her deep under the pub back in Londinium. Arrow didn't even try to fathom how that was possible as briny water slapped into her face. It took every ounce of courage not to duck back down into the safer confines of below decks.

Despite the waves hitting over the sides, howling winds and flashes of torture from the sky – she had to find the boy.

Taking the last step up onto the deck, Arrow held herself upright with arms and legs wedged into the wet lintels. This time, when the flash of lightning came, she didn't shy away but used it to scan the deck nearest to her. It wasn't long enough for real sight, but an after-image told her something on one side of the ship felt wrong. Working more on instinct than sight, she stumbled forward, grabbing at ropes and lashed barrels on her way. She looked for crewmen, but the deck was deserted.

Arrow reached the spot her mind's eye had pointed to, by slipping down the deck as it rolled and then hanging onto the ropes at the edge when the wide wooden planks tipped the other way. Her wet hair lashed across her face.

Holding onto the drenched lacing of rope by the sides of the ship with her left hand, she crept her right hand over the edge into the watery darkness, relying on touch where every other sense was overwhelmed.

All that met her fingers was cold wet rope and the outside of the wooden hull, and she started to doubt her gut feeling.

Just as she was about to pull her hand back in, clammy fingers grabbed back at hers. Arrow hung onto them and hauled herself up against the side. To keep balanced, she twisted her left wrist further into the netting close to where she was holding on.

Leaning over as far as she dared, in the next flash Arrow saw the eyes of the young boy, wild and almost senseless, hanging on the outside of the hull.

One of Tor's hands clung onto a single loose rope, and the other hung onto her right hand.

'I have you, I have you. Hold on!' she shouted down to him, not sure if he could hear her through the waves slamming into his body and the force of terror gripping him.

Arrow tried calling, 'Help us! Help!' but the wind ripped the sound from her. Even with the boy's other hand on a rope, she wasn't sure she could drag him on board alone.

Despite his young age, Tor was a large boy. He must weigh near the same as her, with no footing below him. Shouting for help again, it became a near scream as the weight on her arm doubled. Pulled against the side of the boat, her breath knocked out of her, she started to slip over it and down into the darkness. She was only stopped by her left wrist catching hard into the sharp wet twists of the netting.

After a moment trying to gulp air, Arrow managed to look down. The other rope had fallen or been ripped out of Tor's grasp. He now hung on her right wrist with both his hands, being pulled away from the hull when the boat tipped one way and smashed back into it with waves crashing across him when it turned the other. Each time he fell inwards, her arms jerked further apart. Her left wrist caught in the wet netted ropes on deck was all that was holding them both from going into the dark sucking brine.

Arrow managed to call, 'Hold on,' in the loudest voice she could muster, but then a large wave pulled Tor back away from the ship again and she felt the tendons and ligaments of her arm stretch beyond their capacity.

The joint of her right shoulder left its socket.

Clenching teeth against the searing pain of bone slipping against bone, she willed herself to stay conscious.

The memory of dangling from Barro's arm back in Londinium

thrust into her mind and she whispered to herself, 'It's just a rope,' as the ship tipped back.

The drags on a dislocated shoulder tried to loosen her mind.

The boat tipped out again, stretching her, with Tor's hands slipping from her wrist below, now wrapped only in her wet and frozen fingers.

'Just a rope,' Arrow whispered to herself as her knees collapsed and she lolled, a soaked figure crucified between the wrist wrapped in netting and the arm stretched over the side. There was no before or after, only a line of pain from wrist to shoulder, across her chest and to the other wrist. If the boy let go, she wouldn't be able to save him.

Again and again the boy was slammed against the hull, each time dragging her dislocated arm. Arrow didn't know if she screamed.

'Rope,' she whispered, half-senseless, to a shadow that reared up before her.

Then her back felt like it rested against a warm wall, and she could hear shouts from far off. The weight on her left arm lifted and the tight ties of netting slipped off her wrists, releasing the warmth of blood where the friction had serrated her skin.

'I have you,' a voice spoke into her ear. 'You saved him, Empire woman, but I still must save my ship.' The voice went on, 'I will do what I can for your arm.'

With that, fingers moved up to her shoulder, and then palms rested either side of her chest. 'Forgive me,' the voice said as strong hands pressed together and turned with a force only a lifelong sailor could harness.

Arrow screamed as her bone slipped back into its socket.

This time, even the gods would've heard it.

CHAPTER XIV

'Cook made this for you. With the little honey left.' Tor slid the plate over.

A small pastry balanced upon it, folded over into an intricate circle, the smell of cinnamon floating up.

'It looks delicious, Tor, please thank Cook for me.' Arrow smiled. 'But tell him that if he keeps feeding me like this, you'll have to take me out of the porthole when we hit land because I won't fit through the door. Let's share it.'

Livy carefully cut the bun into three pieces and Arrow was solemnly handed the largest one. Livy hadn't been happy to find her governess injured again and there had been a few tears. Earlier she'd tried to push Tor back out of the room so Arrow could rest. But the boy had just stood mute at the doorway and Livy had relented.

Now the children wolfed their sections down and started bickering about who was going to lick the last of the honey off the plate.

Arrow had been pleased to see Tor. The boy was bruised from head to toe and with a nasty cut above one eyebrow, but he was alive. She was slightly less comfortable that he now worshipped the woman who saved him, whether she be a god or not.

All that day, other exhausted-looking crew members kept gently knocking and slipping their heads around the cabin door to thank her, bow or even leave her little presents, despite Livy's jealous nursemaiding. Arrow had received small carvings of wood and a wrinkled but sweet apple carefully preserved for a long voyage. She even accepted an embroidered cloth patch of such stunning detail and beauty she couldn't quite believe it came from the rough and calloused hands of the large silent sailor who handed it over.

Her most welcome visitor was the small rodent-like Cook, with broken teeth in his broad smile. The plates of stew and sea-bread they had been eating were replaced today with delicately filleted and steamed fish, fresh-baked small rolls and a very ripe cheese. Cook displayed unexpected skills, and she wondered if they were usually reserved for the Captain, and if she therefore did have a few feminine tastes.

Neither Llund nor the Captain came. Arrow guessed the ship had taken a beating in the Godstorm and Captain Baja was trying to patch it up. Tor said parts had flooded in the storm and most of the crew had been below decks shoring up when he'd gone over the side.

Right now, Arrow felt the crew would forgive her almost anything for saving the boy.

'Tor, have you seen my friend, Barro?'

'I don't think I'm allowed to, Lady Inguz.' The boy didn't look up, scuffing his shoe against the floor.

'Well, I think I am. Could you help us?' Arrow stood, testing her balance with her incapacitated arm tied across her chest.

Livy grabbed Tor's hand and smiled like a daybreak. 'Oh yes! Tor, pleeeease. You can have the last of the honey!'

The boy didn't speak; her he looked between his friend and the woman who saved his life, then stood up, nodding. Cradling her healing arm, Arrow followed him out of the cabin.

Arrow was glad of Tor's help navigating below decks and getting down the steep ladder to the hold. Her arm didn't enjoy the jolts of the swaying ship, but she hid her grimaces from both the children when they accidently bumped into her.

They found Barro lounging on the pallet bed in the brig, reading from a book in one hand, with the other under his head. When he spotted them, he jumped up and pushed a bucket behind the bed with his foot.

Barro looked a little hollow-eyed, but his grin was its familiar span when Livy ran up to take his hand through the rusty metal bars. Tor hovered at the bottom of the ladder.

'Looks like you survived the storm in one piece,' Arrow said.

Barro's smile tightened but still held. 'Better than you.' He nodded at her arm. 'Don't worry about me, dear ladies. It's easier down here than it was scrubbing pans and chopping potatoes. It's quiet, and I even got my hands on a few books. Almost like a holiday.'

Arrow glanced at the book on the bed. It was an Empire tome she was intimately familiar with: *On The Nature Of Effula* by Dia Agrippina Severina. She'd written up hundreds of pages of notes for the Dia as she was compiling it. Arrow suddenly wanted to calculate the effula levels in the hold, worried that Barro's breathing might build up in the confined space.

Then she remembered he was in more danger from her than a creeping gas.

'You're a stupid, crazy, loose cannon of a mess, Barro. But I promise, I'll beg Captain Baja to release you, if I can find her.'

Barro raised an eyebrow and half a smile at her. 'I already have! Where do you think I got the books from? She came down here first thing this morning. I was hardly decent, but she strode up to the bars asking about you and Livy. I think she's trying to find out what she's got herself, and her crew, into.' Barro leaned to whisper, 'I've even found out a few things myself. You're not going to believe this, but we're heading to the Amazonial shore. Apparently, we'll make Rioh Port in a few days. Gods know how we've crossed the Atlas sea so fast.'

Arrow frowned; she'd expected to have much longer to work on the Captain or get her hands around Llund's throat. Heading to the Amazonial sounded like a fairy tale.

'That's barely part of the Empire,' she said.

'Out in the forests, it's not part of the Empire at all. But all the ports are held by the Legions.' Barro reached out through the bars to grasp her shoulder. 'We'll find a way, Arrow, I promise.'

Arrow racked her brain for what she knew of the Amazonial nation. A land of rivers and forests all under a humid sun. Only part of the Empire for a generation and, if the Londinium news-papers had it right, the Amazonial people hadn't fully accepted their luck in being annexed. A wildness still ruled there. But, if Rioh Port was held by the Legions, could Barro and she fight their way free and reach them?

The magic of Consul Derain's name would then find them a ship home. Arrow would be tried as a bonds-breaker and strung up, but she'd try to save Barro if anyone would listen. Livy would be safe and on her way to the Academy and a life of freedom.

Arrow's shoulder started to throb. She had to think fast. 'Livy, we need to plan how to get out of this. Before we reach port.'

'Because you want to take me home?' The girl's brows were wrin-kled with a worried look Arrow didn't remember her ever having back in Londinium.

'Yes, dearest, back to Consul Derain.' Arrow wanted to hug her, but that would soon no longer be allowed. 'As a Citizen you're going to have the best, safest, life in the world. Don't you want that?'

'Only if you come too. I don't want to go to the Academy on my own.'

'Livy, I'm just a governess. I will be sent on to my next job.' Arrow used her clipped governess voice. Barro turned away and sat on his pallet, and she was pleased she couldn't see his face as she lied.

'What? You'll go and look after other children, and leave me alone?'

'Livy, I couldn't have stayed with you forever anyway. I was preparing you for a life that I was never going to be part of.'

'But, what if I want to stay with you?'

'Livia, I'm a governess, not your mother.' The words were horrible to say, horrible to watch Livy's face as she said them.

'I know that,' Livy said with a voice older than her years.

Arrow reached out for her hand, but Livy pulled herself away and ran off up the ladder out of the brig, Tor fast on her heels. Arrow watched her leave, then slumped against the bars of Barro's cage and he sat down beside her, their shoulders almost touching between the bars.

If her arm wasn't throbbing with pain, Arrow wondered, could she have handled that better? Maybe.

'Kids, eh,' Barro said.

'*Gods.* What am I supposed to do?'

'Staying indoors during Godstorms would be a start.' He nodded at her shoulder, cradled in the crook of her other arm. 'First losing Livy in one and now an injury like that. So far, the Godstorms have won every bout you've fought against them.'

'Well, the priests back in Londinium blame them on our lack of piety.' Arrow snorted, then winced.

Barro inched a little closer, his arm now pressed against hers, warming the cold metal bar between them. How could just one strip of skin touching another be so comforting and unsettling at once?

'Honestly, Arrow, I don't think that girl wants to go to the Academy, or to Derain,' he said. 'Even if you can get her back there.'

'That's because there's so much that she doesn't understand, about the world and what all this means.'

He sniffed. 'I blame her governess.'

'Thanks a lot, Barro. When we reach Rioh Port, there won't be any time for discussion. It might take both of us to hold off Llund and the crew, to give her a chance to find a Legionary and tell them she's Derain's ward. We might not make it, but she will. That's if . . . if you'll stand with me.'

Barro leaned his head back against the bars, face close to her own, but staring up beyond the beams of the hold.

'I'll stand with you, Arrow.' Her shoulder relaxed a little with relief. 'But Livy's not going to be easy to convince. You've raised a girl who thinks for herself.'

Confirming that Barro had her back was Arrow's only plan. If Livy ended up hating her, so be it. The girl would be back in Londinium, safe.

Even if Arrow got herself and Barro killed in the process.

She remembered giving Barro his name. The Arena bosses just numbered them in their first few days as novicii gladiators, like they numbered the swords and shields. He'd been IV and she was V. They were strictly warned against sharing anything from their previous lives. So, the children invented names for each other, and if they lived long enough even the bosses eventually used them as battle-names.

The other trainees named her Arrow after their training Lanista threw her out of target practice. That same night the tall, blond boy had snuck into the novicii's cramped barracks, pushing a barrow of food scraps he'd pilfered from the Arena kitchens. As he'd started trying to negotiate with the other hungry but penniless children, Arrow had blurted out, 'No sale, barrow boy!'

The name Barro stuck, although he never seemed to hold it against her.

'I don't know why you're still helping me, after everything I've done,' Arrow said all these years later, a locked cage between them.

'What? Leaving me heartbroken in the Arena, without a word of explanation, when we'd planned a life together? Or disappearing for years, then turning up and getting me kidnapped and transported across an ocean? Or making me a bonds-breaker and condemning me to death?'

Even with the smuggled spices, oiled wood and tang of the sea, she recognised his scent. Perhaps, after her fleeting time of lying in his arms at night, and wrestling against them in the Arena by day, she'd never forget.

'Yep. All that.'

Her fingertips touched his, their hands slipping between the bars. Could you forgive someone with touch rather than words? If she'd been in the brig with him, she might have tried to wrap more than fingers.

'The girl doesn't know, does she? About you being indentured and what that means if you're captured.' Barro's voice was as gentle as his fingers stroking her palm. 'If you take her back without her knowing, and give yourself over for execution, she'll never forgive you.'

'What does that matter?' Arrow said, but in that moment it mattered more than anything. 'As long as she goes back.'

Barro turned towards her, and she could feel the heat from his cheek so close to hers. His eyes weren't the bright blue of their youth when he was always high-hearted and optimistic. Now they were an ice blue, with something trapped behind them, frozen. Arrow felt a shiver wondering what Barro had to work so hard to keep hidden.

But still she held his hand.

'There's something you could try with Livy, that you never gave to me,' Barro said.

'What's that?' she asked, more from bravado than any desire to hear the answer.

He dropped her hand and closed his eyes. 'The truth.'

There was nothing she could say to that.

Arrow hauled herself up the bars with her good arm. Then navigated the ladder without a backward glance.

Time discovers truth, but she'd had so little of either.

Tor and Livy must be up on deck somewhere, swinging, jumping and death-defying on the ropes and jibs of the *Flyer*. Arrow made her way to the cabin with a few agonising bumps against bulkheads and then crawled onto the pallet bed. Should she have told Barro the truth back then, when she left the Arena . . . or perhaps even now? She cradled her belly with her good arm, the memory of that old ripping pain never far enough from the surface. There were no words to explain to a man what had happened, the horror he'd perpetrated, all unknowing. No. While the cause remained hidden, the result was obvious. She didn't hate Barro nearly enough to tell him the truth.

Arrow expected that her stinging shoulder, combined with the thoughts pounding the inside of her skull, would deny sleep. But her eyes closed moments after her head hit the mattress. There were no dreams.

Waking with a start, she winced at the pain in her arm at the movement. Then she caught her breath, aware that someone else was in the small cabin, as motionless as she was. With her eyes closed, other senses felt sharper, and she could smell the sweet tang of cinnamon in the air, and the distant cawing of the goslings, who had survived the Godstorm without injury. Letting her heart rate slow, she relaxed. Arrow knew every soul on this ship by now, and, if they wished her harm, she'd been in more vulnerable moments than this.

It was strange though, that someone would feel they could wait here, in her cabin, as she slept. With a growing sense of affront on her privacy, Arrow let herself move, pushing out her legs and even faking a small yawn.

'Did I wake you?' a soft voice asked her.

'Captain?' Arrow slipped down from the bunk, tugging her shirt into a more respectable place with a little difficulty. 'Is the ship repaired?'

'Well enough to make port. Only a few days now, anyways.'

They stood in silence with the gentle rocking of the waves. The ravages of the storm were etched onto the Captain's face. The woman looked like she'd come from an Arena battle, one that hadn't gone well.

Captain Baja's voice was still soft as she asked, 'You saved my son. Why?'

'Because he's a child.' Arrow tried to shrug, and winced. 'Anyone would do the same.'

'Anyone? I let a sobbing girl be smuggled aboard my ship. I carry that same child, and you, against your wishes to a distant shore, without knowing what fate Llund plans for you. Without Tor . . . ' Baja stopped and her voice cracked. 'I owe you my life for saving him, my heart. For more too. On this sailing, my boy has been happy for the first time since his father passed. You and the girl brought him back to himself in a way I could not. You should have had my gratitude for that, even before you saved him.'

Arrow nodded. 'Tor is a brave boy, smart and kind. I tell you truly, Captain, Livy herself has never had any friend but me. These past weeks have given me nothing but fear and worry, but they have been freedom and joy for that little girl.'

'But you want to take her back to Derain? He is not a man built to love. We Frisians have felt the end of his spear, and blood runs from it.'

'What choice do I have?' Arrow said. 'I have no claim to her.' Now it was her turn for her voice to break. 'Derain can give her the life she deserves.'

Baja hesitated a moment before asking, 'Is that what you want?'

'What else is there?' Arrow's shoulder stung and it make her eyes prick. 'I am nothing in the Imperium. All I can do for her – is give her back.'

Why was everyone questioning the only logical decision?

'I think that girl wants you, more than any life Derain could offer her.'

'Then I have raised a fool. I told you, I have nothing. No wealth, no home, I don't even have my own name. I'm nothing, no one. You all call me Inguz, or Yngvi, or even Arrow. It's all *bloody* lies.' Tears started when she expected her fists to fly instead.

The Captain moved closer to her as she stood there, weeping like a maiden.

Baja wrapped her arms around her, one hand on her back, the other in her hair, fingers brushing against her skin. The pirate woman smelt of the sea, of salt and power and sunlight on waves. You could breathe it in until tears would be lost in deep waters.

Baja's voice sounded far off, even though they were close. 'Of all the crimes your Empire has committed, and there are many, the trade in people is foulest. Of all the lies it's told, telling a person they are nothing is the worst.'

Their chests rose and fell in time as if locked in combat. Arrow didn't try to defend her neck, left exposed to the touch of breath from Baja. If she trembled, it wasn't because of fear poisons flooding her blood. This was a different type of shaken.

In the Academy, the handsome Citizen boys were more interested in love affairs with other boys than with the girls their parents plotted for them to marry. The girls traded kisses between each other for honey cakes and gossip. In the Imperium Romanum, love affairs were often safer within sexes, as marriages between sexes were for property not poetry. The newspapers had touted that Frisians believed that love must only be performed between a man and woman as further proof of their uncivilised barbarity.

Arrow wondered if the reporters might be wrong.

Pulling back a little, Baja's hand stroked her cheek.

'What do you want, woman of Inguz?'

There was nothing but the sound of waves and rocking of the ship as it sliced through the water.

'I . . . I want Livy to know everything,' Arrow said and found she could finally look up, 'to understand.'

Baja stood, and Arrow admitted to herself her first estimation of the woman had been wrong. The Captain was neither striking nor hard. She was a young widow fighting to save her son's inheritance in a man's world. The woman was beautiful.

'I want her to know the truth,' Arrow said.

'That, perhaps, I can give you,' Baja turned. 'I will fetch Livy, Llund and even the sunshine boy. Then, above wave and under sun, we will decide our own fates.'

The woman smiled at her and strode out, mistress of every plank, rope and sail.

Hugging her arms around herself where Baja's had just been, Arrow stood alone in the cabin. When she was Livy's age, she was fighting for her life, and her freedom, on the Arena sand. Arrow had desperately wanted to shield the girl from even a part of the pain and fear she went through herself. To let Livy build an inner strength of safety, knowledge and hopefulness rather than an outer shell of scars, cunning and sacrifice.

It is easier to find men who will volunteer to die than to find those who are willing to endure pain with patience.

Arrow steadied herself against the bed, holding on harder than she needed to, as if she was trying to steady the whole vessel, then she managed to follow the Captain.

As Baja had promised, the sun was shining up on deck, with the wave tips catching the light. This was the same sky as Londinium, Arrow knew enough heavenly astronomy for that. But the gods had painted in richer colours out at sea. She was comfortable in Tor's rough shirt and trousers, her hair tied back with a piece of twine. Barefoot on the smooth wood below her, which thrummed with the working of the ship.

How soon a place could come to feel like home.

As Barro emerged from a hatch across the deck, he stretched and turned his face up to the sun, eyes closed so even she heard the grunt when Livy jumped down from the rigging onto him. Barro threw the girl back up and, with a laugh, she landed near her former governess.

'I'm sorry, Miss, I shouldn't have run away.' The girl's contrite face was a perfect mirror of so many times when she'd spilled the ink pot or tipped an oil lamp back in their Londinium garret.

'No, Livy. I'm the one who should apologise to you.' She felt Barro move closer and others come up on deck, but she didn't look away from Livy. 'There are some things you should know.' *First things first.* 'When we get back to Londinium, dearest, I won't be able to look after you anymore.'

'I know, you said.' Livy's frown pressed down on her again.

'But I didn't tell you the whole truth. Even if I wanted to, I couldn't stay with you. Because I'm a slave, Livy, I'm one of the indentured.' Livy just cocked her head as she did during difficult lessons, and didn't jump backwards or sneer as somewhere deep down Arrow had feared she might, 'All I want now . . . I very much want for you to be safe, and go to the Academy.'

Livy's face was more serious than any child's should be. 'Miss, what will happen to you if we go back?'

Arrow's smile was frozen, struggling to hold onto her mouth. *Maybe there is too much truth.*

'She'll hang.' Barro said. *Damn him.*

'What?' Livy's panicked eyes flitted between them, 'You haven't done anything wrong!'

'Yes, I have, Livy. Derain told me to stop looking for you, but I didn't. I disobeyed him. But Livy, this is very important. I still want us to go back.'

'But he'll kill you!'

'Perhaps,' Arrow kept her tone imbued with the authority of a teacher, 'but this is how important being a Citizen is, Livy. I would die for you to have that chance. This isn't about an exciting adventure; this is a future I would happily give my life for you to have. Do you understand, do you see, how much I want this for you?'

Livy was shaking her head as if it would remove what she'd just learnt.

'Livy, we must go home. To Consul Derain and your place in the Academy,' Arrow repeated.

'No!' Llund was standing beside Captain Baja, but he looked like her prisoner rather than the reason they were on the voyage at all. 'Livia must reach her destined shore!'

'Destined, you say?' Arrow held her voice steady. 'You took more than a hand in forcing this fate.'

'It matters not,' his amulets rattled with every head shake, 'Livia must be delivered to Rioh!'

Captain Baja stepped between her and the Druid.

'Llund, my people vowed to serve your quests in return for a great gift given by yours. In defiance of that, I tell you now, I would rather lose my own honour, my ship and shore rather than transport these people like cattle any longer, against their will,' she said.

'You will break troth with your people's promise?' Llund spat out.

'My vow is already broken. None of these folk will be forced from this ship when we make port. I will return them to Londinium or elsewhere, as is their wish. The Inguz will decide.'

Llund's head jerked up, and he turned to her.

'Well, woman chosen of Inguz. Will you take Livia, ward of Consul Derain, and go back to Londinium,' Llund's voice grew to a shout, 'denying her forever the right to know her true family?'

'What family? You stole this child, Llund.' Arrow wanted to pummel the truth out of him.

'I didn't take her.' The man's face was as inscrutable as the carving back in the Green Man pub. 'I am returning her.'

'What?' Arrow and Livy said at the same moment.

Arrow tried to concentrate on Llund rather than Livy's gasp. 'You're returning her?'

'Yes, this ship takes the girl towards her true family.' Llund finally looked at Livy. 'Livia is the daughter of the Amazonial River Queen. She was stolen by the Empire as a baby.'

Each of Llund's words hit Arrow harder than any fist in the Arena. Baja stared wide-eyed at Livy as if seeing the girl for the first time. Barro just shook his head, in denial or disbelief, either would match Arrow's own feelings.

'Miss, is it true? Is my mother an Amazionial?' Livy looked older somehow.

'She was the River Queen herself.' Llund's voice softened a little. 'She died in child-bed with you. The Amazonials have great power and wisdom, but the Empire has medicine even they do not. Your mother knew she was gravely ill when her birth pangs lasted too long, so she sought medicine from an Empire encampment. But it was already too late. The Empire doctors told the river clan that their Queen and infant had both died.'

'The doctors pretended I was dead, but my mother really was?' Livy asked.

The girl had gained and lost a mother in a moment. Her eyes didn't stray from Llund's face, but her fingers floated out from her side. It took a moment for Arrow to realise Livy sought the comfort of her governess, rather than a weapon.

She took Livy's small palm in both of hers.

Llund answered the child. 'Yes, your mother died. But even then, the Amazonials suspected something was amiss. Garrison slaves told of a newborn babe spirited away on the same night the Queen perished. The clan's wise woman tugged at that thin thread of gossip and discovered the baby had been seen in the port city, Rioh. A man, one whose own newborn had succumbed to fever, hired his wife to a group of Empire men as wet nurse, and they left on a ship bound for Britannia.'

'Who took Livy?' Arrow asked, although the knot of pain in her stomach told her she already knew. She heard Barro mutter, '*Damnatus*,' behind her.

Llund swept his arms open. 'None of the Amazonial people could get aboard the ship. But we are one family with them, and their messages reached across the water, smuggled in with amulets and other goods.' Llund shot a glance at the Captain. 'We Anglish followed the trail for the Amazonials. It took time, and many bribes, but we discovered that a powerful man had been at the port in Rioh. He ordered the child to be stolen and then took her across the sea with him, away from her family and home. We have been searching for her ever since.'

Arrow made herself ask again, 'Who took her, Llund? Tell us his name.' *Damn all gods and their games.*

Llund stood a little taller, gathering his threadbare robe around him.

'His name is Consul Derain.'

'My guardian. He stole me?' Livy finally turned towards Arrow. 'Then he gave me to you?'

'Livy, I didn't know. I promise you, I didn't know.'

The girl started to cry, not like a child weeps, but like an adult who isn't even aware tears are running down their face. Arrow knelt before her, holding the child's hand as if she were a supplicant. There was already Derain, the Academy summons and a noose for Arrow waiting to separate them. Why did discovering that Livy had her own true family somewhere make Arrow feel more sundered from her than by execution?

One thing was clear, she no longer had any right to make choices for the girl. She hadn't even known who Livy was.

No one moved. Even the goslings fell silent.

'Well now,' Barro looked around at everyone, 'as everyone knows, I'm not much more than luggage on this trip. But seems to me it's time to decide the turn of our sails. If Lady Baja here will take us wherever we want, what's it to be?'

Llund looked between them. 'We must take Livia to her people! The river queens don't come into Rioh Port. Charnot convoys leave for the oil stations deep in the forest, and we will buy passage on one of those. We must go to the Amazonial and take the child home!' he cried.

'If that's what is chosen.' The Captain spoke to Llund but she looked at Arrow. 'The river queens might be Livy's people, but it's a long way to their forests, and the girl has never known any of them.

They don't come to the port, you say? Well, that's because they are at war with the Empire, in all but name. Arrow, you would be taking the girl into a battle, without clear friends on either side. When I said I would take you anywhere, that includes back to Frisian shores with us. You have friends on this ship.'

Arrow looked at Livy.

The girl wouldn't meet her eye, but kept hard hold of her hand. Arrow wanted to scoop her up and tell her it was all going to be safe, and easy. But that would be another lie. And her entire life with Livy had been a falsehood.

Gods, she'd been part of Livy's kidnapping. She'd raised the girl in near isolation when Livy was supposed to have grown up surrounded by her family. Arrow was nothing more than a slave with less claim to decide for her than Llund had to take her in the first place.

The girl had a life waiting, somewhere over this ocean.

'What do *you* want to do, Livy?' Arrow asked, even though other words fought to be said.

Livy looked up at her, tears drying on her face. And Arrow saw something new on the face she knew better than any other. The girl's childhood lay behind her, now as much a fantasy as the fairy tales she had loved so much. There wasn't yet hardness there, but less softness than there had been.

Arrow hadn't expected to grieve watching a little girl grow up.

'Mr Llund, did those river people really ask you to bring me back to them?'

'Yes, Livia,' the Druid answered, 'they have been looking for you for a long time, you are of their blood. They have never forgotten you.'

The girl chewed her lip, looking between Barro, the Captain and Llund. But her hand never left those of the governess who raised her. Finally, she asked slowly, as if carefully writing out neat words on a scroll, 'Miss, will you take me to the forest?'

Barro huffed, Llund exalted, the Captain's lips thinned to a line, but Arrow just nodded.

Preparations for landing busied the crew.

Barro wasn't in the brig when Arrow made it down the next day. She assumed the Captain had released him to the kitchens again. Arrow hoped they'd have a few moments to say goodbye before she and Livy left the *Flyer*.

Captain Baja would take him back to Londinium, or maybe he would join her crew. Arrow thought he'd make a good pirate.

The ship was frenetically busy preparing to port and an injured and inexperienced Arrow was politely asked to stay out of the way by the other sailors. So while Livy and Tor gossiped, heads together, in the rigging, Arrow stayed in their cabin using her left hand to messily finish repairs to the petticoats and blouses they expected to wear in an Empire city, however distant from Londinium.

Her needle stabbed her finger when Captain Baja burst in.

'Arrow, you run from danger into danger.'

The woman spoke as if they were part way through an ongoing argument. Perhaps, in Baja's head, that was exactly where they were.

Holding the smear of blood away from her already much-abused petticoats, Arrow stood.

'Derain stole Livy's life, her family,' she answered the Captain, now pacing within the tiny chamber. 'Perhaps the Amazonials will welcome her. She's their Queen's daughter.'

'Will they welcome you too? An Empire woman, who worked for the Consul? I don't trust Llund not to tell them that you want to take Livy back to him.'

'Well, that's a risk I'll have to take, for Livy.' Arrow wanted to reach out, but didn't know how. 'You have been so kind, Baja, but I can't deny Livy this. I gave her the choice, and she wants a family.' Somehow, those words hurt more than a dagger slipped into Arrow's guts.

The Captain stopped pacing. She'd twisted her leather necklets so hard they'd left thin red lines on the cream of her skin.

'What if it's not her only chance to have one?' Baja asked.

'There isn't anything else. She won't go back to Derain.'

'I don't mean that. I mean the family Livy could have here. Tor already loves her like a sister.'

'You mean stay here on the ship. Working for you?'

Baja sighed. 'For a god, Arrow, you can be very stupid.' She raised a half-smile Arrow hadn't seen before. 'I mean you and Livy stay here with Tor and me, as our family.'

Then Baja kissed her.

Her mouth was warm, lips gentle against her own. The leather of Baja's jerkin pushed against her, and the other woman's long curls brushed at the nape of her own neck. Arrow's skin tightened, and she softened into Baja, the contours of their bodies sliding into each other.

Baja's eyes were dark like a Godstorm at sea as she released lips but kept arms encircled. 'I want you, Arrow. You are fierce, brave and beautiful, and I would lead this ship with you and raise our children to be as you are.'

Arrow pulled away, shivering as if she were already living on the frozen Svalber tundra.

'I . . . I can't.' The words hurt her lips as she said them. 'I love Tor, and I would be proud to call him son,' her voice cracked on that last word, 'but I can't choose for Livy. Please, Baja, please don't make this harder. I must keep my promise.'

Every one of Arrow's sinews ached to step back to Baja's arms, like she was a fish hooked through the heart, and Baja reeling her in.

'Even if you both perish in the keeping? Or the Amazonials take her but turn you away, or kill you?'

'If I must. They are Livy's true family.'

Laying her hand over Baja's heart, skin soft and warm under her palm, Arrow tried, 'Please. I'm sorry.'

The Captain stood with head bowed and then stepped away.

She turned back to Arrow at the door. 'Word will pass through the fleet. Help will be granted by any Frisian you ask.' A tiny bite edged her voice. 'Ask in the name of Tor, the Frisian boy you saved.'

The cabin door closed quietly as the Captain left, but to Arrow it felt like another life closed with it.

The Kalends of Quintilis, Amazonial Forest

MDCLVII, Aurelian Calendar

CHAPTER XV

The female cabin was a box of wet air.

Moving slowly in the heat, Arrow fingered the treasures in her sash. Knife (demanded back from Llund), handkerchief and stone. Of the three, she feared the knife might be the most useful where they were heading.

Arrow raised her voice against the constant drone of the engines that thrummed through the metal. 'Which Emperor directed the alchemists in Rome to ignite Gaea's blood?'

Livy lolled against the cabin window, as the unending parade of green forest passed outside. They had spotted what looked like a small monkey in the giant trees a few days ago, for only a moment, and Livy had eagerly scanned for another for hours afterwards. Now, Arrow wasn't sure what the girl was watching for.

'Livy dearest, I asked you a question. We're travelling in a charnot convoy burning Gaea's blood to travel through the Amazonial forest. Do you realise how amazing that power is? That thick black oil can fuel a giant vehicle like this. Now, do you remember who discovered it?'

Livy didn't turn from the window, and muttered, 'Doesn't matter.'

'Of course it matters.' Arrow forced enthusiasm into her voice. 'Oil is the heart of the Empire. Without it, there would be no charos or charnot convoys like this one, not even chain-trains. We couldn't make lamps or win wars.'

Livy hunched a little lower in her hard seat.

'You mean win wars against people like my mother?'

If patience truly is the remedy to every misfortune, then Arrow wished the gods would grant her more of it.

Each day their convoy of gargantuan supply-charnots churned along the rutted muddy road sliced deep into the Amazonial forest. Their cabin perched atop the final monster in the group, like the humans were a forgotten addendum to the more important cargo of oil-extraction equipment and supplies the convoy carried.

And each day, Livy swung from giddy and thrumming with nerves about meeting her family, to limp and tetchy with boredom. Both should be manageable by an experienced teacher, but Arrow was struggling. Livy was right to feel betrayed, by both fate and her former governess, and Arrow didn't know how to answer her.

Llund and Barro rode ahead in the men's cabin on the leading charnot, in even dirtier and more cramped confines then this. Arrow wished she had someone other than a furious and frightened child to plot their next move.

Livy turned towards her, cheeks pink and shiny, not just from the heavy heat and humidity. 'I don't need to learn any of this, anymore. I wasn't born in Londinium. I'm not even a Roman.'

'Livy. I know everything's changed, and that's scary. But education is never wasted, even where we're going.'

Livy's hands were curled into fists as tears started to trickle down her reddening cheeks. Her mood flipped like pages of a book.

'But what if they don't want me? I was a baby when I was taken. Now I'm an Imperium person, one of their enemies. What if they *hate* me?'

On the last words, Livy's voice rose higher, and the horribly organic snoring from the opposite corner of the rough cabin juddered to a stop.

Damnatus. They had woken her.

The only other occupant of the women's cabin shuffled thick muscled limbs, raising a head too small for her neck. After they boarded, their travelling companion had grunted out that she worked as a washerwoman in the oil camps for six months, then trucked back to Rioh to 'live free' for a week. Clutching a bottle of dark, foul-smelling spirits to herself day and night, the woman worked to empty it before reaching the oil camps, where alcohol was banned.

She covetously cradled her bottle like a newborn, as if Arrow or Livy plotted to snatch it. At least when she wasn't snoring off its effects.

Awoke, she levered her bulk upwards. 'What'd you say about me?'

'Nothing,' Arrow placated, now used to the paranoia the woman wore like a warm scarf tight around her neck. 'We were thinking how much nicer it would be to sail on the great river we've heard so much about, rather than be stuck on this nasty charnot.'

'Go by river?' The woman snorted a huge laugh even louder than her usual snoring. 'Your Empire don't have enough guns to stop the she-devils' attack on the river. Ghost women don't want oil, though they try to sink Empire fuel boats anyway, to feed crocodiles for fun. But cargo? Food and arc guns, maybe? Axes for chopping trees. Trees are their husbands, they say.' She laughed again. 'On the river, they would kill us all.'

Then the woman frowned, as if surprised at herself for talking to them, dug out her bottle and turned away to start slugging from it again.

Arrow and Livy leaned back into their places, too spent to continue arguing.

'Fuel stop!' came a shout up from below their cabin.

In the sudden silence with their engines off, it took a second for new sounds, of bird calls and even rustles from the sea of trees, to reach them.

The large woman laboured up and threw herself at the cabin door, and started climbing down the gigantic vehicle, huffing and puffing all the way. Well, if the time the washerwoman had taken to get up into the charnot when they embarked at Rioh was anything to go by, they would be stopped here for a little while. Perhaps enough time for Livy to run around and shake off the mood that plagued her.

Arrow followed down the ladder, helping Livy jump to the ground from the bottom rung. She gyrated her shoulder, expecting a twinge of pain, but the heat of the Amazionial seemed to have accelerated her healing. It almost made up for every other discomfort the vicious humidity dished out.

The fuel stop was nothing more than a large area cut out of the forest near the river, with barrels of fuelling oil buried into the soft soil. Grease-stained drivers wound out a long hose, proboscis-like, from the lead charnot to suck from the drums.

The passengers had seen almost nothing of the famed Amazionial waterway itself since they set off. Only occasionally had the road threaded close enough to glimpse wide sand-coloured water between the screens of foliage. Here, though, the clearing ran right down to the edge of the water.

Trees towered up around the convoy, but that made the scale of the three charnots all the more shocking. Each vehicle was near the length of the *Flyer* and painted a vivid but chipped canary yellow, with six sets of wheels each taller than Arrow. Enormous bales and boxes like small houses sat securely tied to the flat cars. The engineering was extraordinary, yet they evidently weren't invulnerable. Each charnot was mounted with arc guns manned by Legionaries and the leading behemoth was topped with a pressurised Vulcan machine – which could belch spouts of fire for several feet. Years ago, a Vulcan had been deployed in the Arena for a battle enactment. After the flaming stands had been doused and spectators carried to infirmaries, it was banned.

Out in the open air, if the humidity could be called open, Livy practised hops and kicks on the bare earth, while Arrow used a little of their precious soap to freshen their linen in a small bucket.

Barro wandered over. Arrow didn't look up.

More than a week ago, back on the *Flyer*, Arrow had prepared a whole speech of thanks for how he had helped her find Livy and had practised until she'd crafted a perfect goodbye.

But he couldn't be found amongst the ranks of *Flyer* crew who came to wave them off as she, Livy and Llund disembarked.

Then she'd spotted him standing down on the dockside with a small pack of supplies lent by, or possibly won off, the crew. After meeting her eye for the briefest moment Barro had stridden off ahead through the bustling pier, and, before Arrow could catch up and ask why he wasn't heading back to Londinium, the new city had engulfed them and she was left just trying to keep pace and tight hold of Livy's hand.

Rioh had left her speechless, anyway. The one thing it had in common with Londinium was crowds. Although, these weren't a single people at all, but rather all sorts of different peoples, and most of them wearing much less than would be acceptable even in a bathing house back at home. The buildings had been made by sticking anything together: planks of wood, sheets of fabric, even the trellis from a thick green plant – all then painted in the brightest colour possible, as long as it was a different colour from the place next door, or even the plank above. Barro waited for them to catch up lest they all lose themselves in the chaos. Then the overawed visitors weaved between the buildings, turning corners only to find a sharp slope ahead of them covered in dense jungle, or a wide plaza filled with merchants loudly hawking wares laid out on multicoloured cloths beside them. The sun beat down and insects chirped in their millions.

As they navigated between novel sights and sounds, Arrow had tried to ask Barro why he was still with them. Had Captain Baja refused to carry him back to Londinium, or was he afraid bondsmen would snatch him if he returned? With his skills in violence and commerce, she wondered if he hoped to make a new life for himself in Rioh.

But he dodged her questions with the same skill he'd dodged her punches back in their Arena days. Once they'd found an inn, and

Llund had purchased their places on the charnot convoy, she hadn't seen Barro at all.

Now, deep in the jungle, he stood beside her, staring out over the wide river with the squawks and rustles from the forest cutting through the heat.

Scrubbing a little harder than necessary, Arrow spilled water over the side of her bucket.

'Aren't you travelling with a washerwoman?' Barro asked. 'You might want to learn a thing or two from her.'

'Don't worry,' she spat back, 'I don't intend to make a life of washing clothes, thank you.'

'If not washing clothes, Arrow, then what, in the name of the gods, do you intend to do?'

Arrow dearly wished people would stop asking her that. She didn't know, or particularly care, what happened to her, if Livy was finally safe and loved.

'I promised to take Livy to her people. That's all the plan I have. She deserves to have a family, Barro, everyone does.'

His feelings were betrayed by a slight flaring of his nostrils, but Barro turned away without answering. Then he wiped away the sweat from his eyes and spun back, colour rising.

'I will never understand you, Arrow. If she wants a family, weren't you offered that on the *Flyer*? A family for Livy and freedom, even a home, for you?'

'What?' Arrow stood, knocking over the bucket to spill on the ground. 'How do you know that?'

'The Captain asked for my permission to offer herself to you. She wanted to check you and I didn't have an arrangement first. Said she would take you and Livy to safety, away in the north, free of the Empire. I told her I was all for it. Just drop me back at home first.'

Arrow stood staring at him, the sodden slip of linen in her hand. 'She asked you – and you told her she should?'

'Of course I bloody did,' Barro snapped and stepped closer. 'All this is madness, running into a war in a jungle – with a kid! Bad things are coming, Arrow. You and Livy could both be safe with Captain Baja by now and I'd be back in Londinium going about my business. I'm in this gods-awful forest because for some insane reason you turned down a sensible offer from a fine woman.'

'You didn't want to come with us?' Arrow regretted it as soon as the words hung in the damp air. It sounded so pathetic, as if she was hurt that Barro had come unwillingly. She dropped her head. Barro would prefer her tucked up with Baja in Svalbar and himself back to smuggling and carousing in Londinium.

Now he turned towards the river, not even looking at her.

Going to grab his arm, she realised that everyone was facing the same way. The guards by the river had raised their arc guns and pointed them out over the water. A soldier on the lead charnot behind them started winching the huge flamethrower around.

Arrow didn't bother trying to see what had caught everyone's attention, instead searching for Livy amongst the gathering crowd. She bent down and, as suspected, spotted the girl right down closest to the water, bouncing on the balls of her feet and pointing. The soldier nearest barked at the girl to move back.

Arrow elbowed past an oil-splattered driver to get to Livy and grasp her shoulder. Once she had hands on the child, she looked around to see what all the fuss was about.

'Look, Miss!' Livy turned to her while pointing out over the water. 'There's a girl in a boat.'

Close to the opposite shore, across the vast expanse of flowing buttery water, was a small boat, or perhaps a canoe. Within it sat a girl, no more than ten years old. Her sleek black hair was held back with three bright yellow and blue feathers, her coppery skin wrapped in a hessian-like dress. The young canoeist was ignoring everyone on the bank, dipping her small paddle into the water.

Arrow understood Livy's excitement. Spotting another child, and one in charge of a canoe, was a welcome novelty in their long, dull journey. But why were the soldiers, and all the other passengers and drivers, so intent on the girl?

'Shoot her!' their washerwoman bellowed. 'She-devil. Shoot her, and let the fish eat her.' Hades, the woman was mad with drink.

Barro must have thought the same. 'It's just a kid in a dinghy. I think we can defend ourselves, don't you?'

'Fool,' the woman spat, 'feathers means river woman. She'll call up ghosts and devils, make the trees come alive. The soldiers know.'

And it seemed the soldiers agreed with her, at least in terms of fearing the little girl in the wooden boat. The legionary closest to Arrow and Livy turned. He was a scruffy mess compared to the soldiers back home; no breastplate or helmet, and his red shirt was filthy with stains. But his arc gun was steady, and he rammed it towards them.

'Get back. Or get burnt,' he grunted.

The soldiers marched away from the water's edge, and Arrow felt a deep thrum from the metal of the lead vehicle as oil pumped up to the Vulcan on its roof. No, *oh gods*, her guts crunched as she swept up a protesting Livy and stumbled back towards the charnot.

Looking over her shoulder, Arrow watched the little canoe turn towards their shore. The girl was holding the paddle over the side as she moved forward against the current of the river. Arrow could now see a broad face with a wide brow, and eyes so dark they looked black from this distance. So similar to Livy, it could be a slightly older version of her. The girl's feathers moved a little in a breeze on the river, which couldn't be felt on the shore. She'd paddled to almost the midpoint in the river, moving towards them.

One solider barked an order to the man on the charnot's roof.

Oh gods, this can't be happening. They wouldn't.

Arrow thrust Livy against the vehicle and then swung back towards the shore, but Barro seized her waist. Struggling against him, all she could do was scream out, 'WARE! FIRE!'

The girl in the canoe stopped paddling and looked up towards the clearing on the beach.

A click went above them.

Arrow spun back and threw herself against Livy, blocking the girl's body from a storm of searing heat over their heads.

The ignited oil shrieked, and the stench of burnt chemicals rained down on them. Another and then another long stream of fire streaked out above them and out over the water. When it stopped, Arrow heard Livy screaming into her shoulder, fingernails tearing at Arrow as the girl shuddered.

Holding Livy, Arrow turned her head. Where the canoe had been was now a long flame dancing on the water. It smouldered out as the last embers slipped under the dark river water.

'They burnt a child,' Barro said.

He'd leaned in between her and the fire as Arrow had crouched over Livy.

'They burnt her,' he said again as if saying it would make sense of it.

All Arrow could do was nod, while Livy sobbed.

She should leap onto the roof of the charnot. Barro would have her back and could probably dispatch the other soldiers while she crushed the neck of the murderer behind the flamethrower. Barro's body was tense, and his breathing steady beside her. They had stood beside each other like this before, waiting in the dark corridors under the Arena, perfectly prepared to do battle with whatever they found above.

They could kill every gods-damned solider and guard here, between the two of them.

Leaving them alone in a vast forest.

Arrow rocked Livy as the child cried herself out. Then she picked up their few items from around the fuelling camp.

Barro ignored the strict prohibition against a man entering the women's dormitory and carried the girl up the steps. Livy, exhausted by tears, fell asleep in their cabin. Llund hadn't witnessed any of it, Barro said, the travel was taking a toll on the old man, so he'd used the other passengers' absence to snatch a nap.

Arrow didn't say much. She appreciated Barro helping her gather their clothes and Livy's water flask, which she'd left by the river.

Despite the heat, she couldn't shake the chill down her spine.

In the Arena, both she and Barro had seen terrible things, had done terrible things. She once sank her sword deep into the guts of a man whom she'd counted a friend because they'd been drawn against each other in a death match celebrating the Ides of Mars.

Barro broke her arm in one fight, and she'd left him with a sword scar on his forehead that his hair only just covered.

But even in the blood and filth of the Arena sand, there were rules. An unmatched duel, between a condemned criminal and a seasoned gladiator, was still a fight, with weapons on both sides. 'We are in a show, dearest,' her mother had explained, 'not a war. In performance, how you fight, the chance of an unexpected win and the thrilling or tragic manner of your death all matter. The crowds are paying to feel something. In a war, all that matters is that you die.'

In the cabin, the women were in the same positions they had all been in before the stop, Livy by the window, the monstrous laundress swigging from her bottle, Arrow trying to move as little as possible in the heat. As if the stop at the fuelling station never happened.

Arrow's jaw churned and the knuckles of her fists were white, placed unmoving on her lap. While she'd seen more violence than most serving soldiers ever faced in their tours of duty, she now knew she wasn't one of them.

She had killed to order in the Arena, taking lives to entertain Citizens. But she would have plunged her knife deep into her own heart before pressing the small button on that flamethrower.

All cruelty springs from weakness.

CHAPTER XVI

The view from the windows was the only thing not bleak.

Once they left the fuelling station, the road kept closer to the river and the life it carried. Huge flocks of wildly plumaged birds would soar to the air as the charnots growled past them. The majority vibrant pink, but others black with red-tipped wings. Arrow and Livy watched them in silence. They turned away from birds with blue and yellow feathers.

Occasionally, during the humid nights, the washerwoman's snores would stutter and stop. Before the refuelling stop, Arrow had crept over to check she hadn't swallowed her tongue or drowned in vomit. Now Arrow turned over on her hard bunk, not caring if the snoring started again or not.

At least Livy and she still had fresh bread with salted cheese to eat, wrapped in huge green leaves and tied with vine. They'd discovered the food leaves in a bazaar back in Rioh, drawn in by a bright red and yellow awning, painted with exotic birds and fruits.

As she and Livy had browsed that treasure trove of a shop, the two former Londinium residents tried not to stare at the Rioh women's bare shoulders and outrageous calf-length skirts. The local women gossiped over bales of embroidered linen and brightly printed cotton. Arrow had wondered why they bothered to buy cloth in the first place if they were going to wear so little of it.

Nevertheless, the quality of the clothes felt acceptable, and the shop's owner had helped them buy travelling clothes less likely to kill them from heat exhaustion than their thick Londinium petticoats.

Livy had loved the whole experience and kept twirling in her new dress. The azure skirt had wafted around her, and she'd gone up on tiptoes in leather sandals, the laces strapped around her legs almost to the knees.

Arrow's new frock wasn't quite as minimal as Livy's but would still have elicited gasps on the streets back home. The new green dress hung like a starved version of her former heavy fabric frock. Made in the same basic outline of respectable Empire attire, with a full-length skirt, bodice and small jacket, it was missing several layers. The dress had no petticoats, the skirt held in place just by thin strips of a light metal stitched into the cloth. Although it was near full length, her legs missed their concealing petticoats. Without a corset, the thin silk of the bodice only lightly touched her skin, her midriff and chest felt almost naked with nothing but a slip between them and the world – as if her old corsets had served as armour.

At least the sandals laced up with familiar ties from her Arena days, even if it felt wrong wearing them under a dress.

The elderly owner had served them in a private, muted corner of the general store. She helped them choose water flasks, fine mesh nets to hang over themselves when they slept, and a large patchwork bag with a neat wooden handle to carry it all.

'Why are you going to the forest? There's just spiders and ghosts in those big trees, and everything wants to bite you,' the old lady had joked as she bustled around them.

'It's a secret!' Livy had blurted out with the discretion of a child with a mystery to share.

'Don't confuse this nice lady.' Arrow used the placid smile she'd perfected as a governess, and told the shopkeeper, 'We're travelling with my husband, on an Empire inspection.'

The crone shot her an incredulous glance from the side of her eye, but bustled on, placing a wide straw hat on Livy's head. 'You can move in it, girl? Can raise your arms?'

Testing the fit of her new dress, Livy had jumped up and landed in the attack pose Arrow taught her on the *Flyer*. Firm but relaxed, knees slightly bent, body turned at an angle to present the least surface area to her opponent and fists curled, ready for a punch or a block. The girl gazed at the old woman. Then, after a heartbeat, Livy laughed and pirouetted.

'It's very comfy, thank you,' she said.

The woman, who had stepped back when Livy took her fighter stance, now grabbed the girl's jaw, tilting her head up and examining every inch and angle of Livy's face.

Arrow had pulled the old woman's hand away. 'Do not touch her,' she said, then, seeing the fear in the woman's eyes, she went on, 'She's just a child, she wasn't going to hurt you.'

The crone shook her head as if to free it from a web. 'Perhaps the ghosts will welcome you, after all,' she muttered.

Then she had bustled away to pack up their purchases, and Livy wheedled for a necklace of polished shells to go with her new dress (too expensive and too long for her).

Arrow had thought it was shock in the ancient woman's face when she saw an eight-year-old girl in fighting stance before her. As the charnot wheels churned on, thinking about the girl on the water, Arrow now realised it was recognition.

A driver broke Arrow's reverie by pounding on the cabin roof and shouting, 'Arrive tomorrow,' and then jumping on.

The washerwoman groaned and gulped down almost half a bottle of her dark brown spirits. Arrow girded herself for bone-rattling snores tonight as their cabin mate tried to finish every drop before they arrived.

Hopefully, Llund had means of contacting the river queens. In case they needed to make a quick exit from the convoy, Arrow packed up their belongings. She wasn't even sure if Llund had paid the full bill for their transport. Baja had pressed a fistful of silver coins into her hand on the *Flyer*, but after all their purchases in Rioh it was now just a fingerful.

As if to test the last of their patience, the humidity soared.

The forest around them, usually so loud with clicks and whistles of insects and the calls of birds, always audible even over the throbbing sounds of the charnots, went silent. It was as if the only thing moving in the jungle was them.

In the hot, wet air the sound of their vehicles grated on Arrow's raw senses.

Then a bird call cut through the heavy silence, three very loud squawks that carried across the forest. An answering set of calls came from ahead.

Arrow tensed.

'Livy dearest. Go into the little latrine room, now.'

'Why? It's horrible in there and I don't need to go.'

Arrow turned to her, face steady. 'Now, Livy.'

Livy's long training kicked in. Without another word, the child stepped into the cramped little metal box. Arrow checked she was hiding with minimum exposure to the windows, and then drew the knife out of the sash she'd demanded they add to her new dress back in Rioh.

Another three bird calls rang out, now from the left of the charnots, with three from the right following moments later. *Damnutus.*

They were surrounded, and Arrow didn't think it was by anything with feathers – unless they wore them in their hair.

A screech of metal in deathly pain rocked their cabin.

The colossal transport shuddered to a stop, Arrow stumbled, and the washerwoman rolled out of her bunk, groaned and clasped her head.

Arrow checked Livy was safe, if shaken, and then tried to warn their cabin mate.

'Be ready! It's an attack. They must have hit the charnot in front of us.'

216

The washerwoman looked at Arrow with a slack jaw. 'The ghosts, the she-devils? They've come for us? Eieeee!'

'Shut up,' Arrow hissed. 'We have soldiers with arc guns, be ready to move.'

But the woman started to tear at her own hair and shriek about demons who would eat her alive. For much of the journey, the washerwoman had just flopped on her bunk or heaved herself over to the fetid latrine. Standing in panic revealed a body at least a head and shoulders taller than Arrow, and hysterical.

Over the woman's wild shrieks Arrow could hear arc-gun fire and men's raised voices.

'Sit down! I must see if anyone is coming behind us!'

The washerwoman jerked, then turned to look out of the rear window. 'They are coming! They'll kill us all,' she sobbed. Then threw open the door to their cabin and clambered out. Arrow tried to haul her back in, but the large woman slipped off the ladder, landing with a groan.

The injured washerwoman limped a few steps back down the dirt road they'd driven up. While the road was lit with the sharp sunlight, the tall trees either side sucked up the sunshine into darkness. Where did she think she could go?

Stopping in the middle of the pot-marked road, the washerwoman looked around and drew out a small arc gun from the folds of her dress. Arrow's jaw tightened; the woman had hidden a loaded arc gun in the cabin, all this time?

Then the madwoman started to fire into the trees on one side, and then the other. The pop of arc-gun bullets echoed the ones Arrow could hear being fired at the front of the convoy. Arrow was about to lean out of the cabin and call to her again when she recognised a twang in the air.

The large woman stopped.

Two more sounds rang out. Arrow saw the shafts, each piercing a side of the woman's body. The first must have hit her front. Each arrow bolt was weighted with feathers in yellow and blue.

The big woman dropped to her knees, then started crawling forward, still holding the arc gun and firing. Five more bolts hit her, in shoulders, neck and haunches. She dropped onto one shoulder and jerked to the ground.

Then she was still. But Arrow could see movement in the trees. *Get to Barro.*

Arrow pulled Livy out of the latrine and pushed her towards the cabin door, away from the window that looked back down the road to the fallen woman.

'We're going up front, we'll jump between the charnots like the drivers do. We need to find Barro,' she said.

'What's happening, Miss? Why have we stopped?'

'Climb forwards out of the door, Livy. Don't look back,' Arrow ordered.

If they climbed forward, then most of the charnots' bulk would be between them and the invisible archers behind.

Arrow had hoped this might be a welcoming committee from the river queens, organised by Llund. But when the first shaft hit the drunk washerwoman, she knew there was no welcome here. This was a raid, and she doubted they would ask for the passengers' life stories before slaughtering them.

Arrow imagined shouting out, 'Hey, you've made a mistake. I've got your stolen princess!' She doubted she'd get past the 'hey' before a weapon cut her off.

Livy scrambled along the charnot's vast wheel rims, and Arrow sent a tiny prayer of thanks to young Tor for the little girl's climbing skills.

They clambered over metal spurs and boxes of equipment as fast as they could manage, passing the huge cargo containers full of whatever it was their attackers wanted to get their hands on.

As they got close to the driver's cab at the front of their charnot, Arrow reached out to stop Livy. She climbed over her, Livy pressing herself close into the warm metal of the charnot. As Arrow's body was over the child's, a blast from the flamethrower flared out ahead of them, and a rattle of arc-gun fire followed it. They had fled from hidden killers, right into an open battle. But this wasn't her territory, and Arrow needed Barro alongside her, between Livy and whoever was attacking them.

Arrow peered into the driver's cabin, but there wouldn't be much help there. The man was impaled through his stomach on a long shard of metal where the two giant charnots had crashed into each other. The cabin was littered with broken glass, but Arrow felt around the cooling body for an arc gun. Nothing but blood and glass. She wiped her hand on her dress and indicated that Livy go forward, putting her body between the child's view and the bloody mess in the cabin.

What the Hades had Llund got them into?

Arrow lifted Livy onto the back of the next charnot in front of theirs. This one carried no passenger cabins, but they needed to cross it before reaching the lead vehicle with the men.

Livy started to scramble up the metal wheel rim again, then stiffened and edged backwards, never taking her eyes off what rose before her.

A woman covered in yellow, blue and red zigzag stripes of fine mud or paint, with feathers in her hair, looked down at them from the charnot's roof. Arrow didn't see much more detail because her attention was fixed upon the razor tip of the spear that hovered one inch from Livy's forehead.

The woman stood above, with her shaft hefted and eyes slowly rising from the child to where Arrow stood behind her. Their eyes locked, and Arrow held, assessing her opponent.

A tiny raise of the woman's eyebrows hinted that Arrow's behaviour was unexpected. The spearhead wavered almost imperceptibly.

Then another discharge from the flamethrower lit up the forest.

As the attacker let her eyes flick back to the light, Arrow pushed Livy down and sprang over her.

The heel of Arrow's left palm hit the woman's solar plexus but recoiled off concealed armour, painted and moulded to her body. The warrior didn't fall, but the blow was enough that she dropped her shaft, curling forward and grabbing at Arrow's neck as she did so. Strong fingers pressed into Arrow's windpipe as they both hit back against the metal roof and almost rolled off the charnot.

Avoiding the armour and trying to reach up to her enemy's face, Arrow's chest was on fire from the lack of breath, sapping her strength. The warrior woman watched her, pressing down, keeping her face out of Arrow's biting distance.

Arrow's hands fumbled downwards, head swimming and gagging for air. The attacker watched without visible emotion as Arrow's eyes widened and lost focus.

Then the warrior woman stiffened.

Her hands loosened from around Arrow's throat and she rolled away, feathers falling from her hair as she slipped from the charnot.

Arrow's knife was slicked with blood.

She coughed and rasped for breath as Livy crawled up to her.

What had her mother said? Your enemies' expectation of you is a weapon in your hands. The Amazonial woman hadn't thought an Empire woman would be carrying a knife. Or that she'd know the weak spot between armoured plates, however well concealed.

Arrow wiped the blood on the inside of her skirt and slipped her blade back into the sash.

'Keep moving,' she managed to croak at Livy. The girl's face was like a simply drawn child's picture, devoid of emotion.

Arrow didn't think she'd managed to hit her assailant's heart, perhaps just a lung. And anyway, that woman wasn't the only enemy out there. They were close enough now to hear screams from the leading charnot, which in Arrow's judgement were only coming from the throats of men.

It sounded like the river women were winning, even though they carried only spears and arrows against the power of arc guns and flamethrowers. She and Livy reached the middle charnot drivers' cabin, but it was deserted. Livy had started shaking and sweating.

'Livy, look at me.' Arrow crouched down and turned Livy's face to hers. 'You must hide here, while I fetch Barro.'

Livy started to mouth 'no, no, no' over and over again, not even able to make any sound. The girl had watched her former governess almost throttle and then stab one of the people she had hoped would be her family. Arrow wanted to hold the girl, listen and explain, preferably back in their cosy little garret, surrounded by books and a few beloved toys.

But Arrow needed to leave Livy alone, fast.

'Crawl under the panel there.'

She bundled Livy into the empty cabin and under the driver's dashboard panel. Livy's body stiffened, and she kept shaking her head.

Arrow hugged her tight unmoving body, then pushed away.

'If everything goes quiet, then come out. Cry loudly if you can.'

Arrow backed out of the cabin and closed the door. She straightened her flimsy bodice and jumped between the two charnots onto the lead vehicle, her heart left back in the cabin with Livy, but her head in charge of her actions.

In both Academy and Arena, Arrow had been taught military tactics devised by the Empire's greatest generals. Each of those heroes would agree she now fought an unwinnable battle. Because all the arc guns had fallen silent as she and Livy had reached the forward cabin.

Now all Arrow heard, every few moments, was the scream of a man. It sounded like an execution. And Arrow needed to hand herself over to it.

She couldn't think of anything else. If their attackers were bent on slaughter, then that was what they would have. There was no way to evade them in their own forest.

But she still held onto one wild hope.

If Livy was alone, perhaps they would spare her. Men might willingly believe what they wish, but as a desperate woman, trying to save a child, she had seen what a man might miss. While the warrior woman had attempted to kill Arrow without qualm, she had stood, for a few moments at least, without loosing her spear into Livy.

The warrior woman had hesitated to kill a child.

That was the tiny thread of hope that Arrow hung onto as she climbed over the charnot. Leaving the girl felt like death, but worth it if Livy lived. She inched past the front wheel, and, if she was surprised that no one stopped her, that was quashed by the sight that met her.

Before the lead charnot, the male soldiers, passengers and drivers all knelt in the muddy road, hands laced behind their heads. Barro was halfway along the line, but there was no sign of Llund.

Warrior women paced around the group, their bodies painted in different patterns, circles like eyes, and zigzags. Most carried spears. Others bore curved swords and hoisted crescent-shaped shields. Archers aimed heavy bows, their arrowheads glinting in the dappled forest light.

Swordswomen held the tip of their weapons pointing towards the men. Or at least, the remaining men. Arrow counted only two-thirds of those she'd last seen in the refuelling clearing. These living wretches were the lucky ones. The feet of a dead solider were just visible at the edge of the forest.

Another woman stepped out from behind a perimeter of archers. This warrior stood taller than the others and her entire body was concealed by paints. Her face was drawn like a skull, with deep black pockets around her eyes and shades on her cheeks and jaw to resemble sharp bone.

Without bow, spear or sword, she stood as if she herself were the weapon.

The man on the end of the line closest to her started to shake and weep. He was a driver Arrow didn't recognise, and younger than the others, his filthy trousers stained where his bladder had opened.

The bone-painted woman walked over to him, speaking so softly that Arrow couldn't hear what she was asking. The boy curled over in a defensive posture. Tears rolling down his oil-streaked face.

The bone woman bent and started to stroke his hair, repeating her question over and again. Now he almost melted, tiny shakes of his head in answer as she brought her face right down in front of his, and held his frizzy mat of hair tight, forcing his face up to meet hers. The bone woman half-smiled, asking her question again and again. A tiny spit of foam flecked the corner of his mouth. Then he groaned out a loud 'Nooooooo' that even Arrow could hear.

The bone woman jerked up, yanked his head back by his hair, exposing the skin of his neck. The nearest swordswoman swiped forward with her blade.

'Stop!' Arrow heard herself shout.

Two of the warriors turned towards her, while the others didn't break their concentration on the captives. The bone woman barked an order at them and released the boy, who crumpled trembling and weeping at her feet.

The archers raised their weapons as if they were one person.

Tilting her head at Arrow, the bone woman shouted, 'Come down, or be shot down.'

Watching Barro's eyes blaze into her from where he knelt, Arrow stepped forward to the high hood of the lead charnot.

Then jumped, landing lightly despite her skirt.

Two warriors stepped forward, their curved swords held one at her head and one at her heart. The bone woman strolled up to her, looking her up and down.

'You're the one who pricked my Kepes? I didn't believe it when she said an Empire woman stuck a knife in her. Skirts don't fight.'

'I fight,' Arrow said, her voice gravelly from her damaged windpipe.

The two women took the measure of each other. There was no bravado in Arrow, no desperate defiance or desire to deceive. She locked eyes with the black irises of the river woman as a warrior trained, knowing her own power and able to judge that of others.

'You fight, you say? Then why didn't you fight when this fire-monster breathed flame at the girl on the river? Why not stop it?'

So, not a raid to steal the cargo. This was revenge.

'I should have,' was all that Arrow could say.

The bone woman grunted, then shrugged as if disappointed. One warrior pulled Arrow over to the line of men as the other kept a sword trained on her. She dropped to her knees in the mud with her arms raised like the others. Barro didn't even try to meet her eye.

The bone woman tilted her head on one side like a teacher repri-manding a class as she paced before them. 'Maybe I'll let you all go. Even after you burned up the little canoe.'

She stopped pacing. 'But first, you must answer my question. Where is the old man? We know he's travelling in these fire-monsters with you. Where'd he go, eh?'

She stood, wide-legged, before Arrow, and waved to a warrior to step behind, sword held against Arrow's back.

'In the Empire, the men protect women, they say. You call it honour. So, before I kill this strange fighting lady, one of you boys tell me,' her voice rose to a roar, 'WHERE, IS, THE, OLD, MAN?'

Arrow could drop and roll, then perhaps the blade would just hit her shoulder. She might even struggle to her feet before a spear found her heart.

Death is a debt that every one of us must pay.

'He's with me!'

Livy's light voice rang out as she and Llund stepped up onto the hood of the lead charnot where Arrow had jumped from.

Both wore the symbol of the Inguz, the crossed lattice, daubed in mud on their foreheads.

Arrow struggled to breathe through her terror, watching the warriors' spears and bows trained on Livy.

The girl's jaw dropped at the sight of carnage before the convoy, but Llund had his hand on her shoulder and gave it a little shake.

'I'm Livy. I mean Livia. I am the stolen daughter of your river queen.' Livy straightened a little, looking down at Arrow. 'You better not hurt my governess!'

Some of the warrior women started to chatter at once in their own language, a few gesturing towards Livy, others to the prisoners.

The bone woman barked an order, and they all fell quiet.

'And you, old man. You come with this girl?'

'Yes.' Llund nodded. 'We have travelled here from far over the sea, as my people promised yours. To return what was stolen from you.'

The bone woman's shoulders tightened. From her knees, directly behind, Arrow scrutinised every move the river woman made.

With the guards distracted, Arrow lowered her arms.

'That will be seen or not, once the child can be tested,' the bone woman said. But at least two of her warriors hissed between their teeth.

'No matter,' the bone woman said, hitting her hand into her palm. 'You, the child and the skirt will come with us. These men will become a warning that the river queens will extract blood debt for every attack upon us.' The warriors raised their spears and swords at the men.

Arrow sprang up and grabbed the bone woman around the waist.

The archers swung around to them.

Then everything went still, as Arrow's blade pressed into the skin of the bone woman's throat, releasing a tiny trickle of blood from where the point pressed too hard.

They hadn't thought to search her, even though she'd already stabbed one of them. What did they think she'd used, a bloody hatpin?

'No one will die before this woman does,' Arrow called. 'Get down from there, Livy.'

Livy and Llund started to scramble down the side of the charnot.

A lecture she'd heard long ago at the Academy swam in Arrow's memory, given by a revered General. 'Your enemy will kill for their honour, unless you give them an honourable reason not to.'

Arrow spoke as reasonably as she could, while keeping close hold of the Amazonial leader. 'These men are not your enemy. They are simply following the orders of their masters. Let them go. The soldiers have been shamed, and the drivers are terrified. Their living stories of the river queen's rage will be more powerful a deterrent than their dead bodies could ever be.'

Holding the bone warrior this tight, Arrow could feel she wore no armour. *Confidence and arrogance are twins only a mother could tell apart.*

Barro slowly stood up from one knee at a time, weapons tracking his every movement. He sauntered a little stiffly over to Livy, who held out her hand to him. The sounds of the forest, chatting and hooting birds, the constant whisper of the leaves, even the swish of the river itself, were all that could be heard.

Would these women react like men? Arrow didn't know if they would attack her, or let her slice open their leader's neck rather than surrender.

The bone woman made a signal with her free hand, not moving her head at all against Arrow's dagger edge. The warriors stepped forward and poked swords and spears into the remaining men's backs, pushing them forward. The boy was first to get the hint. Glancing over his shoulder, he ran forward, up the track ahead of the convoy. The other men then followed him, their feet pounding through the mud and rutted tracks in their eagerness to get away. Silence held until the few remaining soldiers and driver were out of sight.

'You must release her, Inguz,' Llund said. A few warriors gasped at the name.

The last warrior to aim her spear towards Arrow lowered it. Blinking back her sweat in the growing heat, Arrow dropped her arm from around the muscled waist of the bone woman and removed her knife. As the woman spun, Arrow raised it again in an attack hold.

'You claim the name Inguz?' the woman demanded, finally showing surprise rather than anger, the trickle of blood staining the paint on her chest.

Arrow kept her knife in one hand, but her other hand pulled the Inguz stone from her sash, holding it out.

Two of the warriors fell to their knees, looking between Arrow and Livy.

The hot wetness of the air burned her throat. 'I don't know if I'm the Inguz. But Livy *is* the stolen child. Your family.'

CHAPTER XVII

The Amazonial warriors flowed over the charnots.

After riffling through the cabins and cargo, they piled all food and medicine in a heap. Arrow heard no orders. The raiding party was as well trained and disciplined as any Empire legion.

Climbing over the vast metal vehicles, their painted bodies and bright feathers looked tiny against the chipped yellow vehicles. Arrow thought anyone who hadn't been here would find it difficult to believe this small band had defeated the mighty machines of the Imperium.

One warrior carried Arrow's patchwork bag over to her, although she refused the last of the washerwoman's bottle of spirits.

Then the women solemnly carried all the dead out to the road in front of the charnots: four men and the large woman. Crescent shields held at knee height, spears planted in the ground and all arrows quivered. For a long moment, the painted women stood, then several of them plucked a feather from their hair, stepped forward and laid it on one of the bodies. Watching them, gripping Livy's hand, Arrow understood that the women each laid a feather on her victim. The washerwoman was covered in eight feathers while the driver who'd been crushed had one, from the bone woman herself.

The woman Arrow had stabbed wasn't laid out with the other fatalities, but Arrow couldn't see her in the troupe. Had they whisked her away for healing or abandoned her in the forest? As all the warrior women lowered their heads, Arrow decided not to ask.

After a moment, one woman burst out with a piercing bird-like song. The others joined as the sound carried up into the tree canopy. Waves of warbling sound, lasting longer than Arrow thought lungs could bear.

Arrow had mourned before, but this sound cut through you and into an old part of the brain, the part that prepares for your own death. She shivered and held Livy close, as the little girl gave a small whimper.

Once the very last echo of the call faded, all the women jumped up. One of the sturdiest women clambered up onto the lead charnot and wound the flamethrower to aim it at the bodies.

Arrow pulled Livy back, turning the girl away. The nearest warrior looked at them and shrugged. 'Your Empire has strange gods, they don't want bodies to be food for the forest. This is better, no?' she said and hoisted a large parcel of stolen goods onto her shoulder.

A flash of fire engulfed the dead. But the warriors weren't finished with Vulcan's flame. The powerfully built river woman upon the charnot's roof winched it around to face the following two charnots. Perfecting her aim, she let rip with stream after stream of roiling fire. Eventually, the cargo pallets on the nearest vehicle caught the flame, and then the whole convoy went up. The woman who operated it jumped down, just before an oil drum in the lead transport exploded.

Arrow dragged Livy back under the cover of the trees. But the bone woman, her paint now smudged with exertion, strode over. 'It's nearly time for rain. That will douse the fire, but your Empire won't use those monsters again,' she explained with a hint of satisfaction. 'We'll all be wet soon. Step in our step and don't try escaping into the forest. Most things in the trees want to kill you.'

The four foreigners kept together, clambering over fallen tree trunks and dodging thick sinuous vines.

Arrow hissed to Llund, 'How did you find Livy?'

'I watched you from the forest,' the old man replied, his feet squelching through the undergrowth.

'He came into my hiding place and said I needed to help you!' Livy said.

'I thought the river queens planned to rescue us,' Llund said. 'I told Barro to stay while I climbed down to find them in the forest.'

A lazy patter of rain started, huge drops that meandered down through the wet air, gaining bulk as they fell.

'But it was an attack, not a rescue. I knew that as the Inguz you would be protected by destiny, so I waited and then climbed up to Livia.'

'Did you think destiny would protect me and the other men too?' Barro asked. 'Or did that slip your mind while you hid in the trees?'

'He knew I would protect you!' Livy smiled up at Barro and took his hand. 'Llund said you needed me, that I must be brave and tell them I'm their lost girl!'

Livy looked quite excited about it all. The river women kept smiling shyly at her, and she grinned back at them but stayed close to Arrow.

'Well, as a show, it had some flair,' Barro said, a little too loud.

The rain started to become so heavy that the huge drops hurt where they hit bare skin. Soon it became impossible to talk as they slipped around, trying to see through wet eyelashes.

The downpour didn't bother the warriors, and a few even smirked at their flailing. Arrow lifted Livy up onto Barro's back when the child stumbled with exhaustion from trying to slog through the sloughy wet undergrowth. The nearest warrior woman stopped laughing then. She waved others to take their bags on top of the large packs they already carried, and one even offered Arrow help across the logs, slippery with moss, and vine-crossed hangings.

Arrow's long skirt, torn edges catching on every twig, dragged mud as she weaved through the forest for what felt like hours.

Every step felt like a test, where rain made organising sodden fabric, waterlogged sandals and chafing blouse nearly impossible. She wanted to scream out in frustration, trapped in heat, and rain and ruined silks.

So taken up in her discomfort, Arrow walked on when the others stopped. Only when the light made her blink did she stop at the sight before her – mud and skirts forgotten. The wet sunshine lit an open clearing before them, the sky boasting a giant rainbow, its colour shining with a vivid clarity impossible in charo-fumed Londinium.

But the rainbow wasn't what halted Arrow in her tracks.

A massive stone pyramid soared up in the centre of the clearing. It glinted like gold, although Arrow felt ridiculous for thinking that. Fronted by a sweeping staircase of high steps running up to a covered platform, twenty people would be able to climb up it in lockstep.

Wooden lodges and leafed shelters around it were dwarfed by the pyramid as if two different scenes had been superimposed upon each other.

Barro carried Livy up to her and asked, 'What in Jupiter's name is that supposed to be?'

'It looks like a Nubian pyramid. Or even the Spire back in Londinium.' Arrow shook her head, as if to make it change to something that made more sense.

'I hope it's dry inside.' Livy sniffled a little, too sodden to be impressed.

But they weren't led towards the grand golden structure. The warrior women, all standing a little straighter and carrying their packs as if they weren't bothered by the weight, indicated that they should follow to a simple shelter. It was covered with tight-woven reeds, and set near to the forest edge, far away from the other buildings.

There was a platform to sit upon and fabric hangings keeping out the worst of the weather. Inside, food was set out on leaf plates on the floor. Roast meats, flatbreads and abundant piles of fruits of every colour were piled before them.

The warriors dropped their packs and set to eating, ignoring their visitors. No one else could be seen or heard. Like they'd all stumbled upon a gift from invisible spirits.

The woman closest to Arrow ripped a yellowy-pink fruit open, to get at the soft flesh inside. She grunted and bobbed her head towards the food a few times.

Livy got the message and dropped to her knees, picking a small bright red dappled fruit. Barro shrugged and followed her, reaching out for the meats.

Arrow struggled, stomach still tight from battle. But Livy handed up the other half of her fruit, one they'd been shocked by in Rioh and then were delighted to discover the juicy, citrusy flavour under its garish pink skin.

'It's our favourite, remember?' Livy moved to sit beside her former governess, as if they were at teatime back in Londinium.

Arrow remembered the feasts that followed every major fight in the Arena. Mountains of breads, cheeses and vegetables were provided to the gladiators, occasionally with an entire roasted pig. The surviving fighters would devour it all with silent determination as if their touch of death drove a desire to fill with food. The feasts were always lavish, but never cheerful or comforting.

The rain pattered out as they ate.

Then the meal finished abruptly when the bone woman stepped up onto the platform. She hadn't been at the feast, but, like all the warriors, her paint was streaked with rain, blood and sweat. Every woman on the platform stood, then turned towards Arrow, as if they expected something of her.

'We must cleanse off blood. You fought too, skirt-woman, stabbed Kepes. Now you must wash away the taint of it before entering our village,' the bone woman said.

Arrow's hands flexed back into fists. 'I won't leave Livy. If we are your prisoners, then we will stay together.'

The bone woman laughed, cracking even more of the paint on her face into hundreds of tiny lines.

'We're not prisoners,' Llund pleaded with Arrow, 'we came to bring Livia to these people. Please, Inguz. Purification rites are important. We do the same in Britannia. You must be cleansed.'

Arrow looked at Barro. Livy sat close beside him, and they resumed eating.

'Livy will be safer with that lot gone anyway,' Barro said with a shrug. 'We've got the food, so I'm happy. I won't leave her.'

The heat and humidity had soared since the rain stopped. Arrow held no desire to go anywhere with the women who killed the convoy. But she needed to know more about their captors.

'Know your enemy at rest, as well as you know him in battle,' her mother had taught her. 'Understand his tastes, his faith and his pleasures, because each of these is a weapon in your hands.'

Arrow crouched beside Livy but looked at Barro.

'Be good, Livy. Don't leave Barro. I won't be long.'

As she stood, Arrow smoothed down the wreck of her skirts and jumped off the platform to join the women. They walked back into the forest but now on a clearer path, and, although the rain had dried, the humidity was fearsome. In the wet heat, the forest felt more alive, full of whistles and squeaks, with light dappling down through trees so tall they peaked higher than the staircased building in the clearing. Arrow had never been anywhere quite so verdant; it even smelt green.

After a few moments, another continuous sound started to build as they walked. It sounded like the Godstorm winds that had ripped through the Imperium Museum all those weeks before, a growing rumbling and shrieking of winds. But the vines and leaves around them didn't move, and the sky was clear above.

As the sound swelled, Arrow hesitated, but none of the warriors slowed; those at the front even hastened to reach the source of the growling noise. Arrow caught up with them as they pushed past a clump of leaves each as large as a man and stepped out into a chill she hadn't felt since leaving the *Flyer*.

Before her towered a waterfall, throwing itself down from a sharp cliff above, surrounded by leafy fronds and landing in a wide pool of mirror-clear water. The spray and winds from the tumbling water cleared the air and gave the space around the pool a freshness inviting her to take lungfuls of air.

The warriors stripped off their armour and tunics and threw themselves into the water with naked abandon. A few laughed, and others wept. One woman started a high ululating song, which resonated with victory, while another pressed her head against the cool rocks at the side of the pool, shaking and crying.

Arrow stood in her frayed and soiled long dress, chosen to try to mimic the respectable wide skirts of her Londinium life, looking out over the pool of naked women releasing the grief and glory of their battle.

In Londinium, newspapers relished tales of Amazonial barbarian women slicing off their right breast for better aim as archers and spear-women. Here by the pool, Arrow saw it was just how their armour was shaped, moulded to suppress the right breast for tighter draws and throws. Perhaps with a breastplate like that she'd have performed better in archery at the Arena.

One woman turned towards her. Without her bone paint, her face looked less fierce and younger than Arrow expected. Arrow tried not to even glance at the dark skin of her naked body and stared up at the top of the waterfall.

'Come. You have legs under those skirts, no? Clean off the battle and blood. No one will look, if the Empire lady is shy!' The bone woman laughed.

In the baths of the Arena, Arrow knew, the male gladiators almost always washed together. Because there were so few gladiatrixes, she'd had the female baths to herself.

Whatever is natural cannot be shameful.

Arrow peeled off her dank garments and untied her skirts. Despite the strangeness, she saw sense in this ritual. The water bit cold and clear as she lowered herself into it. It felt pure and her new bruises were soothed by the coolness. A warrior threw over a black lump to her and Arrow sniffed it. It smelt astringent even though it wasn't proper soap. Several of the other women scrubbed similar blocks of the stuff into their hair or wiped it over wounds and scratches.

It stung her grazes, but in a clean way. Sweat, mud and oil sloughed off her. She immersed herself in the water, alone under the sparkling blue and green.

Down here the real world was far away. The reality in which Livy had watched her fight, stab, and threaten to kill.

It is better to think before doing something than to repent later.

When she emerged, some women were leaving the water, and they carried away her clothes.

Arrow waded towards the shore, shouting. The bone woman snorted. 'Clothes covered in blood and mud must be washed. Don't worry, Empire woman, we will keep your skirts safe,' she said, and then leaned back, eyes running over Arrow's body. 'More under them than I thought.'

A few of the other warriors laughed as Arrow ducked back down under the water.

One pointed at her and gesticulated to another as they helped to wash each other's hair. They traced shapes on each other's bodies and mimicked different fighting stances as if trying to complete a puzzle.

They were tracing Arrow's own scars out on each other, with grudging smiles and nods.

Seven raised whiplashes ran from her left shoulder down across her back. Her upper arms, ribcage and belly held a patchwork of scars from slashes and stabs, some so old as to be nothing more than white lines. Her right hip carried red marks where a spiked ball had lodged during a very nasty bout. A long-puckered sword cut decorated one thigh and a nasty jagged score from a trident the other.

Arrow had fewer disfigurements than most gladiators, and had kept all her limbs, eyes and fingers. But back in Londinium, she tried to hide these wounds even from herself as she washed. Reminders that she could never deny her past.

Although the worst scar of all wasn't visible on her skin, and she could feel it in her guts every day.

Today, her mutilations were approved of, admired even, in this land of women who chose to fight. Arrow pulled the water out of her hair. She needed to remember that respect for her scars wouldn't stop them from killing her, or Livy. *Where there is doubt, there is freedom.*

A younger woman, not one of the raiding party, stood by the pool. She wore a long simple shift of soft fabric, almost a wheat colour. As the women left the pool, she handed them each a similar dress.

The women threw them on and started to plait their own long dark hair. The bone woman riffled in the basket the girl carried and lifted out the palest of the plain shifts and held it up to Arrow as she stepped out of the pool.

'You Empire people call us ghosts of the forest. Now you look like a spirit too,' she said.

Arrow slipped on the soft garment, plaiting her own hair in a similar way to the other women. The sun began to set in a warm blaze of yellow and orange over the trees, and the birds called out their sunset songs.

'Now, we'll test the girl you bring us. See if she is of our blood, or if you are spies in our nest.' The bone woman frowned as she turned from Arrow and walked back into the jungle.

Arrow's muscles, which had almost unclenched from her joints in the cool water, tensed back into battle readiness.

Being amongst these women was distracting, familiar, and even comfortable because they were so like her – they were all killers.

CHAPTER XVIII

As the day dropped beneath the trees, hundreds of dots of light began to glow. The wide plain was ablaze with blue.

Every one of the wooden lodges hung with them. Delicate poles Arrow had earlier mistaken for reeds were each topped with the unusual bluish light. They nagged at her brain until she connected them to the lights on the *Flyer*. The god Inguz wasn't the only connection between these worlds beyond the Empire.

The steps leading up the pyramid blazed with hundreds of them. But just like the blue lights on the ship, each lamp's light didn't extend far, only deepening the shadows. A fitting metaphor for her own patchy grasp of this new reality.

Arrow walked across the plain behind the silent women, grinding her jaw and trying to think. The air was warm against her skin. She could hear the night noises of the forest following her: rustles and hoots as the day creatures hid or nested, and the night animals emerged to lurk and hunt. The encroaching darkness at her back propelled Arrow forward, but, even with the strangeness of the forest behind her, she was uncomfortable on the speckled blue plain.

But Livy was somewhere within those lights, and even if the child belonged to these people Arrow should be beside her.

The women chanted. So faintly at first, she thought it the movement of leaves in the forest. Once they stepped into the plain the sound grew. Repetitive, deep and rhythmic. *I-ano-ka, I-ano-ka, I-ano-ka. Do. I-ano-ka, I-ano-ka, I-ano-ka. Do.*

Arrow didn't join in with the sound, even though after a few moments the rhythm of the chant crawled into her head. She pressed her lips together and curled her fists. The gentle warm wind, deep leafy smell and blue lights were in danger of dulling her senses. Joining a hypnotic chant wasn't going to help keep her reflexes sharp.

As the line of women weaved around the lights, it became clear they headed towards the pyramid, which still glinted, holding onto the memory of sunlight.

Arrow stared into the shadows with her remaining night vision from the forest. No one else could be seen in the wood cabins they passed. Only the chanting women, with her as a silent witness, following.

Where was Livy?

An answer suggested itself as they drew closer to the great pyramid. In the darkness between the blue lights on each step, hundreds of silent people stood, facing upwards – all so motionless that she hadn't noticed them in the darkness. Old people, their wrinkled skin and sunken muscles beautiful in the blue light. Tall, wide-shouldered younger men, with leather around their waists and paint on their backs, in the same style that the warrior women had worn during the attack on the convoy. Arrow could see streaks of dark and light lines, swirls and dots but couldn't make out colours; the blue clouded over other tones. Stouter women, older than the warrior women but their backs standing proud. And children. Arrow spotted the curves of little ankles with smoother skin than the rest, delicate ribs and hands clutching the older women's hands.

The walking warriors broke neither stride nor the rhythm of their chant as they started to climb the stairs between a line of lights where no one else stood. The silent figures either side made no acknowledgement they were there, except that, at each step the leader took, all the people on that stair joined the chant. The sound came from around the pyramid. She wondered how those in the darkness on the other sides knew the moment to begin the song.

Arrow hesitated on the dirt of the plain.

Joining the women at the river had been a mistake.

Since the moment she'd left the Consul's office, she'd had to run to keep up. Neither her training in the Academy nor the Arena had prepared her for the jolts of strangeness she faced. Barro had swept through it all with a sardonic smile, and Llund was fuelled by religious zeal. Even Livy adapted to sights and habits with more ease than her former governess.

Arrow's shoulders drooped, and she stood mute, staring up at the pyramid. Should she run up the stairs, knocking people aside, and try to defend Livy from whatever test they wanted to subject her to, whatever the cost?

But, these were Livy's people, her real family. She belonged in this strangeness in a way her former governess didn't.

Two tiny lights flashed in the darkness just above Arrow – the whites of a child's eyes as they turned to look back down, perhaps confused as to why the foreign woman hadn't followed the others or just curious about the stranger. The child mouthed the words of the chant while staring back down the few steps at Arrow and then, for the briefest instant, grinned at her. The mother tugged, and the child turned back, melting into the still, ghost-like throngs chanting together.

'Everyone bleeds, dearest, and loves, and cries in the dark,' Arrow's own mother had said, so many years before. 'There are no demons in the Arena, whatever crazy armour they wear or bloodied skulls they tie to their helmets. No monsters, only men. And all men and women are the same in most respects. I know they all die the same.' Her mother had been sewing up a deep laceration in her own thigh as she said that, while her four-year-old daughter wept in the corner in fear of a giant gladiator, who'd strode into their mess hall wearing a full-tusked boar skull over his helmet. Her mother told her that she'd cut the man down, nevertheless. Once she'd dealt with her injury, she'd taken her little daughter into her arms and sung the tears away.

A few years later, barely older than Livy was now, Arrow had watched as her mother was slaughtered in a death match commissioned by rivals, to settle a squabble over a debt.

She had been sneaking to watch her mother for weeks since the first time. Horrified, fascinated and unable to look away from every thrust and parry. The mother in their tiny room was firm, loving and caring only for her daughter. A different woman to the gladiatrix Britannia on the sand. There she was a goddess of battle – bold, ruthless and proud. Taking risks to perform ever greater feats for her adoring fans to scream their adulation.

Slowly, fear for her mother's safety was being replaced with pride at her death-defying tactics and slaughter of men who towered over her.

Mother was beautiful, glorious. Gladiatrix Britannia bestrode the sand, and her daughter thought her invincible.

Until that day.

Mother had done nothing wrong, no misstep or failure. A shaft of sunlight caught on one of the copper bowls of burning oil momentarily blinded the gladiatrix. Just for a heartbeat, but enough for her opponent to plunge his sword into her midriff. Arrow knew the man; he had taught her to play catch in the mess hall years before. But they were all just gladiators after all.

Arrow had stood transfixed, deafened by the cheers and screams of the watching throng, as her mother fell to the sand, arm clutched over a long deep gouge in her belly. For many steps' lengths around her, the sand darkened with her blood.

In a trivial match to settle a debt, the undefeated gladiatrix Britannia became just another dying slave.

The girl had wanted to run away, but, with timing only the gods' cruelty could engineer, Mother looked up and locked eyes with her.

Her face was spattered with shock at seeing her daughter. For a moment, it seemed like her mother might move, or even stand up. Instead, she half-rolled over, so they weren't facing anymore. Mother didn't move again.

The gladiatrix's daughter knew her mother must have been angry at her, as she breathed her last under the sun on the sand, with the Citizens laughing and cheering at the sight. Perhaps the gladiatrix had wished she'd never had a child at all.

Despite the warmth of the Amazonial, so far from grey Londinium, Arrow shivered.

Killers shouldn't be mothers.

Think of all universal substance, and how little portion of that makes you. Think of universal time, and what a short interval has been assigned to you. And of destiny itself and how tiny a part of it you are.

But perhaps killers could be guard dogs.

Arrow was tempted to growl as she rushed up the steps in the heat of the Amazonial night, the sounds of the forest drowned out by the chanting, her soft dress and slippers offering no protection, and without the dagger they'd taken away with her clothes.

But she could claw and shred anyone who threatened the girl.

The upper platform was partly covered by a high wooden roof. The blue lights hung all around the edges, and a large pit filled the centre, burning with fire. The heat and acrid smell made Arrow blink.

The line of warrior women had divided, and they now stood along all the edges that Arrow could see. And there were men here too, with bows slung across their bare shoulders and quivers at their sides. While the women only wore the dresses they'd been given at the river, many of the men carried knives, slung on hips or even strapped to their calves.

All chanted.

As Arrow started to circle around the burning hollow to search for Livy on the other side of the white-hot fire, all the singing stopped.

Not in a wave, as people further down the pyramid recognised what happened. All at once.

Arrow's heart skipped a beat at the shock of silence. The raging fire in the centre, which till that moment had burned with such ferocity, immediately extinguished itself, with only a haze of rising smoke to suggest it had ever been there.

As the smoke cleared, the tip of a bobbing blue feather appeared to rise out of the pit. The feather was attached to others, atop a pile of white and grey hair, hung with silver amulets. The rising apparition's head was turned away, wearing a hessian dress much like Arrow's own, if a little crumpled and dusty in places. A wide golden girdle held the dress close, embroidered with silver moons running from waxing crescent through to waning sliver.

A spindly arm used a stout staff to help lever the bent back of the creature up the steps, which must be within the pyramid itself. When almost out, the figure paused, bent over to cough and spit.

'That blasted smoke smells like burnt rats' piss, every time.'

The face that turned towards Arrow was a set of wrinkles stacked upon each other, like a poorly built wall in danger of falling. But the eyes that peeped out of the ancient dark folds pierced Arrow.

'Guess you can't smell it though, being as you've stopped breathing.'

Arrow's chest burned. As she took a ragged inhale, the crone let out a deep squawk, which might have been a laugh. Then she turned to a dark corner and rapped her staff on whatever she stood upon.

'Here, girl. Don't just stand there watching. I can't fly out.'

The woman who ran forward was the bone warrior. She helped the crone to step out onto the platform, standing close even after the old woman shrugged off her helping hand.

'Right then. Where's that old rune-thrower and the miracle child?'

'Grandmother, the girl claiming to be the daughter of Queen Teuta won't come without the man who travelled with them. But he is unconsecrated. I will kill him at your command and drag her to you.'

244

'No, you won't.' The old woman smashed her staff down as her amulets shuddered. 'There has been blood enough today! If a poor witch like me and the old Druid from over the sea aren't holy enough to hallow this place, then we have a god here too, or so I'm told.' The woman waved a scrawny arm circled by bracelets and hung with charms. 'That should be enough sacredness to balance against one unconsecrated male, don't you think? Now, go and fetch them, and try not to massacre anyone while you're at it.'

The crone waved her off and then turned towards Arrow. The bone woman bowed towards the old woman's back but flashed a look at Arrow that, in the Arena, would have made her grip her weapons and prepare for attack.

As the bone woman slunk off, Arrow saw tiny releases in the shoulders and fists from the silent throng watching around the edges, especially from the men.

'You speak like you could live next door to us in Londinium.' Arrow spoke before the old woman could reach her.

The crone barked out a spit of laughter.

'Ha! Most of the rest here might do too if they let themselves. Think we only live here in the forest? Most of us have worked in the rigs or mines, and a few even in the cities. When your old Emperor was a young man, he built Imperium schools and even an Academy here. Welcomed us out of the forest and signed treaties of friendship. But when they found *ikha* here, then we ran back to our trees to hide. Turns out your Emperor liked *ikha* more than he liked friendship. But I remember how to talk your talk, and curse in it, too.'

'*Ikha?*'

The crone spat. '*Ikha* is poison, but the Empire treats it like mother's milk. Pouring it into their great mechanical beasts with no thought for the filth they puke out after drinking it.'

No one liked charo fumes, but here in the forest how much problem could it be?

245

'But oil isn't our business here tonight, is it, girl? You've brought the child back to us, through danger, I hear. I patched up poor Kepes after you stabbed her lung. Eager to tell she was, once she could speak without coughing blood. The Empire skirt who fought like one of our own. Not heard anything like it before. Are there others like you, or is the god truly within you and our Kepes was fighting him instead?'

Arrow controlled her every muscle and reflex. 'Only if he trained in the gladiator Arena since childhood and has killed as many men as I have.' She raised her voice. 'Although I have never had the chance to equal the number of men I've killed with women. Until now.'

Everything about this old woman was designed to distract, but as she cackled Arrow saw Llund, Livy and Barro walk up the steps into the light. Llund and Livy both looked crumpled and miserable, and Barro wore a cracked lip, his arms tied behind him and held by the bone woman.

The crone didn't turn to follow Arrow's gaze but stood transfixed, head cocked and staring at Arrow as if listening to a sound no one else could hear. After a moment she stamped her staff absent-mindedly.

'Gods and gladiators. *Ikha* and blood. This is not the day I thought it would be.' She shook her head and turned to the newcomers.

'Daughter, untie the male. With every warrior and hunter up here, I hope we'll all be safe enough.'

The bone woman drew a blade at Barro's back and Arrow tensed. But Barro pulled his arms around to rub at his wrists, using the action to make a tiny hand signal as he did so. Arrow's shoulders released; if he could be bothered cursing in finger flicks then he was well enough to fight if necessary.

The old woman stepped away from Arrow, raised her arms and shook the charms on her wrists and hair. Then she turned in a circle, striking her staff towards each face of the pyramid. A great cry came up from all the watchers on the platform and down below, ululating out and across the forest.

Livy crouched down and covered her ears. Arrow dodged around the crone and over to Livy, the child turned inwards, and Arrow felt the girl's small shoulders shiver as if she was cold and wet back in Londinium. Arrow wrapped an arm around her, and the shaking stopped. As did the sound. But as the crone turned back towards them, the fire exploded back up with a shower of sparks. It roared behind her, and Arrow couldn't believe the old woman wasn't burnt.

'Children of the forest, HEAR ME!' The old woman's voice carried out to all those on the pyramid steps and even to the trees themselves.

'Mothers who have come before. Daughters who have died in blood. Sons lost to the dark. HEAR ME!' The fire flared up again.

'One has come who claims our blood. Comes from our old enemy across the sea. She says she is the stolen child, daughter of my daughter. A rune man brings her, but I know him not. A woman protects her, but our warriors know her not.'

Here the old woman's eyes flashed. 'An unconsecrated man comes with her, but our hunters know him not. And we have been deceived before!'

Barro inched closer, so his shoulder touched Arrow's. He didn't turn towards the old woman's show but out into the darkness. Arrow was grateful he protected his night vision in case they had to fight down the dark steps. Not that it would do them much good. Three lost souls shipwrecked in a sea of trees.

'The stolen child was born from deception. Conceived in a lie. And then taken by falsehood. How now shall we know if she is ours? Or if our enemy seeks to plant a false egg within our nest?'

At this, a howl of indignation flowed up from the crowd, not ordered song anymore. The haphazard roar a guttural cry of defiance and denial. Arrow stepped forward a little so that Livy was squeezed between her and Barro as they stood back to back, arms raised to a defence posture that might give them seconds if the warriors and hunters on the platform rushed them.

'HEAR ME!' Llund's voice rang out higher and clearer than Arrow thought possible, and the fire burned a little lower.

'Llund I am. He who walks the dark green. Head warden of the wood and keeper of the waters. Green Man, of the Iceni, am I. We are a captive nation of the Empire, but we have not lost everything we were. In the heart of the Emperor's own home we walk, we watch, and we fight. Great gift of light did the People of the River give us, a boon never to be forgotten and debt we can never pay.' Here the old woman sniffed, but Llund went on.

'A child was stolen from you and brought to our shores. And we have searched for her, for you, ever since. Hidden she was. Given to a protector with no family or name – a slave. For years we looked, paid bribes, listened at doors, and darker things.' Llund looked around the throng, without ever looking at Livy herself.

'This is the child we found. You know she was taken eight years ago? This child arrived in Londinium soon after, motherless. You know the snake Derain stole your Queen's baby? This child is Derain's legal ward. And you know the destiny prophesised for her. She will lead us all. She will smash the Romans and grind their Temples into dust. She is the spear the true gods chose to pierce the heart of the Empire!'

Arrow heard whispers from the disciplined rows below. If that nonsensical rant helped, she might even hug the crazy old Druid.

Then Llund turned to her. 'See? The gods even sent the spirit of Inguz to protect her, who you call the Panthera.'

What the Hades? Trying to follow the two old lunatics' arguments while keeping track of every armed enemy on the pyramid wasn't helping Arrow's nerves. Or was she supposed to call herself Panthera now? No chance.

'Words!' the crone spat back at Llund. 'Would our Panthera come to us in skirts? In an Empire convoy? The child has no parents, you say. How do you know she isn't a bastard of the snake Derain himself? The girl cowers there between the Empire pair when our children of her age are already in the hunt or battle. Yet she will break the Empire? My youngest granddaughter challenged the filthy convoy from her canoe and took the measure of them before our ambush. Yet this girl, who you say is my blood, who you say is our weapon, she hides behind her nursemaid. Bah! We should kill you all, rather than give Derain the chance to laugh at us!'

During the speech, Arrow could feel Livy begin to tremble again, and she reached behind to try to comfort her without losing eye contact with the warriors who raised their weapons.

But Livy shot out from between her and Barro.

Arrow hadn't expected the move and jumped forward to grab her. A forest of spears rose against her and Livy. Arrow stopped, arm outstretched to Livy.

The girl stood with her hands clenched at her sides in her torn and dirty dress, filthy bare toes curled against the stone. Her body thrumming with what could either be terror or rage. Arrow could no longer tell the difference.

'I am *not* Derain's daughter! I don't know if I'm your lost girl. But I don't belong to him! If you don't want me, then let us go. You hurt Barro because he wanted to stay with me. He'd said that he would look after me, then a lady hit him because he tried to keep his promise. I don't want to be your granddaughter, anyway. You're horrible. And I bet that fire isn't really magic, it's just an oxidised updraught.'

Despite the likelihood that they would all die any moment, Arrow couldn't help the tiny surge of pride that Livy remembered her alchemy lessons.

The old woman took two steps closer to Livy, who shivered but didn't budge. Arrow promised herself that, if the crone tried to hurt her, then even archers' shafts wouldn't stop her breaking the old woman's neck before she fell.

'So, the girl may have a spirit of her own, after all, eh? You know that since you've arrived you've broken almost every one of our laws? And insulted our customs even more. If those men with their spears raised are forced to kill your friends, they will have to leave this place and never return. None are allowed to spill blood up here. Except me, of course.' The old woman gave Livy a wide, unpleasant grin.

'Hmm, now. Blood. That *is* an interesting idea.' As everyone on the platform held their breath, the old woman scratched one buttock. 'Well now, blood is an old magic . . . but this is an old problem.' The crone turned to the bone woman. 'Bring me the Icar knife.' The bone woman ran to one far corner of the platform and down the steps without a word.

The crone swung back to Livy, her amulets clanking against each other.

'Child. Will you be tested in blood?'

'Yes!'

'No!'

Livy and Arrow both spoke at the same time.

Llund scurried over to Arrow.

'This might work,' he hissed. 'We have rituals like this at home. They will just give her a tiny nick and test her blood.'

'How in Hades' name will they do that?' Arrow spat.

'We taste it. But there are other ways.'

At the thought of Llund tasting Livy's blood Arrow wondered if all the rumours about the Druids might be true. But the crone whispered to Livy, the girl's shoulders relaxed, and she even gave Arrow a tiny tight smile.

The bone woman leapt back over the lip of the top step and walked over to the crone holding out a long white blade with a black hilt across her palms.

'The Icar knife.' The crone held it aloft. 'Made from a tooth from the cursed lozibon, man made to wolf. Blood cut with this knife will prove the truth.'

The crone gripped the dagger's hilt, held out her own left wrist and made a small cut on her wizened mid-forearm. A trickle of deep red blood seeped out, and she held the flat of the blade against her arm to catch it – red blood on white blade.

The crone carried it over to the fire and, as she stepped near, the flames rose up.

'I am the blood of the river,' the crone chanted and thrust the blade into the fire. Flames licked the hilt, and then the bloodied knife. The fire roared up again but this time with a strange blue glow, the same colour as the lights across the plain.

The watchers gasped. While the people below may have heard rather than seen what happened above, the colour of the flame was visible to all.

The crone smiled to herself and carried the knife back to the bone woman, who almost dropped it. If the knife had become hot, the crone had shown no sign of it.

'Now, we test the child,' the crone said.

'No! Test me,' Barro shouted.

Arrow jerked and was about to demand what the Hades he thought he was doing, but he squeezed her arm tight and stepped past her.

'After the way you have treated us, the way you have treated her, there's no way we're letting you have Livy because of a crazy trick. Maybe all blood burns blue in that fire, or the knife itself does it. I am most definitely not the blood of your damn river, unless it's the Thames back home. I want to see what your knife says about me.'

Everyone looked horrified, and their bows raised to readiness again. But the crone narrowed her eyes at Barro and nodded.

'Very well, boy. If I've already committed sacrilege by letting an unconsecrated man up here, I don't suppose bleeding him will make any difference.'

She grabbed the knife from the bone woman, and pulled Barro's arm out straight. Then she cut, long and deep, across it while Barro balled his other hand into a fist. Blood gushed up from the huge slash to spill onto the floor, and the knife was covered in it. Barro pinched the gash closed at the widest part, but blood still pumped out along the wound.

The crone smiled sweetly at him, and then walked over the rising flames and thrust the blood-drenched knife in it.

Nothing happened. The flames didn't rise, and the fire's colour kept to the familiar yellows and reds. She held it in at least three times longer than she had with her own test.

'I can make another cut if you'd like? Perhaps try blood from your guts? Or further down?' The crone laughed her sharp cackle.

Barro stepped back, and Arrow helped to pull his shirt off to tie tight around the cut. The bleeding would be slowed, but she needed a needle and thread to close it off. Not that it would matter if Livy didn't pass her own test. Gods, Baja had been right, she should never have brought Livy here. Arrow wanted to grab the girl and run back down the steps.

The crone arched an eyebrow, 'So, little girl, will you stand to be tested, or shall I tell the hunters to hold you down?'

Livy stepped forward and held up her thin, smooth arm to the old witch. Her hand was steady, but Arrow could see she chewed her lip.

Llund held pressure on Barro's slit wrist, so Arrow had her hands free. If it all went wrong, could she grab the knife?

The crone made a swift small cut to the side in Livy's upper arm, away from any major veins, but enough to gather up the same amount of blood she had used to test her own.

'If this be the blood of the river, I ask the spirits to show us, and none will now dare deny it.' She looked over at Barro. 'But if it is not blood of our blood, then I declare instant death to all those who have come here, claiming a falsehood!'

Arrow scanned the platform. The men with spears were still turned towards them, although their aim did wander as they watched the old woman rather than their targets. Barro was already injured, and if he started to fight would lose blood and then consciousness. But all Arrow had eyes for now was the bone woman, who stood staring between Arrow and Livy, and she held a knife.

It was a nicely weighted, practical blade, with a simple dark wooden handle. Arrow knew it was sharp and well maintained. Because it was Arrow's own knife, taken at the pool.

The bone woman smiled. She clearly expected to use it. Arrow glanced back towards the fire, while keeping the bone woman side-on and trying to inch between her and Livy.

The crone stepped towards the flames, carrying the small smear of red on the white blade. The metal didn't blacken between each test, only the blood burned away. Livy's hand pressed against her little cut, and she watched the bobbing blade as it neared the flames.

The fire burned steady as the crone reached the blade towards it, then, with a quick shove, the old woman pushed it inside.

Nothing happened.

Livy's shoulders fell and the crone sniffed. Arrow spun back towards the bone woman to catch a look of satisfaction spread across her face. Raising the knife, the bone woman lunged towards Livy with a blood lust written across her face.

Arrow was ready and dove to block the strike, turning her back to the bone woman to wrench the blade out of her once it passed her. But the woman was terrifyingly fast, and as Arrow's arm came up her enemy dropped and twisted. Arrow managed to smash her elbow hard down into the bone woman's face, but the blade struck home, tearing into Arrow's body.

As the blade plunged between her ribs, Arrow couldn't help crying out. From all around, it was echoed back.

The entire platform of people, and everyone on the pyramid below, were screaming.

The Kalends of Februarius, Londinium

MDCL, Aurelian Calendar

CHAPTER XIX

'Why are you crying, what do you need?'

The newly minted governess had never been this tired. Oh, Arrow had lain awake many nights before wondering if tomorrow would be her last alive. She'd shivered through days of sleepless fever when a battle wound became infected. She'd even once fought in three consecutive nights of giant Arena combats recreating, with the verisimilitude of blood and death, wars the Imperium Romanum had won.

But compared to caring for an infant, Arrow regretted every time she'd previously complained of exhaustion.

'Do you want milk? To be changed?'

She knew that the small squirming and screaming thing couldn't answer. But after weeks cooped up alone with the baby she had taken to talking to it.

Livia, the child was called. Arrow had called her a few other less pretty names when the shrieking wouldn't stop.

She'd first heard the grating sound before even seeing the child.

After she abandoned the Arena, bondsmen had escorted her to a small garret in the city, giving her no indication of her fate. She'd been relieved on walking up the stairs that the building was far too shoddy and plain to be a brothel.

Far too shoddy and plain for the smartly suited Consul Derain she met standing in the main room.

There were no pleasantries when he saw Arrow.

'Girl, was I correctly informed you attended the Academy and trained under Dia Agrippina Severina?' Even his voice was too resonant and rich for the humble room.

'Yes, sir,' Arrow answered, speaking over the sound of screaming in what she assumed was a neighbouring apartment.

'You are competent in rhetoric, law, history, dialectics and calculi?'

If this was an interview rather than a purchase, she wasn't safe from the whoremongers yet.

'And poetics, music and philosophy,' she answered. If demanded, she would recite, write or perform. These weren't the skills she expected to need when sold on but, gods, they were the ones she most prized. She ground her jaw and, for the first time in her life, didn't force herself to stop.

Consul Derain was holding the bridge of his nose with eyes half shut, as if trying to wish himself away from the piercing screeches through the thin walls.

'I suppose those will be acceptable too, but you will prioritise teaching the grammaticus curriculum. Is that clear?'

'Yes sir,' Arrow answered. Then risked asking, 'Teach who?'

It took him a single step to open a low door, through which walked a wide-eyed woman, wearing the white pinafore of a nursemaid.

Writhing in her arms was the source of the screams, which had raised a decibel now it was in the room.

'I require a governess for this child, called Livia. She is to be fed, clothed and educated.'

Governess. Not whore, miner or latrine cleaner. To become a governess was beyond any dream Arrow had leaving the Arena. Respectable, clean and gentle work.

'You will maintain strict Imperium Romanum propriety and avoid unnecessary – ' for a moment, Derain seemed unsure of the appropriate word – 'coddling.' He went on at clipped speed as if anxious to be away from the ear-splitting sounds. 'You may wonder why I would purchase someone such as yourself for this role. I know exactly what you are: a killer.' Arrow managed not to flinch at his words, her hope now master of her horror. 'But I require this infant to be kept safe, and secret. Her education is secondary to those *absolute* rules. Safe, and secret. Break them and I will sell you on without hesitation. Attempt to contact my office and you will return to the bonds market. You are not a natural governess to a child, but you are naturally ruthless. The Academy and the Arena, you have skills from both. Use them.'

With that, the interview was over. Derain didn't touch the child, waving the nursemaid to hand her over.

The nurse was muttering over the loud bundle. As the two came over to Arrow, the new governess wondered at their similarity. Both nurse and baby had black hair and skin darker than Londinium residents' usual pallor. As she took the bundle in her own arms, Arrow didn't recognise whatever language the other woman used as a last benediction over the child.

Consul Derain hadn't looked at Livia once, and left the garret without any goodbye, trailing the softly weeping nurse.

To Arrow, it felt like the baby had screamed ever since.

Now, with the walls of their garret closing in and sleep a distant memory, Arrow tried again.

'Is it too hot in here? Or do you want another blanket?'

The tiny red face, punctuated with a deep black hole for hollering, wailed on.

Arrow wouldn't allow herself regret. She stood beside the crib wearing a new green dress and petticoats. Petticoats! With the long sleeves and high neck, none of her scars were visible. In the few times she'd left the garret, pushing the giant old perambulator she'd found in the bedroom, shopkeepers and passers-by had nodded or smiled at her. In her gladiator days, they would stare with fright or fascination.

Despite Consul Derain's warning, Arrow had not yet felt the need to draw the blade hidden in her sash. The garret hadn't taken long to secure. There were even a few books, a comfortable chair by a fire and an old nux board with just one or two pieces missing.

If it wasn't for the hysterically bawling baby, this would be the most perfect place to escape from what she had been. From everyone she was refusing to think about.

'You have everything you need, Livia. You're safe, fed, warm and when you're old enough I'll teach you science rather than swordplay. So, why in Hades' name are you still screaming?'

Even Arrow's voice had started to change. The threatening drawl of the gladiator replaced by the pleading fuss of the governess.

Fingers curling into fists, Arrow's scalp constricted with a building headache. Why was this sound so impossible to ignore? She'd heard enough screaming before, she'd caused a great deal of it. Never had she imagined the wailing of a child could be worse than that of a fatally injured man. Of course, out on the Arena sand you knew dying screams would, eventually, stop.

Be tolerant to others and harsh with yourself. That was a maxim she must have learnt at the Academy rather than the Arena.

But . . . there was one thing she hadn't tried. Her heart knew why she hadn't, but her splitting head was finally ready to overrule her reluctance.

Arrow leaned into the crib and picked up the warm bundle.

Rather than handling the child as she had been doing, like a weapon that needed cleaning, instead she held the little body against her own and rocked it. The smell from the baby's head ripped open wounds and memories, but Arrow had been hurt so many times before she didn't falter at the pain. She walked around the room, letting the little head nestle into her collarbone, stroking the child's back.

'Don't cry, Livy.'

The screams became whimpers. Arrow paced as if guarding the perimeter of a tiny encampment.

'Don't cry, dearest.'

As Livy snuffled to a sweet silence, there was no one to see if her new governess smiled, or cried, or both.

The Ides of Quintilis, Amazonial Forest

MDCLVII, Aurelian Calendar

CHAPTER XX

As the blade slid into Arrow on the pyramid, at last a bright blue flame shot up from Livy's blood.

The entire pyramid exploded with screams of people wild with joy. Many wept and jostled each other to embrace Livy, Llund and even Barro. Waves of them crowding up from the pyramid steps below.

The bone woman fell backwards with Arrow's bloodied dagger in her hand, watching the blue fire crackle against the dark sky. She turned back to Arrow, but then stumbled away down the pyramid steps.

For the first few seconds, Arrow's pierced side just tingled. She bunched up a handful of her hessian dress, pushing it against the wound. Then a soaring heat spread out from it, burning like she'd been branded rather than stabbed. She knew a slicing agony would hit soon, and her mind would start to jumble.

Arrow needed to reach Livy. Gripping her side as a slick of warm wetness pulsed out from beneath the dress, Arrow elbowed into the crowd, shouting the girl's name against the tide of people.

The crone parted the sea and grabbed her by her shoulders.

'Livy is safe. My life on it. You are not, Empire woman.'

Arrow struggled, but her hands slipped in her own blood, vision losing focus. The wise woman tore the side of her dress and sucked between teeth as she probed the injury. *Damn*, that hurt now. The crone clicked her tongue, and two other women, older and stockier than the warriors but with strong arms and set jaws, bustled around them. The nearest lifted Arrow away towards the pyramid steps. She tried to struggle but the blood was pulling out her energy as it flowed down her side. Arrow tried to shout for Livy, but it came out as a whimper. As the old witch turned back towards the celebration, Arrow, fighting to stay focused, swore the old woman winked at her.

Half-carrying, half-pushing her down the steps, one of the matrons pinched against the edges of Arrow's wound. The pressure sent more spearing pain stabbing deep into her, but these ladies clearly understood blade injuries. The stumbling group reached a well-lit building, and Arrow tripped when she spotted a face grinning up at her from one of the low beds within it. She recognised those eyes, last seen widening in shock as she skewered the warrior on the charnot roof. Now that woman was here, lying back, bandaged and somehow happy to see her.

Clearly, Arrow had lost way too much blood.

It didn't take much for the two healers to force her down onto a low cot, fold open the hessian dress and start bathing the wound. The crone shuffled in soon after, leading Barro, the shirt held around his cut arm now a wad of blood with a face above it much paler than it should be.

'Livy!' Arrow had meant to demand, but it came out as a hiss.

The crone tutted, 'The girl is safe with my youngest grandchild. All our people wanted to welcome her, but she kept yelling for "Miss, Miss", which I suppose means you. I sent them to rest in a room nearby. She is proved blood of the river, no one will touch her.'

With that, the crone sat Barro on the edge of another bed and waved over one of the matrons to bind his arm.

'Bone, lung or just a scratch?' Barro called over to her, wincing as the matron unstuck the bloodied shirt.

'Scratch, I think.' Arrow coughed.

'Hmmm. Alke tends to cut deep,' the crone muttered, probing around the wound. Then she tutted again, but her shoulders dropped as if releasing tension.

'Perhaps you are the Panthera, with the luck of the gods. It's unlike Alke to miss a killing stroke.'

She waved her arm out without looking away from her patient and a helper handed over a thin needle. Arrow gritted her teeth. She hated this part.

Each stitch pulled at raw skin, sending shooting fire up over her shoulder and down to her hip. The crone jabbed the needle, again and again, making small and neat sutures. That would help the wound heal well in the long run, but for now it extended the agony, piercing and pulling without end.

Arrow lay immobile, clenched her fists and sweated.

She didn't cry out. Not out of pride in front of the Amazonials, but if Livy was nearby she dearly hoped the girl had fallen asleep after such an exhausting day. The screams of her governess wouldn't help with that.

'Alke is a good warrior and leads our defence, but the river didn't gift her with much patience,' the crone said, wiping away a little more blood.

'She didn't want the fire to burn blue,' Arrow replied through her clenched teeth.

'Of course she didn't. Would you want some unknown girl taking your place?'

'What? Why would Livy take her place? She's just a little kid,' Barro asked.

'Who is daughter of a queen.'

The crone dropped onto a small stool and the blue lights in the room deepened the shadows within her wrinkles.

'Livy wasn't taken without reason. Indeed, there is more reason than even Alke knows.' She paused and started to wipe Arrow's blood from her hands. 'Livy's mother, Queen Teuta, was Alke's older sister. Alke always knew she would serve her sister, leading the warriors while the Queen led our people.' The woman looked up from her cloth and met Arrow's eye. 'Alke mourned her sister after she died, but she has asked me to name her Queen, because Teuta died without a daughter. Now, an heir has appeared and Alke must serve her niece? That's a hard ask, for a proud heart.'

The old woman sighed and leaned forward to begin bandaging over her careful stitches in Arrow's side. While Arrow lay back, the pain in her side ebbing, a tightness in her chest began growing.

In coming here, Arrow had imagined Livy running around with other children, carefree, wanted, belonging. But she was so Imperium-minded, the fact that the river queens would have their own power structures hadn't occurred to her. Now Livy faced responsibilities, and rivals. While it may be the mark of a wise man not to rail against the gods in misfortune, Arrow thought perhaps she could be allowed to rail against herself.

'I thought Livy would be safe here.'

Arrow hadn't realised she said that out loud until the crone answered, 'This forest is safe no more. Your Livy is of the river blood, a Queen of queens. And even more than that.' The crone clicked her tongue as her hands felt down Arrow's abdomen, pressing and searching for any internal bleeding. Then, fingers pressing just below Arrow's belly, the crone stopped and sucked air in between her teeth again.

Arrow's eyes flew open, and she grabbed the wizened arm. The old woman's nostrils flared, lips pursed in a dark fury she'd not shown up on the pyramid.

'This was from violence,' the old woman hissed, pressing into an old wound no one could see.

'Long ago.' Arrow held the crone's gaze despite the waves of pain flowing through her.

The old woman turned and Arrow was surprised Barro didn't

fall from his seat, the daggers from the crone's eyes bored into him with such intensity. But he was looking down at a healer bathing his cut.

Arrow slowly repeated, 'long ago', not requesting the crone's silence, but demanding it, as every woman had the right to. She didn't lessen her grip on the arm and the old face turned back and then softened. The woman sighed, as if weary of the world's pains. Then she lifted her hand from Arrow's belly and deftly finished tying off the bandage as if nothing had happened.

No purpose in thinking about old wounds when current ones are so pressing.

'Why does the girl call you "Miss", like you two are strangers? You are the Inguz, or Arrow, as your man names you.' The old woman's tone was chatty as if her rage had never been. Arrow breathed out, even though this question was almost as hard to answer.

How could she explain that, all those years ago, she couldn't teach Livy to call her 'mama', of course, but that hearing her battle-name in the mouth of a baby would be horrifying. So, she'd simply not taught anything, and Livy had picked up the name 'Miss' from what market stallholders and postmen called her.

'Miss' was the only thing she'd ever enjoyed being called, except the secret name her mother had used for her.

'No one knows my real name, anyway,' was all Arrow managed.

'Well then, no-name woman, I have sewn up your wound and my stiches now need you to sleep.'

Arrow almost laughed at the idea, but the draught of milky liquid offered by one of the healers was just out of her hand before her head fell back into the soft animal skins lining her cot. Half-truths and hints swirled in her head. But she fell asleep thinking on her own faults rather than those of others.

The next morning, Livy woke her by sprinting into the healers' rooms, then skidding to a halt. The injured warrior, Kepes, just rolled back over to sleep but Barro sat up, rubbing his eyes and checking his bandage.

'Oh, Miss.' The girl chewed her lip.

Arrow pulled herself up to half-sit and tried to will colour into her cheeks as she smiled. 'Don't worry, Livy dearest. It was just an accident and I'm all patched up now.'

Livy scratched her heel on the packed mud flooring and chewed her lip even harder. Behind her, another girl hovered in the wide entrance. A little taller than Livy and clothed like the other river children, in a hessian wrap dress and long plait of dark hair, with feathers in it.

Arrow couldn't take her eyes from the child's face.

'You! You're the girl on the river. How?'

The girl played with the end of her plait, and said, 'Livy, she told me, you thought I got all burnt up?'

'Yes . . . I saw it. The flamethrower hit your canoe!'

'I was sent to test the convoy. Alke wanted to see how far they would go. I paddled in sight of the monsters, but I didn't think they would attack me. Then, someone shouted a warning, and I was ready.'

'But . . . but, how? How did you survive?'

The feathered girl looked between Arrow and Barro, both staring at her.

Then the girl shrugged. 'Every river queen can swim.'

Arrow levered herself back down off her elbows, hit by tiredness like a long exhale. Since the flamethrower had incinerated the little canoe, that image of the burning embers on the water had haunted her. The memory returned in waking and sleeping, every time she saw a young girl's plait or the red and blue feathers.

Finding the child alive was like waking from a fever she didn't know she'd had.

'Can I take Livy to the river?' the girl asked. 'She can't swim! I must teach her before the others find out.'

'Oh, please, Miss, me and Sosia will be so careful, pleeeeease.' Livy's smile lit up.

Barro turned to Arrow. 'That's not a bad idea, considering where we are.'

Sosia. The name of Livy's true cousin.

'Very well,' Arrow said, pleased the girls had even asked. Because who was she to still decide Livy's fate now she was back with her family? Livy gave a whoop so loud it made her new friend jump. 'But stay in shallow water,' Arrow added.

'Yes, Miss!' Livy grabbed Sosia's hand, and the two ran off.

Arrow stared up at the simple roof of neat bundled dried reeds. Livy off playing with other children in her true family. It was what she'd wished for, yet her heart felt as pierced as her ribs.

The sunlight was warm, and the humidity wasn't too unbearable yet. The whistles, whoops and chirps of birds were constant, a strange music at different tempos and rhythms that somehow made a coherent whole. Deeper calls sprang from other beasts, swinging between the vines or digging into the wet soil. A burst of laughter from children and chatter of families on the lodges nearby filtered through.

'Not quite what we expected, is it?' Barro said.

'I read about the Amazonial back in Londinium, in the newspapers. It just sounded like the Britannia countryside, but with bigger trees. It's more than that, though. I feel slower here, deeper—' She stopped herself, and snorted. 'Must be the bloody heat.'

'Do you miss home?'

'I miss proper tea, reading books to Livy, playing nux together.' Arrow closed her eyes.

'You know that old witch isn't telling you everything.' Barro's voice carried an edge to it. 'She keeps making little hints. Staying here might not be as easy as you think.'

Arrow rolled over towards him, wincing a little.

'I know, Livy becoming the Queen here was more threat than promise.'

'Well, as an unconsecrated bloke I'm basically the lowest of the low. Like a little boy, one of the healers told me last night. No one is going to tell me anything, especially after I was so rude and challenged their test, even though I got sliced for my trouble.'

'Why did you do that, Barro?' At the time she'd wanted to punch him. 'Bringing Livy here was our only plan. By doubting the test, you risked everything.'

Barro's face had been soft, but now his sardonic smile flicked back into place.

'For a god, Inguz, or Panthera, or whoever you are today, you can be bloody stupid.'

People seemed at pains to keep pointing that out to her, as if she didn't already know. But the healing women bustled in before Arrow could reply, and they started to push her back down into the cot to rest and drink more healing draughts.

Barro turned away to have his dressing replaced. The woman treating him clicked her tongue. 'The skin heals well. You can go with hunters now, become a man.'

Despite feeling she'd already offended him, Arrow couldn't help a burst of laughter.

'I'll bloody hunt whatever you want, if that's what it needs to be taken seriously around here,' Barro said to the women shooing him out of the healers' rooms towards a rather nervous delegation of teenage boys who were waiting for him. The Amazonials were eager to consecrate the rogue male in their midst. Well, he was good with a bow and had more training than the other men could even begin to understand.

'Go consecrate yourself, Barro,' Arrow called to his retreating back through the open door. His tall blond head stood out as the men slipped under the trees, but he matched their fluidity and stealth.

Arrow rotated her shoulders a little to test her side.

The stab wound was fresh, but the healing skin hadn't swollen or puckered overnight. Whatever they were giving her to drink was fortifying her blood better than anything medicinal the Arena had offered her. The fresh pain layered over an older ache, from her shoulder's dislocation aboard the *Flyer*. Wounds upon wounds. Well, another scar wasn't going to lose her any friends here.

Through the open rattan blinds next to her bed, Arrow watched women plaiting large red and yellow flowers into the awnings of buildings. Men built up an intricate, tall bonfire in a cleared space at the centre of the plain. The sound of the maize she could see being pounded and children getting in the way of everything rippled across the clearing.

'Feast tonight!' Kepes had woken and followed her gaze out of the window. 'To welcome back Livy-girl, blood of the river.'

Arrow tried to smile. Lying around an unfamiliar camp without any reconnaissance was making her squirm.

Her green Empire-style dress, the full skirt clean but frayed, had been left at the end of her bed, along with her sandals. The sash was there, with the Inguz stone resting on Octavia's folded handkerchief. But no knife.

All she had worn in the healers' tent so far was a light loin cloth under a soft blanket. She struggled into her skirt and blouse, grimacing at every movement. In Londinium, a dress without petticoats would be indecent. Here the wide metal-boned skirt would mark her out as a stranger.

Arrow briefly wished she could be as comfortable as Livy and Barro, who had both changed into Amazonial clothing. But as she fastened her small mother-of-pearl buttons she knew it would take more than a day to convince her to wear nothing more than a hessian slip.

Before one of the healers could order her back to bed, she went to slip out. Kepes frowned at her and even tutted – pointing at her wound – which admittedly throbbed, and her head felt foggy. Arrow blinked at the warrior woman. On the charnot she'd pierced Kepes' lung; her own wound was a graze by comparison.

Arrow had to get out, to see this world she'd brought Livy into.

As she wandered, the men and women of the camp smiled and nodded at her, but none approached. Children either hid behind parents or ran up to her with great boldness, only for their courage to desert them as soon as she turned to say 'Hello'. Then they'd run back to their parents, who lifted, hugged and laughed indulgently at them. Scrutinising these people of the forest Arrow noticed how close they stood to each other. An older woman was peeling the green leaves off maize corn, her daughter leaning her head on the mother's shoulder. The girl was older than Livy. A man ruffled a boy's hair, then kissed his forehead before shooing him away to play. None of them stood in tense propriety, as if the gods were judging them.

Or perhaps their own gods were watching, and they wanted their people to show something other than indifference and decorum.

Her feet took her past storage sheds, with crates and boxes stacked under leaf roofs to keep the afternoon rain off. Arrow expected stolen cargo from charnot convoys and banditry, and she did spot some oil barrels and even a tumbled pile of oil lamps. But as she leaned into the darkness, the speckled light through the reed walls let her pick out Frisian markings on large containers. Perhaps they had travelled in the hold of the *Flyer*, as she had done.

Arrow felt a sharp twang of pain in her chest thinking of Captain Baja. Then she caught a familiar smell on the air, sulphur and sweat, which drew her to a group of outbuildings set away from the main village. Hammers rang upon metal and her nostrils burned with fire sparks from heated steel.

As a girl, she had loved to watch the blacksmiths beat and temper the weapons for the Arena.

Here in the Amazonial smithy, older people in thick hessian wraps worked the metal. A white-haired woman was even blowing delicate glass. It was mesmerising to watch, and Arrow knew better than to get too close. Giant, sweaty and soot-covered blacksmiths had chased her away from Arena forges enough times in the past.

A man and woman lifted a cylinder, then poured the white and red molten steel, running with the consistency of toffee before it set. The smiths' movements were steady but swift to beat and cool. Weapons were piled in every corner: arrowheads, swords, knives and things like arc guns, but larger and with wires dangling from them. Even as the rest of the camp busied themselves with cooking and decorating for a great celebration, the blacksmiths didn't stop their labour.

'Soon, the Empire will feel the bite of those weapons.'

The old Druid, Llund, stood by her shoulder, the sparks from the forge flickering in his eyes.

Arrow snorted. 'The Arena in Londinium boasts a forge larger than this, day and night it runs, making swords merely for mock battles and circuses.'

'You felt the touch of our light rods. The Empire has nothing like them!'

Llund gestured towards where an elderly woman tested one of the strange large arc guns against a straw-filled dummy. Where the tip touched the hessian covering, lightning sparks were visible even in the bright sunlight, and the smell of singed fabric wavered over.

'That's what you hit me with, under the pub.' Arrow's voice was flat.

Llund bowed low. 'Pain without death is a powerful weapon.'

Arrow wouldn't let him see her shudder, remembering the shafts of heat coursing through her body. But the trained killer in her assessed the weapon coldly. It had dropped her, but not ended her. And you could only use it on one enemy at a time.

'The Legions are armed with *millions* of arc guns and Vulcan machines, and they are designed to kill again and again. A little lightning won't stop them. You dream, Llund.'

'I dream of freedom, Inguz. A slave should understand. Especially one trained by the Academy.'

Arrow wondered if Dia Agrippina Severina would be able to

maintain her genteel politeness if introduced to Llund. Perhaps she'd want to analyse him, like a dove in a jar.

'You know a lot about me, Llund.'

The old man smiled as if he hadn't noticed the edge in her voice. 'Oh yes, Inguz, we studied you and Livia for months to be sure she was the child we sought.'

Arrow had thought about that day in the museum so many times, the rabble coincidentally turning up. Her failure to spot Livy was being watched.

'You followed us to the museum, didn't you, you'd already planned to take Livy?'

'To liberate the child from her captor, yes.'

Arrow's fists clenched, but Llund turned and bowed to her.

'Had we known you were the Inguz, her champion, we would never have attempted to tear her from you.'

'Stop with that god crap, Llund. You deliberately left the damn stone for me to find.' She pulled it out of her sash and watched him deflate a little. But he didn't dispute it, and his silence was as good as a confession.

'What else have you lied about?'

He pulled himself straight. 'What does it matter how the stone came to you, Inguz? You carry the greatest talisman of the Iceni, the most powerful in all Albus itself.'

'It's just a stone.' Arrow was going to throw it into the forest, but somehow still gripped it in her clenched hand.

'You are the Inguz, whether you hold the stone or no. The sword, her protector.'

The pain in Arrow's side throbbed in offence at the word. She'd failed Livy in almost every way. Hadn't searched for answers about her origins, so happy in their little bubble together. She'd been too witless to protect her from abduction. Livy had to save *her* in the charnot battle. Only some stupid blue flame had prevented Alke killing her on the pyramid.

Worse than it all, for years she'd played at being a 'respectable' governess, doling out rules and reciting long-dead philosophers to the girl. Livy would get more hugs and warmth here than Arrow had ever given in cold Londinium.

Arrow's laugh cracked. 'She has a family, Llund. Wasn't that the whole point of you taking her? I'm nothing more than baggage, now.'

'Your destiny is together – to end the storms!'

Arrow blinked, trying to understand the madman's ranting. 'What the Hades, Llund? The Godstorms?' He'd said something like this on the pyramid, but she'd assumed it was just bluster to impress the old witch.

Arrow realised she had seen faces like Llund's before. In Londinium, condemned criminals were offered a choice – hang, or fight in the Arena. Most often the bouts were unpopular 'opening acts' on a festival day. Untrained, desperate men, hastily armed in ill-fitting armour, wielded weapons they'd chosen because they looked big and powerful. Facing a trained gladiator, a killing machine. But in the felons' eyes, there was always a wild, feverish hope. Perhaps, against all odds, they would win their freedom.

'Yes! Together, you and Livy are fated to throw down the false gods of oil! Break the drills that despoil Eiocha, stealing her blood and fouling the air. Melt the Empire charos into ploughs, raze their cities back to farms! You will lead Livia's armies and crush the oil-glutted Citizens so our gods can breathe again!'

Of course, out on the sand, the true gladiators cut down the criminals like they were corn, every time.

'Lead her armies? Llund, your gods have left you mad.'

Arrow went to walk away, but Llund darted around her, panting and red-eyed, his hands in supplication.

'A child raised by a sword; a sword hidden by a gown. Livy coming here, to the Amazonials, is the spark! I will return to Britannia and raise our people in her name. Stories of your courage already circulate across the Frisian Sea. You saved the Amazonial girl from the

Vulcan flames by calling a warning. You fought their champion. Whispers travel across the forest to the other river nations. Multitudes prepare to follow your child into battle.'

'Livy's not my child, Llund, and she isn't yours either.'

Arrow's wound throbbed and temples ached. It was too hot, and her dress stuck against her. Although her heart felt cold in a burning body.

'You cannot hinder it. The Inguz is the weapon. Livia is the war child. We have waited for a legend like yours, and it has begun. The rivers will run with Empire blood, and we *will* be free.'

Spit was caught in the edge of his tangled beard. The forest was too hot for this zealot rot.

'I'm not a sword, nor a god. I'm a slave,' Arrow said.

Enough.

Enough of gods and storms and invented prophecies.

Her hands whipped out by their own volition and grabbed Llund by his throat, his oily beard scratching against her fingers as she pressed, hard, into his windpipe. Arrow dragged him towards her face, despite sudden pain in her side, his weak grip clutching at the green silk slicked to her arms.

'I'm a slave, Llund. A brutal, violent guard dog. And I swear, I will break your neck if you whisper any more of this madness to Livy. Now, nod if you understand me.'

He winced affirmation and fell to the ground massaging his neck as she released him.

Arrow strode back across the lush, springy grasses and deep rich earth. Wishing she had Londinium cobbles under her heels. Where was Livy?

'No one can escape destiny!' he called after her.

That was what the gods taught man. Why each class within the Empire – Citizen, Plebeian and indentured – must accept their place as foretold. Why the child of a slave gladiator must also fight and kill in the Arena. Why a child without a family must remain an orphan.

Why Livy must start a war.

Well, sod the gods, both old and new. Arrow pressed her palm against her wound.

She would either find a way or make one. *Livy would be free.*

As the afternoon wore on Arrow rested, had her dressing replaced and drank more of the healing tonics. She watched the grandiose sunset spill over the wide clearing across which busy people gathered. Clean hessian, bright feathers and carefully applied paints reminded her of the top hats, satin dresses and colourful toga sashes of Citizens gathering before an Arena bout.

Livy returned damp and beaming from her first swimming lesson. She now darted through the gathering people with Sosia, both girls giggling with the excitement. Sometimes, Livy would stop in her tracks and glance back to Arrow, grinning. Satisfied her governess was there, she would grab Sosia's hand again to continue getting under everyone's feet.

The slip of Octavia's handkerchief was folded in Arrow's sash. She shook her head; too much of frail hope to hang a child's future on. Was Livy to be a Citizen, orphan, Queen or some prophesised warmonger?

The option of just 'child' wasn't being offered by anyone.

As the sun dipped below the line of the trees, it shot out a final burst of light, and the bonfire erupted with a roaring flame in the same moment. In the gathering darkness, pipes welled up, both hollow and deep. The crowd started to stamp along to the sound, clicking with their fingers and swaying. Meats, freshly cooked and running with juices, were handed around spiked on sticks.

The smell made Arrow's stomach growl, but she walked away from the healers' lodge to the far side of the fire. In the shadows, she watched.

'I caught it, you should eat it.'

Barro could have been any of the hunters, with paints darting across his bare chest, wearing a hessian skirt and feathers in his quiver.

'Hunting has made me a man now, apparently.' His lopsided grin was in full force. 'Still can't fight people though. Only women can take a human life here, because they also bring life into the world. Men feed whoever's left.'

'I'm not hungry, Barro.'

He turned to look at her in the firelight, grin replaced with concern.

'Doesn't matter, Arrow, you know that. Meat's best for a wound.'

She ignored him. Close to the fire some of the warrior women, painted and armoured as they had been the day of the charnot raid, started to spar. It wasn't serious, more like dancing, as they lunged and parried with curved swords and shields. The gladiator in her thrilled to the movement.

'What's up, Arrow? You look like you lost a fight to a blind Andabata in a festival bout.'

Barro looked so comfortable, fitting into the river camp as a natural. She stood there, in her mock Empire dress, trying not to notice the sly glances and half-looks directed at her. She moved further back into the covering darkness, with Barro following behind her.

'Why are you here, Barro? Don't you have a life, even a family, back in Londinium, waiting for you?'

It had been years since she'd walked out of the Arena. A rich merchant would have slave women and servants, and Barro could be charming if he chose. What life and loves had he left to follow them to this jungle?

'Doesn't every man want to see the world, Arrow? Oh, Londinium does have its charms, and I've enjoyed most of them. But today, I wrestled some black snake the length of two men, and then hunted a giant long-nosed pig for our dinner. Beats another day cheating at cards in the back room of pubs, trading for city gossip.'

'You're here for an adventure, then? Bored of the Londinium whores and taverns?'

Arrow expected him to storm off in offence, or at least quip back a barbed comment. Instead, he just stood in flickering firelight, watching the river people celebrate Livy's return.

'The boys here, we talked a bit on the hunt. They're all certain, as sure as Londinium rain, that in the deep forest the trees will protect you. They will feed, clothe and shelter anyone – if you learn their ways. You can live out a life without ever coming across another person. We could answer only to the birds, the leaves and the sky.'

Years ago, they had whispered to each other about freedom, wrapped together on the sand of the Arena. Of escaping – no bosses, no orders, no fights, no gods.

'You'd run away then, Barro? To live in this wild forest.'

In the half dark his answer came as a whisper just above the drums around the fire and haunting clicks and whistles of the night forest: 'Yes . . . with you.'

Without realising it, she leaned back against his chest. As if in rhythm with the drums, Barro's arms circled her waist. His breath slow against her neck, he dipped to kiss a small scar behind her ear. She'd got it many years ago, one of her first in a bout with him. Barro remembered her body, to know where to brush his lips.

In the darkness one hand moved down her body, the other hand moved up, her body stiffening against his featherlight touch even in the warmth.

She turned into him, and their lips met. They had always been the softest part of him. The smell of his body so familiar it was like her own. To feel the lips of the man she'd last known so long ago swirled so many memories that none could land.

The thin silk of her dress was like another skin, trapped between their bodies. Barro's fingers traced a seam from her waist up to breasts more used to the protection of a corset.

Falling back into tall grasses on the edge of the forest, she found a body she already knew. Arrow could tell the story of his scars, some wounds she'd sewn up herself, others she'd given him. He should taste of distance, a life she didn't know. Instead, he felt like coming home.

His hand moved up under her skirts, along the inside of her thigh.

Disappearing into the trees together was the most beautiful idea that Arrow had heard for a long time. Two misfit souls, living out their lives in the deep forest's heart, far from Empires, wars and hard decisions. Hunting, loving, forgetting.

From the darkness, Arrow caught sight of Livy.

The girl's eyes were blazing and feet dancing, spinning around with her new friend in the light by the fire.

Arrow sighed, in danger of it falling into a sob, but she pulled away from Barro, trusting that his hands would fall.

'Barro, all I want is a home for Livy, nothing more. I hoped she might find it here. And she would, I know it. If they let her.'

His voice was thick, 'I don't know what you're worrying about, looks like she already has.'

Down by the fire, Livy and Sosia mock fought each other. Sosia was taller, but Livy used every trick her governess had taught her, darting under strikes, blocking and ducking. She even managed to land a few hits on her older opponent, which she then undermined by bursting into giggles.

Warriors and hunters stopped to watch the two girls, nudging and nodding to each other.

'We might be happy, Arrow.' There was no cheap laughter in his voice.

She turned to look down at him, the warm red of the flames tracing the shapes and patterns painted on his body.

'Every new beginning comes from some other beginning's end,' he breathed.

But from here she could see Llund, almost out of view across the circle. The bone woman Alke was with him, as was the old crone. All three stared at Livy as she boxed and mock fought with her friend by the fire. They weren't looking at a little girl, but at a plan, an icon, a weapon.

The soft warmth she'd let her body feel was doused by a cold wave of fear.

'That may be true, Barro. But fate still tends to find a way.'

CHAPTER XXI

Arrow didn't sleep well that night. Not least because healers nursed a birthing mother in a curtained-off space behind her.

Now consecrated, Barro slept in the unwed men's building. No labour shrieks to disturb him.

The woman's screams (and curses) had started while it was still dark. Now the first pink touches of dawn sidled into the room but the shouting never lessened.

'Kepes? Are you awake?' Arrow asked.

'Yes, Panthera. Are you hurt, do you need help?'

'I'm well, Kepes. But, I want to make a gift to Alke. To prove we can be friends. Do you know where my bag is, from the convoy?'

'Good! Warriors are strong, together!' Kepes hit her chest with the palm of her hand. Arrow had known so many like her at the Arena, those who could fight like demons from Hades, but just wanted everyone to be friends.

'Yes. But I need my bag. Is it in the pyramid?'

Kepes' brows narrowed and head tilted.

Arrow tried again, 'The big Temple, with the fire on top? Is that where my things are?'

'Queen Molpadia lives in the Temple, the Mother of the River.'

That was what Arrow had hoped. She levered herself up, covering any signs of effort or pain so Kepes wouldn't call for the healers.

'I'll go and ask Livy and Sosia to find my bag for me. Perhaps I'll eat with them this morning.'

The injured warrior woman glowed as she smiled, in a way that made Arrow turn as she buttoned up her dress. Outside, the morning air was fresh before the wet curtain of humidity descended. The earth smelt of green sap and dew warming on leaves.

Arrow dodged around the edge of the lodge where she could hear Livy's piping voice chatting away to Sosia. Through the reed walls, she caught the girls discussing Londinium. Livy described their rooms: the big old chair by the fire, her few but very beloved dolls, their nux board.

There was a catch in the girl's throat telling her cousin about 'home'. Arrow stopped, arms listless at her sides. She took a step towards the door, from which girls' laughter spilled out, but didn't go through.

'Why do you say Miss, rather than calling her Inguz?' Sosia asked.

'Because she's my governess,' Livy said, as if that answered everything.

'What's a governess?'

Arrow thought that perhaps she'd missed Livy's answer, too faint to hear through the wall. But after a moment the voice came, each word careful and slow, as if Livy were thinking through her answer.

'A governess takes care of you. You live with her, and she makes your food, puts you to bed, and teaches you. If you get hurt, she looks after you. And if you get lost, she finds you.'

'So, like a mother, if you don't have one of your own,' Sosia said, without any question in her voice.

'Yes,' Livy was still talking with more deliberate care than her usual chatter, 'like a mother.'

Arrow turned on her heel and walked away, fists clenched.

If she weren't a slave. If Livy weren't daughter of a river queen. If Derain wasn't Livy's guardian. If Molpadia wasn't hiding something.

In a different world, she would have rushed through the door and caught Livy up in her arms and never let her go. Instead, the trained killer, escaped slave and failed governess walked herself away over the plain.

The blue lights hadn't been dimmed or tapered since they'd been there, another of the mysteries of the place. Well, everything unknown seems magnificent. Arrow's jaw clenched. Time to change that.

She strode on with head high and decisive steps, trying to look like it was normal for her to be heading towards the pyramid at dawn. No one stopped her and, when she reached the side closest to the jungle, she was out of sight of the buildings. Now closer to the pyramid than she'd been since that first night of Livy's testing, she stood and gaped up at it.

In the early sunrise, the pyramid glinted like solid gold. As large as the Spire back in Londinium but somehow made of bullion.

As she walked closer, it became glassier. When she crouched down to touch it, the glassy-gold was revealed as thin sheets, attached to ordinary stone beneath it. Each sheet had veins of darker metal running through to thicker arteries every few feet between the panels. It was intricate work and seemed elaborate considering that simple gold alone would be impressive enough.

The workmanship was reminiscent of the delicate but incomprehensible Druidic instruments back in the Imperium Museum. Brows knitted, she pondered the hints and riddles about 'light-lenses' on the *Flyer*, and the same blue lights hanging off their hull.

Arrow stood and allowed herself another moment to review the scale of it all. There must be thousands of the glassy gold sheets, all the way to the top. There was a purpose here, to have those panels everywhere.

Except in one spot. There was a small rough stone gap, near the base of the upper platform.

Arrow couldn't prevent a half-smile. The old crone Molpadia had her own private entrance into the pyramid.

Checking back around, she slogged up the steps, legs heavy and muscles demanding to be returned to her bed. The spot bare of panels just below the pillar wasn't easy to get to, with smooth stone around it. There must be a trick to reaching it.

Arrow jumped from a step near the top.

The puffed sleeves of her blouse didn't allow a full range of movement and her wide skirt didn't help her balance. She wished she'd accepted a hessian slip rather than wearing her Empire dress again. Especially when the rough stone scratched up her arms and calf as she scrambled for a handhold after her leap.

Once steady, Arrow checked her side; there was no sign of blood. She hadn't reopened her wound.

The small gap in the stone led to a cramped stairway downward, and Arrow cursed herself for not swiping one of the blue lamps to light the way. But it was a straight stair, and if she found no light below she could always retrace her path back upwards. As she stepped downwards into blackness, the sounds from above became distorted. She hesitated, her vision focused to reveal the edge of the steps in front, rather than finding them by feel. A soft blue light flickered ahead.

The staircase became so tight, Arrow was forced to bend double down the last few steps, her knees almost hitting her nose. At the end of the stairs hung a thick hessian curtain, with the tiniest chink of light coming through one crumpled corner. Moving with practised care, Arrow even suppressed the sound of her breath. She could hear a thumping in the space behind the curtain, as someone moved around.

Shuffling in, bowed over with head down, would be foolishly vulnerable. If it were the bone woman Alke rather than old Molpadia in there, then Arrow needed to be ready.

So, she curled herself over while perched on the final step, ignoring the tug at her wound, and then threw herself forward down the stone steps, bowling through the curtain and pouncing to her feet, hands raised and body tense.

She was surrounded by towers of metal and glass, everywhere.

The haunt of the old crone should be like a witch's lair, with animal skins hung on the walls and potions brewing in caldrons. But this room was reminiscent of the Academy — filled with tall pillars of stacked metal discs, all encased in glass, hundreds of them spaced like trees in the forest.

It was like being inside one of Dia Severina's experiments. The pillars generated a deep hum and Arrow felt like she'd bitten on a metal denarii; the tang of it set her teeth on edge.

'Those steps are designed to force a bow as you enter, to show reverence. But it does horrible things to my back, so I enjoyed your alternative.'

Molpadia stepped out from behind one of the giant grey metal coils, her amulets and bangles revealed as the same metal as the thrumming discs.

'You opened your wound.' She nodded towards Arrow's side. A small stain peeked out under the green silk. Arrow was a little ashamed she'd undone the crone's careful work.

Riffling in a drawer under what looked like a charnot control panel, Molpadia threw over a wad of bandage. 'If you take such risks with my neat stitching at least tighten the dressing.'

Catching the bundle, Arrow unbuttoned her blouse a little. She pushed the bandage in and trusted the tightness of her Empire jacket to hold it in place.

'This,' Arrow waved around her, 'it's not what I expected.'

'You're surprised? Well, consider that feeling mutual.' Molpadia sniffed. 'An Empire woman in skirts who fights? I had to order the warriors and hunters away from the healers' lodge. Everyone is cooing over your scars. The girls who were at the pool gossip constantly about the pink pucker marks on your rear. Kepes is already a little in love with you, I think.' Molpadia's sniff became a soft chuckle.

At the thought of the river women talking about her body, describing her scars, Arrow's mouth went dry, and she struggled to swallow. She wanted to shake the old woman, but her training kept her controlled. No doubt Molpadia sought to distract. But where wisdom is called for, force is of little use.

'Enough, Molpadia.' It was more of a bark than she had intended. 'Livy came here hoping for nothing more than a family. But now you say she will be Queen? Well, there's one boss here, and that's you. I'm not afraid of Alke, and Livy might be happy here. But will you let her be?'

The old woman tinkered with dials and switches on the tall pillars and the metal tang in Arrow's mouth became worse.

'Your little girl, she has our river blood, that is true. But that's not all she has in her veins. Your man, with the sun-gold hair, he knows.'

'Barro knows? He doesn't know anything. He's here by accident.'

'Perhaps. But he knows my tricks. Of course your Livy is my lost grandchild. But Alke and the others needed a little more convincing.' She smiled and clicked her tongue. 'Your man, he knew how to put on a show for the people.'

Barro had demanded his blood be tested before Livy's. To Arrow, it had seemed nothing but a stupid risk.

'It was a trick, the blue flame? And Barro knew?'

'Sometimes tricks tell the truth, and sometimes tricksters help each other. By insulting my test, your man made it easier for the others to believe.'

Arrow pressed both hands against her bleeding side, turning away from the crone. Barro, Llund, Molpadia. Everyone knew secrets about Livy; only the silly naive not-a-governess didn't understand. Perhaps she should have slunk back to the slave market and left Livy to them.

The ache demanded her attention, and the humming metal slipped into her mind, disorientating her. Molpadia was sparring with her, with words rather than weapons. Arrow's knuckles itched. She could stride over to Molpadia and shake the straight truth out of her.

Burst open the hints and riddles.

Alke wasn't here, nor any of the warriors. Just one old woman, testing her. Arrow took a deep breath even though it twinged her wound. Being angry is easy, but to be angry with the right person and to the right degree and at the right time and for the right purpose, and in the right way – that is wisdom.

'What else is in Livy's blood?'

Molpadia nodded to herself as if Arrow had passed a test.

'River water, mixed with oil.'

What stands in the way, becomes the way. If river water was the metaphor for her mother's blood, then oil . . .

'Livy's father, he's from our Imperium Romanum?'

Molpadia sighed out as if she'd been holding in a breath for a long time.

'Not *from* the Empire.' Molpadia's eyes pinned her. 'Her father *is* the Empire. Your Livia is the daughter of your old Emperor's son. She is heir to both realms.'

A coldness spread out down Arrow's limbs that had nothing to do with the spreading red seeping from her side. Livy was the old Emperor's grandchild, bastard child of the Heir Augusto.

Like all dark fairy tales, being a princess could be as much a curse as a blessing.

'The Heir came to our forests, almost ten years ago now, seeking friendship between our peoples.' Molpadia snorted. 'Searching out secrets, more like. That oil station the charnot convoys rip through the trees to reach, it was just an Academy research outpost back then. The Heir had been sent away in hope or anger by the Emperor to join their exploration. The Dias studying our forest swiftly grew bored of him and sent him to us on "diplomatic missions".'

'The Heir came in here?' Arrow asked, looking around the metal and glass interior of the pyramid.

'Hah! No, I may have trusted him with my daughter, but not with our light-lenses. What does that say about me, Empire woman? What mother nurses her secrets more than her child?'

'It's dangerous for children in your forest.' Arrow thought of the girl Sosia sent to face the flamethrower.

'The children of the Imperium Romanum are only safe because children everywhere else aren't,' Molpadia bit back. 'My daughter, Teuta, was always too entranced by Empire trappings, and when she took your Heir hunting too many times she became the prey.'

Arrow looked around the room and wondered how much that young queen had shared with her lover. How safe anywhere was for Livy now.

'Is this what you hid from him? This . . . magic?'

'There is magic here, child, it's in the souls of our people and the life of the forest. But I don't need to hide that from your Empire, they don't value it anyway. But light-lenses, yes.' Molpadia thumped her foot on the floor of the room in a proprietorial way. 'Have you smelt the stink of oil in any one of our lights?'

Arrow hadn't, nor on the *Flyer*.

'We don't pollute ourselves with oil's effula.'

Academy lessons slammed back into Arrow's memory – recollections of cooing doves and spiritus pumps.

'You know about effula? I'm sorry, Molpadia, but you're wrong. That comes naturally from living things breathing, not oil.'

The old woman's cackle was almost too theatrical. 'All those Academy lessons. But they don't even teach you oil comes from the ancient death of living things. That's why there's so much here, under our forest. And every time you spark oil alight in those monstrous engines of yours, pure effula is released.'

Arrow thought of the doves, dead in the bell jar. The smell of exhausts in the city. The calculation clicked itself together in her brain: burning oil released effula.

She could risk everything and return to the Academy and seek out Dia Agrippina Severina. Perhaps a revelation like this would nullify her crimes, win her a place as a permanent assistant. Arrow could wash beakers while Livy studied.

'You're losing blood, girl. But never fret, if you die here on my floor, the Academy won't suffer lost knowledge. Because they already know. Oh yes, the most senior Dialectics have known for years.'

'No, the Academy wouldn't hide a threat like this.' The Academy existed to serve the Empire, and effula was a poison. If it truly came from charos, then cities would be death traps.

'They're hiding more than that. Effula you call it. Poison it is, unbalancing the sky itself.' Molpadia shivered, and Arrow didn't think it was for effect. 'Nasty name for a world-killer. Not just a poison for a person, or for a whole city. It could kill off Eiocha, who you call Gaea.'

Arrow remembered the feeling of charo fumes in her throat back in the city. Crawling up her nose, making her hair and clothes feel soiled if she stood near a road, leaving the taste of metal in her mouth. She remembered the child in the slum beside the road coughing like she would never stop.

It was suddenly easy to believe those fumes could kill more than a few doves in a jar.

'I see you, little Empire woman. The god in a skirt. The sword. You now realise the world is bigger than you knew, and a lot worse, yes?'

Arrow didn't resent the jibe, she deserved it.

'I'm sick of secrets,' she said.

'Then you're living in the wrong Empire, my dear.'

Her heartbeat was pounding in her ears, but Arrow wasn't going to let either of them leave until she knew everything.

'What is this place, Molpadia? Really? The golden glass, the blue lights. The Frisians have them too. What else are you hiding?'

'Nothing can be concealed from the Panthera, you are a god after all.' Molpadia's tone was only half-mocking. 'You saw correctly. Our Temple works like those Frisian light-lenses. Long ago, my people learnt how to harvest light and warmth from above rather than from below. Using our alchemy and geometry to capture Sol's rays, not

Gaea's blood. We shared our knowledge with the Anglish Druids, who gifted it to the pirates. Our golden panels are an idea, another way, spread carefully amongst those who stand against the Empire. It's why we go to war against oil. Their world-killer isn't even necessary.'

Arrow wanted time to think, to work out Livy's role in all this. 'You should have shown this place, this power, to the Heir,' she said. 'If they know oil causes effula they must be searching for something exactly like this.'

Molpadia pulled a small wooden stool from behind a thrumming pillar. Rough-hewn and simple, it made the tall light-engines in the room even more fantastical.

'You misunderstand me. Your Emperor, Consul Derain and the senior men of the Academy have known about our light-lenses since they first visited us. We taught those Dias, and they listened politely, dissecting our glass panels and blue lights we gave them. I expected to see giant light-lenses spring up across the Empire.' When Molpadia laughed, this time Arrow thought it was at herself. 'Instead, as soon as they discovered oil in our forests, they started seeking out our panels, and our wind catchers. They smashed them into nothing but shards. As many as they could find. Academy men along with Legionaries, dragging those with knowledge of this power away. I was one of the last with the knowledge, which is why I shared it beyond our kingdom. Believe me, I was not hiding knowledge from the Empire when I sent my daughter into the arms of your Heir. I was hiding myself.'

Arrow remembered so many lectures, held in halls built like small amphitheatres, where the great men of the Academy revealed, layer by layer, the nature of the universe, of life itself. Teaching her, however unwillingly they did it, what she needed to know.

They wouldn't lie or destroy knowledge like this. Why would they need to? Students were taught that findings from an experiment were never 'right' or 'wrong', they were just data, more evidence on the road to enlightenment. If burning oil in charos caused effula, and if effula was dangerous, then study it. And build giant temples of the glassy gold panels everywhere. Plaster them all over the Spire itself!

The Spire of oil. The Temples to Gaea's blood.

The Imperium Romanum *was* oil. Arrow massaged her forehead as if trying to fit a new model of the world into it.

Oil formed the bedrock of the Empire's power. The Londinium papers often accused the Jade Empire of squeezing oil prices in exchange for tea, spices and precious silks. Revealing that Gaea's blood might cause sickness when burned, or even whatever worse damage Molpadia hinted at, that would give the Eastern traders even more reason to cut their payments. And if there was an alternative, one that the Empire didn't have a grip on? With another source of energy, why would anyone need to trade with the Empire at all?

Of course the powerful men would hide their knowledge, and keep destroying every hint of it apart from a few blue lights they couldn't reach out at sea, or in the deep forest.

Arrow remembered Dia Severina fighting for years to publish her paper on how effula killed the doves. Even though it didn't even hint at any of this. Back then, Arrow had assumed her teacher's troubles were caused by gentlemen of the Academy recoiling at a lady scientist making such a discovery. Dia Severina herself had certainly thought so, raging at them confusing skirts and science.

But perhaps Dia Severina's revelations were a small truth far too close to a big secret.

The Empire would burn the oil, even if that burned them all.

Unless someone forced their hand. Found a way to rouse all the peoples suffering under the heel of the Legions. Arrow understood why the Amazonials and Frisians wanted war. Even though she knew they would likely lose it.

Consul Derain must not sleep very well, thinking of all the ways the Empire could be rocked by this.

'Livy's a threat.'

'More than you know.' Molpadia nodded. 'A child of Imperial blood? She can be a powerful tool in the war to come. The Consul knows this. He took her as insurance against us. Perhaps even as a weapon against the Heir. To be used at the right moment.'

'A tool? A weapon?' Arrow forced words out. 'She's just a little girl.' It felt like a hand had her by the throat. 'Livy came here for a family.'

'This is a family of warriors, and we are at war.'

The ache in Arrow's side, the metal tang, the stupid dress. Who could Livy ever be safe with, be a child with, wanted and cared for? 'Gods!' she spat out.

Molpadia's eyes lit up, reflecting the blue from the metal around them. She rose from her stool and clasped her hands together.

'Yes! You truly are the Panthera if you see it!'

'What?'

'Some crave war with the Empire,' Molpadia said. 'Llund, and the Frisians, perhaps even my Alke too. But there is another way. Your Livy, she is more than the child of two warring worlds. She can be the bridge between warring gods.'

The old woman paced, white curls shaking, and beads clacking against each other. 'Those cold Roman gods are dying in the world of oil. They are more marble than magic now. Your people worship in the markets and avenues, idolise Eastern silk, pray to shiny new charos, build mansions rather than Temples.'

The crone raised her face upwards as if speaking to more than Arrow. 'Your gods were born in forests and rivers just as ours, and they've fallen silent in the dark of cold Britannia. Livy was sent to wake them. Why lead warriors to war, if she can lead believers to worship! Wreck the shrines of baubles and rebuild those to your gods!' Molpadia upstretched both arms, a sheen of sweat on her brow. Arrow felt the woman vibrate with the strange machinery all around them. 'End the storms!'

Llund had said the same.

'The Godstorms?'

296

Molpadia spun back and grasped both of Arrow's hands in her own, the old skin like cool, crumpled silk, while her pupils filled her eyes with a deep blackness.

'The gods hate oil, Panthera. The burning effula chokes even the heavens. While oil burns, the storms will get worse. Livy, she can end it, lead the Empire back to their gods.'

'She's a little girl,' Arrow said again, although she didn't expect any argument to reach the old woman. 'Perhaps war will come, but a child can't lead it.'

'Who better! An innocent. Even your own priests are searching for a symbol, a message from their gods, to rouse their people and lead them back to piety. They will smash the markets, banish oil, return to the simple ways, all in her name! I can hear the gods now – they are calling for her!'

Arrow was also listening. Not to the mad ranting about sacrificing Livy to some spiritual uprising. Forcing a child to solve adult problems.

Instead, Arrow heeded a sound reverberating through the stone. The sound she had heard through the walls of the museum, and on the *Flyer*.

'Godstorm.' Livy was outside.

Arrow grabbed a handful of Molpadia's frock and beads, pulled her closer until the old woman's face was tilted up to hers.

'The fast way out, now. Otherwise, you'll face your gods, today.'

Molpadia was pale, spent from her sermon, but she shuffled forward and pulled open a hatch.

Howling winds and water invaded the room, cracking glass pillars that shattered around them.

CHAPTER XXII

'Livy!'

The winds stole Arrow's voice as she hefted a large plank sideways. It was as dark as if night had fallen. Sounds of a million trees ripped and swung in all directions.

'LIVY!'

Arrow had almost lost her footing racing down the huge pyramid staircase, winds buffeting every step. The blue lights whirled against their posts, tricking any sight still possible in the mess of gale. Grabbing one, Arrow tugged, but part of the post was attached – a long cord running to the next lamp.

Gritting her teeth, she tore the light from its connecting link. The blue light went out. *Hades.* Arrow threw it aside and ran on in the dark to the cabin Livy shared with Sosia, the winds buffeting her forward and then back.

It was a pile of torn thatch and fallen planks.

Bodies crashed past her towards the Temple, people clutching children or carrying old folk. A tree shrieked as it toppled, high boughs pulled to the extremes as if by a giant invisible hand. A man screamed as the tree fell faster than he could run.

'LIVY!' she yelled again, pushing at the wrecked pillars of the destroyed cabin, searching with touch, in the splintered wind.

Something soft brushed the back of her leg, and Arrow twisted to yank up a jagged piece of wood. Two yellow eyes bored into her, and a deep growl cut through the noise, carried as vibrations through the very soil itself.

A giant cat, like the dark killer she'd seen back in the Arena, struggled up out through the opening she had made. Rising like a silky black monster from the deep.

Arrow stumbled back, never looking away from the snarling jaw of long sharp teeth. The animal was free, but maddened, with ears pinned back and shoulders rippling. It didn't run and Arrow didn't move, but she noticed something from the corner of her eye.

On her knees, Arrow inched her hand forward. The Panthera scrutinised every movement as the winds buffeted them both. The animal snarled flashing white and yellow teeth so close that Arrow felt the warmth of its breath.

Every movement of fingers kept slow and deliberate – the eyes of the crazed creature speaking to her own heart – Arrow pulled the wood away a little further, freeing a small paw.

Tiny black ears popped up from the hole, with small whiskers fluttering in the wind.

The Panthera grabbed her little cub's neck scruff in her mouth and pulled it out. Then crouched back to leap away.

'Yah! Yah!'

A yellow oil lantern flared out beside her, swinging madly but bright in the darkness. The black Panthera careened towards the trees with its young clamped in its jaw. The mother and child were free.

'Is she here?' Barro shouted, holding the bright lantern above them.

Arrow shook her head.

'The pyramid?' he shouted again.

'No! The healers?'

They clung to each other, bending into the wind as the splinters of wood and grit tore at their skin – half-pulling each other through the screaming gale as they reached the healers' cabin, which still stood. They found Kepes, clasping her side and bleeding from her forehead, but hanging onto one of the thick wooden posts.

'Livy-girl at the river, with Sosia. Not come back!'

Arrow appraised the wounded woman. Her lung puncture may have reopened, as she knew her own wound had also done. Kepes' skin was grey, and it looked like she'd been hit by flying debris. The woman needed urgent treatment, safely in the pyramid.

As if reading her mind, Kepes grabbed Arrow's arm.

'You be lost in the forest. I'll take you.'

Arrow should object, send the woman to safety. Instead, she gave a curt nod and turned to Barro. Together they lifted Kepes and stumbled back out into the wind, each step a victory against leaves and twigs that sliced against their skin as the winds beat them. Once they reached the treeline at the edge of the clearing, Kepes seemed to gain strength and waved them forward while hanging onto Barro's arm.

The storm raged less under the trees, but the sound was eerier. Every bough, vine and leaf slapped in one direction and then another. The creaks of tortured wood confused Arrow's senses.

Every few moments a huge crash cut through the wind as, nearby, another giant tree tore up from its roots and toppled beside its siblings. Birds flew into them in a confusion of wings and talons.

'This storm is wrong, not natural. Animals fear. Take care,' Kepes shouted.

The forest did feel wrong, a taste of madness filled the air. But Kepes stumbled on, leading them over felled trees and pushing past vines like long arms grabbing at them.

Arrow recognised the pool by almost tripping into it. The waterfall itself careened in the wind, with fallen rocks and ripped-up trees littered below it.

Barro and Kepes tried to call out into the winds, but Arrow fell onto her hands and knees, holding the yellow oil lamp out over the waters. In the chaos of the storm, it was going to be impossible for the two girls to hear them.

A Godstorm in a forest, with a mad witch and war-hungry old Druid fighting over who would get to use Livy. Arrow winced as the winds pulled the lamp in her hand, tugging at the weeping gash in her side.

None of us are born for ourselves alone.

Please, Livy, please see the light.

A terrified creature jumped up before them, wild-eyed and howling. Arrow raised her arm to defend herself.

'Help! It bit Livy!' the maddened Sosia screamed at them, pulling at Arrow's arm.

'Show me,' Arrow shouted and stumbled forward with the girl, Barro supporting the wheezing Kepes to follow.

They found Livy sheltered in a lee of the waterfall rock face. The girl looked like she was sleeping, but when Arrow reached down for her she felt heat from her small body even through the chill of the winds and storm. Under the swinging light, Livy was deathly pale and sweating, her eyes rolling under her closed eyelids and her body limper than any child should be, even in sleep.

'What's wrong with her?' Arrow turned on Sosia.

'The storm came fast, so we climbed out of the water. Livy grabbed a root, but it was a *radikor*. It bit her.'

Livy's arm was swollen and turning to a blotched and purple colour. Sosia had tied it with a tight tourniquet below the shoulder. Arrow touched the knot; it had been done well. Kepes fired a series of questions in her own language. Sosia's answers got higher-pitched as the girl stuttered.

Arrow shouted, 'Can Molpadia help her? Do you have an antidote, a medicine for her?'

Kepes looked down. 'Snake bite is bad, very bad. My brother, he died from it.'

Sosia stared down at Livy and then stammered in her own language, gesturing away from the pool. Kepes shook her head, slumped against Barro.

'What, Sosia? Can you help her?' Arrow begged, on the ground cradling Livy's head in her lap.

'The oil place,' Sosia whispered, as if worried they might be overheard.

'What?'

'The Empire oil place,' Sosia said. Kepes tried to shush her, but the girl shouted over her, 'I went to spy on the workers once, and saw a man bitten by a *radikor*. I was sad, even though he is an enemy. I thought it was a bad way to die. They took him to their healer. Then one week later, I saw him working again.'

The oil station their charnot had been heading towards. It must have an apothecary or even a hospital for the workers and soldiers.

'Take us.'

'No! They'll kill you. Steal Livy-girl again.' Kepes staggered towards Livy, but Barro held her back. 'Livy is a river queen!'

Arrow lifted Livy up, carrying her like a little child again. She ignored Kepes and turned to Sosia.

'Take us. Now,' she demanded.

'No! You risk one girl to save other.' Kepes grabbed at Sosia and pulled the girl to her. 'It's an evil place. Sosia cannot go.'

A guttural yell of frustration ripped from Arrow. With Livy on her shoulder, she reached out to seize Sosia's arm and force her to lead them.

'I can find it,' Barro said.

'What?' Arrow released Sosia. 'How?'

'There are hunter marks on the trees, left by the men. I know I can find it.'

Kepes hung onto Sosia. 'Livy-girl has strong blood, she will fight *radikor* in her heart. Come back with us.'

Arrow hefted Livy a little higher on her shoulder. 'Sosia, take Kepes back to the pyramid, she's losing blood.'

Sosia nodded, holding the weight of the larger woman against her. They started to shuffle away with Kepes still pleading with them not to go.

Arrow shouted, 'Wait! What did the snake look like? In case they don't know what *radikor* means?'

'Black snake with red neck,' Sosia replied over her shoulder.

'Let me carry her.' Barro reached to take Livy.

'I've got her, Barro. You clear the path and watch for those hunter marks.'

He stared down at her, face empty of either lopsided smile or clouds of anger. 'It's too far, Arrow, in that dress. And you're bleeding. I'll take her and bring her back to you.'

Livy wasn't heavy, but Arrow's side throbbed. She checked the child's shallow breathing and then hoisted her over onto her stronger shoulder.

'We'll get there faster if you start moving,' she growled at him.

He looked at them both, woman and child, then nodded and set off through the trees, pushing aside vines and giant leaves for her to follow.

After a few steps through the swirling trees, Arrow started talking in a soft sing-song voice. 'Livy, dearest. We're nearly there. We'll find the healer. They'll have medicine. And when you wake up, I'll be there. I promise. I promise.'

Arrow wasn't sure if Livy could hear her, so she panted out her soliloquy, and the wind tore the words away from her lips as soon as she said them.

Once again, the girl's pain and danger were all her former governess's fault. There was no fighting the panic-poisons, the chemicals for guilt and pain, coursing through her now. The dark, wet forest pulled away each layer of her, as she struggled through it. Fearing that every weak breath would be Livy's last.

A child was dying, because of her.

When the memories came this time, Arrow could do nothing, she had nothing left to hold them back.

* * *

It had been a gloomy day in Londinium, twelve weeks after the grand Saturnalia festival. The night when she'd forgotten to drink bitter-fennel tea after lying in Barro's arms.

She knew that brief time in between with Barro had been happy. She could remember their tender moments, their plans, their love. But it always felt like those few months had happened to someone else, because of what happened after.

The gloomy day was no festival. Two Citizens wanted to settle a bet, not a particularly important one, so no death match. Just two gladiators wrestling to first blood.

Another day in the Arena. And to spice things up for the men, the bosses chose a gladiatrix to fight for one side. Barro fought for the other.

He was larger, but Arrow was faster. The fight wasn't interesting for either of them. Perhaps because the two lovers knew each other so well, there was nothing to discover in their combat. Of course, they didn't pull their punches and Barro got a fat lip and a cracked rib. He finally brought her down with a hard kick to the stomach.

Usually, it wouldn't even have dropped her. But today, Arrow didn't even know why, she wanted to run the moment his calloused foot left her belly.

So, she used an old gladiator fake, biting the inside of her cheek and spitting out a mouthful of blood onto the sand.

First blood – the bet settled.

Of course, Barro knew what she'd done and whispered, 'Don't blame you. Not worth a decent fight for just two blokes watching, eh?' He'd even winked as they were led off the field.

Arrow had made it to her tiny room just in time.

The blood poured out from between her legs. Within minutes she'd used up all the wadded rags she kept for the days of her menses.

Cramps pounded her guts like Barro's heel was still slamming into her belly again and again. Waves of nausea pounded her, and tears mingled with beading sweat. She'd been sliced, stabbed and beaten before, always a sharp spike of pain followed by the long ache of recovery.

This was more like a flogging, where each crippling seizure of pain would slowly loosen its grip, but you couldn't relax, knowing another lash would fall in a moment.

Those hours were still a haze to remember, even all these years later.

When the crushed lumps were all out of her, there was so much blood in bowls around the room Arrow wasn't sure how to hide it. If she went to the Arena apothecary, they would know what had happened, everyone would know.

Barro would find out he'd killed their baby.

Even though she'd only recently suspected herself pregnant, even though she'd told him nothing, even though it wasn't his fault. Knowing what he'd done would kill him.

So that night, pale like a ghost, and bent over from the pain, Arrow had snuck the bowls out to the Arena floor. Then mixed her blood into the sand. It was the one place, in all of Londinium, where the pools of dark red wouldn't be remarked upon.

Her failure, her loss, and her dead future now in the sand. Her and Barro's baby, buried where her own mother had died.

The next morning, Arrow walked to the airy offices of the bosses and declared she'd never fight upon the sand again. They thrashed her of course, but she was so numb it didn't hurt. Not once did she raise hands against the whip.

Within a day they'd sold her on. Barro hadn't understood, of course, and she was careful to leave him confused.

For years after she'd comforted herself that perhaps Barro's blow had been sent by the gods. That it was better for everyone that she'd miscarried.

She'd told herself over and over: killers can't be mothers.

* * *

Now, Arrow stumbled in the dark wet of the forest, crashing onto her knee. Pain exploded up her leg, dispersing the memory.

Livy was still safe on her shoulder. As she hauled herself up on a vine, she had to bite her cheek against crying out as a slow gash ripped down her leg.

Pulling her skirt aside revealed that one of the thin metal stays that kept her skirts in their wide Empire shape had snapped and cut through the inner fabric to her skin. The jagged metal wire now poked out of the silks sideways. Arrow ground her teeth against the sharp sting of the cut and rammed the rod back into the cloth, then wiped matted hair out of her eyes and pushed forward faster through the forest.

Barro's light bobbed ahead, waiting for her.

Trees and wind and darkness. Livy's skin burned against her own, but the girl didn't stir or speak. Minutes, hours passed. Years even. With the girl's breathing becoming shallower with step after step after step.

Arrow's legs stomped through the deep moss and leaves like lead. Gasps stamped out in bursts from lungs running on acid. She was a charo, made of metal and oil – a machine.

She shook her head. *No!*

Livy's soft cheek was against her own. Two warm living hearts beating.

Panthera, Inguz, Sword, Arrow, Miss.

Pushing through the Godstorm, with a dying Livy in her arms and blood seeping from her side, for the first time her past lives fell away. Now she was one person: a mother fighting for the life of her child.

That was all that mattered, all that ever mattered. Livy was her child because she was the only person who truly loved the little girl.

Mothers might fight, kill and fail, it didn't stop them being mothers.

'There.' Barro dropped into a crouch and lowered the lantern.

They'd reached another clearing, with another huge pyramid at the centre.

But this one wasn't made of stone. This was a metal tower, fathoms high, with the oil drill at its centre still pumping despite the Godstorm.

Piercing Gaea's veins for the oil within.

Familiar yellow oil lights shone from within the windows of low buildings, made of wood reinforced with stone or metal, cheap but sturdy. She could see the outlines of charos parked between buildings. Further off, Arrow could see a few windswept men climbing around on the giant extractor or rolling large barrels of crude oil between buildings, slipping and fighting against the tempest.

Barro didn't look at her, but said, 'Give me Livy. I'll take her in, say we escaped an attack on the convoy and got lost in the forest.'

'Barro, I'm not leaving her. That story works as well for three as for two. Let's go.'

A whitewashed cabin had the mark of Aesculapius, the apothecary sign.

'No, Arrow, it's too dangerous. You're a runaway slave, what if word of that reached Rioh? Anyway, it's safer for a man than a woman in there.'

Matted hair had slicked to Livy's forehead. Arrow picked the strands away, fingertips gentle on skin so hot, as if Livy's veins pumped with Gaea's burning blood.

The girl didn't even moan as Arrow hoisted her limp body back onto her shoulder. Leave Livy again? Wincing as she stood, Arrow turned towards the compound. Barro could follow her, or not.

The Godstorm tried to push her back towards the trees, her sudden tears from the grit carried on the winds.

'Whatever happens, Arrow, I will try and save her.' Barro's voice reached over the gale. He'd come with them.

The jungle lurched as a vine snagged her foot; a strong hand closed on her elbow. Barro's skin against hers felt almost as hot as Livy's. Together they reached the rough wooden door, peeling white-wash, on which was daubed a serpent-entwined staff in black paint. Arrow whispered a prayer.

I beg to Aesculapius. Let there be an antidote.

Barro dropped his hand but didn't try to open the door. Gods, was he so worried she'd be caught? It didn't matter. Nothing mattered but Livy.

She banged on the crude snakes with her free hand. No answer. So, she pounded and kicked against the thick wood.

The door opened an inch and yellow oil light spilled out. 'Go away,' a weedy voice said. 'This is a private consultation.'

'We are Imperium Romanum!' Arrow yelled back. 'I have a sick Citizen child. We need a healer!'

A small man stood in the doorway, wearing an off-white apothecary's overcoat that had seen better days. His nose wrinkled as he peered over thick-rimmed glasses.

Wrapped in her bloodied and torn green dress, carrying a naked child, her claim to be Empire must look far-fetched. Her words tumbled out. 'Our convoy was attacked in the forest. The child is sick, we need an Empire doctor, now.'

The little man's mouth dropped open, but he didn't budge. Other figures were just visible in the room behind him. Perhaps a real doctor, with more sense.

Arrow called over his shoulder into the room, 'I have a Citizen child here, legal ward of Consul Derain! She's hurt.'

The apothecary shuddered backwards, and Arrow pushed past him. The glow of a single lamp at the far end of the room cast a light onto the floor. She felt, rather than saw, that Barro followed her.

The room held a few chairs, a long, high table near the lamp, and a small medicine cabinet nailed to the far wall. Two men were between her and the white box, both turned away from the door. One of them buttoned his shirt as he stood up from the table. The other, a broad-shouldered soldier, stood at attention beside him.

'Please, we need medi—'

Both men turned, and the yellow light picked out the contours of their faces. The man who had been seated now fastened his final button.

Her throat closed with it.

Consul Derain smiled at her.

'Well now. Look at this, Mal, such serendipity. My errant slave and the troublesome child.' The Consul nodded. 'But perhaps this isn't a boon from the gods after all. Isn't that Barro too, costumed like a ridiculous native?'

The blood pounding in her skull sounded like the voice of her mother trying to tell her something. The soldier's scar was familiar, running from eye to lip. He was the man Barro had been fighting on the Arena sand. Who Barro had spoken to so quietly before setting off with her to find Livy.

'I will admit to being pleased to see you, bondsman Barro. I travelled to this gods-forsaken oil station to organise a proper defence of my supply convoys. Not a moment too soon. Another one was attacked just before I arrived. And now, you appear. I should have anticipated your diligence, I suppose. Always so dutiful.'

The Consul had been looking over Arrow's shoulder, but now he stepped forward, shaking his head at her.

'And look at what you've collected for me.'

The Consul's eyes ran over Livy, then he turned towards the scruffy man who had let them in.

'Apothecary, I believe I am finished with your services.'

The weedy man scurried to the back of the room and began to shuffle away pots and apparatus.

Bastard.

Bondsman Barro. Derain's dutiful servant. Sent to track, collect and return property.

The pounding in her head stopped, and for the first time since leaving Londinium Arrow felt cold, the hairs on her arms rising. Everything had been a lie, and she was the ridiculous fool who had fallen for it.

Tears started and she made no effort to stop them.

Her Academy lessons, victories in the Arena, years as a governess. Barro had proved none of it mattered. She was just a stupid slave girl after all, exactly what they all had told her she was.

Nobody can escape destiny.

If it wasn't for Livy's unmoving weight in her arms, she would have crumpled to the floor.

'Please. I need medicine.' She raised her voice, directing her supplication to the little apothecary. 'This child was bitten by the black snake with a red neck. She'll die without the antidote. Please, I entreat you in the name of your god, Aesculapius. Help her.'

Without looking back at her, the apothecary opened the cupboard and lifted out a blue vial.

'Set that down, my good man, and leave, now,' the Consul snapped.

The little, white-coated man stiffened, then lowered the vial to the bench below him. As he raised his other hand to close the cupboard, he made one swift movement, as if knocking back an imaginary drink.

Arrow blinked, but she understood.

The vial was tiny, and the blue glass caught a glint of yellow lamplight – Livy's life, mere steps away.

The apothecary fled past them all, and the door slammed behind him.

'My Lord . . .' Barro spoke.

'Oh, don't fuss, Barro. Mal will fetch my own man, a physician. He was scared to venture out in the storm, but Mal will drag him if needed. I wouldn't trust a mere apothecary with Livia's life. Mal, inform my man I have a child and a woman here, who both require urgent attention. While we wait, my bondsman will provide his report.'

Mal followed the apothecary out, and Barro stepped so close behind Arrow that she could feel the heat from his body. Then he started to catalogue everything; the Green Man, details of the

Flyer and Captain Baja, the location of the Amazonial city, and the deployment of their guards. Barro's voice was clipped and formal – information only. Such a professional bondsman.

The Consul nodded to it all, ignoring Arrow and Livy. He even snorted when Barro outlined their meeting with Scratch in the Gaen Temple.

'Oh yes, the Pontifex is rather upset with you, Barro. But I explained I expect my agents to use their initiative in securing intelligence.'

Standing like this, Arrow could feel Livy's heartbeat against her own skin, fluttery and weak as if a dying moth were trapped in the girl's chest.

Each of Barro's words was a reminder that she had been led, manipulated and sent down a path of his choosing with every step. He had always been unexpectedly patient, and inventive, when he wanted to be. When she had turned up at the Arena, Barro went along for the ride, letting Derain know via Mal that he was with them.

Gods, had Derain actually wanted the Druids to take Livy? Perhaps he'd known Arrow's instinct would be to seek help at the Arena. Then Barro could collect intelligence about the Anglish, Frisians and Amazonials that he could get no other way.

Arrow felt hollow, like any sense of herself had been scooped out to be reviewed, critiqued and laughed at. *Fool.*

'The Amazonials prepare for war against the Emperor,' Barro finished.

'Which one?' Derain chuckled. 'We have a new Emperor now, my old friend having coughed his last. Indeed, also an Empress. I had the pleasure of her mother's company for days on the airship journey here. The newlyweds on their wedding tour, giving thanks at every temple.'

He lowered his brows.

'Oh yes, I have you to thank for this too, don't I? Introducing Augusto to Miss Octavia Troak. Sorry, her glorious majesty, the

Empress Octavia. Not whom I would have chosen, but perhaps her soft-headedness will temper him. Now he is Emperor I suspect the river whores are right – war will come.'

Barro's voice became hesitant. 'They blame the Empire for these Godstorms. Because of burning oil.'

Derain snorted. 'Oil is power, that's what they hate.' He glanced out of the thick window at leaves whipped by the frenzied wind, talking as if rehearsing familiar arguments. 'Without oil, the Empire would fall, and with us, civilisation itself will end. Our Academy will invent some way to control the Godstorms, have no doubt. And a few squalls are preferrable to living in caves, like filthy Druids, deprived of Gaea's blood.'

Rulers have the privilege of lying, to everyone, if it's for the good of the state. Arrow couldn't remember where she'd learnt that.

Livy moaned a little, so Arrow laid the girl on the floor, crouching beside her to wipe her fevered brow. Nothing mattered except Livy. Perhaps her mistake had been thinking that anything else could.

'Now, Barro, I need more details of the cultists' encampments, armaments and capabilities. And of how those pirates crossed the ocean at such speed. I should like to track down that ship with the blue lights.'

Barro nodded. 'Of course, sir.' Then he reached down to Livy. 'But the child needs—'

Arrow was ready.

Pivoting up, she yanked Barro's hunting knife from his calf sheath and got it to his neck in one smooth movement.

He held himself motionless in her arms. Arrow could feel the heartbeat in his chest against her skin and smell his sweat and blood.

'Hand over the vial, or your loyal bondman dies,' she spat out.

The Consul looked at her as if she were a child trying to recite a poorly remembered lesson. He stepped back to the bench and lifted the blue vial with his thumb and forefinger. Then he turned and walked towards her, holding it out.

Before the bottle was in range of her hand, Derain stopped, and held the vial out in his fingertips, like Arrow had held the Inguz stone over the water.

'Come now, girl, you must release him. This isn't helping Livia.'

They stood. Her eyes locked onto the wavering bottle. Then Derain softened and tilted his head to one side.

'Enough of all this, child.' He lowered the vial a little. 'Your whole silly escapade is over. Barro has been leaving messages for me, in Rioh, and then with the charnot soldiers. Livia has been very useful, luring the Empire's enemies into my hands. But Barro was protecting her at all times, after *you* put her in harm's way. Thankfully, it's all over now and you're both safe again. You must learn self-control of your violent temper, being around little children. Now, don't let your ignorance hurt Livia, again.'

Her knife wavered a little.

'My personal doctor saved the girl once, when her mother dragged herself to this very encampment. The poor woman begged me for aid because the river madwoman just chanted over her. I wasn't going to send a Citizen child back to that. So yes, I took Livia back with me to civilisation. Sentimentality on my part, I admit.' He smiled, then lowered the bottle onto a bench in time with Arrow lowering her knife.

'Now I will save Livia once again. Once my man has checked this antidote, he will help her. Then back in Londinium, Livy can take her place as a Citizen, with all the privileges and power she deserves. The girl will be protected, properly. You must admit, my dear governess, that you have consistently failed her in that regard. Now, can you put down that silly knife? Livy is my sworn responsibility, on my honour.'

Livy as Citizen, protected, safe. The side where Arrow's wound had opened felt very warm now, even though the rest of her was cold. She swayed a little where she stood, as Barro plucked his knife out of her hand.

'Now then, let's get this whole sorry affair cleaned up. Barro, you'll have to secure her to that chair after such an outburst.'

Barro wouldn't meet Arrow's eye as he led her to a wooden chair near the table and secured her wrists and ankles with twine carried at his waist.

'Check her, please. We don't want her hurting anyone, even herself.'

Barro lifted Arrow's filthy and torn Empire skirts, but she wore no knife sheath below them. Then he dug at her waist and pulled out the handkerchief.

Olivia's handkerchief had held such hope. But, of course, it had all been a silly game; Arrow was nothing more than an inconvenience to everyone. Livy would be better off without her. With proper doctors, and Derain, and *bondsman* Barro.

'Silence her with that, will you?'

After gagging Arrow, Barro lifted Livy and laid her on a bench nearby.

The wind screamed as the door opened.

'Ah, here he is.' The Consul turned, but Arrow couldn't see who entered. Her chair faced the blue bottle.

'This child urgently requires your services.' Consul Derain looked down at Livy, lying immobile on the bench. 'Then administer to her governess with similar care. Be diligent and swift, their lives concern me. Come now, Barro, you must help me through the storm.'

The Consul walked to the door, but Barro wavered, still looking down at Livy.

'I think she needs that vial,' he said with a thick voice to whoever had come in. Then with head bowed, Barro followed his master, without once looking at Arrow.

'I know exactly what she needs,' a voice drawled.

A man walked into Arrow's field of view as the door clicked shut behind Barro.

Arrow froze. Then tried to scream and bite through her gag. She dragged against the ties around her wrists with all the force she had left in her.

Caligo licked his lips, watching her struggle.

CHAPTER XXIII

'Well, hello again, little slave.'

Caligo stalked towards her, just as he had done back in Consul Derain's office in Londinium.

Panic flooded her body, pulling at every muscle, the gag stifling her lungs.

He appraised her like an animal sent for sale, or slaughter.

'Derain promised me this, if we found you again.' He fingered a livid scar across his forehead; she remembered the blood spilling from it on the Spire staircase. 'I appreciate him trussing you up so carefully. After you were so naughty last time.' He sighed as if ending a race. 'You have caused me so much work. Tracking bondsmen, organising airships. Why couldn't you just leave the brat to her fate?'

White knuckles clutching the chair, Arrow's nostrils flared, desperate for air, chest pumping as she struggled.

'Discovered too many secrets while galivanting with heretics, did we? Nasty talk about oil making storms? Perhaps you even saw those blue lights that don't need Gaea's profitable blood. Oh yes, that's all well known. By the right people.' When the clerk smiled his lips pursed. 'That child was meant to start the war while the old Emperor lived. Allowing us to destroy all their heretic energy once and for all. But now, it seems you've both become liabilities I must administer to. I will be diligent, as ordered. But perhaps not as swift as Derain would like.'

Bending forward, he ran his fingertips over the ties at her wrists. Then his hands swept up her arms, to her shoulders. He caressed along her collarbone, his head tilted and his breath coming faster to match her own.

She'd sat down in this chair willingly, letting Barro tie her. Derain had bested her without raising a hand, sapping her will out with poisoned words.

Oh gods. Livy.

Caligo grabbed her neck, then pushed her back so hard that the front legs of her chair tilted up.

He squeezed her windpipe again and again. Not tight enough to fully choke but holding her on the edge of suffocating. If she swallowed, he pushed harder.

'Poor . . . little . . . slave.'

Arrow whimpered, and his sneer widened into a smile at the sound. He teased the gag from out between her teeth.

No screams, or headbutts. No one would hear her over the storm anyway. Even if they did, no one would come for her.

'You didn't train at the Arena, I would have remembered you,' she croaked when she caught breath.

'Oh, but I did. Just not at your little circus in Londinium.' He stroked her cheek and watched the muscles clench in her jaw. 'I trained in the true Arena in Rome. They teach death as art there, not as silly swordplay to entertain the unwashed.' The smile spread out across his face, like ripples from a stone thrown into a still pond. 'And of course, in Rome, women only perform on their backs . . . or their knees.'

The windows juddered with the violence of the storm, but the construction was solid.

He leaned in closer, staring into her eyes, moving his hands down her chest, more urgent now, tugging at the fastenings of her blouse.

'Now, where were we back in Londinium? Oh yes . . .' He leaned back and slapped her, far harder than in the Consul's office. Her head jerked sideways.

'You won't speak unless ordered, you will move exactly as I say and, this time, I'll finish what I started.'

Arrow suppressed a shudder. Now she knew Barro's true nature, the clerk's intention, horrific as it was, seemed almost less grotesque than Barro's caresses.

Because the clerk hated her openly. Barro had just used her.

Caligo's fingers slipped against the small mother-of-pearl buttons and he ripped one off, pulling her face closer to his with the force of it.

Men have no greater enemy than themselves.

He cried out and staggered back, clutching his crotch, curses pouring out of him.

Barro hadn't been attentive when he tied her. By twisting her ankle back and forth, Arrow had loosened one binding enough to pull it down off the bottom of the chair leg when Caligo had tilted her back.

She knew a better way to use her knees than to go down on them.

'Bitch,' was all he managed to groan, turning from her.

Heaving herself up on her free leg, Arrow hurled herself backwards with all the force she could muster.

The chair shattered under her, jarring every bone but freeing her arms. Rolling, she yanked broken wood from the ties on her wrists.

Just in time to duck, as the hard side of his palm sliced to where her neck had been. His miss didn't put him off; his other hand came down in a hard-balled fist to her stomach.

Keeling inwards, Arrow grunted as the wind was knocked out of her. But she managed to grab his hand with both of hers, and twisted backwards, jerking his arm.

His ulna should have broken, but her left arm was too weak, almost unusable. Caligo kicked out at the back of her knee. He slammed her down to kneeling, and his forearm was across her, crushing her throat for real now.

The pain fought to be felt, but Arrow snarled it back.

Grabbing a handful of her hair with his other hand, he dragged her head back to expose her airway to his full pressure. Facing the small blue glass vial, Arrow watched it wobble close to the edge of the bench. Her sight reduced to a pinprick as he squeezed.

'I would have killed the girl quickly,' he snarled, 'but just for that, little Livia and I will play a while.'

A clump of her hair tore out as Arrow turned her head closer into his elbow, giving her a second's more breath. He leaned over her, trying to drag her head back up again. Their grunts drowned by the Godstorm's screams outside the window.

He was better than her, stronger than her, more skilled than her.

She hung on, even pushing her shoulder up, forcing him to lean further in, chin inching closer to her.

Gladiator. *Governess.*

Arrow's hand shot up, scratching her nails into his face, tearing into his eyelid. A woman's move.

As he pulled away, his arm loosened, and she shoved back against his left leg.

Caligo hissed, wiping at the blood running down his cheek like tears.

Arrow twisted to her feet, gasping. Gods, she needed a weapon against him. She knew she lived only because he wanted to torture before killing.

Dodging towards the broken chair, she grasped for a leg, a wooden shard... anything. But her fingers closed on empty air.

His weight slammed into her, throwing her back down against the floor, like a rag doll she'd made for Livy once.

Too much blood was spilling out of the reopened wound on her side, and her bruised windpipe wouldn't pull in enough breath. The room swam around her. She couldn't believe she was still conscious.

Despise not death, but welcome it, for nature wills it like all else.

All artistry gone, Caligo pressed his advantage in size and strength, punching into her chest, stomach and hip. The thuds of his fists audible even over the storm. Arrow tried to move away. But there was nothing left. No one to help.

Her ribs cracked under his blows as she curled over, hugging her skirts.

One arm now lay twisted by her side, and blood slipped down her face from her torn scalp. Too many wounds. Too much blood.

Again and again, each of his blows forced out a little more breath that didn't come back in. The warm rust of blood filled her mouth. The red behind her eyes fading towards black.

I'm so sorry, dearest.

Arrow hoped she'd at least bought the girl enough time to die peacefully.

'Remember, dying is easy.' Her mother stood over her and the frenzied strikes as Caligo rasped through his work. 'It's so much harder to live.'

I'm sorry, Mother. I'm sorry, Livy.

Across the room a gentle sound floated. 'Miss . . .' Livy's voice, cracked and low.

The clerk glanced over as if surprised by the sound.

Arrow gagged, broken fingers fumbling down her body. They closed around the only weapon she had. Not even a weapon, not as any Arena instructor would recognise it. But it was sharp, and hard, and hers.

Arrow drove the wire upwards.

Up through the soft point between his chin and neck. Up into the artery to his brain.

The man stumbled back, skewered by the broken metal rod she'd pulled out from her skirts.

Her mother turned to him and raised her sword, slowly disappearing. 'For those about to die, we salute you.'

Caligo dropped. Not crumpled, but like the trees that fell in the forest storm, ripped up by their roots.

Pain kept beating her, nerve endings wracked and jagged bones screamed. Breathing was so painful it would be easier just to stop.

Livy, get to Livy.

Dragging herself through the widening pool of blood where the clerk lay, Arrow reached the bench and lifted the blue vial in quivering fingers. Shuffling lopsided on her knees to Livy, smearing blood across the floor, she pried open the girl's lips and poured a little of the liquid into her mouth.

A trickle ran down Livy's cheek, but some went in.

Arrow poured more, being careful not to tip too much while the girl struggled to swallow. Livy drank.

Once the vial was empty, Arrow tugged the girl down onto her lap and curled herself around the little body. She rocked Livy like a baby, her heart praying, her lips too broken and bruised to make the sounds.

All she could think of was the long necklace of shells Livy had begged for back in Rioh. The girl had been entranced by them, but they were frivolous and expensive. Arrow desperately wished she'd bought them for her.

Every time Livy had been excited for something, or happy, or hopeful, Arrow wished she'd encouraged it more. Hugged her more. Let the girl know how much she loved her.

The Godstorm must have blown over; all she could hear was the bubbling of her own breath against broken ribs.

She who is allowed to make mistakes, makes fewer mistakes.

The Consul would send Mal to check on them if Caligo didn't return soon. Or to help the clerk with their bodies. She needed to get Livy out of here.

As Arrow leaned over the girl, mustering the strength to try to raise her, the front of the building blew off with a thunder of wind and raging fire.

Arrow staggered. Her back stung like she'd been lashed a thousand times, and all she could hear was a deep ringing, like a bell in her head. She feared she'd lost her sight too, but as she blinked Livy's face swam into view. She wasn't burnt; Arrow's body had protected her. But the girl was still unconscious, covered in black sooty filth. Arrow rested her hand on Livy's chest – it was moving.

She turned to check the devastation of the building, but it was hard to make anything out with the wind and rain now pouring through it.

She spotted light outside. *Hades.*

It wasn't the strange blue lights of the river queens, nor the yellow of Empire oil lamps. This was vivid red. Fire.

In every charo engine, a tiny, ignited spark danced on the edge of destruction, teasing bursts of energy from oil, without ever letting the trapped power rip outwards.

The flamethrowers on the charnots gave that force more rein, sending controlled streams of incandescent oil to destroy the Empire's enemies. But even that ferocity was managed with levers and locks, each drip accounted for, and the alchemy controlled.

Every child in the Empire learnt one rule before all others: never let fire and oil meet. The power of Gaea's blood and blaze combined, like the meeting of two lovers, would destroy everything in an orgy of flame.

Arrow dragged herself up and stumbled out, coughing and spluttering, carrying Livy tight against her body. A fire at an oil station was like igniting a gigantic bomb. She had to get Livy safely away. Broken bones and punctured lungs would have to hold a while longer.

A flicker of obdurate gratitude passed through Arrow's mind. Thanks for every beating, every wound, every time an Arena boss sent her back out on the sand before she'd healed. Even for the night she'd lost the baby, then pulled herself upright through the agony the next day. Every former hurt now helped her, they'd taught her that pain wasn't powerful enough to stop her.

It is a horror not to be able to bear horrors.

Thick smoke billowed everywhere, and, through the soles of her feet, she could feel rumbles and explosions, even if the sounds came muffled through her damaged ears. The chemical smell made her gag.

She tripped over a burnt body. One of the workers? He had two arrows sticking out of him. Tipped with blue and yellow feathers.

Her hearing returned in time for another explosion behind her. Arrow hunched over Livy and wasn't sure if it was droplets of oil or rain that patted down on them.

Huddled as she was beside a crate for protection from the worst of the blast, Arrow's senses were so dulled it was hard to tell if fever still burned through the girl's little body. She put her cheek against Livy's and felt more than heard the deeper and steadier breaths the girl now managed. Arrow's own breath eased with hers.

As she leaned back against the wood, relief almost conquered Arrow where pain hadn't. As if the gods themselves felt her lightness, a breeze rose up and cleared the smoke before her.

To reveal, not twenty paces away, Barro lugging a large body wrapped in what looked like soaking wet sheets.

Barro's left shoulder and half his torso looked like burnt crackling on over-cooked meat, his skin now blackened flakes, with bright red showing beneath. The scalds licked up his neck almost to his cheek, as if the ruined skin were a torturous armour.

The body she had known, the scars she remembered tracing with her fingertips, scorched away.

The pain must be exquisite, considering the tears running down his face. But Barro handled his burden with almost as much care as Arrow nursed Livy. He carried the load towards a parked charo, through the chaos. It was Consul Derain by the size. *Gods*, she hoped Barro held nothing but a blackened carcass.

She should run and hide from him, or rip a shard of wood off the crate as a weapon and challenge him. She should call down curses upon him from any god still listening.

The man who had, almost, killed both of her children.

Instead, when he looked up and caught sight of her, Arrow could do nothing. Whatever she expected to see on his face – shock, shame, anger – there was none. He met her gaze, gently hoisting the man he carried a little higher on his shoulder.

Then Mal came out of the building behind. Barro broke his gaze away and edged his own body around as if to block the soldier's view of her. If he hadn't, Arrow might have wondered if Barro had seen her and Livy at all.

But that tiny moment was enough to jerk her out of torpor. If Mal saw them, Arrow had no doubt that arc gun on his hip would be used to dispatch both her and Livy without hesitation.

She rolled them both further behind the crate, heart pounding, waiting for the first splintering crack of arc-gun fire to hit them.

None came, nor any call to guards or soldiers. Barro had shielded them from Mal's sight.

She didn't want to think about him, but her whirling mind reviewed his actions as if it were studying the habits of an opposing gladiator. Derain had needed to trick Barro into leaving her and Livy with Caligo, ordering their death in code. Barro had wanted her safely off with Baja, or even to run away into the forest together, even though that must have been against his orders. Perhaps the Barro she had thought she knew was still there, hiding within the loyal bondsman.

Whatever feelings fluttered in Arrow's heart were still fledgling. All she knew was that, whoever she was now, she wasn't a slave anymore. But whoever Barro was, he wasn't free. Perhaps this was what pity felt like. She'd never had cause to feel it before.

Another boom rang out and a cloud of black smoke roiled out to cover the scene of the three men.

Barro was, quite literally, not her problem anymore.

Lifting Livy, she pushed up and on through the crazed Hades of the oil station. A little further and they would be out of it. The sound of arc-gun fire and screams were hidden in the smoke. She bumped into crates and almost sprawled over pipes hidden in the smoke.

They needed to get to the forest, hide in the wet welcome of the trees, find the Amazonials. Whatever happened next, it would be away from this burning bomb of the place. She needed for Livy to wake up.

Arrow tried to find the edge of the treeline.

But the forest rose up before her.

The bone woman in her paint and feathers, with a spatter of gore across her face, stepped out of the smoke.

'Thank the gods. Alke, help us,' Arrow managed.

'Give me the war child,' Alke said.

'What?' The noise and smoke lay between them. But Arrow had heard those words before and kept tight hold on Livy. 'We need to get out of here, save her!'

Alke shuddered, all the rage and bravado fallen from her. Arrow felt every inch of her skin tighten.

An arrogant, angry and cynical Alke she knew how to handle. That warrior was like every ambitious young gladiator sold to the Arena after thrashing all comers in the provinces. Their confidence was exploitable on the Londinium sand.

But the woman now standing before her looked confused, scared even. Deciding what must be done rather than what she wanted to do.

Alke shook her head. 'I need to save my people from her. From what she will do.'

The bone woman was unsure of herself, and for the first time Arrow felt afraid of her.

'For the *gods'* sake, Alke, please think.' Arrow's crushed windpipe made speaking difficult. 'Livy did nothing. She's been used by everyone.'

'You should have kept her in your cold country.' Perhaps it was the soot and heat, but Alke was crying. 'Not bring her here to lead a crusade and end my people.'

'Your bloody witch and the crazy Green Man, they want the war. Not me. They are using Livy to start it!'

Alke stared at Livy.

'Then, I must end it. Blood of my blood.' Alke stopped shaking, 'May the river forgive me.'

The bone woman drew out a dagger, the one that had already tasted Arrow's blood; her own knife.

Alke moved forward, clutching the hilt in both hands and chanting.

Shuffling back, Arrow twisted and near dropped Livy behind her. Then half-stumbled up, hunched, her breath coming in rasps and eyes swollen, one arm useless.

Crouched in her burnt and bloodied dress, Arrow had no weapon or shield except her own body between the murderous warrior and her niece.

'Don't do this, Alke,' Arrow tried, aware she'd started to sway. 'I promise there is another way.'

'If you wish for peace, prepare for war.' Alke laughed, raising the knife over her head.

A sharp cry rang through the other screams and roars as a black-ened, soot-stained apparition slammed into the bone woman.

Alke slashed at the creature, but he hung on, ripping at her, yelling and biting. Then he stumbled back, clutching at the knife handle sticking up out of his belly.

The old man Llund was burnt down one side of his face, one eye a bubbly red mess, his beard charred black, his precious plaits scorched away. Alke stood, gaping slack-jawed at the medicine man she had just stabbed as he looked down at the knife deep in his guts.

The familiar hilt glinted as if trying to speak to Arrow.

Llund lifted his head from his mortal wound, stared at Arrow and then down towards Livy, curled on the ground behind her.

No mortal can be called fortunate, until you known their ending.

A small sound escaped Llund, like a song of pleading. His hands fell off the handle sticking out of him, bloodied palms open to Arrow, in supplication and in offering.

'Please . . .' was all he managed.

What had he called her back in the clearing? The Sword, destined to protect Livy at any cost. Arrow lurched forward, grabbed his shoulder with one hand and wrenched the knife from his body with the other. A burst of lifeblood escaped him as he fell backwards.

Alke pounced as she saw Llund's sacrifice.

She landed, hands grasping at the knife in Arrow's damaged fist. The bone woman was fresh and unhurt, convinced of her morality. Her strong grip wrenched Arrow's broken fingers, as Arrow bent, burnt and gasping, before her.

It was never going to be a fair fight.

'My mother's knife,' Arrow whispered into Alke's ear as she thrust it into the bone woman's heart.

Then fell beside her foe, wheezing in the smoke.

'Llund.' She rolled onto her side towards the man, hearing gurgling from his throat.

'The girl, she lives?' Llund opened his one unburnt eye, as black blood spilled from his lips.

Arrow nodded.

'Had to find you . . . Barro . . .' He coughed up more gore. 'Don't trust . . .'

'I know. But we're safe. I will never leave her. Llund, do you hear me? I will never leave my child.'

'The . . . sword.' He almost looked satisfied as his eye lost focus, and the bubbling stopped. Arrow had witnessed that silencing of breath too many times.

She rolled on her back, watching roils of thick black smoke dance up into the sky.

Do not indulge in dreams of having what you have not, but reckon up the chief of the blessings you do possess, and then thankfully remember how you would crave for them if they were not yours.

Arrow took as deep a breath as she could through cracked lips and ribs.

Accept the things to which fate binds you and love the people with whom fate brings you together and do so with all your heart.

Now, move yourself, woman.

Before they reached the deep forest, Arrow was crawling, with Livy slung across her back. The battle frenzy that had blocked most of the pain now deserted her. Scorched skin and broken bones were her master, demanding she stop, trying to force her into unconsciousness. She no longer had will enough to hold her agony back.

Perhaps she did whimper, a little. But she kept inching forward over fallen leaves and vines, pulling Livy under the trees.

Fleeing a war, mind racing as to how to prevent another one.

Dia Agrippina Severina had always valued Arrow's brains over her blades. Perhaps it was time she tried the same.

The wet thick air felt like a caress on burnt skin. She hauled Livy onwards, following no path, ignoring time, until the pattering of rain and calls of forest birds blotted out the chaos behind.

The tall trees reached over them like the great hall of the Imperium Museum.

Livy moaned and stirred a little. Dragging her own ragged body up against a giant tree trunk, Arrow rested the girl's head on her bunched skirts, what was left of them. Was that colour returning to Livy's cheeks below the filth?

Caligo. Alke. Llund. She prayed that the fire had killed Derain, and he would sink to Hades. She didn't think about Barro.

They'd escaped from a civilised Empire camp into a wild forest she'd never been alone in before. A bird chirped and a tiny smile bubbled up from inside her but couldn't make it past her bloodied lips. The trees rustled like they'd picked up the laugh from her.

Molpadia would find them. Because the old crone wanted Livy to lead a battle against oil. As if war was ever the right way to find peace.

Well, the warriors couldn't have her, no one could. *Needing the child wasn't the same as loving the child.*

Livy was hers, and she'd almost lost her.

Holding the girl, Arrow wondered at this little person, with her own passions and preferences, who lay in her arms. This miracle that she'd almost let go, long before Caligo tried to end her.

Livy's love was given freely, but Arrow hadn't deserved it. Lacing herself into a box more confining than any corset. Following the rules of Empire more than the needs of a child. She'd been so stupid. But if there was one thing Arrow knew from both her Academy and Arena training: she could learn.

In her life so far she'd been a successful gladiator and a failed governess, according to her respective masters. As a mother, only Livy would get to judge her. Although Arrow thought she might not ask that question for a little while.

'Miss?' The girl's eyes fluttered open. Livy squirmed a little in her lap and rubbed at her dirty face, then coughed.

'You smell like a Vulcanalia festival, Miss.'

'I'm sorry, dearest. We'll have a good wash back in the Amazonial village.' Arrow had thought she'd need to force speech through her broken lips, but for Livy her voice endured.

The girl blinked, then frowned. 'Will . . . will you leave me there?'

The child hadn't asked why she was bleeding, what had covered them in burnt ash, or how they were in the jungle.

The worst monster children fear is being left alone.

'I'll *never* leave you, Livy . . . we're family.'

In the end, it was so simple to say.

Livy just nodded as if that had been obvious all along. Perhaps it had.

Light dappled down through the canopy so far above them. Everything was such a vivid green. No, that wasn't quite right, there were millions of greens, from a dark earthy olive on the tree bark to a translucent pale jade of thin leaves. The forest was so alive, Arrow wanted to drink it in, like an antidote.

'We'll rest for a little.' Arrow fingered the gag hanging around her neck, Octavia's signet with its half-burnt and filthy-yellow nasturtiums. 'Then we can go anywhere. Back to Molpadia, or to Captain Baja, or even to find an Empress who offered you patronage.'

She bent and kissed the girl's forehead. Livy smiled as if she were being tucked up in bed back at home.

Mother and Child, Oil and River, Arena and Academy. There seemed to be two parts to everything. Including a solution for every problem.

'Sosia told me you used to be a gladiator. Were you really?' Perhaps Livy had noticed the blood and bruises after all.

'Yes, I did fight in the Arena, long ago. But I also studied at the Academy, with a wonderful teacher. She taught me that words, not just weapons, have power. That we can use them to change the world.'

'Did she? Change the world?'

'Not yet, Livy. But perhaps one day she'll get the chance.'

'I hope so, Miss.'

Mere mortals might not force the will of fortune. But perhaps the gods would allow her to nudge it a little.

'Livy, I don't think you should call me Miss anymore, nor Arrow.' Their hands met and clasped together. 'Would you like to call me by the name my mother gave me?'

Her daughter nodded.

'Then, dearest, you can call me Kal.'

To Citizen Dia Agrippina Severnia – Academy of Natural Sciences.

My honoured teacher,

I write this missive in strange circumstances. I can only imagine how it will reach you, passed from hand to hand across forests, oceans and continents. Many of those who will risk their lives to bring you this letter are of ilk and kind that might shock you.

But I assure you, none wish ill will to yourself and, despite great provocation, most crave only for peace with the Imperium Romanum.

If I had used our Imperial post service, I am convinced this letter wouldn't reach your hands. Its contents run against the interests of those vested in a great wrong being perpetuated against Citizen and Barbarian alike.

If you have the strength of character to read thus far, which I am convinced you do, then what follows will pique your scientific interest, horrify your better nature and, I dearly hope, spur you to action.

Attached are two treaties, written in the scientific style you so kindly taught my lowly self. One is on the nature of effula, its emergence from burnt oil and how it causes devastating Godstorms. The second may be even more shocking. It is a set of diagrams for production of a golden 'light-lens' that generates energy without oil.

Many years ago, you taught me that effula and spiritus gases were Janus-like – the bad and good together balanced. These two papers follow a similar pattern. The first revealing the destructive impact of oil, the second a beautiful solution to that threat. I will leave you to decide which of Janus' faces you will follow.

Your everlasting student,
Arrow, Ward of the Arena.

ACKNOWLEDGEMENTS

Thank you to everyone who has helped build this world of *Godstorm*.

My dear friends Liza Ravenscroft and Bryony Randal swiftly followed my family as early readers, and their support convinced me to continue. My dear friend and fellow solutionist, Lucy Shea, kindly shared my draft with a friend in publishing and began this journey.

Thank you to this book's godmother (and publisher) Laura Fletcher, who has been an unfailing champion. To my wonderful agent Alice Saunders for gently nudging me, the book and career in the right direction. And to Flora Rees for editing with a light hand and creative heart. Also to Kira Jones for checking my Greek and Roman quote attribution (although I may have slipped a few extras in since her corrections).

I must acknowledge my friend and mentor of 25 years, Chris Tuppen, who 'peer reviewed' the science of *Godstorm*, including calculating the amount of oil I'd need to burn to spark climate change by the 1800s. But please note: all scientific or engineering clangers in this book are entirely mine and justified as poetic licence!

I'm incredibly lucky to have visited the real Amazon rainforest, but the stories of indigenous and traditional communities who preserve that precious place are not mine to tell. Instead, my river queens are based upon the ancient Greek and Roman conception of female warriors. I'm grateful for Adrienne Mayor's incredible book *The Amazons*, for creative inspiration on customs, weapons, dress and naming.

Thanks to Matt Sexton, Karen Boick, Lola Young, Stefan Kyriazis, Martin Wright, Joel Makower, Hannah Jones and every friend who has listened to me rant about climate storytelling.

I offer lifelong gratitude and love to my family: Mum and Dad, Sian, Francesca, Grace, Wynter and Alanna. Without your unfailing support, I wouldn't be able to write a word.

Finally, all my thanks to everyone who cares about their kids and the climate. Our situation is immeasurably better than that of *Godstorm*, if we choose to make it so. Now go save the damn planet.

CLASSICAL QUOTES

The wisest lines in this book were written thousands of years ago by ancient Greek and Roman philosophers, historians, emperors, generals and early scientists.

Some of these quotes have disputed attribution, others I've translated or adapted myself (with no small amount of poetic licence). All helped to inspire this story.

- *War, detested by mothers* – Horace
- *Not even the gods fight necessity* – Plato
- *Let us live, since we must die* – Seneca the Younger
- *Disturbance comes only from within* - Marcus Aurelius
- *Some things are within our control, some things are not* – Epictetus
- *Fear is the foundation of salvation* –Tertullian
- *Poverty is the lack of many things, avarice is the lack of all things* – Publilius Syrus
- *We are dust and shadows* – Horace
- *To overcome an inclination and not be overcome by it is reason to celebrate* – Plautus
- *She gathers strength as she moves* – Virgil
- *Laws fall silent amidst arms* – Cicero
- *It's a bad plan that can't be changed* – Publilius Syrus
- *It's better to keep at home* – Hesiod

- *Kindness begets kindness* – Sophocles
- *The first and greatest punishment of the sinner is the conscience of sin* – Seneca the Younger
- *A wrongdoer is often a man who has left something undone, not always one who has done something* – Marcus Aurelius
- *Avoid doing what you would blame others for doing* – Thales of Miletus quoted by Diogenes Laertius
- *Men act as wolves to other men* – Plautus
- *Nature loves nothing solitary* – Cicero
- *Fear was the first thing on earth to make gods* – Publius Papinius Statius
- *If I cannot sway the heavens, I will raise hell* – Virgil
- *Whom the gods love dies young* – Menander
- *While there's life there's hope, only the dead have none* – Theocritus
- *Necessity dictates law without itself having one* – Publilius Syrus
- *Confine yourself to the present* – Marcus Aurelius
- *Either don't try at all or make sure you succeed* – Ovid
- *We suffer more often in imagination than in reality* – Seneca the Younger
- *Let them hate me, as long as they fear me* – Suetonius
- *Docendo discimus (by teaching, we learn)* – Seneca the Younger
- *God has endowed children with magic charm* – Euripides
- *Twice victorious is the one who conquers himself in the moment of victory* – Publilius Syrus
- *Great fear is concealed under audacity* – Lucan
- *Life is one long struggle in the dark* – Lucretius
- *The manner of death is sadder than the death itself* – Martial
- *The existence of the gods is a helpful thing, so let people believe in them* – Ovid
- *Education is an ornament in prosperity and a refuge in adversity* – Aristotle
- *Practice is everything* – Periander

- *No one dares challenge one who he realises will win if he fights –* Vegetius
- *Time reveals truth –* Seneca the Younger
- *The cause is hidden; the strength of the spring is well known –* Ovid
- *It is easier to find men who will volunteer to die, than to find those who are willing to endure pain with patience –* Julius Caesar
- *Patience is the remedy to every misfortune –* Plautus
- *All savagery is from weakness –* Seneca the Younger
- *Men willingly believe what they wish –* Julius Caesar
- *Death is a debt all mortals must pay –* Euripides
- *Think of the universal substance, of which thou has a very small portion; and of universal time, of which a short and indivisible interval has been assigned to thee; and of that which is fixed by destiny, and how small a part of it thou art –* Marcus Aurelius
- *Be tolerant to others and strict with yourself –*Marcus Aurelius
- *For this is the mark of a wise and upright man, not to rail against the gods in misfortune –* Aeschylus
- *I will either find a way or make one –* Seneca the Younger
- *Fate will find a way –* Virgil
- *Everything unknown seems magnificent –* Tacitus
- *Where skill is called for, force is of little use –* Herodotus
- *Being angry is easy, but to be angry with the right person and to the right degree and at the right time and for the right purpose, and in the right way, that is wisdom –* Aristotle
- *What stands in the way, becomes the way –* Marcus Aurelius
- *Not for ourselves alone are we born –* Cicero
- *The rulers of the state are the only persons who ought to have the privilege of lying either at home or abroad, they may be allowed to lie for the good of the state –* Plato
- *Despise not death, but welcome it, for nature wills it like all else –* Marcus Aurelius
- *It's not death that a man should fear, but he should fear never beginning to live –* Marcus Aurelius

337

- *Those who are about to die, we salute you* – Suetonius
- *It is misfortune not to be able to bear misfortune* – Bias of Priene
- *If you wish for peace, prepare for war* – Vegetius
- *No mortal can be fortunate until his end* – Euripides
- *Do not indulge in dreams of having what you have not, but reckon up the chief of the blessings you do possess, and then thankfully remember how you would crave for them if they were not yours. Accept the things to which fate binds you and love the people with whom fate brings you together and do so with all your heart* – Marcus Aurelius
- *It is not for us to force the will of fortune* – Euripides

ABOUT THE AUTHOR

Solitaire Townsend is a climate expert by day, and storyteller by night. After decades of teaching governments, global brands and even movie studios how to communicate sustainability, she now has stories of her own to tell. She blogs for Forbes, has a popular TED talk, and wrote the critically acclaimed non-fiction book *The Solutionists*. While some of her characters might not know that they are 'LGBTQIA+' or 'neurodivergent', Solitaire does because she's also both. She lives in London, and once visited an oil-rig in the Amazon, which caught on fire. Visit www.solitairetownsend.com for more of her story.